Firelight

Bill Dughaille

They travelled in winter
they travelled from town
to find that welcoming glimmer
was the farmhouse
burning down

Chapter One: Tuesday 20th December

'I hear the vicar's pig got out again,' George Browne chuckled, leafing through his morning Times, flicking the pages to make them crack. 'That nasty little newspaper delivery boy told me. The one with the freckles and runny nose. They found it in the village trying to eat another lamppost. Stupid animal.'

'Oh, dear, not again,' replied his wife. She had just finished putting their breakfast plates in the dishwasher – toast with a dash of Marmite for him, toast with diabetic honey for her – and was peering through her reading glasses at a list she was making. 'That reminds me. Cheese biscuits, I must add those to the list. What is the name of those cheese biscuits Hope used to love when she was little? I wonder if she still has a fondness for them.'

'I don't know who's the bigger idiot, the vicar or the pig. The vicar for deciding to keep a pig, or the pig for leaving a perfectly comfortable warm sty to ramble around in the middle of winter with the fields bare of anything for the damned thing to eat. Won't make good bacon if it keeps running around like that.' He looked across the kitchen towards the fireplace. 'Has that fire gone out? I think it could do with another log. Feels warm enough, doesn't look too bright.'

'It's just the morning sun shining on it, George. It's burning nicely.'

'Pretty feeble sun. I'm sure we had better sunrises in our day.'

'That's a point. Do you think Gail's new boyfriend will be a vegetarian?'

'You know, pigs need company. Social things. Can't keep a

pig on its own. Got to have a few of them together. A boar and three or four sows. Maybe a couple of logs, eh, Win?'

'So many young people do seem to be vegetarian these days. It does make things difficult. And with a name like Garant, well, you never know. He could be a pop-singer or something.'

George Browne stretched his broad, wrinkled neck and frowned at the fire.

'Probably a, what do they call them?' he said. 'Vogon? The ones that don't eat anything apart from soya beans and organic dirt. Bound to be a pouf anyway, name like Garant. Feel sorry for the poor buggers sometimes, these days, stupid names their parents give them. You know, I'm sure logs don't last as long as they used to. There's definitely something wrong with smokeless logs. It goes against nature. Logs should smoke. That's the whole point.'

'George, really, I wish you wouldn't come out with nonsense like that. Words like that. You know you don't mean it, and you know that others think you do. Remember what happened when little Tommy Dawkins overheard you calling Mrs Haggerty an old witch.'

George Browne chuckled again and folded up his Times. Noisily.

'Teach the little brat to eavesdrop outside people's windows.'

'You knew that he was eavesdropping. That's why you said it. And I heard what you said to that poor little boy when he delivered the newspaper. Putting ideas into his head, suggesting that we were going to turn this old house into a lunatic asylum again. Really, George. You know he's going to repeat it, and the villagers will probably tease him enormously. You'll only have yourself to blame when he gets scared and refuses to deliver again.'

'That's if,' she continued before he had a chance to speak, 'the villagers themselves don't believe it, and begin a demonstration, or a protest, or something.'

His lips twitched. He looked at the newspaper, and then changed the look to one of scorn. 'Why you insist on ordering the Times I don't know. It's not even a shadow of a shadow of itself. Nothing in it these days but society gossip, tittle-tattle and adverts. And American gossip at that. That Birtney thing. Or the one who grew up in Wales. Or Scotland or somewhere. Oh, and crises. Crises after crises after crises. We're all going to die of bird flu or mad cow disease or mad Islamic terrorists or global warming. Ha! We didn't go through crises, did we? Just got on with life. Even when the bombs were falling. And even when there is some hard news you can't believe a word they say. Might as well buy the bloody Guardian and have done with it. At least you know what their lies are. And they have better columnists. Probably burns better, too.'

'George, you know I only order it because you always complain when I don't.'

'No need to. I could stroll down to the village shop if I felt I needed to waste good money on it. Old Jameson keeps hinting that I could do with some exercise. Silly fool. As I've said before, how many doctors do you read about dying of old age at ninety or a hundred? Whenever you read about the oldest man in the world, is it a doctor? Never. Always someone who's enjoyed a good life and a whiskey every day.'

Winifred Browne returned to her list.

'I wonder if we should get some tofu in, just in case anyone is vegetarian. I don't know what you're supposed to do with it, but I daresay they do. I wonder what it looks like.'

'Feed the buggers boiled rice. Though you'll probably find

that that's against animal welfare these days. The idiots probably eat it raw. Like that Japanese rubbish, that fish, suki-saki or whatever they call it. Bloody Japanese! Slant-eyed ... Look at what they did in the war, and now we're buying raw fish from them. As if they had some superior culture. Raw bloody fish!'

'It's supposed to be good for you, I hear. I don't understand why, myself. Oils, or something.'

'I really do not understand people today. More money than sense. Fads and fashion, that's all it is, blasted fads and fashion. What happened to good old fish and chips?' He pummelled his newspaper and looked at his wife from underneath his eyebrows. It was almost a cajoling look. 'Now there's an idea. A good old-fashioned dinner of fish and chips. Like we used to have in the old days. Only you'll have to cook it, there aren't any places left around here that sell fish and chips. I couldn't believe that the old shop had been turned into a hairdressers. A salon. Bloody French word, salon.'

Winifred Browne added "M and S – oven-ready fish and chips" to her list.

'Finish your coffee, dear. Then we must make a start on the shopping. You can drive me into town and order the drinks from Hoxleys while I go to the supermarket. I've made a list for you. If you feel up to driving that is, we can always get Stevens to send a car.'

'Nonsense. Never felt fitter in my life,' he said, waving the rolled-up Times to prove his point. 'And the Jag is a joy to drive. Automatic, power steering – marvellous beast. Even you could drive her if you wanted. But I'll take my walking stick – the one I bought when we were in Austria, remember? One thing the Austrians are good at. Lovely piece of workmanship, that stick.'

He stood up and walked slowly and purposely across the room to the window, taking care not to show a limp. Winifred Browne briefly closed her eyes at the memory of their holiday in Austria. Something about the way his large shoulders blotted out the sunlight reminded her of a scene in a restaurant there. One where a diner at the table alongside had leaned across to politely inform George Browne that many Austrians could understand English. Including the rude words. Sometimes especially the rude words.

'There's still a bit of mist at the end of the garden,' he noted. 'Whole garden is frosted over.' Then he muttered something under his breath. 'You know, I told you that someone is stealing bricks from the top of the back wall,' he said, perhaps to prove that he could still see something the size of a brick over a hundred feet away without his glasses or even binoculars, if ever he had been able to. 'They must be using ladders during the night. One of these days we'll wake up and there's be nothing left. They'll bring a lorry in and cart away the lot.'

'Crackers,' said his wife.

'What was that, Win?'

'Crackers. Christmas crackers. I almost forgot them. I had crackers on the list, but those were meant to be cheese crackers.'

He stomped back to his seat.

'Ah, Christmas. Season of goodwill and offspring coming to sponge off us. Along with their latest weird boyfriends and girlfriends.'

'Now, George, stop that. You know you're really going to enjoy it. It's the best chance you'll get all year to complain and insult people. Why the children have bothered to make the effort I've never understood. As for the grandchildren, I can only presume that they appear to have inherited insanity along the line.'

'Haven't noticed them making much effort over the last few years. When was the last time Gail or Claire came around at Christmas time? Hmm? Tell me that. It must be at least five years. Longer! Too busy with their precious boyfriends and girlfriends. And always a new one, every year. Talk about the disposable society. Remember when –'

'Well, this year is going to be different. And it's one of the real reasons you decided to buy this rambling old manor house – apart from the one we are not going to discuss – so that you can impress the grandchildren. And you know that you've been looking forward to it for the past few months.'

George Browne harrumphed, nodded several times, and took a few seconds to calm his blood pressure.

'They'll have to know some day. Maybe we ought to leave a diary, or something like that. You know, after we ... well, something, at least. One day.'

'Whatever we do, it won't be this Christmas, George. We are going to have an old-fashioned Christmas, with the children and grandchildren.'

George Browne nodded.

'Well, at least this year we'll have space for them. No excuses about not wanting to travel with the children on Christmas Day this time, they'll all be staying over. All of them!' He smiled as an idea struck him. 'You know, we could set up a patrol roster for the walls. Catch those thieving little ... thieving little ... brick snatchers at their own game.'

Winifred Browne smiled fondly.

'Grandchildren,' she repeated. 'That makes them sound as if they were still in their nappies. And now they've got little ones of their own. Great-grand-children. Who would have thought of it?'

'I'll have to put a tie on. If we're going into town,' he said looking down at what he was wearing, white shirt and comfortable old grey flannels. 'Do you remember me telling you about that young idiot at the men's shop in town who didn't know what flannels were?'

'Yes, George. Several times.'

'I bet he didn't know what slacks are, either,' he said. His wife was wearing a cream silk blouse and fawn slacks. 'Funny how things turn out. Quite acceptable for young women to wear slacks to church these days.'

'George, you know very well I would never wear slacks to church. There is a difference between going to church and domestic shopping. And in winter one has to compromise between the acceptable and the practical. Though I am glad to hear that you have your attention on the important things on the rare occasion you attend church with me.'

George Browne looked at his newspaper and gave it another squeeze.

'Definitely a tie,' he said.

'As you wish, George.'

'You know, I don't think I will. It's not really necessary to wear a tie whenever you go out. Not these days.'

'As you wish, George.'

'But it does show a standard. Being retired doesn't mean you have to go around dressed as if you couldn't be bothered. It shows respect, both for yourself and others. You know, there was a news presenter on the local news last night not wearing a tie. And it was the BBC! Or was it that other one? That other channel. Number seventy-six or whatever number it is. It was one of them. Not wearing a tie on the news!'

His wife frowned at the list and added "rocket?" to it. He tapped the table with the fingers of the hand holding the newspaper.

'We aren't buying the turkey from that blasted supermarket, are we?' he asked. 'Ninety-percent water, that's what they said in the paper the other day. Ninety-percent water! It's almost unbelievable what they do to food these days. More additives than the original article. One of these days we won't need to worry about children not knowing that milk comes from cows because it won't. They'll make it in a laboratory from recycled cardboard or something.'

'Farmer Giles has promised to take care of all the fish and meat, dear. We need to collect them tomorrow. Or he can deliver for a small extra charge. Probably best that way.'

That brought a burst of something which could have started as laughter.

'Good old Farmer Giles, eh? You'd think he'd at least make an effort to live up to his namesake. I'm not sure a scrawny little farmer like that should be trusted. Doesn't look as if he eats any of his own stuff. And all those complaints about costs and prices. I'll bet he has a tidy little fortune stashed away. Much good may it do him when he's old and nothing to show for it apart from boxes of shekels in the basement. A real – what's the name of that character in Shakespeare? Sherlock?'

'That reminds me. Pickles. I must remember to get some pickles. In sour vinegar.'

'Shylock, that's it. Shylock the Jew. Sherlock's the detective chap. Know why Shakespeare made Shylock a Jew?'

'Valerie might be coming with Gail. You do remember Valerie, don't you, George?'

'Valerie? One of young Anthony's ex-girlfriends, isn't she?

Used to wear tops that showed everything.'

'No, George, Valerie's an old school friend of Gail's. You're thinking of – oh, what was her name, now, Chrissy? Yes, that's it, you used to call her Missy Chrissy to annoy Anthony.'

'Ah, that Valerie. Yes, come to think of it I do remember that Valerie. Had a large bosom, didn't she? Large for her age, I mean.'

'I thought you might remember that. I wonder if it's worth getting avocado pears. They're so expensive for what you get. And Christmas just seems like the wrong time for avocados.'

'Waste of money. All pip and no pear. You know, we're going to have to make them wear name tags. And who they belong to. Be damn confusing otherwise. That's a thought. Name, status and gender orientation. Don't want to make any mistakes.'

'You mean you don't want to insult anyone by accident, you'd much rather do it on purpose.'

George Browne nodded.

'Blue, I think,' he said. 'Blue tie and blazer. Maybe the one with the Legion badge. What you wear is important. It says something about who you are.'

Winifred Browne sighed quietly.

'I do hope Adam can make it. He didn't sound very confident when I spoke to him. You would have thought that he could take a break from his work for a few days.' She made another note on her list. 'I'm sure he'll do his best,' she murmured.

'You must have a word with him about Peter and Rebeccah. I don't care how modern a world we live in these days, they've got little George now. It's time he did the right thing by her and married her. I don't care if she is ... well, you know. She could always convert.' He hesitated as a thought struck him.

'That religious freak Adam married isn't coming, is she? Susan the saint?'

'George!'

'Well, I know she's good for Adam's image, but, really, Winifred! There are some limits. The questions she comes out with! And she isn't improving with age, you know. Remember, I told you, the last time she asked –'

'That reminds me. I must ask Gail whether she and Garant are sleeping together.' That was met with a splutter from her husband. 'If they are then they can have the green bedroom. If they aren't then Gail and Hope can share the green bedroom – unless Hope's bringing her boyfriend. I'll make a note to call her. And try not to make those comments if they are sleeping together, George. You know very well that times have changed. What was right for us isn't necessarily right for them.'

George Browne folded his newspaper one more time to punish it. He appeared to be about to make a comment about the times.

'Hope has a boyfriend?' he asked instead, his mouth twitching again, with a small smile. 'Well, well, that only took her ten or so years. Let's just hope he isn't a limp-wristed save-the-whales tree-hugging long-haired liberal leftie like the last one was.'

'George! You know very well that the only reason she finds it hard to get a boyfriend – and keep him – is that you always used to scare them off. Ever since she first came home with that poor boy – what was his name? Jeremy? No, not Jeremy. Anyway, I don't think she's ever forgiven you for that, and I don't blame her.'

'I hope they've grown up a bit. All those silly little arguments they used to have.'

'You hope they haven't grown up at all. You used to start those silly little arguments deliberately. Well, you aren't going to do that this Christmas, George.'

George Browne stood up. With his large body slowed by age it appeared, as all his movements did, to be an announcement. 'I'd better get the car warmed up,' he said. 'It looks like it's going to be a bit chilly this morning.'

'I don't think the fire needs any more logs, George. Not if we're going out. And don't stoke it again, please.'

Chapter Two: Wednesday 21st December

'Onions,' murmured Winifred Browne to herself the following morning, going through another list in the pantry, notes in one hand, a cabbage in the other, a large yellow pen hanging on a lanyard from her neck. 'I wonder if we have enough onions?' The slow, muted bongs of an electronic doorbell filtered through to the kitchen. 'Now who on earth can that be?' she asked the cabbage as the sound died away, echoing through the house. 'I know, it will be a delivery. Adam's flowers four days before Christmas. He always sends them four days before Christmas. He's very good that way. He never forgets.' She put the cabbage down gently amongst the potatoes and made her way at a steady pace along the passage, the doorbell bonging again before she arrived at the front door. She opened it to find two women waiting with suitcases at their sides, both wearing thick parkas with the fur-lined hoods turned closely in and their hands rammed into their pockets. One parka was a bright red, the other a dusty-pink. The dusty-pink one had on a thick denim skirt down to the calves, with flat-heeled shoes, the bright-red one skin-tight jeans folded into brown boots with three-inch heels.

Winifred Browne peered at them through her glasses. They obviously weren't flower delivery men. Or flower delivery women. Certainly not what she expected. On the other hand, they didn't look like Jehovah's Witnesses, her second thought. Perhaps they were collecting for something. One never knew these days.

'Yes, can I help you?' she asked.

'Gran, it's me!' said the one in the skirt. 'Don't tell me you don't recognise me!'

'Gail! My darling!' exclaimed Winifred as the skirted woman took down her hood to reveal flowing, chestnut hair and eyes with a hint of having experienced a heavy night of drinking. 'Come in, I didn't expect you until tomorrow. I thought it was the flowers. And with that hood on. Well, I couldn't tell who you were!'

'Flowers, gran?' Gail asked, giving her grandmother a kiss and a hug. 'I did call to let you know. I left a message with granddad. I suppose he forgot to pass it on.'

'Yes, I suppose he must have done. I was expecting a flower delivery. Those hoods do wrap the face up well, don't they.' Gail grimaced.

'The heating in the car broke down a couple of miles away, gran. We've been freezing since then. It even woke Valerie up. Oh, you remember Valerie, don't you?'

Valerie took her hood off. Her blonde hair was in a pony-tail and she had full make-up on, the red lipstick showing an echo in her slightly blood-shot eyes, with a hint of more than just one heavy night of drinking.

'Valerie! Of course, my goodness, it's been ages – when was it? Your school leaving do, wasn't it? Yes, that's it. My, you have grown. Come in, come in, it's cold out there. Bring your suitcases in. You used to have light brown hair, didn't you? Or is my memory going? Come in, come in.'

'Almost fourteen years, Mrs Browne,' replied Valerie as they entered the hall, bumping wheeled suitcases over the threshold. 'Gail and I were discussing it on the way here. Funny, that. It feels as if it were yesterday and years ago at the same time. And, yes, it was light brown, but my hairdresser and I decided I was a more natural blonde. For the moment. I might be a brunette next month.'

'Time does fly. Just a second while I shut this door. There's a trick to it, it's a bit old and slightly warped.'

'Gran, this place is absolutely huge!' exclaimed Gail, looking around the large hallway as her grandmother began to placate the door into closing properly. 'I know you said it was an old country house, but I didn't expect anything on this scale.'

'I think it's called a manor house rather than a country house,' Winifred said, keeping an eye on the closed door. 'You know, it often appears quite happily in its place, but waits until you're elsewhere to swing open. We bolt it at night so that we don't wake up frozen dead one morning.' She frowned. 'Though I'm not sure what the difference is.'

'Difference, gran?'

'Between a manor house and a country house. It's a bit like a terraced house and a maisonette. They do seem to be rather much the same thing.'

'But, gran, it's so – huge!'

'Well, my dear, it isn't really. Not by the standards of its time. There are only three floors, and the top floor used to be the servants' quarters, so that would never have counted.'

'Gran, you could fit my flat into here about twenty times over. And as for the garden! Or are they called grounds? Or am I confusing that with something else? Gran, it's huge!'

Winifred Browne nodded, continuing her perusal of the innocent looking door. Valerie looked at her back, one eyebrow raised.

'Well, we call it the garden. In its day it would have been much larger. Quite a bit of the land has been sold off over the years. Thinking about it, I suppose it's the wrong size, really. The house, I mean. Too large for a single family, too small for, what do they call them, a business park? Those offices they build in the country for some reason.'

'Oh, gran, go on. Too small? It's like a mansion. How many

bedrooms? Twenty? Thirty?'

'No, only ten, my dear, it's not that large.'

'Oh, gran, really! Only ten bedrooms? You make it sound like a pauper's place.'

'Yes, well, perhaps you are right. Different times. But there is a story behind it – why we bought it. Your grandfather claims he wanted it as an investment, but as usual he's – what's that terrible modern phrase, "being economical with the truth"?'

'Lying to himself, as usual, you mean?'

'Now, now, Gail, he's not that bad. I think it's closed,' she said to herself, and turned her attention from the now apparently happy door towards them.

'So what's his real reason for buying this place? He isn't aiming at becoming a lord or earl or something?'

'Oh, to impress you, of course. He dotes on you, all of his children and grandchildren. Even if he's not very good at showing it.'

'If you say so, gran. Why is it called Maid's Manor? And what's with the Big Ben doorbell? If it's as loud inside as out – it's enough to wake the dead.'

'Ah, well, it isn't called that, really. Maid's Manor, that is. Your grandfather had that sign put up to annoy some of the villagers, the older ones who complain about city people coming to buy up properties and change everything. To them it's simply known as the Manor, or Lord's Manor. Putting up "Maid's Manor" was mild compared to some of the other ideas he thought of. As for the doorbell – well, your grandfather thought that we should be able to hear it in the garden as well as in the house, in case we were outside. His hearing isn't quite what it used to be. But that's between us, he doesn't like to admit it.'

'I bet you could almost hear it in London.'

Winifred Browne looked absent-mindedly around the hall.

'He wanted to put up a stuffed lion's head in here.' She shook her head at the thought. 'There's a terrible wind blowing this morning, isn't there? Not very strong, but sharp. It gets through everything. Every single crack. You learn to find out the cracks in this old place, to seal them up.'

'I feel sorry for the villagers, gran. He's not up to his usual charm-them-one-minute-insult-them-the-next tricks, is he?'

'He hasn't changed greatly in that respect. Yes, well, let me show you to your bedrooms, you can put your cases down and then we'll have a nice cup of tea in the kitchen. Your grandfather is watching television in the television room. Which is to say that he's probably fallen asleep with the television on.'

'Television room? You have a television room?'

'Oh, yes. Yes, we're lucky that way,' Winifred Browne said as they followed her to the stairs. 'But then your grandfather and I are – what would you call it? The pre-television generation? Era? I have to say that I would rather read a good book than watch some of the programmes they put out. It is nice to have a room where you can watch a programme you want to, and then switch the set off and do something else. Oh, Garant will be coming later, I take it? Come along, your room is on the first floor.'

'No, gran, Garant isn't coming,' Gail said, her mouth curling. 'I've broken up with him.'

'Oh, dear, dear, dear, that is terrible,' her grandmother tutted as she led them up the stairs, the two lugging their suitcases along. 'Are you sure it isn't temporary? I'm afraid that these old wooden stairs tend to creak a lot, but you don't notice it after a while. Watch out for splinters – we had hoped the carpet people would have been by now, they did promise, but they still haven't turned up. I must say, your generation seem to have so many more problems with relationships than we did. Do you think you could make up if you wanted to? What was the name of that boy you seemed to have so many break-ups with?'

'Gran, I'm more likely to cut Garant's –' She tossed her hair, trying to think of a more delicate word than the one she had intended to use. 'Well, let's just say that I wouldn't take him back if he came crawling to me on his hands and knees. With a rose stuck up his – nose.'

'Oh, dear. You think he won't? Come back, that is. With or without the rose. In the nose. Is that where they put them these days? Strange place to put it, with us it was between the teeth, if the idea ever occurred, that is. Like the Spanish, you know. That was uncomfortable enough, a rose doesn't really taste of much. But then I do find modern fashions so strange. Pierced noses and eyebrows and such. To me it just looks so ugly. But there you are, we probably shocked out parents and grand-parents in our day. Yes, I'm sure we did. People always do. Have you definitely broken up with him, or might we need to set another place at the table in case?'

'Not a chance, gran. It turned out that he was already married. He seemed to think having a bit on the side quite acceptable. "All's fair in love and war", he actually used those very words. Just before I slapped him. We were in the middle of dinner in a posh restaurant, I really enjoyed that. And dumping his steak over his head. I was just sorry we'd finished the soup course. It would have made a better mess.'

Winifred Browne nodded.

'Good for you, my dear, good for you. And much better his steak than yours, I always think. You can always ask for a doggy bag for yours. No, he doesn't sound a pleasant person.

You're much better off without him. Mind the corner, some of the plaster needs replacing. Apparently you can't see it behind the wallpaper. The builders said that if we wanted to move in before Christmas it would be best just to paper over the old, otherwise it would have taken months. Married, was he? I don't know, the things you read of. They always seem so far away. No, not a very pleasant person at all.'

'Him and the rest,' said Gail, struggling with her suitcase, trying not to grunt with the effort. 'You know what men are like, gran. Not snips and snails and puppy dogs' tails, that would be an improvement. Bloody seventy-five percent ego, seventy-five percent pride and a hundred percent me-me-me. And I know that's, what, two hundred and fifty percent, but that's men for you. There always appears to be more to the bastards than there is.' She paused and smiled awkwardly. 'Sorry, gran, I shouldn't have sworn.'

'That's alright, my dear, it's more acceptable these days, isn't it? But I wouldn't be too hasty in condemning all men, you know. I've always thought of your uncle Adam as the perfect gentleman, and I'm sure there are many others out there like him. Or some, at least. But, speaking of swearing, I don't want to sound like an old fogey, but somehow I can never get used to the sound of ten-year-olds using words like – well, like the F word. I couldn't believe it when I first heard it. I was visiting an unmarried mother on an estate a few years ago, when I still belonged to the WI there. I must find out whether they have a branch here. But I just could not believe the language the children were allowed to get away with. Unbelievable. It really was unbelievable. How on earth are their children going to get out of poverty if they allow them to get away with that?'

'I agree, gran, there are limits, and that's one of them. When I have children, if I ever catch them using language like that they'll get a good belting, and sod the liberal anti-corporal-punishment do-gooders. They don't seem to realise that sometimes a child does need a good smack. Call someone the working class, impoverished, victims of society, and they're allowed to get away with anything.'

'Ah, yes, speaking of that, if Garant isn't coming, would you two mind sharing a room? I'm really not sure how many of the others are coming, it might be a case of sharing or having two rooms each, if you see what I mean.' She sighed. 'It is a little bit up in the air at the moment, I'm afraid. Your uncle Adam is going to try to be here, but he doesn't quite know. He works too hard, really. But he does have such a responsible position.'

'Course not, gran. It'll be like boarding school again, won't it, Val? We'll sit on our beds sharing a bottle of wine while gossiping about everybody, being right little bitches. We've got a lot to catch up on. Val and I haven't really seen much of each other since 97.'

'Good, good. Here's your room, then. It's what we call the green room. Because of the wallpaper. We can re-arrange things later depending on who turns up. The oil heaters are working quite well, I switched them on in here just in case, so you shouldn't be cold, as long as you don't leave the door open too long. Heat seems to evaporate so quickly into the corridors. I'll leave you two to unpack. I'll put the kettle on. Come down when you're ready, turn left at the bottom of the stairs and go straight down the passage, the kitchen is right at the end. Oh, and if you need it, the bathroom is at the end of the corridor.'

She sighed.

'Your grandfather, I'm afraid, keeps changing his mind. One

minute he talks of having en-suite bathrooms for all the bedrooms, the next he thinks that it's too much pampering, and people should have to suffer cold floors if they need a midnight pee.'

The other two women looked at each other. Then Gail turned to her grandmother with a mischievous smile on her face.

'The main bedroom has en-suite, gran?' she asked.

'Well, yes, of course. It's the way it was built.' She looked out of the window as if lost in thought. 'Yes, it was the way it was,' she said. 'All those years ago.'

'All those years ago, gran?'

Her grandmother started.

'Sorry? Oh, just wandering a bit, my dear, just wandering. I must remember to lock the door to the stairs, the one to the servants' quarters. It's at the end of the corridor. The builders haven't finished there. Everything is still in a bit of a mess, wires everywhere. Nails poking out of the floorboards. And still many boxes from our old house. It's not dangerous, but when the children arrive, well ... Better safe than sorry. Children always want to explore, and I'm worried they might do something up there. Pull some heavy boxes down on top of themselves, that sort of thing. Play with some loose wires. Jump on floorboards until they break.' She shook her head at the thought. 'Right, I'll put the kettle on. It's definitely time for tea. You come down when you're ready.'

'It isn't haunted, is it, Mrs Browne?' asked Valerie with an impish smile.

'Oh, all houses this old are haunted in one way or another, my dear, all of them. You just learn to live with it. It can't harm you unless you let it. Tea. I'll see you downstairs when you're ready.'

Firelight

Chapter Three: When We Were Just Little Girls

Valerie laughed when Winifred Browne had left.

'I think your grandmother was wondering if we were gay,' she said.

'You've got to watch her. She likes to pretend she's an absent-minded old housewife whose only thoughts are about what to make for dinner, but she's as sharp as two pins. Asking if we were willing to share was her way of letting us be lesbians if we were without mentioning it. Granddad, on the other hand, would take malicious delight in it. He'd call it a perversion, and then ask which bits go where. Who's on top, that sort of thing.'

'Funny that. The last time I saw your gran was when I was wondering if I was lesbian. That ten minute time when you're growing up and aren't sure, and the PE mistress with the moustache looks inviting. Lousy time, being a teenager.' She paused. 'No, wait a minute, that wasn't the last time I saw your gran. Oh, it doesn't matter. I'll take this bed, if you don't mind.' She took off her parka to reveal a tight, red v-neck sweater and white shirt. She dropped the parka on the floor and bounced onto one of the single beds.

'Yes, go for it, I'm not fussy,' Gail said, turning, opening a chest of drawers and looking inside.

'These beds are a bit on the small side if one of us gets lucky this week,' Val noted. 'We'll have to come up with a plan. Leave your shoes outside if you don't want to be disturbed while you're having a hump, something like that.'

'Val, really. This is a family reunion, not a — whatever the word is for what you're thinking.' Val laughed again, lay back, put her hands behind her head and stretched her legs, watching Gail unpack her suitcase.

"'Val, really!'" she quoted. 'You sound like your gran. What happened to good old "Oh, for fuck's sake"? You said that often enough while we were on the way here. Twice when we took wrong turnings, several times to tractors.'

'Well, you know how it is. Gran's a really lovely person, I don't want to upset her. After all it is their home. You have to make allowances.'

Valerie made a face.

'Let's explore the slave quarters later,' she said. 'Might be a good place for a bonk if something happens. They're usually soundproofed. So the mistress of the house couldn't hear the lord and master having it off with the serving girl.'

'Servant quarters, not slave quarters, dummy. Anyway, you heard what my gran said. Loose wires, nails sticking out, dust, dirt, the rest. Not my idea of the ideal love nest.'

'Oh, go on, use your imagination. Sweat, dust, lust, must, excellent stuff. I used to know a man who got kicks out of having electrical shocks while he was doing it. Great sex. Best I've ever had.'

Gail's eyes widened.

'Electrical shocks?'

'Not massive ones. Carefully controlled, he had a little machine. Pity I had to give him up.'

'What happened to him then?'

'Oh, he had body odour problems.'

'Yuk. That's gross.'

'Yes, it was. Can't stand body odour. Apart from the usual when you're at it, but not continuously.'

'I meant the whole thing is gross. Sex in a time of dirt and dust and electrical shocks. Give me clean sheets any day.'

'Sounds like you're ready to get married, settle down and start whelping. You'll be a paid-up member of the WI in no time. Like your gran.'

'I am, as it happens. Maybe not the WI bit, but let's face it, we're both thirty, single – it won't be long before we're on the shelf. I want to get married, settle down and have kids. I've had enough of this brave new world. Might as well call it the bland new world. With added doom and gloom. Fuck that for a game of soldiers. I just want a normal life now.'

She pulled a rueful face as she looked at a skirt which brought back memories.

'I often wish I hadn't dumped Nick. Okay, so he wasn't perfect, but who is?'

Valerie looked at her with raised eyebrows.

'Nick? Do I know Nick? Am I supposed to know Nick? Jesus, Gail, it's hard enough trying to remember who your uncles and aunts are. Never mind your cousins. Who the fuck is Nick when he's at home? Or was.'

'Nick Moore. You remember, medium height, wavy brown hair, sexy smile. A little bit shy. Serious looking, but – well, with a smile, you know? A bit overweight, but that's because he lived on take-aways. I think that's one of the reasons I dumped him. I had this fear that I'd end up doing all the cooking and cleaning if we got together permanently. The good little woman.'

'Nope, can't say I remember him. Are you sure that I met him? I didn't fuck him, did I?'

'You must remember me telling you about him pushing me into the swimming pool in Gran Canaria when I still had my t-shirt and skirt on. Bloody expensive skirt that was, it was ruined. Shrank, almost totally.'

'I remember you coming back from Gran Canaria. You were tanned all over. I think I vaguely recall someone called Nick.

But that was the time we drifted apart. Well, more than before. I was busy with work and the divorce, you were busy with Nick, I suppose.'

'I was thinking about that in the car while you were sleeping. As I said to gran, we haven't really seen much of each other since 97. I don't think she caught that. But you must remember that night.'

'A night in 97? Gail, I have problems remembering a night last week.'

'Oh, go on. When we stayed up all night to watch the election results coming in. And then we caught an early bus to Downing Street, singing Things Can Only Get Better.'

'Oh, that night! I remember that night. I was trying to pull that Polish student.' She laughed. 'The whole time I was flashing my tits and legs off as much as I could. All he could do was go on about how Lech whatsisname had betrayed the workers. Well, I don't know whether Lech baby screwed the workers, I certainly didn't get a screw that night. Really pissed me off.'

'I wish I'd listened to him. There we were, fired up with the idea that out generation would bring real change, we'd end the iniquities of modern capitalism, overturn Thatcher's evil legacy of privatisation ... and the rest. And look at what happened. Now we're all sitting in a pea green boat in the middle of a cesspit and the thing's fucking sinking. And if I do have children, and they ask me, what did you do to make a better world, what am I going to tell them? "Honey, I worked in advertising. It's not a bad job if you don't mind being fired for no reason twice a year." Let's face it, what have we actually achieved?'

'No, Gail, there you were. I warned you not to get all excited about politics. Or anything like that. Most of our generation just wanted a good time, and that's all you can hope for. A good drink, a good party, and a good fuck. All generations at that age want that. It's just the weirdos who see some bright new future. Probably smoked the wrong dope.'

'Well, you might not have scored with the Polish student, but we sure as hell all got screwed by the government we trusted. Never again. They're screaming like stuck pigs now. "We're listening." Like hell they are. So what if the Tories get back in. Who cares? From now on I intend to look after myself. Myself, my husband when I find him, and our children. Maybe Thatcher was right. There isn't such a thing as society.'

'Nor is there such a thing as a happy marriage. I found that out the hard way. I thought I was going to have a husband who would keep me in style and only turn up once every so often. Instead he gets promoted and lands a job where he doesn't have to travel, and I'm supposed to have to live with him turning up at six every evening complaining about his day at the office. As if I could give a shit. Put a right bloody crimp in my sex life.'

'You don't mean –'

'Course I bloody mean. You never would accept the reality. Remember what I kept on telling you about Nelson and Lady Hamilton? Old Charles the Second and Nell Gwynn?'

'Not really. I can't remember you concentrating hard on history when we were at school.'

'That's your problem. You believed all the shit they give out. You always have. They tell you that our dear hero Nelson was having an affair with Lady Hamilton. Bollocks. She was having an affair with him. He wouldn't have made it to her boudoir if she hadn't decided to have him there.'

Her face had become animated. She sighed, shook her head and leaned back.

'Whatever. Tell me about this Nick you were so busy with.'

'Not that busy, I dumped him a couple of months afterwards'

'But Gail, that was over five years ago.'

'It was five years ago, now I come to think of it. That was around Christmas time too.'

'You're mooning on about some git you dumped five years ago? Sure it's not premature menopause or something?'

Gail pursed her lips and looked at a bright pink jersey she was about to pack away.

'I like the idea of celebrating Christmas with a man in my life, Val. Preferably a husband. I definitely don't like the idea of ending up sitting in my flat all by myself watching other people celebrate on the telly. Finishing off the second bottle of gin and crying into my pot-noodle. If I can be arsed cooking the damn stuff. Or boiling it. Or whatever it is you do with pot noodle.'

'Nothing wrong with a good gin to make life look better. Anyway, you've changed your tune. What happened to the all-men-are-bastards song you were singing not so long ago? Coming up the creaking stairs, I think it was.'

'That was that shit, Garant. Two-timing little piece of rubbish. Waits until we've got to the going to bed stage before admitting he's married with a kid on the way.' She slammed a drawer closed. 'But there's got to be someone out there. Gran and granddad have been happily married for ever. Uncle Adam and Aunt Susan, ditto. Well, sort of. There has to be someone, there has to be. I just have to accept that you have to make certain sacrifices for happiness.' She sighed. 'I suppose even Cinderella had to make sacrifices after the fairytale. Prince Charming probably farted in bed or something.'

'Sacrifices such as not losing your rag when boyfriend comes home pissed? That's what Nick did, wasn't it, if I remember correctly? I do remember that bit. Or was that someone else?'

'That was Nick. Coming home pissed wasn't the problem. It was irritating, it always is when you're sober and they're not, but I could have handled that. No, coming home every night for weeks on end pissed was the problem. Especially the night we were supposed to be going to his folks' place for dinner. Four days before Christmas, it was. I had to phone his parents to tell them that we couldn't come because their darling son hadn't come home, that he was no doubt pissed as a parrot somewhere else. I'd put the decorations up that day. Since I wasn't doing very much else.'

Valerie's eyebrows rose.

'You told them that? That he was lying pissed out of his mind somewhere else?'

'Yup. I told his mother. I'd just had enough of Nick's behaviour. I was hoping to get a bit of sympathy from her, I knew his father was pretty much a heavy drinker. Oh, no. Know what she said?'

'What?'

'She basically implied that there must be something wrong with me if Nick had to get pissed before he got home every night. That any decent woman would make allowances for her man, make sure he had something to look forward to in coming home.'

'You're joking!'

'Nope. That was the last straw. It reminded me of all those evenings I had hoped he would come home sober so that we could go out for a drink together, or just stay in with a bottle of wine and a good meal. How I felt I couldn't have a drink until he got home, and then when he turned up drunk it just put me off the whole idea.' She grinned wryly. 'You know the funny thing?'

'There's a funny bit? Please, tell me. I like the funny bits. They stop me from feeling depressed. Which I'm beginning to feel now. In fact, I think I could do with a drink.'

'In a way. The funny bit is that I did end up doing all the cooking and cleaning, and it never crossed my mind that that might be unfair. All that feminist stuff we learnt at university, and I never once stopped and asked myself why it was that I was doing all the domestic work. I was quite happy with that. No, what really got me was him coming home pissed.'

'So you dumped him.'

'I told his mother to go fuck herself, preferably with something large and painful, went down to the local corner shop, got as many old boxes as they could find, went back to the flat and packed all his stuff – threw it in, rather than packed. Put them outside the door. And then left a note telling him to clear out.'

'Did he?'

'Damn right he did. Tried the "I'm so sorry it won't happen again" routine the next morning. That's when he finally turned up. Had a hangover, he'd slept at a mate's. I told him he was right, because he was out. It was my flat – I wasn't sure that that was a good thing, packing my stuff and walking out would have been a lot easier. In the end I was screaming at him to get out, the neighbours were complaining about the noise, and someone called the police.'

'Oh, boy, wish I could have been there.'

'The cops didn't. Two young blokes, the types who would rather face an armed burglar than an angry woman. They advised Nick to leave – I think they thought it would be temporary. I told Nick to take his stuff with him or it would end up in the rubbish. I don't think he believed me. As they left I began carrying all the boxes downstairs and put them down next to the bins. At first he tried pleading, but then gave up and packed everything he could in his car. He looked so pathetic – but he was good at looking pathetic the morning after – I almost felt like giving in and forgiving him. Until the last trip, when I noticed his beers in the fridge. I threw those out the window and told him to catch. It was a second-story flat. They splattered all over him and his car.'

'Bit of a waste. I don't like beer really, but a bit of a waste.'

'True. I realised that afterwards. But they made a cracking good explosion all over him.'

'And that was the end of Nick?'

'Not quite. He phoned a couple of times, left a few messages, promising to be good, begging to be taken back. I told him I'd report him to the police for harassment, and that was the last I heard of him or saw him, until two years later. I bumped into him and his wife, pushing a pram – he was pushing the pram. We didn't chat for long, but I heard later that the two of them had got together on the rebound, rushed into marriage. She turned out to be a right little bitch. Held him on a tight leash.'

'Sounds like you had a lucky escape. He sounds like a total drip.'

'Ah, no, that's the point. I spent that Christmas feeling terribly sorry for myself. Instead I should have realised how lucky I was.'

'Lucky to have broken up with Nick the drip.'

'I shouldn't have broken up with him. I should have let him come crawling back, slowly. Make him grovel. Gradually let him feel forgiven, but make sure that he understood that he couldn't treat me the way he had. He'd have to ask my permission to go out drinking with the lads.'

'You really want someone that feeble?'

'I wouldn't call it feeble. Just teaching him to have some respect. The thing is, all couples go through problems like that. The question is, do you build on them or let them break your relationship?'

'Let it break, I say. Life's too short. Move on to the next. Girls just wanna have fun, after all.'

Gail sighed, and then chuckled.

'I suppose maybe what I regret about breaking up with Nick was that I didn't get to see his mother's face. It would have been great to turn up at their place with Nick and make sure she knew I didn't regret telling her to go fuck herself. I would even have repeated it if necessary.'

'Bit of a cow, was she?'

'Oh, one of those mothers who thinks their little boy can't do anything wrong, it's always someone else's fault. Number one son, that sort of crap. I hope I don't fall into that trap.'

'Funny how every mother thinks so much of their kids, but they turn out to be pretty much the average.'

Gail paused, as if contemplating the idea that any children she might ever have were doomed to be just average.

'Wasn't it one of the French philosophers who said that most people live great lives without doing great things?' she asked. 'That's kind of what I feel like doing now.'

'I had a French lover once. Spent his whole time banging on about how good the French were at love, and food, and music. So much time he didn't have much left for the real thing – banging, that is. His cooking was pretty shit, too. Olive oil and garlic. All the time. Every single fucking meal.'

Gail sighed.

'All I want is a man I can look after and love, is that so much to ask for?'

Valerie smiled a memory smile, a half-bitter smile.

'From what you say you won't find one here. Not this Christmas. Not unless there are some hunky young peasants in the village. And that I doubt. Too many Landrovers. Four-by-fours. Yuppies, I expect.'

'No, guess not. Nope, it's a time for comfy old pyjamas, thick towelling dressing gowns, and sitting in front of log fires wearing those silly furry slippers with the cute little rabbit's heads on the front. Getting pleasantly pissed, but not totally sozzled.'

There was a pause.

'You didn't bring those slippers along, did you? They must be ancient. And they look stupid.'

'I like those slippers.'

'Well, you know the ancient Chinese saying.'

'What's that?'

'Men don't make passes at girls wearing rabbit arses.'

'They aren't made of real rabbits, Val, you know that.'

'Same principle. There's only one type of fur men are interested in.'

Gail shook her head and looked at her friend.

'I wonder if I should warn gran that there's something more dangerous than loose wires in the servants' quarters.'

'There is?'

'Yes, loose screws in this bedroom.'

Chapter Four: Who's Who

Valerie laughed, looked at her, the side of her lips curled up. She took out a hip-flask.

'Fancy a nip?' she asked.

'A bit early for me, Val.'

'Suit yourself, I need a bit of the hair of the dog,' Valerie said, taking a swig. 'So how are Adam and the others these days? Last time I saw him was that week we all went over to France. When we were sweet sixteen. I'll never forget that week. Best week I'd ever have.'

'Now you're talking ancient history.' She pushed a hand through her hair, remembering. 'I'll never forget that week either, though I've tried my best. I was in bed the whole time while you lot were swimming or sunbathing or whatever. Bloody food poisoning. Either in bed or the loo. It was only the second last day I was able to get out. Took me years to face French food again.'

'I remember it was your Uncle Adam, his wife Susan, your dad and mum, us two and – who else was there?'

'A lot of French bacteria. It was another world, Val. It happened to people who no longer exist.'

'The first thing your mum said to me was, "Please don't call me Mrs Green, Valerie, it makes me feel old. Just call me Jane – and not Aunt Jane, just Jane." That made me feel grown up for the first time. Funny that. The things you remember.'

'Val, I prefer to forget some things. Being sixteen is one of them. Having a crush on your uncle is another.'

'Hey, remember the bikini I wore? That bright red one, the one my mother didn't know about?'

'No, Val, I was in bed the whole time, remember? In bed or

on the loo.'

'Good times,' Valerie said, looking at the ceiling. 'Your folks, Adam, Peter – I'd forgotten Peter was there. Ah, well, that was then, this is now. How are they all doing these days?'

Gail glanced at her. She lay on the bed looking up at the ceiling, apparently too lost in memories to notice Gail's look. It lasted for several seconds before Gail continued, taking out a white towelling robe.

'I don't know, really. It's been ages since I saw most of them.' She stopped unpacking and looked at her open suitcase. 'You know, I think that week was probably the last time we were all together as a family. After that – well, we finished school, went to university, and ...' She resumed unpacking. 'I haven't seen dad since he and mum split up. Mum's been travelling all over Europe on business. As far as I know Peter's shacked up with a partner, they've got a kid but aren't married, which sounds very strange for Peter.' She paused. 'You listening? I said that Peter's got a kid, but not married.'

'I heard. What about old Uncle Adam, the Stern Prophet?'

Gail threw a pile of panties into a cupboard drawer.

'Uncle Adam's going to be something big in politics, though I'm not sure what. Whatever it is will piss mum off, she tries not to show it, but she gets hacked off when anyone sings uncle Adam's praises, especially gran.'

'I remember you saying that once. Remind me, why was that?'

'Oh, usual story – number one son, again. Uncle Adam was the first born, and a boy. Took me a while to work that one out – why my mom was jealous of him. Light of his mother's eye – my gran, that is – top of his class, always in the first team in every sport, cups galore. Mom felt side-lined, I think. She was just a girl, something to be brought up and married off as soon as possible. Different days, then. After all, we're talking about – when, just after the war? Mom was born in the mid-Fifties, Uncle Adam sometime before that, just after the war, I think. Wooden coat hangers, good quality,' she said, as if suddenly noticing them in the cupboard. 'That'll be gran. She can't stand plastic or wire coat hangers. You can tell by the way she looks, blinks her eyes and says "that's interesting". It's her way of calling something crap.'

'I think it's something to do with motherhood,' said Valerie, stretching and yawning. 'Pregnancy scrambles the brains somehow. A man can be screwing half the world but to his mother he's still a little angel. And if she finds out then it's someone else's fault. His wife's normally. Show me a serial murderer and I'll bet you his mother will be there somewhere blaming his friends. Or the victims. Women are born to be victims. Well, fuck that, I ain't going to be one.'

'Must be boy babies. Incompatible with our hormones, or something. Maybe men should have boy babies and women only little girls.'

'Thank god I've never had the maternal urge.'

Gail paused in hanging up a dress.

'You know,' she said, 'talking about that week in France, when I was hoping I was going to die because living didn't seem worth it – well, come to think of it, mum was at my side every time I woke. I think she was really worried about me. I don't remember seeing dad once. I can only presume he was out enjoying himself. Mum was always there when I needed her, dad only turned up in the good times, and who did I hate when I was a teenager? Mum, of course. There's definitely something wrong – a design flaw in humans. Why do we women do it to each other?'

Valerie rolled over, leaned on her arm and looked at Gail. A smile played over her lips.

'Will they be here for Christmas – your mom and your devastatingly handsome dad?'

'Mum's in Italy, so she can't make it. I can't see dad turning up. I get the feeling that everyone has said they might come. Or maybe not. I think it's a case of A will come if B doesn't, or C will turn up only if D will. E hasn't been speaking to F since – since they had a falling out over G's wedding or something. Who made the better trifle for the school fete, something stupid like that. Normal family sort of stuff. I like to sit on the side-lines enjoying the spectacle. It's better than blood sports.'

'What about Adam? Good old Uncle Adam.'

'I don't know. I hope he and Aunt Susan turn up. You remember my Aunt Susan always had a bit of a religious fixation? I'd like to see if she still has it.'

'A bit? Christ! She was a nutter. More Catholic than the Catholics.'

'Not that bad, surely? Anyway, she's Church of England, not Catholic.'

'High Church. Bloody high. Still, whatever ripples your knickers.'

Gail closed a cupboard door with some force.

'Val, do try not to use language like that downstairs. Remember this is my grandparents' home, not some watering club in Soho.'

Valerie shook her head.

'Any chance of waking up on Christmas day to find Z in the billiard room with a knife in his back?' she asked. 'Or her back?'

'Oh, I doubt if things will get that bad. Maybe a punch-up at best. Just don't let granddad wind you up though, he's good at that. He has a cruel sense of humour. But you probably remember that.'

'He's okay, so long as you know how to flirt with him, I remember that well enough,' Valerie replied, taking out her mobile phone. 'At least he's pretty harmless compared with some others I've known. Hey, I can't get a signal on my mobile. This isn't a black spot, is it?'

'Better not be. I'm preparing a special Christmas present for that bastard.'

'Garant?'

'Yes, his wife is going to get a rather nasty call on Christmas day. I'm going to make sure that both have a very crappy histmas.'

Valerie laughed.

'I think I'm going to enjoy Christmas this year,' she said. 'I might even start singing Jingle Bells.'

'You do that, Val, and you'll be bloody Z in the bloody billiard room. With the knife. Sticking out of your back. Or possibly somewhere else.'

Valerie laughed, and then stopped.

'Was that the doorbell?' she asked as the booming noise flowed slowly around the house.

'Certainly sounds like it. Let's go downstairs for that cup of tea and see whether any of the other victims have turned up.'

Chapter Five: To Have and to Hope

Winifred Browne had just put the kettle on when the distant bongs of the doorbell came through.

'Definitely the delivery man this time,' she told the large teapot. She made her way along the passage, and opened the front door.

'Hope!' she exclaimed, finding a young woman and man waiting. The woman had short, dirty-blonde hair and a sallow face. She was smiling. The man was wearing gold-rimmed spectacles, a brown leather jacket and a serious look. 'Come in, come in. Oh, dash, I meant to call you before you got here. Still, never mind, come in. This must be the boyfriend.'

'Hello, gran. Yes, this is Tom. Tom, this is my gran.'

'How do you do, Mrs Browne? Maria – Hope has told me all about you. Apparently we'll all be obese by the time the New Year arrives.'

He had a soft, deep voice, slow, with a faint suggestion of a burr in it, Scottish or Irish, possibly.

'Oh, I wouldn't put it that way, Tom. But it is the festive season, after all. And there are plenty of walks around here to stimulate your appetite before, and work things off afterwards. Come in, come in. Let's get you unpacked. The kettle's just boiled, I was just about to make some tea.'

'It's much larger than I expected, gran,' the girl said as they carried their suitcases in. 'And those walls at the entrance! They must be at least ten feet tall. Were they built to keep people in, or keep people out? They look a bit crumbly now, though.'

'A lot of it is crumbly, I'm afraid. We will definitely not be spending any money on the outside walls. Not for a while.

Though whether we'll sell them for scrap, or whatever the term for old bricks is, I don't know. We might just let them crumble away in their own time. We'll just have to hope that they don't fall on anyone.'

'Why on earth did you buy it?'

'That was your grandfather's idea, Hope. He claims it's an investment, but I think one of the reasons was so that he could have you all around for Christmas, and probably the summer. You know what he's like.'

'Still as bloody-minded as ever? Granddad?'

'Well, you could put it that way, my dear. Now, will it be two rooms or one?'

'Do you think it would upset granddad if we shared the same room, gran? Do you have one with two beds?'

'He'd be scandalised, my dear. Just a second while I close this door. The latch doesn't catch if you don't do it properly. It's a bit old and quirky. That's one thing you will have to watch when you go out. It often appears to be closed, but swings open when you're not looking.'

'In that case we'll share, gran. It'll be an early Christmas present for granddad. He loves having something to be scandalised about.'

'Quite right, my dear, quite right. I look forward to telling him. Ah, Gail, Valerie, you're coming downstairs, good, the kettle has just boiled. This is Tom, Hope's boyfriend, Tom, this is my granddaughter Gail and her friend Valerie.'

Gail and Valerie paused as they came down the stairs. Gail's eyes locked briefly on Tom's. Valerie's stayed on Hope's. They continued walking down, Gail blushing slightly. Tom took his glasses off and began cleaning them with a handkerchief.

'How do you do, Tom?' Gail said, smiling and holding her

hand out. He dropped his handkerchief, shook her hand, and bent down quickly to retrieve it.

'Hope, I don't remember whether you and Valerie ever knew each other,' Winifred Browne continued, as if not noticing the sudden clenching of Hope's jaw, nor the slightly curled sneer in Valerie's lips. 'They were all at the same boarding school, Tom, I'm afraid you might find yourself having to listen to hours of reminiscing.'

'Yes, gran,' Hope said slowly, 'Valerie and I know each other very well, don't we, Valerie?'

'It's been a long time, Hope,' Gail said as cheerfully as she could, glancing from Valerie to Hope. Tom's eyebrows rose as he too looked from one to the other, before resting on Gail with an inquisitive glance. She shrugged her own eyebrows, scratched the side of her head and then looked at the floor. She noticed that Tom's shoes were scuffed. They had the appearance of the type of shoes worn by someone who rated comfort over appearance. If he ever thought about it. His baggy brown corduroy trousers suggested the latter to her. His chunky leather jacket spoke not of fashion, but of something designed with one purpose, to keep the wearer warm.

'Some things you tend to remember,' Hope said, her eyes still locked with Valerie's. Valerie smiled back, amused.

'Right, well I'll take Tom and Hope to their room,' Winifred Browne said. 'You two go on and say hello to granddad, he's in the television room, just along the corridor. I'll be down in a second.'

'I'd forgotten about old Hopeless,' Valerie said as she and Gail went in search of the television room.

'I'd forgotten about you and Duncan.'

'Hope obviously hasn't.'

'Well, be fair, Val, he was her boyfriend.'

'Rubbish. She was besotted by him. He didn't even know she existed. Let's face it, she always was a bit of a wet. I'll bet you that she's still a virgin, even now.'

'I think it might be better to pretend it never happened. Otherwise it could turn out to be a rather bloody fortnight.'

'That Tom looks like a bit of a hunk. Wavy brown hair on a man just gets my hormones going every time.'

'Anything on a man gets your hormones going, Val.'

Valerie laughed.

'I prefer them when they haven't got anything on. You can tell what you're getting.'

Gail shuddered.

'Thank god for clothes,' she said.

'I wonder what he sees in her,' mused Valerie. 'Maybe she's just something to keep the bed warm until something better turns up. And you know, I think I just have.'

'Don't even think of it, Val,' Gail warned. Valerie laughed.

'Come off it, Gail, I could feel you quivering next to me yourself. Don't tell me you weren't thinking exactly the same thing. I could see where you were looking.'

'I was not quivering. In fact I was having a bout of deja vu. I could have sworn that I've already met him, but I know I haven't. It's almost as if we knew each other in a past life – or something. Gave me the shivers.'

'I think I know what gave you the shivers, and it wasn't anything to do with a past life.'

'Val, he isn't even your type. He's the type of man who – who needs a woman to look after him. I noticed that straight away, that jacket, and his shoes – '

'Oh, come off it, Gail. He's ideal for a Christmas fling. Men definitely are just for flings, not for life. Stop pretending you don't fancy that too.'

'If you really want to know, Val, I think he looks like a decent young man who happens to be my cousin's boyfriend, and consequently out of bounds. Even if I fell head over heels in love with him he would be out of bounds. Which, of course, I haven't.'

'You know what, Gail? I am ever so grateful I don't suffer from your morals.'

'Just don't try anything, Val. I'm warning you. I mean it.'

Valerie looked at her.

'Because she's your cousin's boyfriend, or because you fancy him for yourself?' she asked.

'Try to control yourself for once in your life, Val.'

'I will if you will.'

'Of course I will. I mean there's nothing to control myself about, after all.'

Valerie laughed.

'Bet you won't be wearing those rabbit slippers after all.'

She paused.

'And I bet you I'll have him before you do.'

Chapter Six: The Odd Couple

Upstairs Winifred Browne ushered the young couple into a large bedroom.

'Here you are, Hope. We call it the red room, because of the wallpaper. Personally I think of it as more maroon than red, but your grandfather insists that it's red, especially when he's not wearing his glasses. And there's a nice view over the fields. It gets the afternoon sun. Much better in the summer, of course, the days are so short at the moment.'

'Oh, it's lovely, gran! Look at those duvets! I'm not sure I'll be able to get out of bed in the mornings.'

'There are a couple of oil heaters which warm the room up quite quickly. So long as you remember not to leave the door open too long. Your grandfather wants to have central heating installed, but he wants to keep the fireplaces. He also wants to have double glazing, but keep the original windows.'

'Still expecting the impossible, then?'

'You could say that, my dear. He's full of plans for the future, anyway. When he's awake, that is. Come down when you're ready, turn left at the bottom of the stairs and go straight down the passage, the kitchen is right at the end. There's a nice fire going and the tea will be ready.' She carefully closed the door behind her as she left.

'Your gran is quite a woman,' Tom said to Hope, putting their suitcases down. 'Asking straight out like that – whether we wanted one room or two, I mean.'

Hope jumped onto one of the single beds and lay there on her back, sprawling.

'She's great, I love her to pieces. I'm sure she meant to phone me and ask about us more subtly, but failing that she's quite happy to ask straight questions. And she makes it seem perfectly normal. Funny, that.'

'Funny?'

'She's very religious. Church every Sunday – High Church, preferably. Good works, looking after the poor, giving to charity, the sanctity of marriage, all the rest. Yet she never seems fazed by what other people do. I think she believes it's up to each of us to choose our own paths.'

Tom wandered over to a chest of drawers and opened the top drawer.

'Better get unpacked, I suppose,' he said.

'I suppose so,' she replied, standing up and throwing her suitcase on one of the beds. Tom looked at the beds.

'Don't get any ideas, Tom. I've told you before, there's going to be none of what you're thinking of until I'm sure you really love me. Until then we'll be in separate beds.'

Tom took his glasses off, looked at them, and began cleaning them.

'Better find a dragon to slay, then,' he murmured.

'What's that?'

'Oh, nothing. Just wondering how I'm supposed to prove my true love.'

'You'll know when the time comes. You'd better get unpacked. Come on, the others are waiting downstairs.'

Tom began transferring his clothes to the cupboard. It was done in the automatic manner of someone used to packing and unpacking.

'Will I have to call you Hope as well?' he asked. 'It's very confusing.'

'My name is Maria. Let that lot call me Hope if they want to. They know I don't like it. I can't blame gran, she's always thought of me as Hope, but the others do it deliberately.'

'Bad blood, eh? Sounds like it might turn out to be an interesting Christmas.'

'I'm sure there'll be blood on the carpet before long.'

'Valerie's?'

'I certainly hope so.'

He paused.

'Maria?'

'Yes? I think I need to get changed before we go down.'

He watched as she stripped off her clothes and began rummaging for new ones. Off went the baggy old jumper and men's jeans, revealing what she called her "old but comfy" knickers and bra, on came the short and tight white t-shirt and tight white jeans she had to lie down to get into. She wore a silver chain and crucifix around her neck which was carefully tucked into the t-shirt after a brief kiss. That was followed by a baggy black sweat-shirt which saved Tom from having to look at the small roll of stomach pushed out between the white jeans and the t-shirt. He had known her for six months. She had moved into his flat a month before, taking over the spare bedroom, after an argument with her landlord. He was still trying to get used to her lack of embarrassment in changing clothes in front of him, or coming out of her bedroom for breakfast wearing only a long t-shirt which kept sliding off her shoulders. Yet refusing to share his bed until he had found the secret of how to prove his love for her.

'What I've been trying to work out,' he said slowly, concentrating on a pair of trousers in his hand, 'is the way you kept changing your mind about coming here.'

'I wasn't changing my mind,' she replied, putting on earrings and then applying make-up in the mirror. 'It was purely a question of whether we should have a quiet Christmas on our own or not. That's all.'

'Until, strangely enough, when you heard that this Valerie person was going to be here. And then, suddenly, we were definitely coming down. Maria,' he continued, coming up behind her and putting his arms around her waist, 'what exactly is going on?'

'Tom, stop that, I'm trying to put some make-up on.'

'Sorry,' he said, sitting down on the bed, elbows on his knees.

'Right, that should do. How do I look?'

'Exquisite,' he replied without looking up, rubbing his forehead as if he was getting a headache.

'Good. Let battle commence.'

'Maria, I am not here to do battle. I thought it was going to be a quiet Christmas with your grandparents in some old country house they'd bought. That was the whole point. Quiet walks along the river, snuggling up in front of log fires, forgetting about work and everything. The perfect Christmas, right out of the picture books.'

'Do you think this shade suits me? The lipstick, I mean? Not too red, is it?'

'It's perfect, Maria. Would you mind telling me what's going on?'

'Oh, shush, Tom. Let's go down.'

He looked at his toes, as if to ask them a question. They curled up. He pulled at the shoelaces on his feet.

'So what did Valerie do to you?'

'Never mind, Tom. I'm not going to rake it up.'

He looked at her.

'I'm not going to rake it up,' he quoted slowly. She smiled back. Or at least her scarlet lips turned up.

'No,' she said. 'A rake isn't the implement I plan on using.'

Chapter Seven: Memories

In the kitchen Gail and Valerie sat sipping tea while Mrs Browne carefully put a tea-cosy over the teapot and patted it.

'This place must have cost an absolute fortune, gran,' Gail noted. 'A real fire in the kitchen! I've never seen one of those before.'

'Well, your grandfather has always been good at bargaining. And it was more or less run down. The builders have been in and out over the last six months. Oh, while I think about it, be careful which cupboards you open. The electric box under the stairs has some loose connections, or something. The electrician has promised to fix them first thing in the New Year. Apparently it is safe enough, but if we fiddle with it the whole house could go up in flames or explode or something. Perhaps we'll just lose power. I suspect he's just exaggerating to make sure we don't hire someone else. They do, you know, these builders.'

'It must be wonderful to wake up on a winter's morning and come down to a roaring log fire.'

'Yes, my dear, it probably would be if you didn't have to light the fire yourself. Did you say hello to your grandfather?'

'We popped in, but he was sleeping. We thought we shouldn't disturb him. Don't you have anyone to help you out? Cleaning lady, something like that?'

'Oh, there's Mrs Toodle from the village, she comes in three times a week. And her son delivers the coal and fills up the scuttles. The logs we have delivered from a company. Apparently they're one of the few remaining companies to do so. Deliveries, that is.'

'Mrs Toodle? You have a cleaning lady called Mrs Toodle?'

'Yes, I think her first name is Martha, but I call her Mrs Toodle and she calls me Mrs Browne. You know, most of the villagers are quite old-fashioned – or perhaps they still see us as strangers. Everyone is Mr or Mrs or Miss. Definitely not Ms. Apart from Doctor Jameson, who is of course called Doctor. And the vicar, Reverend Wilkins. He, for some reason best known to himself, decided to keep a pig. It keeps escaping and trying to eat lampposts, for some reason best known to itself.'

'A pig? The vicar owns a pig? That's fantastic! I mean, a vicar would be good enough, but a vicar who owns a pig? Is it a vicious pig?'

'Oh, my goodness, no. It's very friendly. It likes having its back scratched.'

'That's a pity, gran. But, you know, when people ask me what sort of Christmas I had, I think I might make it a slavering, wild, man-eater. Roaming the streets at night, that sort of thing. Or the fields or whatever.'

'Yes, dear. Biscuits, tsk, I've forgotten the biscuits.' She stood up and went to a cupboard. 'You used to love pink wafers when you were a child, do you remember?'

'Pink wafers! I'd forgotten about those. Uncle Adam used to tease me about that. Everyone else wanted chocolate, I just wanted the pink wafers.' She hugged herself. 'This is going to be great, gran. I feel as if I'm an eight-year-old kid again. Pink wafers! Whoo-hoo!'

'Here you go, I bought a selection. I'm not sure how good they are. The supermarkets are so full of boxes of biscuits, Christmas puddings, you wonder how on earth they can make so much without losing something, some of the quality, that is.'

'I can't stand Christmas pudding,' Valerie said, helping herself to a chocolate biscuit. 'Ever since we got back to boarding school one January and had Christmas pudding every evening for a week. It was absolutely vile. And the custard! Eurgh, I can still taste it.'

'I remember that,' said Gail looking at a pink wafer in her hand. 'I think they must have bought a load cheap. I remember we argued over what it was made of.'

'Not even the pigs would eat it,' said Valerie. 'We had some as part of some project or other.' She giggled. 'Remember your little sister? How we –'

'I can hear voices,' a loud voice said, slow, heavy steps coming along the passage, accompanied by the regular thudding of a walking stick. 'Which one of the little buggers has turned up?'

'I think your grandfather has woken up.'

'Gail!' George Browne exclaimed on entering the kitchen. 'My gorgeous granddaughter! Come, give your gramps a kiss. Winifred, why didn't you tell me that Gail had arrived?'

'We didn't want to disturb your afternoon nap, George,' Winifred replied as George Browne threw both arms around Gail, narrowly missing Valerie with his walking stick.

'Nap? Nonsense! I wasn't having a nap, I was watching a very interesting documentary. Probably why I missed the sound of the doorbell.'

'Hello, grandad. This is Valerie. We were at school together, do you remember?'

'Valerie! My goodness! The last time I saw you, you were wearing ... a school uniform.'

'A gymslip, I think you remember best, George.'

'You know, I think we should have tea in the front parlour. To celebrate.'

'Later, George, when everyone else turns up. This kitchen is quite large enough at the moment, and I'm not fetching and carrying unless it's absolutely necessary. Anyway, the front parlour, as you insist on calling it, will be far too cold. The fire hasn't been lit. And there's no sense in wasting good logs while we have a fire in here.'

George Browne put his walking stick against the wall and sat down, smiling at Gail. His wife got up to get him a cup.

'Let me give you a hand, gran.'

'No, that's okay, Gail, I think we've got everything at the moment. I'll just get a box of shortbread from the cupboard. Your grandfather likes shortbread. He did yesterday, anyway.'

George Browne changed his view and bristled his eyebrows at Valerie.

'So, Valerie, didn't I hear that you got married a few years ago? Where is he, looking after the little ones?'

'Married and divorced, Mr Browne. Now happily single again. And no children, thank – heavens.'

'Married and divorced? Still, not surprising, I suppose. Young men today don't know they're born. Don't know how to appreciate a fine-looking woman.'

'Oh, he knew how to appreciate a good looking woman, Mr Browne. The trouble was he appreciated them so much he had affairs with as many of them as he could.'

Gail looked at her with raised eyebrows.

'Shameful! Ah, I feel sorry for you youngsters today. When I was a young man the thought would never have even entered our heads. Fidelity, that was the word. Fidelity. Until death do us part. That's what we said, and we meant it.'

'To honour and obey, I remember that bit,' his wife said, sitting down. 'They don't use those words any more, do they?'

'More's the pity. Damn feminism came along and ripped the family apart. And look at the result. Single mothers all over the place, whining that the country owes them a living. Should be at home looking after the children while their husbands earn a living. That's the way the world was designed. And those wet leftie politicians spouting nonsense about equality won't ever change nature, no matter what they say.'

'Now, now, George. So, Valerie, what is it you do these days? Weren't you in advertising with Gail?'

'I was until a few days ago, Mrs Browne – a different company to Gail's. I gave up the job. I'll have to start looking for another in January. It happens.'

'What about you, Gail?' asked George Browne. 'Your grandmother told me that you were going out with something called Ganant. Not coming, is he?'

'Garant. No, granddad, we split up a few days ago.'

'Split up? Good for you, my girl. Can't have you going out with someone with a silly name like that. But you'll have to do something, my dear, you're getting on. How old are you now, thirty? Thirty one?'

'Thirty, grandad.'

'Thirty? Unmarried and no children at thirty? Your grandmother was nineteen when she had Adam. And we had the war. And after the war rationing continued for years. No money. Hardly any food. Would have been easy to use that as an excuse but we didn't. I don't know, you youngsters today.'

'Would you have done the same, Mrs Browne?' asked Valerie. 'I mean, if you had the choice, would you still have got married young and had so many children?'

'I think this tea has gone cold. I'd better make a fresh pot.'

Chapter Eight: Photographs

'I think real men went out with your generation, Mr Browne,' Valerie said as Mrs Browne emptied the teapot into the sink, straining out the tea-leaves to be put into the compost bag. George Browne's reply was interrupted by the appearance of Maria-Hope and Tom at the kitchen door.

'Ah, Hope, Tom, there you are,' said Winifred Browne, 'come in, sit down. Tom, this is Hope's grandfather.'

'Hope! Come here, a kiss for granddad, there's a good girl.'

Tom watched as Maria-Hope gave her grandfather a quick kiss and then retreated to help her grandmother.

'How do you do, Mr Browne?' Tom asked.

'Not bad considering my age, boy. Pretty well, in fact. So, you're Hope's boyfriend, are you? He doesn't look as bad as I expected, Hope. Probably the best you could hope for, eh? I tell you, Tom, the girl was always so useless with boyfriends we thought we should rename her Hopeless. Eh? Ha ha ha.'

'Sit down, Tom. Would you like tea or coffee? Or perhaps something stronger? Or orange juice or blackberry – we've got quite a selection, just in case the great-grandchildren turn up.'

'Tea sounds great, Mrs Browne,' Tom said, taking a seat which left a gap between himself and George Browne on the one side and Gail and Valerie on the other.

'So, Tom, what is it you do?' demanded George Browne. 'Not another librarian like Hopeless here, are you? Got a proper job?'

'Tom is a photographic journalist, grandad.'

'A what? A pornographic journalist? A pornographic journalist? In my house?' George Browne glared at his walking stick leaning against the wall as if wishing it was within his grasp so that he could thump the floor with it.

'No, grandad,' Maria-Hope almost shouted, 'a photo-graphic journalist.'

'No need to shout, Hope, I'm not deaf. A reporter, then? Don't tell me you're one of these popporotsi crowd I read about? Disgusting! Unbelievable the things they get up to. All those shots of young women in bikinis taken from a distance with a telephoto lens or whatever it is. Some dirty grubbing pervert hiding a mile away under a bush. Still, bloody Italians, can't expect any better from them. During the war –'

'Hope's grandfather dislikes it so much, Tom, that he spends half an hour every day perusing the tabloids in the local news-agent to make sure that they're as bad as everyone says.'

'Nonsense, Winifred! I don't even go down to the newsagents every day. So, Tom, not one of the grubby crowd, are you? I hope not. There's that word again. Hope, your parents must have been mad or drunk when they christened you. Much prefer the name you decided to call yourself. Mary. Much better. A good old-fashioned name. Comes from the bible, you know. Not many things do, but that's one of them.'

'That's Maria, gramps, as you well know.'

'That's what I said, isn't it? Well, Tom, are you a muckraker?'

'No, Mr Browne, I'm not one of the paparazzi. I cover the political scene mainly.'

'Tom was a war reporter, until he was put into hospital when he was hit by a shell about a year ago.'

'It was only a little piece of shrapnel, Maria. No need to exaggerate. Just caught me in the wrong place. A calf wound. Meant I couldn't run as fast when I needed to. So I was transferred to the political department for a few months. Been there ever since.'

'Does that mean you meet the people in power?' asked Valerie. 'The prime minister and that sort of thing?'

Tom smiled.

'No, I'm afraid not. Well, not very often, anyway. Most I can manage on a good day is a shadow cabinet minister, and then it's normally off the record. They prefer off the record. And even then they never tell you more than they absolutely have to. Quite often you find that they're asking you the questions.'

'I'm sure you're just being modest, Tom,' Gail said, smiling at him. 'Come on, tell us some of the gossip of Westminster and Whitehall, or wherever it is. All the juicy scandal. Who's being a naughty boy. Or a naughty girl.'

Tom blushed slightly and looked down at the table.

'Have you met Hope's father, Adam Browne?' Winifred Browne asked, returning to the table with the fresh pot of tea. 'He's quite well known, so I'm told. He does work a little too hard, though.'

'The success story of the Brownes,' George Browne said. 'Or one of them. All the Brownes have been success stories. I brought my children up to work hard and play hard. No namby-pambying. None of this modern nonsense. Adam is a fine example of what a young man can achieve if brought up properly.'

'Have you met him?' Winifred Browne asked Tom again.

Tom nodded and put his teacup down.

'Yes, Mrs Browne, I have, several times, strangely enough. I'd interviewed him twice before Maria and I met. It took a while for the penny to drop that he was Maria's father, you don't expect a coincidence like that. I mentioned it to him the last time I met him, which was about, oh, about a year ago. I haven't seen him since, apparently they're busy as hell planning for the next election. Whenever that's going to be.

Could be in February. Maybe much later, the year after, possibly. It's the bane of our lives, trying to second-guess when they'll call it. It makes me think that the Americans have the right idea. At least they know exactly when their elections will happen. Though I'm grateful ours don't last as long as theirs.'

'There was an article in the paper the other day saying that if their party get in he'll probably get the Foreign Office. Is that true, Tom?'

'I wouldn't put any money on it, to be honest, Mrs Browne. That sort of thing starts as a rumour in Westminster and becomes news by the time it gets to the editor's room. Actually, sometimes it starts as a rumour and becomes news in the editor's room. Even when there is a hint of truth it could be true today and gone tomorrow. Politics is a strange world. I'm just glad I only report on it rather than work in it.'

'He has an entry in Who's Who, doesn't he?' asked Valerie.

'Quite a small one. Not very much to go on. University, degree, married with two children, that's about it.'

'Just as well,' George Browne said, nodding his head. 'It's ridiculous the amount of trivial information people seem to insist on forcing on you these days. What every celebrity did the night before, what they had for breakfast, the problems they had teething. Most of it made up, of course. Pure invention. Made up by those spin doctors and that sort. We aren't even in the telephone directory. I made sure of that. Don't want any Tom, Dick or Harry ringing us up to find out our opinion on some nonsense in the news as they do these days.'

'What made you want to go into journalism?' asked Gail.

Tom smiled again.

'I'm afraid I grew up with this rather idealistic notion of

55

journalists as being dashing heroes, racing all over the world, surviving danger at every turn, to bring back crucial news to the people at home. Oh, and they were all extremely honest and never told a single lie. Fortunately that ethos does still exist in little pockets. Only little pockets, but it's not quite dead.'

'What about your parents?' asked George Browne. 'Old family, I take it? Sons become soldiers or bishops, that sort of thing.'

Tom blinked at the sudden change of topic.

'No, Mr Browne. My father was a bus driver. He's retired now. Both my parents are very proud of me, perhaps too much so. But my father has always been staunchly Labour. I think he found it difficult to become accustomed to a son who has been through university. He's not quite sure whether it's a good thing or not. Unfortunately I don't have any brothers or sisters to compare with.'

'You never told me about that,' said Maria-Hope. 'About your parents, I mean. You just said they were retired. A bus-driver?'

Tom appeared to think about this for a few seconds. He was about to reply when George Browne took over the conversation.

'And you, Gail? How's my favourite granddaughter doing? How's work?'

'So-so, granddad. Things are changing in advertising. The Internet is the big thing these days. It's becoming quite complex. We used to be able to rely on television and the newspapers, radio, that sort of thing, but it's much more diverse. Viewing and reading figures have dropped over the last few years – plummeted, really. It's a different world. Has journalism changed that much, Tom?'

'I'm not surprised,' George Browne said, 'the rubbish they have on the television these days. Only themselves to blame. So-called comedy shows which are filled with swearing. Schoolboy nonsense. And all this Opera Woodfrey rubbish. In the old days we would have been embarrassed by people like that, kept them out of sight. Now they parade their inadequacies in public view. Sickening, that's what it is, sickening. As for that Big Bother – I couldn't believe that we as a nation could sink so low. No wonder the army's having trouble in the Middle East. Not enough discipline.'

'Gran, you were talking about the walks around here,' Maria-Hope said.

'Yes, my dear. It's a lovely place for walks, even now, in the winter. Oh, I hope it doesn't snow too soon. Or at least not too heavily. Some of the older villagers come up with terrible stories of being snowed in for weeks.'

'Used to be much more open in my day, around here,' George Browne put in. 'Far too built up now. Hardly recognised the place. Just lucky the old village remains the way it was.'

'You used to live here, Mr Browne?'

'Indeed, Valerie. Adam – our eldest son, don't know if you ever met him – he was born here.'

'Yes, I know Uncle Adam. Or knew, I suppose you could say. I was saying to Gail earlier that I haven't seen him or the others since we left school. We seem to have drifted apart.'

'I think Tom and I will go for a little walk,' Maria-Hope said, standing up. 'Unless there's something we can help you with, gran?'

'Goodness, no, plenty of time before dinner, you and Tom get off. Speaking of which, does anyone have any special requirements? I believe that there are so many allergies going around these days. Gluten, that's the word I remember. I can never find anything that explains what gluten is, but so many people appear to be allergic to it.'

'I'm vegan, gran,' said Maria-Hope. 'But I'm okay with milk and cheese. And eggs. And organic chicken. And fish that come from the proper sources.'

The only people who seemed unfazed by this announcement were Tom, George Browne and Winifred Browne. Tom had heard it before. George Browne was staring at the floor, occasionally risking a glance at Tom, a glance which was an equal mixture of dislike and admiration. He appeared to be itching to ask a question. Winifred Browne had taken out another list and was scrutinising it, her lips moving.

'Then we'll be able to manage,' said Winifred Browne, nodding at the list. 'Now off you go, and have a good walk.'

'You sure, gran?' asked Maria-Hope.

'Well, if you get back in an hour or two you could help me peel the potatoes and the carrots, if you really want to.'

'We'll do that, gran, won't we, Val?' said Gail.

'If you really want to, Gail,' replied Valerie, inspecting her fingernails while not looking at Tom.

'What about you two?' Mrs Browne asked as Tom and Maria-Hope left. 'Don't you fancy a walk?'

'I think I do,' Valerie said, springing up. 'If we hurry we might catch the other two up. Let's grab our coats, Gail.'

Gail shot her a puzzled frown and then stood up and followed her.

Chapter Nine: A Walk in the Woods

'I suppose you realised that Valerie was flirting with you?' Maria-Hope asked as they strolled through a wood of leafless trees.

'Was she? I didn't really notice.'

'Oh, come on, Tom, it was obvious. She flirts with every man she meets. Don't tell me you didn't realise she was coming on to you. She was even flirting with grandad when we walked in, you heard her.'

'Honestly, Maria, I really didn't notice anything. People – both men and women – do seem to think that I've got the inside line to the latest political gossip which can't be printed, that's all she was asking about. I had rather hoped to get away from that. At least for Christmas.'

'Right, I believe you. Not. Any fool could see that she was making eyes at you.'

'Maria, even if she did, she would be wasting her time. I'm here with you, aren't I?'

Maria-Hope did not reply. She carried on walking, hands forced into her jacket pockets, scowling at the ground.

'Oh, come on, Maria, give me a break. I can understand that you're pissed off with her for some reason, but does it have to affect our relationship? Can't you just forget it and ignore her? Why are you having a go at me because of her?'

'I wasn't having a go at you, Tom. You don't understand.'

'Damn right I don't. I could understand if you were pissed off with your grandad, he's a right rude old git. Calling Gail his "favourite" granddaughter while you're sitting there.'

'He's always been like that. He does it deliberately. The great patriarch playing with people's lives. You get used to it. Just ignore it.'

'What I also don't understand is, why did you come? And why ask me along?'

She smiled thinly.

'I came to lay some ghosts to rest. And I asked you because I'm probably going to need some moral support.'

'Ah, good,' he said, 'I knew I was going to be useful for something. Just such a pity I never did quite understand what morals are supposed to mean. Everybody seems to have so many different ones these days. And all at the same time.'

'Nobody has any morals in that house. Apart from gran.'

'Bugger,' said Valerie, arms folded tightly and hood pulled close, 'they must have gone a different way.'

'Why on earth did you want to catch them up anyway?' asked Gail. 'You don't like Hope, and you certainly aren't enjoying a peaceful stroll.'

'It's bloody freezing. And I've never seen the point of going for long walks in the countryside.'

'Well, exactly. So why the sudden enthusiasm?'

'I didn't fancy the idea of being stuck in the kitchen with your grandad going on about the old days and how terrible modern women were, while we peeled potatoes like those good little women he prefers. Last time I peeled a potato was at school. I get other people to do that these days.'

'I did warn you about grandad. Though he does seem worse than he used to be. And I told you that it was out in the sticks and there wouldn't be much to do.'

'Oh, I don't know. A good old game of wind Hopeless up sounds like fun. And Tom looks interesting. Working class, eh? I could do with a bit of rough.'

'Val, the only rough you're going to end up with is what you find on golf-courses. Buried in it.'

'This looks nice,' noted Tom, changing the conversation. 'A pond in the wood. Must be great to come here on a hot summer's day. It even looks appealing now, though I think you'd freeze to death before long if you fell in.'

'I wonder if Valerie has brought her bikini along. Maybe we could convince her to take a dip. A long dip.'

'What is it about you and her? And what's this about a bikini?'

'She and Gail were right shits to me when I was a kid. At boarding school. Gail wouldn't have been so bad, but Val was a total and utter bitch.'

'Wasn't that a long time ago, Maria?'

'When you're a kid the memories stay with you for a lifetime. Until you do something to balance the books.'

'There's a spinney over there,' Tom said, after a pause. 'It looks like the type of place someone would take cover in during a thunderstorm.' He smiled. 'Spinney. I like that word. Cosy. The sort of place young lovers would get together in bygone days. To be out of sight.'

Maria-Hope looked at where he was looking. She smiled thinly.

'You must point it out to Valerie,' she said. 'I can imagine her going there for an assignation.' She pulled her hood tighter. 'I wonder where I can get some petrol from. Could we get some out of your car?'

Tom's mouth was open. It was only the freezing of his teeth that forced him to close it.

'Sod this for a game of monkeys,' said Valerie. 'They've probably already gone back. Let's go back before we freeze our tits off.'

'Even if we have to peel potatoes?'

'They've probably done them already. It's the sort of thing Hopeless would do.'

'Well I intend to give my gran a hand whenever I get the chance. She might be going strong for her age, but she's still old.'

'Okay, okay, I'll help with the fucking potatoes. At least it will be something to do. And in a warm kitchen rather than this blasted heath.'

'It's not a heath,' replied Valerie. 'It's a wood.'

'Heath, wood, forest, glade, bloody moor, whatever. It's outside. And it's bloody freezing.'

'It's not that bad. I think it's quite refreshing.'

'I'm a hot-blooded woman. I'm sure I was meant to live somewhere like Spain.'

'You'd have to dye your hair black.'

'I'll dye my hair black! Oh, please, Gail, let's get back. Back into somewhere warm.'

'Okay, let's go face the potatoes.'

'What's that noise?' asked Maria-Hope, stopping suddenly.

'Something in the undergrowth. Probably a pheasant or something.'

'It sounds too large to be a pheasant. Oh, Tom, it's an animal!' she cried, hiding behind him.

'It's a pig,' smiled Tom as the animal broke cover. It looked at them with curious eyes. 'Hello, Mr Porker, what are you doing wandering around the countryside?'

The pig came up and sniffed at him as Maria-Hope cowered behind him.

'Just want some company, don't you, Mr Porker?' asked Tom, scratching the pig's neck. The pig grunted agreement and sighed with enjoyment.

'He could be dangerous, Tom.'

'Nah, he's just lonely. If he were wild he wouldn't come near us. Anyway, there aren't any wild pigs in Britain. France, yes, not here. So, Mr Porker, where do you come from?'

The pig moved around and presented his back for scratching.

'Look, I can't stand here all day,' Tom said. 'That's enough. You get on back home and so will we. We have some potatoes to peel.'

He turned. Maria-Hope took his arm on the opposite side of the pig and they began to walk away, Maria-Hope throwing a fearful glance back at the pig.

'Tom! He's following us!'

'I shouldn't have mentioned the potato peels.' He chuckled.

'Funny sort of dragon.'

'Dragon?'

'And I'm not going to slay him, whatever you say.'

'Tom, what are you talking about? He's still following us.'

'Shoo, Mr Porker, go home. We can't take you with us. It's bad etiquette for a guest to bring a stranger back unannounced.'

The pig looked at him with sad eyes. It grunted in a resigned manner, shook its head, turned around and ambled back the way it had come.

'You know,' mused Tom, 'I like to think that I've seen a lot in life, but that's the first time I've ever been made to feel guilty by a pig. Poor thing.'

'Poor thing? Tom, he was huge!'

'A bit over-weight, maybe. But basically your average-sized pig.' He paused. 'What am I saying? Of course, he was huge. And terrifying. With tusks. Slavering at the thought of munching on you. His favourite food, a vegetarian. And, single-handedly, and empty-handedly, I saved you. Surely that proves my love for you.'

'Stop being silly,' Maria-Hope replied, letting go of his arm and walking on. 'It was just a silly pig.'

He looked at her retreating figure. His eyes locked on her backside.

He paused, and then emulated a rugby player kicking a drop goal.

The effort made him grunt with pain as his calf protested. He limped on after her.

Chapter Ten: Signals

'So how are your parents, Valerie? We haven't seen them since you and Gail finished school.'

'Oh, so-so, Mrs Browne. Where shall I put the carrots?'

Potato-peeling, it had turned out, had not been an arduous job, as George Browne had bought his wife an electric peeler some years before. With just the two of them it normally sat in a cupboard and gathered dust. With the increase in numbers it had proved practicable to use.

'Just on the sideboard there. Surely they must wish you with them at Christmas?'

'I don't think so, Mrs Browne. They got divorced twelve years ago. Dad's got himself a girlfriend half his age. She doesn't like me very much. And mum's got herself a toy boy, so she probably sees me as competition. We were never really close as a family.'

'Dear, dear, dear, that is terrible. Terrible.'

'The way things go, these days.'

'Gran,' said Gail, shaking her mobile phone, 'my mobile phone can't pick up a signal. This isn't a black spot, is it?'

'A black spot, Gail? Funny term to use. It's a lovely area, in all seasons. It might not look that way at the moment, but when you live here you come to appreciate the passing of the seasons. It might even snow for Christmas, like it used to in the old days.'

'No, gran, I meant a place where mobile signals don't reach.'

'Oh, yes, I see. Yes, they were planning on putting up a mast of some kind. Your grandfather got the villagers to sign a petition against it.'

'Grandad went around collecting signatures? I am amazed.'

'Don't be silly, dear. He got someone else to do it. He just gossiped in the local pub about the dangers – apparently they can give you cancer. Oh, and how more yuppies, I think he called them, would start buying the village up, how not being able to use their mobile telephones would keep them away, that sort of thing. You can use the telephone in the passage if you need to call someone.'

'You can't get a signal anywhere in the village, Mrs Browne? Nowhere?'

'Well, I believe that there's a mast at the supermarket – about twenty miles away. I don't know what its range is. But for some reason it appears that it doesn't reach here.'

'Twenty miles? You mean we're stranded here for two weeks with no contact with the outside world?'

'Hardly no contact, Gail. We have a television and a telephone. There's the village right next to us. And Adam should be arriving tomorrow morning, and Anthony later on, so I'm sure there will be plenty of company.'

Gail put her mobile phone back into her pocket. Her mouth twitched as she looked at her grandmother.

'Is dad still not talking to Uncle Adam, gran? Dad and Uncle Adam had a great falling out when I was about sixteen, Val. I never found out what it was about, but I was never allowed to mention uncle Adam's name again. For a few years at least.'

'Now, now, Gail, it wasn't that bad. And I'm sure that's all water under the bridge. No use in gossiping about it now.'

'Who else is coming?'

'Well. They all seemed so uncertain. Peter and Rebeccah might be able to make it, which means little George will be along. And Claire said she'd come.'

'Oh, god, not Saint Claire,' muttered Valerie.

'How is Claire these days, gran? Still baby-faced little sweetness and light? Shining blonde hair and pretty little bow mouth?'

'Really, Gail, that's no way to speak of your sister. She was a little angel as a child.'

'Just joking, gran. She was a bit of a pain, though. A bit of a goody-two-shoes.'

'I suppose it might have seemed that way from your point of view at the time, Gail, but when you have children you'll find that it's a relief to have one who doesn't seem to want to make your life as difficult as possible. And when you're a grandparent it's even more so. No matter how much you love them, children are a lot of hard work for the most part.'

Gail nodded reluctantly.

'I guess you're right, gran. It was just a little bit embarrassing to have a sister who brought her dolls to boarding school. And kept them with her the whole way through.'

'There was a reason for that, you know.' She sighed. 'I've always felt sorry for little Claire. She was a sensitive child. I think she realised that your parents weren't getting along very well. You were at boarding school, so perhaps you weren't affected as much by it, or perhaps you had grown beyond the age where parents are so important. I think she thought that she could make things better if she was good. The dolls were her way of creating the happy family she wanted. And she did so want to be part of a family. Poor thing.'

'I hadn't thought about it like that. I didn't really notice that mom and dad weren't hitting it off. Or perhaps I just thought that that was normal. I didn't think there was a serious problem. Not until mom called to say that they were getting divorced.'

'And by then you were at university, if I remember correctly.

Claire was still at school. She hated that boarding school, poor, poor little thing.'

'Poor, poor little Saint Claire,' murmured Valerie to Gail. 'The original martyr.'

'Ah, yes,' Gail said quickly, 'I haven't seen her for a while. How's she keeping these days?'

'When did you last see her?'

'Hmm – about five years ago? So she'll be what, twenty-four now?'

'Well, you'll find that she's changed. She's been through some pretty bad problems recently. She needs support from her family. A lot of support.'

'Oh, good, serves her right,' muttered Valerie.

'What sort of problems, gran?'

'Five years without seeing your own sister. I don't know, the way your families have parted. Not seeing your own sister for five years. It's not as if you have any excuse, you know.'

'A bit like you and grandad and Uncle Adam and Aunt Jane, then, gran?'

'I think it's time to turn the roast. The stove can be quite temperamental at times. Your grandfather refuses to buy a new one until it's absolutely necessary. One of these days I shall start feeding him on cold meats and see how long it takes before he gives in.'

Chapter Eleven: Saints and Sinners

'Oh, be a dear and see who's at the door, Hope, I can't go with my arms in flour up to the elbows. I think it might be Peter. At least I hope so.'

They were in the kitchen. Tom stood next to Winifred Brown, kneading dough. Maria-Hope shot out to attend to the bongs.

'Maria –' Tom started. 'Hope, that is – is looking forward to seeing Peter, Mrs Browne. She said that they were very close as kids.'

'Very close, Tom. I'm not sure it wasn't too close. Are you sure you're okay with that dough? It isn't really a man's job, is it? Or is it these days? Of course bakers were all men in the old days.'

'I'm a modern man, Mrs Browne. And I find kneading dough both creative and relaxing. Besides which, I have an ulterior motive.'

'An ulterior motive? My goodness. What would that be?'

'Well, Mrs Browne, Maria – Hope – is very fond of you, so I have to get in your good books to keep her sweet.'

Mrs Browne smiled.

'I'm sure you don't have to go to the bother, Tom, you strike me as a very nice young man. You remind me of my son Adam in many ways. And I'm sure Hope is very fond of you too. I'm sure she is.'

'It's Peter I'm worried about, to be honest.'

'Peter? Peter is a lovely boy. A bit too serious as a child, but I'm sure he's grown out of that. His mother, you know, she had a tendency to take religion too seriously. One must keep sight of practicalities in this world.'

'Oh, I know Peter is a lovely person, Maria – Hope – keeps on telling me how lovely he is. In fact I've been ordered to like him. Which means I have to get into his good books too. If Peter decides he doesn't like the cut of my jib then Maria – Hope – will dump me sooner or later, and that is not going to happen if I can help it.'

Mrs Browne looked at the dough.

'It's been ages since I kneaded dough the old-fashioned way,' she said. 'There is a machine in the pantry, but it's a terrible bother to clean properly. And doing it by hand is much more satisfying, I find.' She sighed. 'Not that I have the strength these days. One does grow old. But, Tom, you're still very young, you know. And, I hope you don't mind me saying so, but – still idealistic, if I can put it that way.'

'I don't mind at all, Mrs Browne. I know I am. In fact I'm a little proud of it. It's too easy to be cynical these days. I think we need to fight for ideals, for dreams. There don't appear to be many left.'

'I'm glad to hear it, Tom. There does seem to be too much pessimism in our world today. But – and I'm only speaking as someone who has lived quite a while – there come times when you realise that you've backed the wrong horse, as I believe the saying goes. It is so much harder to accept that you've got things wrong when you believed so much in the first place. I suppose that's why people find that being cynical is easier.'

Tom grinned.

'Funnily enough I see it the other way around. I think it's easier to believe in something.'

'Peter!' cried Maria-Hope, opening the door to a young man and woman, the woman holding a swaddled baby in her arms.

Both were wearing knee-length winter coats, his black, hers navy-blue. 'Oh Peter give your Maria a hug and a kiss!'

'Hello, Maria, come here then.' Peter flung both his arms around his sister and gave her a long and hard hug.

'Oh, Peter! It's been ages. How are you? Are you okay? Got over the flu? You're looking pale. Almost Byronic.'

'Just a little cold, Maria, nothing to worry about. Rebeccah, this is my sister, Maria, known to the rest of the family as Hope.'

Rebeccah was slightly taller than Peter. She had long black hair, a pale face and watchful eyes.

'How do you do, Maria?' she said. 'Peter has told me all about the two of you growing up.'

'And this is your little nephew, Little George,' Peter added. Maria-Hope turned her attention to the little bundle in Rebeccah's arms.

'Oooh! Hello, George! Georgie! Say hello to your Auntie Maria. Oh, he's so cute, Peter. Six months and he looks just like you.'

'What, old and wrinkled, you mean?'

'Silly. Come in, it's freezing with the door open.'

'How's the old tyrant?' asked Peter, as they brought their suitcases in. 'Learnt a little humility in his old age?'

'Nope, still as obnoxious as ever. Worse, perhaps. I think he's dozed off in front of the telly in the television room. Apparently he does that quite often. Leave your suitcases here, come along to the kitchen, there's someone I want you to meet.'

'Let me guess. Tom, that handsome man you keep making noises about.'

'Peter, I'm serious, you have to like him. For my sake. If you don't I will never speak to you again.'

'Now that sounds like a good idea.'

'Stop teasing. Just a second, this door won't shut properly. I think gran is the only one who actually understands it.'

She struggled with the door as they watched. Each time it appeared to close, before swinging back slightly ajar.

'It's warped a little,' said Rebeccah. 'And the top hinge is out of line. I think you have to press the handle down a bit.'

'Oh, to hell with the door!' said Mariah-Hope. 'I'll get gran to have a look at it in a while. Come along.'

She took his hand and almost dragged him towards the kitchen. Rebeccah looked at the door. She held George in one arm and gently pressed it closed. The latch caught. She nodded to herself. Then she followed the other two.

'Peter!' exclaimed Mrs Browne as they entered. 'Oh, my dear Peter! Let me clean my hands and give you a hug. And Rebeccah! And Little George! Oh, what a sweet little thing.'

She hurriedly washed her hands while Maria-Hope pulled Peter over to where Tom stood putting the dough into a bowl to rise.

'Peter, this is Tom, Tom, my brother Peter. You two get to know each other, I want to get to know my little nephew.'

She skipped over to the table where Rebeccah and Mrs Browne had sat down. Little George looked out from his blanket at the women cooing over him. The two men looked at each other. Tom grinned.

'How do you do, Tom?' Peter said.

'Greetings, Peter. Just a sec while I get rid of this flour.'

'You're into baking?'

'Only at Christmas and on special holidays – the only occasions I have the time.'

'Rebeccah does all our cooking. That's my partner, Rebeccah. She's the only one with the time.'

Tom's eyebrows raised.

'You're not – er, married?'

'Not in the eyes of bureaucracy. And no intention of doing so. People have this strange notion that marriage is some type of unbreakable bond. In most divorces it's exactly the opposite. You know that saying – when a man marries he thinks his wife will never change, and when a woman marries she thinks she'll be able to change her husband, and they both end up being wrong. If people looked upon marriage the way they should, as a bond between two people before God, with each accepting the other for what they are, we wouldn't have the problem with divorce we have today.'

Tom opened his mouth to say something. Then he closed it. He coughed a little as he dried his hands, and cleared his throat.

'Mmmm, I can see a problem there. I'll put the kettle on. The women are going to be busy with little George for quite a while.'

'A problem?'

'Well, I'm a little old fashioned, you see. I want to get married to Maria. Settle down, have a family, that sort of thing. Kids, you know.'

Peter's pale face was expressionless, as if he either knew or wasn't interested in knowing.

'Will she want to marry you, though?' he asked.

'That's the other side of the problem. Tea or coffee?'

'Coffee. You're quite domesticated, I see.'

'Not normally. Don't have time for it. Until I met Maria meals were oven-ready from Marks and Sparks or take-aways. Pizzas, mainly. Had a bad experience with a kebab once, can't face them these days. Keeping the house clean – well if it wasn't for my cleaning lady, I don't really want to even contemplate what a state it would be in.'

Peter considered this, and then nodded slightly.

'And now Maria's moved in with you?' he asked.

'Sort of. As a lodger, really. Different rooms at the moment. And we're at the feeling guilty stage.'

'Feeling guilty stage?'

'Yes, I feel guilty if I drop my clothes around the place. I always used to – I had to, my cleaning lady enjoyed complaining about it so much I felt I had a duty to do so. But now I'm extra careful about that sort of thing. And Maria always has a meal ready when she knows I'm going to be home – she feels guilty that she might not be taking care of me properly. She even cooks meat for me. Not very well, and she makes the usual vegetarian comments about dead meat, but she does try. I often wish she wouldn't. I like my meat, but I'm sure I could live on a vegetarian diet.'

'I think that proves my point.'

'Which point?'

'My point about marriage. You two get married and you leave the guilty stage. You start dropping your clothes everywhere, making Maria angry, and she stops making the effort to look after you. No more meat. Next step is the divorce court.'

Tom looked at him. Peter's full dark eyes were on him, unblinking. He looked like a man who was suffering from an ulcer but determined not to let it show.

'You might have a point, Pete,' Tom said.

'The name's Peter, Tom. Not Pete.'

'Sorry.' Tom grinned. 'Stupid, really. In my job I have to be very careful about names and the way to address people. Five minutes in the countryside and I forget my manners. But I'll have to think about that one, the guilty thing.' He turned to the others at the table. 'Tea's ready, everyone.'

'Tea? Oh, Tom, you should have let me do that. I'm not taking care of my guests properly.'

'Nonsense, Mrs Browne. We men have to make ourselves useful while the women adore your little grandchild.'

'Great-grandchild, Tom.'

'Nah, you don't look old enough.'

'Have you always been a smarmy git, or did you practise a lot?' asked Peter in a soft voice.

'All in a good cause, Pete. I wouldn't do it for anyone apart from Maria, mind. Anyway, I like your gran.'

He paused as Peter directed two cold eyes towards him.

'Sorry. Peter. I really am sorry. I'll remember in future. I don't know what's got into me.'

'Did I hear someone mention tea?' Gail called as she and Valerie came into the kitchen. 'Val and I are dying of thirst, the tea-room in the village was closed. We almost popped into the pub instead. Oh.'

She paused.

'Well, hello, Peter.'

'Gail,' Peter nodded.

'You remember Valerie, don't you, Peter?' asked Gail.

'I remember Valerie, yes.'

Valerie arched her eyebrows at Peter.

'I could never forget Petie babe,' she said. 'Could I, Petie?'

Gail looked from Valerie to Peter and then to Tom. Tom was looking at the others, squeezing his top lip with his fingers, as if thinking. His eyes caught Gail's. Both looked away immediately.

'You must be Rebeccah,' Gail cried, turning to Rebeccah, full of artificial gaiety. 'I'm Gail, Hope's cousin, and this is Valerie, an old school friend.'

'How do you do?'

'Ah, so this is little Georgie. He does look a scrunched up little thing, doesn't he.'

'He's adorable,' said Winifred Browne. 'The spitting image of his grandfather at that age. And of you, Peter.'

There was a rumble from the passage. A slow clonk-clonk identified the progress of George Browne. He burst slowly but overwhelmingly into the kitchen. He took in the assembled gathering in a glance. Then his eyes lighted on the baby.

'Little Georgie! Say hello to your great-grandfather! Why didn't anyone tell me you were here? Hello, Peter.'

'Granddad.'

'We didn't want to wake you, George.'

'Nonsense, I wasn't asleep, I was watching television. Hello, little George, smile for your great-grandfather.'

'The great old bull elephant has entered the room,' Tom murmured. Peter folded his arms and frowned at him.

Chapter Twelve: Disputes

'Tom, I've decided. I want a baby. Several babies, in fact,' Maria called as they walked towards the village. She and Rebeccah were walking about fifteen yards behind Tom and Peter. Another fifteen yards behind saw Gail and Valerie. They had decided on a pre-lunch walk and possibly a pint.

'No need to announce it to the entire village,' Tom called back. He turned to Peter. 'Oh, god, Peter, look what you've dropped me into. She's gone all broody.'

'I thought you wanted marriage and kids and everything.'

'One thing at a time, Peter, one thing at a time.'

'He won't marry you, you know,' Rebeccah said to Maria, 'not if he's like Peter.'

'How do you mean?'

'I thought that Peter would propose when he found out I was pregnant. Instead he just gives me lectures about the advantages of not getting married.'

'You want to get married?'

'Of course. Don't you?'

'Not in a million years. Marriage is a curse, for both partners.'

'You and Peter appear to share the same views.'

'Not surprising, really, we are sister and brother, after all.'

'So, Tom,' asked Peter, 'will your mission to make yourself loved by the entire family extend to our mother and father?'

'Funny you should ask that. I hadn't even thought about that. Yes, I should have spotted that.'

'Spotted what?'

'Maria talks about her gran and you all the time. But she

hardly ever mentions your folks. Why do you suppose that is?'

'Why do you suppose that is?' countered Peter.

Tom thought about the question for a few seconds.

'Possibly because they don't mean as much to you?' he suggested. 'Or is that a touchy subject?'

'I think you'd better be careful how much of that journalist's nose of yours you poke into other people's lives.'

'Point. But I can smell a family feud. Knowing what it is will help keep me out of it.'

'Can't see how you can avoid it, if you're serious about Maria.'

'Peter, I'm serious about politics. But a journalist has to be as objective as he can. Politicians use you for their own aims. If you don't keep your ears and eyes open you can be dropped into something worse than a cesspit. And family politics are even more brutal, if that's possible.'

Peter shrugged and looked at the countryside.

'I like bleak,' he commented.

'I want to end up like gran,' Maria told Rebeccah, 'with a large extended family coming to visit me at Christmas – and other times, of course.'

'But without granddad?'

'Well, not my granddad, of course. Tom can be sarky at times, especially when he's tired, but he's not a bully like granddad.'

'You don't think your gran is the way she is partly because of your granddad?'

'Nonsense! She would be lovely whoever she married. You don't know my family. I think you should be careful of making snap judgements about people you don't know.'

'I wasn't making any snap judgements, Maria, I was just asking a question.'

'And if there's one thing I really hate it's being patronised.'

'Look, I'm sorry if I —'

'And I don't think it's very polite poking into the affairs of someone else's family.'

'Peter,' Tom sighed, 'I don't suppose there's any chance of you telling me exactly what this fortnight is about?'

'How do you mean?'

'Come off it, Peter, I'm not blind. You didn't want to come. Maria didn't want to come — apart from seeing you and her gran again, and she would have made it a weekend and stayed in a hotel somewhere. There's something going on and I'd like to know what it is so that I know where to dig a foxhole.'

'No hotels anywhere nearby. Nearest one's at least ten miles away.'

'Jesus, Peter, will you give over?'

'I've warned you about poking your nose into the wrong places, Tom. And I don't like blasphemy.'

'Christ, I think I'll walk with Rebeccah. She and Maria aren't talking to each other. Perhaps Rebeccah put her nose in where it wasn't wanted. Just one bit of advice, Peter. Read Jane Eyre.'

'Jane Eyre?'

'The madwoman in the attic burnt the house down. In this case I think it might turn out to be the mad brother and sister.'

Tom slowed down to allow Rebeccah and Maria-Hope to catch up. Maria-Hope gave him an angry look before hurrying up to join Peter.

His eyes were blazing coals.

Gail watched the others ahead change partners.

'They don't look too happy,' she said.

Valerie looked up and shivered in her parka. She pulled the hood around her face.

'How far is this pub, then?' she asked.

'Well, I don't know, do I?'

'I bloody hope they've got a good fire going.'

'And a bottomless supply of double gins?'

'More like triple fucking gins.'

'Well, that sort of encapsulates an interesting philosophy of life.'

'What's up with you and Rebeccah?' Peter asked.

'Nothing.'

'Maria, don't be stupid. I know you too well. You've been arguing.'

'And you and Tom haven't?'

'That's different. Tom's a prying little sneak, probably comes of being a journalist.'

'Oh, well, in that case you'll be surprised to find out that your precious Rebeccah is a prying little know-it-all.'

They walked on in silence.

'His father is a bus-driver,' she said finally, as if to make amends. 'I only found out yesterday.'

'I was in Sarajevo once, for a short while,' Tom commented to Rebeccah, his eyes on the two ahead. 'I felt safer there than I do here in this leafy village in middle-England. Or, perhaps, considering the season, not so leafy village.'

'That's where you were wounded?'

'No, that was somewhere else. How did you know?'

'Oh, Maria told Peter, Peter told me.'

'Don't seem to be speaking to each other at the moment, do

they?'

Rebeccah stroked little George and looked at the two ahead.

'Do you find it strange – I mean Maria having two names. On the one hand she's Maria, on the other she's Hope.'

Tom nodded.

'Disconcerting is the word, I think. You expect to learn things about a person when you meet the relatives – but it's almost as if there are two different people. Maria and Hope.' He frowned. 'I have to admit to being a little confused.'

Rebeccah received this with a slight nod.

'Tom, can I confide in you?'

'I'm a journalist. So the answer is that you'd have to be mad to do so. Your story will be on the front page before you can say boo.'

'I'm serious, Tom. I don't like it here.'

Tom nodded again.

'Makes two of us. If it wasn't for Maria I'd be long gone. I like Mrs Browne, and old George Browne is a bit of a throwback, though he's not that bad, but –'

'I'm worried, Tom. Peter's acting strangely. Almost the same way he claims that his grandfather does. Bossy, I would call it. It's so unlike him.'

'Let me guess. This strangeness dates back to when you got pregnant.'

She glanced at him.

'Has anyone told you that you're a strange person?' she asked.

'Strange? Then I fit in right at home, here. Why strange?'

'Because you've seen something in a few minutes that I've been trying to deny for almost a year.'

Tom stopped to push a branch out of the way.

'You're Jewish, aren't you?' he said. 'Or your parents are Jewish.'

Rebeccah blinked.

'How did you guess?'

'When I first saw you you reminded me of that cook – chef, whatever – Nigella wotsits. She's Jewish. Okay, I don't think that all Jews look alike, I'd be a fool to have such pre-conceptions in my business. But then there's the name – Rebeccah. Good old Jewish name. Once again, just a pointer, nothing conclusive. The final nail in the coffin was the way the old bull elephant treated you when he walked into the kitchen.'

'You noticed.'

'He might as well have had a neon sign on his head – "I disapprove of my grandson's partner". He totally ignored you. The bull elephant likes attractive young women. In fact he loves them in his own patriarchal way. So why was he so set against the mother of his great-grandson, an extremely attractive young woman? The wrong class? Could have been, because it's obvious to my mind that our dear old bull elephant was not born with a silver spoon in his mouth, though I rather fancy Mrs Browne was close to it. But no, he isn't a raving member of the Socialist Workers. In fact right at the other side of the political spectrum, I'd guess. So what other reason could he have for taking against a beautiful young woman? I come across a lot of disguised anti-semiticism in my work. I won't say that I came to a conclusive decision, but I thought the evidence strong enough to ask you.'

'You're a very straightforward man.'

'Not normally. Not in my line of work. But I am with my friends.'

'You think of me as your friend?'

'I'd like to. We're undoubtedly allies in this situation. We have to be. It might end up a case of my carrying little Georgie out of the burning wreckage while dragging you along.'

'You would, of course, being the man, have to be the hero.'

'Rebeccah, anytime you feel the need to drag me out of the burning wreckage, be my guest.'

He stopped again and looked at her. He put a hand on her arm.

'Rebeccah, it was a woman journalist who dragged me to safety when I got hit by the shrapnel. I had no problem with her being a woman. I was bloody grateful. She saved my life. I don't want to be melodramatic, but that's the way it was. She did save my life. The next mortar landed exactly where I had been. They were pacing them up. They didn't give a shit about who caught it.'

'But you had another problem with her?'

Tom nodded.

'Very perspicacious, Rebeccah. She was in love with me. She thought that, by saving my life, I might return that love.'

'But you didn't.'

'No. I didn't. She was a nice girl, but – no, I didn't. I wish I could have done.'

'A pity.'

They continued walking.

'Yes. A pity.'

Rebeccah turned her dark eyes on him.

'This woman – did she find someone else?'

Tom shook his head.

'No. I – well, if I'm to be honest about it, she was a crap reporter. A lovely person, apart from being mentally deluded, but bloody useless as a journalist. They recalled her. I think the combination of that and my rejection of her after she'd saved my life – well, she got drunk and drove her car off a bridge. Finis. End of story. Another little gravestone lying about someone's life. She was just a fucked-up little girl. They should have put that on her gravestone. Here lies just another fucked-up little person the world never cared about. Born – too late. Died – too young.'

'They fuck you up, your parents – they don't mean to, but they do. Isn't that how it goes?'

'Something like that. Listen, Rebeccah, I'm not a social worker or psychologist or whatever, but I do not like this set-up. In fact the longer it goes on the less I like it. You say Peter's acting strangely – well, so is Maria. I don't mind admitting that I'm in love with Maria – but it's the Maria I've come to love, not the Maria of Wildfell Hall.'

'How long have you known her?'

Tom nodded.

'Only about three months. Logic tells me that that's not long enough.'

'Do you want to marry her?'

'Yes, I do.'

'She doesn't want to marry anyone. Just like her brother.'

'You want to marry him? Peter?'

'Yes. I do. I want to be his wife.'

'His wife, or a wife?'

Rebeccah looked down on little George.

'I think my choice is made, as far as that goes.'

'You could always leave him. We do live in the modern era.'

'You could leave Hope. Maria.'

'She doesn't drive. I drove her up here. I have to drive her back. Whatever happens.'

'So you can't leave her, and I can't leave Peter.'

'Looks like we're both stuffed then.'

She gave a small smile.

'You joke about it. Very English.'

'I prefer British.'

'Am I British, Tom?'

'Well, I thought so. Aren't you?'

'I thought so too, once. I thought I could be English – British – without being a Jewess. I don't believe in the Torah, the prescriptions, the – Tom, I had friends at school, no-one mentioned anything about being a Jew. Or so I thought. Now, suddenly, if you have Jewish parents you are a Jew. Tom, I am frightened. I have read history. Some of my parents' relations died in the Holocaust. They disapprove of Peter. They see it as a – a betrayal. I thought I was a modern young woman, secular, forget the religious nonsense, it has caused so much grief and pain over the centuries. But it seems there is no escape.'

Tom looked around at the landscape.

'Thank god I drove here in my own car,' he said. 'I just hope to hell we don't get snowed in.'

'You would leave Hope? Maria?'

Tom thought for a few seconds.

'You know that question about what you would take with you if your house was on fire?'

'Yes.'

'At the moment I'm beginning to think that the answer is, my own sanity.'

'There's a spinney over there,' said Gail. 'It looks almost welcoming. Cosy. A nook in the winter wilderness.'

'Does it have central heating?' asked Valerie, hooded face pointed towards the ground as she walked.

'Don't be silly, Val.'

'Well, fuck it then. I'm freezing and I need a drink. Which is closer, the pub or the house?'

Gail looked at her. All she could see was Valerie's nose which was uncomfortably white.

'The house, I would imagine. Shall we head back?' she called to the others.

Without saying anything the general agreement appeared to be that they should head back. Gail glanced at the others, Peter looking irritated, Maria-Hope downcast, Tom and Rebeccah thoughtful. Her nose twitched and a brief smile passed across her face. Then she shook her head as if to clear it of some impossible notion.

Chapter Thirteen: Thursday 22nd December. The Prodigal

'Hope, could you be a dear and answer the front door?'

'No problem, Gran.'

'It's probably Claire.'

Maria-Hope hurried to the front door. A man and a woman with two children stood there. The woman looked Chinese. She held the younger child, a baby, while the older, about six-years-old looked up at Maria-Hope with curiosity in her eyes.

'Ah, is this the Browne residence?' asked the man with a distinct American twang.

'Yes. Who were you looking for?'

'Let me guess. You're Hope, arentcha?'

'You could say that. Who are you?'

'You don't remember me? Whal, not surprising, I suppose, I last saw you when you were about three – three months old, that is. I guess I'm your Uncle Bob. And this here is mah wife, Patience, and our two little ones, Angel and Hercules.'

'Lucy!' said the little girl. 'It's Lucy, daddy!'

Hope opened and close her mouth a couple of times, looking from the indignant girl to the man to the woman.

'Uncle Bob?' she said. 'I don't have an Uncle Bob.'

'Now why does that not surprise me? Say, tell you what. Why doan you mosey along to your grandmother and tell her that Robert has arrived.'

'What's up, Maria?' asked Tom, coming up behind here. 'You're letting the cold in. Even more of the cold, that is.'

'This man claims to be my uncle Robert, Tom. Except I don't have an uncle Robert.'

'You mean Bob's not your uncle?'

'Very funny, Tom.'

The man smiled. A wolfish smile.

'Well, I thought it was,' said Tom. 'Pretty quick, too. I suppose a man's wit is never appreciated by his partner.'

'Whal, I agree with you, son,' the man said. 'I thought it weren't too bad. But I see where there might be a little confusion. I thought this here young lady was Hope, my niece. Guess it's just a bit of confusion on mah purt.'

'I am Hope,' said Maria-Hope.

'I did thought I heerd the young gentleman call you Maria, Miss. Perhaps I weren't heering too well.'

'He did.'

The man scratched his head.

'Ah. So you're Hope Browne, daughter of Adam and Susan Browne, born in the year of our Lord nineteen hundred and eighty. Would that be korrect?'

'Yes.'

'Whal, that kinda makes me your Uncle Bob.'

'Do you have any proof of that, Mr – ?' asked Tom.

'Whal, young man, sure, and if Ah'm Hope's uncle, I can only have one surname – Browne. With the E. But you just call me Rob.'

'So, do you have any proof of your identity, Mr, er, Browne?'

'Ah was just suggesting to the little missy here that she call her grandmother – mah old momma – and if she doan confirm mah ahdentity, well, we'll just mosey along. Can't say no fairer than that, now can ah?'

'You'd better come in,' Maria-Hope decided. 'Tom, you take Mr Browne and – his partner and children through to the lounge. I'll speak to gran.'

'Much obliged, Mister Tom, it sure is cold out there.'

'You're an American, I take it?' Tom asked as Maria-Hope

went to consult her grandmother in the kitchen. 'Just a second, this door can be difficult.'

The others watched as he patted the door into position. He stepped back and waited for it to open.

'Well, that seems okay. It springs open all the time if you're not careful. Personally I'd like to give it a good whack, but apparently you have to treat it gently. Come along to the lounge. Sorry, the front parlour. Your luggage is in the car?'

'Now that is an interesting question,' the man called Rob said as they walked. 'About my being an American.'

'A pretty straightforward one, I would have thought.'

'Whal, take my wife here, Patience. Would you say that she was Chinese?'

'Well – I would say that that is a rather rude question to ask – as if she – your wife – weren't here with us.'

'Oh, don't worry about me – Tom, is it?' said the woman. 'I'm used to Bobby. I'm just surprised he's managed to keep up that silly American back-country accent so far.'

'Back country accent?'

'Sorry about that, Tom,' the man said, grinning. 'I put in on just after we arrived at Heathrow. Some idiot made a crass generalisation about Yanks, so I couldn't help it. It's just my sense of humour, I guess.'

'In New York he always puts on an exaggerated English voice for people he doesn't like.'

'You live in New York?'

'Whal, now Noo Yawk –'

'Bobby?'

'Yes, my petal, flower of my life?'

'Put a sock in it.'

'Yes, my sweet. Tom, my boy, be careful of whom you marry – I take it you aren't married, you look too happy.'

'Bobby.'

'Yes my sweet, sorry, my sweet.'

'Robert!' exclaimed a delighted voice from the doorway.

'Hello, mom.' A grin spread across the man's face, an unaffected grin, of the sort a schoolboy might show when his mother had turned up at his boarding school with kisses and tucker after a long, bleak winter's week.

'Oh, Robert! You finally made it! Come, give your mother a hug and a kiss!'

Tom and Maria-Hope watched as their grandmother and the man named Robert hugged each other.

'Been a while, mom,' Robert said. 'Though you don't look a day older.'

'A while!' exclaimed his mother, stepping back and holding him by the arms. 'Robert, it's been well over twenty five years. Oh, my goodness, you have grown. Not filled-out, just more – muscular, I suppose.'

'I suppose I was a bit of a gangling young man when I last saw you, mom. But I did send photographs.'

'I know you did, Robert, but it's not just the same. Oh, my heavens, more than twenty five years. Oh, Robert, my dear Robert!'

'And this is your daughter in law, Patience. Well, as I wrote you, her name's something unpronounceable, which means serenity in Cantonese, but I couldn't go around calling her Serenity, could I?'

'Oh, Patience!' Winifred Brown cried, moving over to hug her daughter-in-law, 'it's so good to finally meet you. And to have Robert back after all these years. Oh, thank you for bringing him back! And these are the children, aren't you two sweet! Now, you must be Angel and you must be Hercules.'

'It's Lucy and David, Mrs Browne,' Patience explained.

'Bobby insists on calling them Angel and Hercules. I try to tell him it confuses them, but he never listens.'

'Well, he hasn't changed then, he never used to listen to me either. Come, come, let's go into the kitchen, it's warmer there. My goodness, over twenty five years.'

'I'm Lucy,' Lucy informed her grandmother.

'And so you are! And what a pretty little thing you are!'

'David's just a baby.'

'Yes, he is, isn't he? And such a cute and adorable baby.'

'I was cute when I was a baby,' decided Lucy. 'I'm sure I was.'

'I never knew I had an uncle Robert,' Maria-Hope called as the others left for the kitchen.

'Surely you must have done,' her grandmother said. 'Your parents must have mentioned him. And I know I always talked about his letters.'

'Yes, but I thought it was just some old friend. Nobody ever called him Uncle Robert.'

Mrs Browne paused.

'Well, I suppose they wouldn't, would they. Yes, come to think of it, they wouldn't. After all he wasn't Uncle Robert to us. Come along dear, the kettle's just boiled. Twenty five years!'

'How are dear old Adam and Jane, mom?' Rob asked. 'I can't wait to see them after all this time. Has age mellowed them? Or is Adam still the teenage would-be patrician? And Jane the haughty lady of the castle?'

'Robert! Really, that was such a long time ago. Now it's Christmas, all the family will be here, so I want you to play nicely. It will probably be the first and last time we're all together, so do try to put some effort into making it work, for your father's sake, if nothing else.'

'How is the old battle-axe? From your letters it sounded as if he were getting old. I just couldn't picture it.'

'We're neither of us spring chickens, Robert. We're at the age when the hereafter could come at any moment.'

'And everyone else is at the age when they hope the hereafter will come to someone else very soon.'

Chapter Fourteen: Who is that man?

'Honestly, Tom!' Maria-Hope exclaimed. 'It's just too weird. To find out that I suddenly have an Uncle Bob, and that he's married to a girl almost my age, and she's Chinese, and they've got two young children – do you realise that that means I have cousins young enough to be my own children?'

'Surely you must have known that you had another uncle?'

'He left before I was a year old. After that my parents hardly ever mentioned him – it was just comments like "mum's had a letter from Rob" – mum being my gran. Nobody pointed out that he was my uncle. And then I became a teenager, and what teenager could be bothered by an uncle she never sees? Then there was uni, moving away from the folks' place, getting a job, the first love affair – well, not in that sense, of course, but ... And now this ghost of the past walks in sounding like he owns half of America.'

'You think so? I don't remember him saying anything about that sort of thing.'

'Oh, it's just the impression I got.'

'Do you remember your Uncle Robert, Gail?' Valerie asked.

'Oh, only vaguely. I was about five when he left – he would have been, what, twenty? Twenty-five? Something like that.'

'He's quite a dish.'

'Valerie! Honestly, you seem to have only one thing on your mind.'

'So? I'm single, unattached, and looking for a man. What's wrong with that?'

'What's wrong with it is that you keep leching after men who are attached.'

'They're so much less trouble, Gail. You can always send them back to their little wives when they become boring. And she does look like such a good little Chinese wife, doesn't she?'

'I'd watch out for that wife of Uncle Bob's. She looks the type who knows all the Oriental secrets about killing rivals slowly and painfully – and disposing of their bodies so that no-one can prove anything. She'd probably feed you to the vicar's pig.'

'She's quite pretty, isn't she – in a sort of Chinese way. But I'd imagine uncle Robert might fancy some home-made delights from time to time.'

'You are going to come to a sticky end if you're not careful, Valerie.'

'That's what I'm hoping for, Gail, a sticky end.'

'Has anyone ever told you that you can be gross, Val?'

'Yes, but they've never thrown me out of their beds because of it.'

Chapter Fifteen: Return of a princess

'My turn,' Gail said as the doorbell rang. When she opened the front door she found a young woman holding a baby, a large, battered suitcase next to her. She wore a thick off-white woollen scarf over her head.

'Hello, Gail,' the young woman said with no emotion.

'Claire! You don't look too well. Whose baby is that?'

'Do you mind if I come in? It's freezing outside. It's not good for the baby.'

'Oh, of course, sorry. There you are, me in the wrong again, you the martyr again, nothing changes.'

Claire stepped indoors carrying the baby in one arm and a suitcase in the other.

'Just a second, this door's a right bitch to close properly.'

'Gail, the only reason I've come is because of gran – and the fact that I didn't want to spend Christmas on my own, with no company or warmth for Sarah. As far as I'm concerned, if you want to play mind games you can go fuck yourself.'

Gail froze in her attempt to close the door. She had been about to say something. Her mouth stayed open but no words came out.

'Claire!' came their grandmother's voice. 'Oh, Claire, it's so lovely to see you again. Come in, come in. Oh, and this is little Sarah, oh she's so cute! Gail, do shut the door, it's getting cold.'

Gail managed to close both her mouth and the door.

'Hello, gran,' Claire said, pulling her scarf back and giving her grandmother a kiss and a long hug.

'Come on, let's go to the kitchen, it's lovely and warm there. A cup of tea, I think. Oh, she's such a sweet little thing.'

'She is. She slept the whole way here. She'll be wanting her feed soon. She hardly ever complains.'

'Just like you when you were that age, my angel. Only four months old. Oh, what a sweet little thing.'

'Just her name makes me want to vomit,' Valerie said. Gail had gone up to their bedroom to deliver the news of Claire's arrival.

'Sarah?'

'No, Claire, your goodie-two-shoes sister. God, she's such a prissy little miss.'

'I'm not too sure about that, Val. Did you know, she told me to go fuck myself? Within a minute of opening the door?'

'You're joking!'

'And what about her baby? Where's the father? How come I wasn't even told that I had a niece? And why does Claire look like some poor little orphan girl out of Dickens, down to her last half-pence?'

'She does?'

'Honest. Cheap, tatty clothes from Oxfam, pinched little face. Still got that lovely blonde hair, though. Still looks after it like she always used to, no doubt. Claire, the hair, the angel and the saint.'

'Makes you wonder, though.'

'What does?'

'How come no-one told you that you're an aunt.'

'So, Claire, my dear, Jack still isn't talking to you?' her grandmother asked as they sat in the kitchen, little Sarah asleep in her arms. George Browne had welcomed Claire, gushed over Sarah, and then decamped to the television room for an important documentary on the mining industry.

'No, gran, I'm afraid father has disowned me for good. He's a hypocrite. Divorced and going out with someone almost my age is okay, having a child out of wedlock and no father around is unforgivable – as if it were my fault that that bastard ran away as soon as he found out. I thought uncle Adam might give me some support, but apparently having a niece who is a single-mother living on benefits is bad for his political image. I'm beginning to think that I've been transported back to the eighteenth century. I think he would have preferred it if I was a lesbian. At least that's politically correct. And you don't end up pregnant.'

'But what about your mother? I'm sure Jane would do everything she can.'

'God knows where she is. Off on the Riviera with her latest toy boy, I would guess.'

Her grandmother sighed.

'I don't know. Sometimes I wonder where I went wrong with my children. We tried to give them a good upbringing, even though it wasn't that easy financially. The best schools, freedom of choice, all the things that ... Ah, well, water under the bridge. Now, my dear, it's obvious that you haven't been looking after yourself. Here, you take Sarah. I'm going to put some soup on, some nice, thick soup, and after that, if you feel tired you can have a snooze until dinner. And you're to stay here as long as you like, it's no time for someone as young as you to be living on her own in a poky little flat in London trying to keep herself and her baby warm on a one-bar heater – no, my dear, you don't have to tell me, I know what it's like. I did many years of visiting single mothers for the church, you know. Such a pity some of my colleagues saw it as a chance to preach rather than to succour, but that's human nature, I suppose.'

'I'd love to stay, gran – not so much for me, but for Sarah. These are her most important months, if I can make her feel warm and secure and loved for the next couple of years she'll have a chance in life. But ... well, you saw how granddad reacted. All cootchey-coo with Sarah and treating me as if I'm the spawn of Satan. He hasn't lost his tongue, has he? Still as sharp and sarcastic as ever.'

'Oh, he's mellowed quite a bit, Claire. You should have heard him when your parents were your age. And he's not very good with strangers, and to him you're a bit of a stranger. I think he really sees you as still the little granddaughter with the flowing golden hair.'

'And he blames me for growing up?'

'Not just you, my dear. I think he blames the world. Especially for letting him grow old.'

She sighed.

'Ah, well. To more important questions. What kind of soup would you prefer? I've got some on the stove, I'm not sure what you would call it, a broth, perhaps. But there are also the things in packets.'

'Broth sounds good to me, gran.'

'Can I hold her? Please, Claire?' pleaded Gail. They were sitting in the kitchen. Claire had just finished her soup. Winifred Browne had gone upstairs to give the oil heaters a chance to warm the yellow room, Claire's bedroom to be.

'Oh, okay. Just be gentle with her.'

'Oooh, hello little Sarah. Helloooo. Who's a cute little thing? Smile for your Aunty Gail, there's a sweet little thing. Go on, cootchey coo, give your Aunty Gail a little smile. Oooh, look! She did it! She's smiling at me! And she's holding onto my thumb with her cute little fingers!'

'Jesus, Gail, you sound like the broodiest hen I've ever heard,' spat Valerie.

'Well, perhaps I am, Val. Perhaps I am. I told you, here I am, thirty, and the clock is ticking. And I want to have children.'

'And a little cottage in the country and a little husband?'

'Why not? I can dream, can't I?'

'What about you, Claire? How did you manage to get up the duff without being married? What happened to our saint Claire?'

'Valerie!'

'Oh, that's okay, Gail. Val's always been a bitch, always will be. It's quite simple, Val, the old story. I met someone, thought I was in love with him, he kept stringing me along with hints about marriage. Soon as I told him I was pregnant he disappeared. I should have wondered about his story of his job needing him to be on the road so much. That's what happens when you're brought up as a lovely little ornamental doll, you're easy prey for any bastard who comes along. But I tell you something, I'm going to bring Sarah up with open eyes. She won't fall for that one.'

'Ah, an Estella in the making,' said Valerie. 'She's about the only Dickens character I could ever relate to.'

'No. Not an Estella. Sweet, but not innocent.'

'The father – who was he?' asked Gail. 'If you don't mind me asking.'

'I don't mind. Someone called Henry. Well, that's what he told me. I thought it was such a nice, old-fashioned name. I didn't realise how old-fashioned. Men like that have been preying on young women since the dawn of time.'

'You never saw him again?'

'I thought I never would, and good riddance. Then one day I was in Oxford Street when I still had my job. A pure coincidence. I spotted him with a woman and twins – a girl and a boy of about four, pretty little things. I guessed that the woman was his wife – intuition. I was six months pregnant and it showed. I walked up to him and asked why he had left me and his child.'

'Oh, boy! That must have been fun,' said Valerie. 'I wish I could have been there.'

'You have a strange concept of fun, Valerie. It was revenge, pure revenge.'

'What did he say?' asked Gail, poking her tongue out at Sarah and smiling. 'Yes, you are a lovely little thing, aren't you?'

'Oh, he tried the old trick – told his wife that I was obviously some deranged madwoman that he had never met, London was full of them. In the old days he might have got away with it, especially if I had lost my temper and hit him, which is what I really wanted to do. I could have knifed the mother-fucking little piece of shit. Instead I turned to her and told her we could have a DNA test done when the child was born – would she accept that as scientific proof? He tried to drag her away, but she wasn't having any of it. It turned out that she owns a laboratory – she's a scientist, and her side is where the money comes from. She's quite a strong-willed woman. She didn't wait. He got the heave-ho two days later. Their divorce should have come through by now, I expect.'

'Good, he deserved it, the bastard. Don't you worry, my little Sarah, Aunty Gail is going to help your mummy look after you.'

'I can look after her on my own, thanks very much.'

'Oh, Claire, please don't be like that. I know I haven't been that nice to you in the past, but ... well, we're supposed to be grown up now, aren't we? Can't we let bygones be bygones?'

'No, I don't think we can. Think of it as a credit card. Sooner

or later the time comes to pay it off.'
She looked at Valerie.
'I think that the time has come,' she said.

Chapter Sixteen: Future present

'I know mom said no presents, my sweet,' Rob said to Patience in their bedroom, 'but – well, surely – just for the kids. It is Christmas, after all. Especially little Sarah.'

'I know. And poor Claire ... "poor" being the literal word. I don't see why we can't pop into town and get something, even if it's only little.'

'Something Claire won't think of as being charity.'

'You have a strange family, Bobby.'

'Now you know why I didn't want to come back any time soon. Any time ever, really. Apart from mom.'

'I didn't say I didn't like them. Just that they seem a little strange.'

'You haven't seen the bad side of them yet. Wait till my older brother and sister turn up. It'll be like an Italian opera, but with subtlety.'

'And without the knives, I hope.'

Rob looked at her.

'Not our generation,' he said. 'Not real ones. I'm beginning to wonder about that weirdo Hope and hers, though. For them I'd keep the cutlery door triple-locked.'

'Maria, this no-presents rule,' said Tom to Maria-Hope. 'Well – well, we could break it for little Sarah, couldn't we. And Claire. She does seem a bit – well, helpless, really, even with the tough front she's trying to put on.'

'Yes. Strange that. I've always thought of her as being such a sweet person. She seems to have become quite bitter – and proud. She's learnt to swear, that's for sure.'

'And she's on a mission,' Tom mused.

'A mission?'

'The same as the rest of your rather dysfunctional family. Not so much lay ghosts as repay a debt of revenge.'

'We're about as dysfunctional as any other family, I suppose.'

'No, Maria, your family have been practising for too long.'

'I think you're overdoing it, Tom. Just one thing, though.'

'For you, my sweet, anything.'

'I doubt it. But, if we do go into town, you just leave your mobile here, okay? We are spending two weeks away from civilisation. I don't want it ruined just because we come too close to a signal and you end up spending a day checking your e-mail and answering fifty thousand voice-mails.'

'Just one call? One, teensy-weensy call?'

'If there is a call box you may make one call from it. But no more than that, and no giving my gran's number, okay? If they ask for a contact number give them a wrong one.'

'I think I know what the problem with your family is.'

'Really? What's that?'

'Too many bosses and not enough slaves. Or enough victims. Christ knows where they found the space to bury the bodies. No wonder your grandparents chose somewhere with a large garden.'

Chapter Seventeen: Mothers

'I'll get it,' Gail said as the doorbell bonged.

'It's okay, my dear, I'm closer,' her grandmother's voice came from the passage. She opened the front door to a woman in her fifties. The woman was wearing an expensive-looking navy coat down to the knees, and fleece-lined boots with short heels which appeared to match practicality with style. Her hands were sheathed in tight-fitting gloves, her car keys in one hand as if prepared to walk away if the door bell had not been promptly answered.

'Jane! Oh, my darling, I thought you weren't going to come. Come in.'

'You didn't leave me much choice, did you, mum?' the woman replied, stepping inside. Neither appeared to feel a kiss was necessary. 'I was going to have a quiet Christmas in Italy until your letter caught up with me. First I'd heard that I'm a grandmother myself. You'd have thought Claire could have mentioned the fact that she was pregnant to her own mother.'

'Yes, you would have thought so, wouldn't you? Let's go through to the kitchen. The others are there. Well, most of them. Just a second while I close this door. It can be obstinate sometimes.'

'Oh, for god's sake, mum! For your information, I have been running around England, France, Germany, Italy, Spain, the whole of bloody Europe for the past few years – on business. I haven't had a decent holiday in years. And I did try to contact Claire. I left dozens of messages on her voice mail until that stopped working. I even telephoned Jack, god help me. Fat lot of good that did me. He just told me that it was my fault and if I had been a better mother it wouldn't have happened. When I asked him what "it" was he told me he had to go and rang off. I don't think he had the slightest clue where she was either. Too bloody busy with his latest little piece of teenage skirt to worry about his daughter. Either that or on the golf course.'

'How is dear Jack?'

'Dead, I hope. Look, mum, let's just get one thing clear, okay? I'm only here for Claire. We both know that you've never thought much of me. Adam was always the apple of your eye. And then Jack couldn't do any wrong, when he turned up, Adam's best friend and the male rampant. I think the only reason I married him was that I had some subconscious hope that it would make you love me. Love me for the grandchildren I'd produce. Well, that's all in the past. Let's just accept it. For the moment I want to see my daughter. You never thought much about yours, but by god I am going to look after my own. And you can stick that wherever you like.'

'You might be right, my dear. Yes, I suppose you might be right. Claire's sleeping at the moment. Why don't I show you to your room and you can unpack your things. Where are your cases?'

'In the hotel in town where I'm staying, mum. You don't think I'd stay here so that you could criticise me every five seconds, while dad made sarcastic comments the other four, did you?'

'But, Jane, it's Christmas. Claire's here, and Gail, and her friend Valerie – and even Robert's finally turned up. He's brought his beautiful wife Patience and their lovely children. And Hope is here with her boyfriend, Tom. He's a lovely boy. And Peter and his partner Rebeccah, and their little son

George.'

Jane's eyes widened.

'Robert? After all these years? Robert's here? He's come back? What the hell did he want to do that for?'

'Yes, my dear, after all these years. So please say that you'll stay. It will make things so much more comfortable.'

Jane tucked her coat collars in as if it had become colder in the hall. Her mother stood looking at the spot where George Browne had wanted to hand a lion's head, as if contemplating whether it was time to redecorate.

'Funny, that. I always thought that he was the intelligent one out of us. At least intelligent enough to get out and stay out.'

'Jane, it is Christmas. Can't we try to make it Christmas?'

'I notice you haven't mentioned Adam turning up. Too busy, is he? Our high-flying politician? The next prime minister but fourteen?'

'He did say he would try to make it. It would make things a little awkward if you stayed in a hotel while everyone else was staying here, Jane. This is an opportunity for the family to get together again. Possibly the last we'll have.'

'Not a chance, mum, forget it. I'm a grown woman now. I run my own company, pretty successfully, if I say so myself. If you think I'm going to give you and dad the chance to treat me like a silly little girl again, well you can bloody well forget it. When is Claire likely to wake up?'

Her mother turned towards her.

'Well, I don't know, my dear. She was awfully tired when she got here, and she's obviously been more worried about looking after little Sarah than herself, she's terribly thin. And —'

'Yes, mum, I get the message loud and clear. She wouldn't be in this position if her own mother had been there for her.

Well, that makes two of us, doesn't it? I'll see if Claire's awake first. Where is she?'

'Up the stairs and third door on the left. But –'

'If she's sleeping I'll go say hello to Robert, quickly catch up on all those lost years. He'll be the fourth door on the left, I presume.'

'Well, no, –'

'Don't worry mum, I'll knock on every door I find. I've become good at that.'

'It's the yellow room. Claire's room.'

'It would be,' Jane said, heading upstairs. 'With pictures of sweet little fucking princesses all over the bloody walls.'

Jane opened the bedroom door carefully and looked in on her daughter and granddaughter. She paused in the doorway and almost gasped at the sight. While Claire was asleep, she no longer had that peaceful, almost fairy-tale princess look that her mother remembered. The silky-blonde hair was still there, but little Claire's face was pinched, almost wan.

A heavy hand dropped on Jane's shoulder, making her start.

'Hello, big sis,' said Robert softly. 'Long time no see.'

'Rob!' she whispered. 'Is it really you? You've grown.'

'I'm officially a man now,' he replied, keeping his voice down. 'Even managed to procreate. Fucking fecund, I am. Two kids so far, and who knows how many more I can come up with? Aren't you proud of your little brother?'

She looked at him. She sensed a controlled anger in his eyes.

'Rob, let's get a few things straight. I might have been your big sister once, but we've all been through the wringer since then. Right now I have only one thing on my mind, and that's to look after my daughter the way I should have. I screwed up. I'm not going to do that again.'

His grip on her shoulder lightened.

'Sorry, sis, I think I'm letting the atmosphere get to me.' He looked into the room. 'She seems like a good kid to me. Needs a bit of feeding up, though. Take care of her.'

'I intend to.' She looked at her brother. 'I know you've never thought much of me. But all that matters to me now is Claire. Any help you can give – will be welcome.'

'What about Gail?'

'Gail can take care of herself. Oh, I don't mean it that way! I love Gail just as much Claire, but Gail doesn't need me as much as Claire does – for the moment. If Gail should need me I intend to be there. You wouldn't understand. You wouldn't understand a mother's feelings.'

Robert smiled. This time his touch was a caress rather than a grip.

'You oughta meet your little niece and nephew some time. They make a man grow up.'

Jane looked at him. She smiled wryly.

'You know, I've often wondered whether you were the grown up one of us. Adam was always so aware of his own importance. I was – I'm not sure what I was trying to be. Miss Perfection, I suppose, in competition with Adam. You – you took one look and got out as soon as you could to live your own life.'

'Three was a crowd. I wanted to do my own thing.'

'And you did.' She paused. 'So, how's it been? Have you found peace and happiness?'

He looked into her eyes for a few seconds before replying.

'I'm happily married. Got a great wife, two lovely kids. Good job, too. Pay's okay.'

'But?'

'But – well, let's say I feel that there's something not quite resolved.'

'You can't leave the past behind you.'

'I suppose that's about it. There's part of me that still feels like a little boy left on the side-lines.'

Jane nodded.

'I remember going back to the boarding school I was at once. Everything seemed so much smaller than I remembered. There was a teacher still there, a Miss Evans. She was a right harridan when I was a pupil. In my mind she was at least a foot taller than I was. When I saw her again I realised that she was actually much shorter. And really quite pleasant. It's a bit like that, isn't it? You need to go back to see things in perspective.'

'I think you've got it there. I need to see things the real size.'

'Well, good luck. I'm going to wait with Claire until she wakes up.'

'Come and see the kids sometime.'

'I will. I'm looking forward to it.'

She slipped into the bedroom and closed the door quietly.

'Mum?' Claire asked blearily, opening her eyes to find her mother sitting on the bed next to her.

'Hello, Claire. I was just admiring little Sarah here. I didn't wake you, did I?'

'No. I don't think so.'

'Your gran was right,' Jane said, stroking Claire's blonde hair gently. 'You do need some rest and some decent pampering.'

'I'm fine.'

'No, you aren't, my dear. But let's not argue about that right now. Or anything, come to that. Not after you've just woken up. I'm going to have to go soon, I'm staying in a hotel in town. There's snow forecast for later, and I want to get back before it's dark. These country roads aren't lit well enough. And some of the drivers could do with taking their test again. And failing.'

'You're not staying here?'

'I'd rather sleep in a cave with the wolves howling outside, my dear. At least I'd know they were wolves.'

'And you want to get back to your toy boy.'

'Toy boy? Ha! Oh, Claire, Claire, Claire. I know you blame me for your father leaving. And other things, no doubt. But couldn't you have let me know what had happened? My darling, I would have crawled naked through thorn bushes to be at your side. If only you'd answered just one of my calls – no, no, let's not go there right now. You're tired, the last thing either of us needs is to play the psychology game – guilt and emotional blackmail.'

'And you want to get back to your toy-boy.'

'Claire, I was having a fling with a young Italian, yes. No commitment either side, just two people passing in the night. Somehow, after your father, I've never been able to see the point of a long-term relationship with a man. They always get in the way after a while.'

'But he came with you anyway. Your toy-boy. Free board and lodging. And free something else.'

Her mother managed a laugh.

'Not a chance. Quite funny, it was. As soon as your grandmother's letter caught up with me he disappeared like a scalded cat. Having a fling with an older woman is macho. Having a fling with a grandmother is just plain embarrassing. I was annoyed at first, and then I thought about it. Hilarious, really, once you put it into perspective. You can't change the world, just accept it and laugh at it.'

'You're on your own?'

'No, my darling, I've got you here. So long as I know you're safe here and being looked after I won't feel alone. I'll be back first thing tomorrow. We've got a lot to talk about.'

'I don't think we have anything to talk about.'

'There's Sarah, for a start. I made a decision on the way over – boy, was getting a flight out of Italy almost impossible. Some sort of strike or other, pure chaos. Oh, dear, there, I'm doing it again.'

'Doing what?'

'Complaining about my problems as if they were your fault. Look, Claire, I said I made a decision. Well, this is it. I'm going to sell the company and buy a nice little cottage in the country, just big enough for you, me and little Sarah – and a spare room for the occasional guest. And one for Gail, of course. Sarah will be able to grow up in fresh air and open fields – oh, there'll have to be a decent school nearby.'

'I don't need your help, or your little cottage. Neither does Sarah.'

'We need each other's help, Claire. Put it this way – when you were growing up your grandmother cosseted you. She had always ignored me, but you could do no wrong. Looking at little Sarah here, I'd love to cosset her. You see what I'm saying? Let's not make the mistake of letting different generations do the same thing to their children and grandchildren. Anyway, it's about time that I admitted that I'm a middle-aged woman. Settle down and start baking home-made cakes, cooking jam or whatever it is you do to make jam, that sort of thing. I'm looking forward to it. Darling, I must go. Let me give you a kiss until tomorrow.'

'Oh, Claire, please, do you have to turn away like that?'

Chapter Eighteen: Entertainment

'Don't you ever get bored out here, Mrs Browne?'

It was after dinner. Everyone was sitting in chairs or lying on cushions around in the lounge. A fire was burning in the grate, casting shadows over a large room otherwise lit by low-watt lamps ranged unevenly around the room. One cast light over Winifred Browne sitting in an armchair, knitting. On the other side of the lamp George Browne sat with a glass of port, benevolently casting his post-dinner eyes over his guests, occasionally trying to focus them.

'My goodness, no, Valerie. But then I grew up around here. Back in those days there was no such thing as television. We were only permitted to listen to the wireless for one hour an evening – my parents, my grandfather, I should say, wasn't at all sure that the wireless wasn't the first step on the path to damnation. It was a totally different world.'

'Made our own entertainment, those days, young Valerie,' George Browne put in. 'I feel sorry for you youngsters these days. No imagination, no need for it. All those channels on television, video shops, the Internet, instant entertainment, just shallow dross.'

'If you're bored there are always the games, Valerie. I made sure we had them. I remember we used to have great fun playing them when Gail and Hope and the others came around, when they were young. Monopoly, Scrabble – and that one you enjoyed, what is it called, Risk?'

'Yes, Mrs Browne, but that was then. Things are different now.'

'Well, there's chess and backgammon – are you enjoying your chess game, Tom?'

'I would if Rob would stop beating me, Mrs Browne,' replied Tom from another pool of light where he and Robert sat with a chessboard on a low table between them.

'Don't worry, you're just out of practice, Tom, my son.'

'And we've got Trivial Pursuit.'

'Did you know that Trivial Pursuit was invented by a couple of men in jail?' asked Gail. 'It's one of those silly things I always remember. Trouble is it's never one of the questions.'

'Was it?' asked George Browne. 'That's one of the problems of today, criminals lying around in jail doing nothing. They should be made to work. Typical of this government. Soft-headed bunch of liberals. Prison should mean just that – prison, not bloody televisions in every cell, and inmates with time to create stupid games – and they should do the time. Judges hand out a sentence of ten years and they let the bastards out in six months. Where's the sense in that?'

'Tom doesn't think the government are a bunch of liberals, do you Tom?' asked Maria-Hope. 'How did you describe them? "More right-wing than Genghis Khan"?'

'An exaggeration, I admit. It was in response to one of their more desperate ideas on security. I forget which, they do appear to come up with some silly notions.'

'I bet you the US government are better at that than the UK lot,' Robert said, pushing a bishop forward. 'We might have a new president soon, but I'm not sure he's up to cleaning the Augean stables.'

'Ah,' said George Browne, 'there you go, you see? During the war we had posters, walls have ears, that sort of thing. We didn't need all these laws they keep making. The government trusted us and we trusted them. Didn't have MI5 tapping your phone or any of that sort of nonsense. But we understood history, you see. The Americans don't have any history, that's their problem.'

'Oh, I think they have enough history,' replied Robert. 'But they have this kind of inferiority complex. And an inherent contradiction. Always trying to prove that their ancestors were noblemen, while at the same time praising the good lord for allowing them to be born in the land of democracy, the land of the free. Commoners, one and all. Except they dote on proving who they're descended from.'

'We could make a family tree!' exclaimed Lucy. 'All my friends are doing it.'

'Well, there's an idea,' said Tom. 'You didn't nick one of my pieces while I wasn't looking, did you Rob?'

'As if I would!'

'Well, it's the only explanation I can come up with for the fact that you've won four games so far. I might not have played in a while, but I used to be pretty good.'

'I play at least three times a week in New York, Tom. Pavement cafes. You have to keep up the practice.'

'Lucy,' said George Browne, 'you know why family trees are a bad idea?'

'No, great-great-great-grandad?'

'Grandad,' said Patience softly.

'But he's so old!'

George Browne blinked. He managed to recover himself.

'Because everybody is doing them these days. That's one. Never do what everybody else is doing. And secondly, the important people are those still alive and with you. Look to the future, my girl, look to the future.'

'But it's interesting, great-great-great-grandad!'

George Browne shook his head.

'Now, my girl, I've seen a lot more of life than you have. There are some things which, even if everyone is doing them, are not a good idea. Take my word for it. I could tell you stories, stories of people who got carried away! Look at the South Sea Bubble business. Bunch of fools are rushed in without thinking. Thought that because everyone else was doing it they were missing out. And look how it all ended.'

'The South Sea Bubble, great-great-great grandad?'

'I think that's a story for later, Lucy,' said Robert. 'It takes a while to tell, and it's getting late.'

'What about a game of backgammon, Petie?' asked Valerie.

'No thank you, Val.'

'Patience?'

'I'm a little occupied with the kids at the moment, Valerie,' Patience replied. 'Be time for their bedtime very soon. No, Lucy, I know you slept on the plane coming over, but that was days ago. You'll get used to the different time zones soon, I promise.'

'Hope I will,' said Robert. 'I'm still feeling disoriented. Another whisky, Tom?'

'I'm still busy, thanks, Rob. You seem to handle the hard stuff quite well.'

'You mean I drink too much.'

'He does drink too much,' Patience said. 'I keep telling him to cut back, but does he listen to me? I'm only his wife, after all.'

'A man listening to his wife?' murmured Tom. 'What a novel idea.'

'Stories!' exclaimed Robert, stretching his long legs and advancing a knight in a casual way that made Tom clench a hand into a fist.

'Stories, Robert?' asked Winifred Browne.

'Rob, do try to concentrate,' said Tom. 'I can handle being beaten, being beaten by someone not bothering to concentrate is a bit much.'

'Old American tradition,' said Robert to the others. 'comes from the days of the wagon trails. Each person had to tell a story – one or two people an evening, depending on how hard the day had been. Everybody had to take their turn, including the children.'

'Of course, like all old American traditions, that was originally an English tradition. Bastards stole it, like everything else about our culture.'

'George! Really! Language in front of the children.'

'Well, yes, perhaps, but – Canterbury Tales. That's where it comes from. The Wife of Bath, that sort of thing. Chaucer. Good old Chaucer. Good clean stories.'

'Can we, daddy?' asked Lucy. 'Can we? I know a good story.'

'Perhaps tomorrow, Lucy. I think it's definitely your bedtime right now. Don't blame me, your mom's giving me the daggers.'

'Yes, Lucy,' said Patience, standing up. 'Time for you and David to go to bed. Come on, let's wash our teeth, I'll tuck you in and read you a story.'

'From that book from great-great-great-grand-daddy's library? The one about the handsome prince and the beautiful princess?'

'If you want, yes.'

'Come on then, mummy. Come on.'

Lucy dragged her mother out.

'Filling my children's heads with fairy-tale nonsense,' Robert sneered, taking a sip of whisky. 'Congratulations, dad, twenty five years later and you haven't changed.'

'Nothing wrong with it, Robert. Good old traditional English fairy tales. If we'd kept them up we would still have an Empire. Look at what happened when we pulled out. Africa. India. And that other country.'

'Jesus! What a crock of shit!'

'Robert!' exclaimed his mother. 'Little Sarah is still here.'

'Little Sarah is all of four months old, mom. I hardly think her first word is likely to be "Jesus" or "fuck" or anything like that.'

'That's enough out of you, my boy,' George Browne tried to roar, leaning forward in his chair, grasping the sides. 'I didn't bring you up to use language like that in polite company. Obviously mixing with the Americans has given you the wrong ideas.'

Robert stood up and downed his drink. Tom looked up from the chessboard, eyebrows raised, drawing back slightly, as if his journalist's brain had engaged.

'I knew this was a mistake. I knew I shouldn't have let Patience talk me into coming back. She kept harping on about how it was only right that the kids should see their grand folks. Know a bit about where they came from. Well, I reckon it's better they don't know where they came from. If you'll excuse me, I'll take a bottle of rye up to the bedroom. We'll leave first thing in the morning.'

'Please, Robert, no, if only for my sake. George! I think an apology is in order.'

'An apology?'

'Yes, George, an apology. Robert might be our son, but he and Patience and the children are our guests.'

'Mmmph.' George Browne leaned back into his seat, breathing heavily. He took a sip of his drink with a shaking hand.

'George?'

'Well, since you put it that way, an Englishman's hospitality is – a bit like his word. He must honour it, no matter how rude the other – gentleman. Very, well, if some of my words have been misconstrued, or taken out of context, or –'

'George.'

George Browne sank deeper into his armchair.

'Then I apologise.'

'I suppose I ought to apologise as well,' said Robert, sitting down. 'I shouldn't have flown off the hook like that. Put it down to jet lag. I'm sorry, mom. Dad.'

'Checkmate!' declared Tom, pushing his queen forward.

'Tell us more about these wagon trails, Robert. They do seem to be part of the American culture.'

'Mom, you always were good at that?'

'Good at what, Robert?'

'Smoothing over things. Coming along with an Elastoplast after a full-on explosion and pretending that it was nothing.'

'I'm not at all sure of what you mean, Robert. Though I must confess, when you get to my age almost everything seems confusing. Go on with the wagon trails.'

'Well, they're part of the American myth, as I like to tell my students.'

'Students, Rob?' asked Tom, trying to keep his attention on the chess board to make sure that he had finally and undoubtedly won a game, especially as Robert appeared to have lost all interest.

'Students, Tom. Remember I mentioned I worked in a university? They normally have students floating around. Most of them pig-ignorant, I grant you, but one or two who realise that they need to rethink the myths and prejudices they've been brought up on.'

'Funny, that, Rob. Yes, I remember the bit about the university. Only, it got somewhat mixed up in all the other jobs you've had – cook in a hamburger joint, chief bottle-washer in a whorehouse, car valet at some swank hotel, bum on the railroads – or does that qualify as a job?'

'It's all true, Tom,' Patience said, returning to the lounge, putting a hand on her husband's shoulder, the light of the fire playing over her face. 'When he gave me those stories I thought he was giving me a line – and especially when he asked me to marry him. I checked up on them.'

'Hi, honey, kids asleep?'

'Fast asleep, they don't realise how tired they really are. Tom, Bobby is a professor of American culture.'

'Cost me a whole fifty bucks for that certificate.'

'Bobby?'

'Yes, my precious?'

'Shut up.'

'Yes, my precious.'

Patience gave his shoulder a squeeze and sat down on the couch next to Gail. She smiled at little Sarah. Several female eyes took in the grace she showed, a strange feminine fluidity in sitting down and smoothing her dress over her knees.

'Bobby earned his professorship the hard way. He didn't pay fifty dollars for it, he took every low-paid job he could find to pay his way. The railroad bum story – that's when I first met him. He was doing a thesis on American culture, I was doing pretty much the same, and I thought it might help if I interviewed people who led that sort of life. I couldn't understand why this apparent bum seemed to be asking me the questions instead of the other way round. Then I discovered later – to my great embarrassment – that Bobby was doing the same research, only he'd turned himself into a bum to see things from the inside – and I was a handy opportunity to find out how so-called academics saw things from the outside.'

'Boy! That sounds fascinating. I'd love to do something like that.'

'Would you, Tom?' asked Maria-Hope.

'Well, Maria, you know, it would be a chance in a million.'

'It would mean you leaving me and living underground.'

'Well, Maria –'

'I wouldn't worry about it, Maria,' Rob smiled. 'Tom's too well known as a political reporter. Too late to go undercover, everyone knows him.'

'You've read his stuff?'

'Of course. We do have the Internet over in the States. Never quite imagined I'd meet him as the partner of my niece, mind you. And while I'm here, Tom, I'd like to discuss a couple of things with you. I think on the whole you're pretty good at seeing things for what they are, but there are some things you've got just damn wrong.'

'Send me an e-mail,' replied Tom. 'Right now I'm on holiday.'

'You're a professor?' George Browne asked, stirring from a drowse. 'Did someone say that you're a professor?'

'Yes, dad, I'm a professor. I did mention it in one of my letters.'

'Tell us about these American myths, Robert,' his mother said.

'Mom, you know myths – every culture has them, and they're pretty much the same whether you're a Yank, a Brit, Taiwanese, Japanese or an Australian aborigine. Though admittedly the Australian aborigines, from the little I know, do seem to make things a little more complex than we do. I'd love to study those in more depth.'

'Bobby's working on a book, aren't you darling?'

'Patience, I told you not to mention that.'

'Yes, darling, I'm sorry, forgive me?'

'Forgive you? That's the first time you've ever been

disobedient to me.'

Patience stiffened and looked at him.

'Disobedient?' she asked.

'Oh, dear!' murmured Winifred Browne. 'I've dropped a stitch. That is a nuisance. And all because of the peas.'

There was a pause as everyone looked at her.

'Peas, gran?' asked Gail.

'Peas, in Marks and Spencer. Fresh peas. At this time of the year. It just doesn't seem right somehow. When I was growing up you could only get tinned peas for Christmas. I'm sorry, you probably think I'm rambling. I suppose I am, really.'

There was another pause.

'I know a story,' said a soft voice.

'A story, Claire?'

'A story. About a wicked stepmother.'

'Excellent!' George Browne said. 'A good old wicked stepmother story. Almost as good as a wicked mother-in-law story. But there are so many of those.'

'Claire? Are you okay? I thought you were dozing there.'

'No, gran, I've been listening, sort of.'

'Just the thing, a wicked stepmother story,' said Robert. 'Come, Claire, let's hear it. First let us charge our glasses. And then, the wicked stepmother story!'

'Just not too wicked, my dear,' suggested her grandmother.

'No, little Sarah's too young for that sort of thing,' whispered Gail. 'Aren't you, my little diddums! Ooh, you are so sweet!'

Valerie put two fingers into her mouth.

Chapter Nineteen: Claire's Story

'Once upon a time there was a little girl with beautiful flowing bl – brown hair who was loved by her father. She was only a young child, innocent, trusting. Everything she did was to please her father. He already loved her to the depths of his heart, yet every day, in every way, he came to love her more.

'She had a sister – a sister who wasn't trusting, older than her, not so innocent, not so –'

'Oh, please, Claire,' begged Gail. 'Please don't.'

'Shush, Gail,' said Valerie. 'This sounds fascinating. Go on, Claire. There'll be an evil friend in it somewhere.'

'The sister wasn't so bad. Oh, she had a cruel streak, a cruel heart, but she was led on by someone she thought a friend, an evil, conniving person –'

'I knew it. Well, at least I get top billing.'

'Val, shut up! Let Claire get on with her story.'

Claire didn't look up as she continued her story. Tom, Robert and Patience regarded her with expressionless faces from the moving shadows. Winifred Browne continued knitting. George Browne had closed his eyes to better concentrate on the story.

'The girl had a grandmother, who looked after her, because her mother was never there. The girl didn't know that her own mother was dead, that she was an orphan. But her life was happy, despite her sister and the evil friend. Until the stepmother turned up. Her father was an innocent, much as she was. He had only known woman such as her own, poor, dear, dead mother. So when Judith turned up he was unsuspecting.'

'Judith?' hissed Valerie at Gail. 'Am I supposed to know a

Judith? Christ, why can't it be Susan, at least I vaguely remember her. Even if she was a fruitcake.'

'Shut up, Val!'

'Now her father worked hard and earned a reasonable living. He wasn't a prince. He wasn't royalty. But he worked hard and earned enough to keep their table and to make sure his daughter wore the clothes of a princess.

'But Judith wanted him for herself. Judith hated this little girl. Judith loathed this little girl – of course, she tried to pretend not to, or the handsome hero would never have fallen in love with her. Which is what she was planning.

'Machinations. Oh, what machinations. Judith gained the affections of the poor man and shortly afterwards the little, innocent girl was sent to a boarding school to get her out of the way.'

'I think I could give the name.'

'Jesus, will you shut up, Val.'

'Boarding school was hell for the poor thing. All the others took against her because of her flowing bl – brown locks. To make it worse her sister and her evil friend were at the same school.'

'Please, Claire? Please?'

'Oh, let the brat go on, Gail.'

'Valerie,' whispered Robert. They looked at each other. He was leaning forward, his face alternatively highlighted and shadowed by the flickering fire. It wasn't a question. She concentrated on her drink. He leaned back.

'Oh, what delights they had with this little child. Such an innocent. So willing to obey, to do the various things they told her were traditional. To prove her worth by standing outside in only her night-dress in the winter to show she did not believe in the ghost that roamed the battlements. Eating dirt. Every cruel trick they could think of. What choice had she, this little girl? Holidays were her only solace. Going home to her father. The only one who really loved her.

'And then she found that Judith had cast a spell on him, her beloved father. A love spell. They were married. Judith tried to convince her that she was really her dead mother. But her spells might work on the pure, deluded prince, but they could not work on the child.

'The child worked hard on her studies when back at school. She had nothing else. No mother's love, her father's love poisoned by the evil step mother. Her own sister – sister – and her sister's evil friend, thoughtless, seeking their own entertainment at her expense – saw her as a toy, a thing, a fly to have its wings torn off so that they could laugh at the poor creature's confusion.'

'Please, Claire, please. I'm sorry.'

'Stuff that, Gail. Go on, Miss Saint Claire, does your story have an end?'

Valerie finished her drink, avoiding Robert's eyes.

'The poor little girl grew up trying to understand. She had been brought up rather silly-minded, to think of herself as a princess. She taught herself to watch, and listen. She watched the evil friend seduce her own uncle. She watched her own sister give herself as a virgin to another uncle. But she never learnt the lesson of what she saw. Her mind was too clouded by the stories she had been told.'

Claire paused, looking at the carpet as if remembering something.

'That's quite a story. Is there a good ending, Claire?' asked Robert. Claire nodded.

'After many troubles she came to understand that what she had been taught was false. She had been brought up to be good. But what does it mean to be good? In her case good meant doing what other people told her to, believing what they said, no matter how obvious it was that they were lying. And so she decided that it was better to be bad. Being bad wasn't easy at first. But it made her happy.

'She wasn't practical – she had been brought up on books, romantic books. Boys did the practical stuff, not her. All she knew about was how to comb her long hair. But she used other books in the library to learn. She learnt how the brakes on her step-mother's carriage worked. She learnt how to remove them. And one winter's night the wicked step-mother rode out to see her secret lover. She never saw him. And she never came back.

'But there was still the evil friend. The girl went back to her books to learn the art of poison. Others had poisoned her mind. So now she poisoned the evil friend. She was found dead in her bed. They sent for a doctor, a specialist, a coroner, a pathologist, but none could work out how the evil friend had died. But the wicked sister understood what had happened. She fled the house, never to return. And now the good little girl who had learnt to be bad stays in her father's house waiting for him to return.'

The others waited for her to continue. But apparently she had finished.

'That's it?' asked Tom.

'What, no happy ending?' asked Valerie. 'Not even a quick shag?'

'What?' asked George Browne, waking up. 'Good story, Claire, very good story. Just goes to show. You always loved reading fairy tales as a child. Important, that, reading. Where are my glasses?'

'Surely there ought to be a happy ending, Claire?' her

grandmother asked. 'Shouldn't every story should have a happy ending?'

'Only in books, gran. Not in real life.'

'I think the moral to that story is that you should never trust Saint Claire's cooking.'

'Shut up, Val.'

'What about you, Tom, have you got a happy story to see us off to bed?'

'I don't know, Mrs Browne. Anything I come up with will have the whiff of politics about it. Not often you hear of happy stories there.'

'Oh, do try. Something funny, perhaps. I don't like stories with too much violence.'

'What?' asked George Brown, starting. 'Violins? Quite like a bit of classical music, don't think we have any violins here though.'

Tom opened and closed his mouth once or twice.

'Do go on, Tom, I'm sure you'll have an excellent story. Perhaps one from your work. You must meet so many interesting people.'

'Well, let's see now ... A true story ... Okay, I think I've got one ... Once upon a time ...'

Chapter Twenty: Tom's Story

'Once upon a time there was a very important minister in the king's cabinet. He was very clever and also worked very hard. Everyone looked up to him, and asked him to make the most important decisions. The king was not a very responsible person. He enjoyed his court, having balls and parties, joking and making fun of other people. Think of Charles the Second – the Restoration period, John Wilmot, that sort of thing. So the minister had to work extra hard to see that the country was run properly. And because the king had no deep beliefs the minister became very religious. He believed that wrong should be punished and right rewarded. He believed that he should be absolutely objective. Everything for the public good rather than self-interested parties. Unfortunately he did not realise that this also made him separate from others. They could admire him, but no-one really liked him. And so he became lonely. He had a wife, but she increasingly began to live her own life, doing what she enjoyed, good works, that sort of thing, seeing him only at breakfast. His children grew up and left. They too could not understand him. He could not understand why people did not like him, as he worked so hard for them. He became to believe it was because they were jealous, and he became proud, as people often do in order to justify themselves to themselves.

'But there was one person who befriended him, a young man, a page at court. The page always volunteered to bring the king's decisions to him – and take his suggestions to the king. He became so fond of this page that he would often give him little gifts, tokens of his gratitude for their friendship. And then, one day, the king's chief minister announced that he was retiring. Now everyone wanted to be the king's chief minister. The position brought power and wealth. There were many intrigues, cabals, much trickery and deception. But everyone thought that there could be no other choice for the position but our hard working and lonely minister. The king did not like him, but he knew that the people would become rebellious should he appoint another.

'And then one of the lowest ministers stood up and announced that he had news. The hard working minister was a liar! He pontificated about right and wrong, criticised his fellow ministers for wrongdoing, told the people that the king was lecherous and slothful, and yet he – the so-called hard working and upright minister – forced the king's own page into bed with him! Yes! Shameful! The hard working minister was a deviant! And all the other ministers stood up and called for the hard working minister to say if this was true.

'The hard working minister denied it.

'But why were he and the page locked up in his office so often? Could he deny that this was the case? He denied that they were locked up in his office. The lad merely came to deliver the king's messages, the door was never locked.

'Bring forth this page! cried the other ministers. Let him have his say.

'The page was brought forth. And he collapsed in tears and admitted that what was claimed was true, that he had fought against it, but the hard working minister had threatened to throw his parents in jail if he did not obey. The hard working minister denied this.

'But what about the gifts? asked his accusers. You deny giving this boy gifts?

'Of course he could not deny the gifts. But they were tokens of friendship, not –

'Enough! cried the king. Begone and never darken the palace halls again.

'And, as it was the word of the king, no matter how he denied the charge, he could not but leave. And so he returned home and sat on his own. He had made his job his life, alienating his very own family, refusing friendship when it was offered, and finally his pride in his own righteousness had made him blind to the intrigues of others. He had nothing. He had no-one. Life had turned to ashes in his mouth.

'That evening his wife returned from her good works to find her husband sitting alone in the darkness.

'When he told her what had happened she said she would speak to the king, for she knew that what was claimed was a lie.

'But he told her not to.

'He told her that if the king could pretend to believe the lies – and he was sure that the king knew they were lies – then it was not worth it. He told her that he had spent the day sitting alone and thinking. That he now realised how he had traded the love of a family and friends for false righteousness and pride. That he was being punished for it, and he deserved the punishment.

'For where were their children?

'Gone away.

'Where were the friends they might have had?

'Nowhere to be found.

'Come, said his wife, you are now committing another sin, that of self-pity. Let us leave this awful city and go live elsewhere. Somewhere where we can live quietly, perhaps a farm that we can work, and achieve a quiet happiness.

'And so they left the city and bought a small farm. At first it was hard work, but the other farmers and their wives helped when they could. They were simple folk who understood that friendship and humility are the most important virtues.

'Then one day their son happened to visit. They had not seen him for years, nor he they. He was astonished to find his father in such poor circumstances, yet also, for the first time he had ever known, happy. The father even smiled often. And this the son wrote to his sister, who could not believe it. So she found an excuse to visit and was also astonished to find it true.

'And from then on the son and daughter, and their families, came to visit their parents often, especially during the festival season, when families celebrated their good fortune, however poor they were. The hard working minister became known and admired as one of them. They looked to him for advice. And so the parents passed happily into old age, their grandchildren all around them.

'And whenever one of the grandchildren should become proud, the old man would take the child upon a knee and tell him he story of the cold-hearted minister who was taught to love his fellow man.'

'Hmmph,' muttered George Browne, who had managed to stay awake for most of the story, his speculating eyes on Tom . 'A good story, young Tom, but I hope you're not suggesting anything?'

'I thought it a very good story, and I'm sure Tom wasn't suggesting anything, were you, Tom?'

'Of course not, Mrs Browne. It's just a story based on a politician I once – read about. Many years ago. When William the Second came to the throne, I think.'

Robert looked at him and rubbed his jaw.

'Well, I think I'm ready for bed,' Winifred Browne said, standing up. 'Has everyone got everything they need?

Blankets, towels?'

'Yes, gran.'

'Yes, gran.'

'I think I'll call it a day too. Don't stay up too late, you youngsters.'

'Night, gran, night, grandad.'

'Night, gran, night, grandad.'

Chapter Twenty-two: Sweet dreams

'Anyone fancy another drink,' asked Valerie once George Browne and his wife had left.

'I think I'll hit the sack,' Robert said, standing up and stretching. 'Still can't work out what time of day it's supposed to be.'

'Well, I'm going to have a nightcap,' Val said, jumping up. 'Ooh,' she muttered, swaying.

'You okay, Val?' Robert asked stepping over and taking her arm.

'I think I stood up too quickly,' she said, leaning in to him. 'Just a sec, I'll be fine in a minute.'

'Try not to grope too much while you're there,' Claire said, gently picking up Sarah. She stood up. 'Right, night all, see you in the morning.'

'Oooh, she has become a right little bitch, hasn't she?' muttered Val, staring at the closing door.

'Here, Gail, take care of Val,' Robert said, dropping her at Gail's feet, 'Patience and I need to check on the children. They have this habit of waking up if they know their momma and poppa are awake.'

'Coming up, Tom?' asked Maria-Hope.

'Yup, bedtime for Bonzo. Night, all.'

'I think we'll turn in too,' Peter said.

'Let's have another drink,' Val said once she and Gail were alone in the lounge.

'Let's take a nightcap up to our room. I'm knackered. Wash teeth, nightcap, and then it's the land of nod for me.'

'Just one? I'll make mine a double, then.'

'Just like the others before it.'

'What's that?'

'Oh, just mumbling. Shows you how tired I am. Come on, bedtime.'

Valerie poured Gail a strong gin, and then double that for herself, before they went upstairs.

'Do you think we should lock the door?' Valerie asked, giggling, once they had finished their pre-night toilette and sat in their beds, covered with blankets. 'In case Saint Claire comes wandering in, in the dead of night, with a butcher's knife?'

'I think I'll lock the door, Val, just in case you suddenly find yourself sleepwalking into the wrong bed.'

'Chance would be a fine thing. Rob didn't even react when I stumbled into him.'

'Give it up, Val, that was so obvious.'

'No, it wasn't. I've just had a drink or two too many, that's all. Could happen to anyone.'

'More like a bottle too many. Good night.'

'Nonsense. Good night, Gail, sweet dreams. Just not wet ones. Especially about that hunk Tom.'

'Val,' Gail said, putting her glass on the side-table next to her, and pulling the blankets up, 'unfortunately there doesn't appear to be a billiard room. Do you have any preference to where else your corpse should be found?'

Chapter Twenty-three: Friday 23rd December

Tom and Maria-Hope were first in the kitchen the following morning, while it was still dark. Tom made up the fire while Maria-Hope filled the kettle and prepared breakfast.

'That story Claire told last night, Maria,' Tom said once the fire was going, looking into the flames. 'Bit strange, wasn't it?'

'Oh, that's just Claire getting a bit of revenge in. Gail deserves it, really, she was a right bitch as far as Claire was concerned. Don't believe all this sisterly love nonsense you hear. For a teenager to have a sister six years younger trailing around can be a right pain. But Gail went a little too far – egged on by Valerie, of course. Valerie was the real cause of all the problems.'

'Oh, I understand that. What I don't understand is why no-one picked up on the story about the evil friend seducing one of the uncles and her own sister being seduced by another uncle. I mean, the evil friend would be bad enough, but we're talking incest here. And no-one said a dicky bird.'

'She was getting a little carried away, Tom. I wouldn't worry about it. I'm sure she just made that up to have a go at Gail. After all, there's only uncle Adam and uncle Rob. Uncle Rob left when Valerie was about ten. Which leaves one uncle, and Claire mentioned two. So mathematically I'm afraid it doesn't work. Now, how many eggs do you want?'

'Two, please. But – just say, for example, that the bit about seducing an uncle was true. There's only one person she could mean – your uncle Adam.'

'Tom, don't be silly. Claire seems to have got this idea into her head that the entire world is sex mad. She's right about that as far as Valerie goes, but the rest is pure invention. In the real world people aren't shagging whoever's available.'

'I'm beginning to think that might be true,' Tom muttered to himself.

'What was that?'

'Oh, nothing, just swearing at this fire. I've often regretted not joining the Boy Scouts. Maybe I would have learnt to light a fire properly. But it's going now.'

'I like it. I don't think I've ever stayed anywhere with real fires. How many rashers of bacon? Two again?'

'Two sounds good. The question is, if it did happen, how old was she when it did? Even if she was over sixteen, he must be a good twenty or thirty years older than her. Even if she was eighteen it could be made to appear as if he had seduced her.'

'Tom, Valerie was sharing herself out long before she got to fifteen. If a man was taken to court for seduction of a minor they'd find him innocent, mainly because she would have shagged all the men on the jury before they got around to agreeing a verdict.'

Tom grinned ruefully.

'Funnily enough I can see her in a school uniform batting her eyelids, pretending to be an innocent school-girl while –'

'Tom, I think I've heard enough about Valerie. If you fancy her, let me know and we can part amicably.'

'Okay, okay! I get the message. I suppose I'm just letting the journalist in me get carried away.' He poked the fire, staring into the flames. 'But that bit about Claire killing her stepmother – who, of course, is her real mother. Talk about the Elektra complex.'

'Like I say, she was just tired and emotional. She's obviously been through a lot in the past year or so. Let's drop it, shall we?'

'Hmm. I suppose you're right. After all, if she hated her

mother that much she wouldn't have agreed to go for a walk with her this morning – unless she planned to push her in front of an oncoming car.'

'Don't be silly, Tom.'

'Now if Claire and Valerie went for a walk I'd put money on Valerie ending up under a car – or in a pigsty, perhaps.'

'Make yourself useful. Make some toast.'

'Zu befehl, mein fuehrer!' Tom said, jumping to the task. 'I think a good walk in the cold will do Valerie good – when she finally surfaces. Did you see that pass she made at Rob? Pretending to stumble into him in the lounge like that?'

'She did? I missed that. I suppose I'm so used to it it seemed normal.'

'Patience didn't miss it. Valerie had better watch out.'

'Patience will have to join the queue. Behind Claire and myself.'

'Still she was a few sheets to the wind – Valerie, that is.'

Maria-Hope peered out of the window into the first light of dawn.

'Hey, it looks like it snowed last night.' Tom joined her, putting his arm around her waist.

'Just a little. I wonder if it will stick.'

'Be nice to have a white Christmas.'

'Let's hope so. Come on, let's eat. And if you mention Valerie again you'll regret it.'

'The name shall not sully my lips again, oh my gorgeous one.'

'You can mention it again when she's in hospital or dead. Preferably the latter.'

Tom noticed that his bacon was burnt, but wisely refrained from commenting on the fact. Nor the state of the eggs, which had managed to make themselves both burnt and runny. He knew he wasn't a chef, but he could at least fry an egg properly.

'Anything wrong?' asked Maria-Hope.

'Oh, no, no, just thinking. I must stop that. Thinking, that is. After all, we're supposed to be enjoying ourselves, having a quiet Christmas in the country.'

'I'm enjoying myself. I'll enjoy myself even more when I've got rid of that thing.'

'Nice toast,' said Tom.

Chapter Twenty-four: Unwelcome streets

'These little villages are very quaint,' Jane Green noted as she and Claire walked through the village later that morning. 'Especially with a light dusting of snow, but they could really do with wider pavements.'

'Next time I'll carry Sarah. These pavements weren't designed for buggies. You'd think they'd try to keep them in good repair.'

'Four by fours, is my guess. Rich townies buy up village cottages and come down on holiday in their four by fours. Since they never walk anywhere they don't think anything of using the pavement as another part of the road when they need to pass another car. Pavements aren't designed to carry the weight.'

'That wouldn't surprise me.'

'Why don't you carry Sarah? We can fold the buggy up and I'll carry that, it's not heavy.'

'I'm okay.'

'No, I insist. I am going to put my foot down. It isn't often I get a chance to earn brownie points in heaven, and you can't stop me now.'

'Well, if you don't mind. But – brownie points in heaven?'

'Oh, it's just a silly phrase I picked up. In France, I think it was. Someone who couldn't really speak English mangling an Americanism.'

'I suppose it must be exciting, all that travelling.'

'Ha! I wish. Travel is only enjoyable when you're on holiday and can relax. Rushing from city to city, country to country, trying to convince boards of directors they need your product – it was exciting for all of the first week, I suppose. But you become very hard-nosed about it after a while, especially when you're facing hard-nosed men – directors are almost always men, and when you find a woman director you realise that she's even worse than the men. She has to be to survive. And then one day you wake up alone in yet another bland hotel room with yet the same bland lighting and the same bland radio and the same bland television and wonder just what you're doing and whether you like the person you've turned into.'

'At least that's one good thing. People tend to end up lying in the bed they make.'

'Try not to say that as if you enjoyed the idea so much, Claire. Anyway, I don't believe it's true.'

'Don't you.'

'No, I don't. Take you and Henry. You could argue that you deserved all you got for sleeping with him before you were married. That would be what I would call the male point of view – it's always the woman's fault. On the other hand, the view I would take is that he's a low-down scumbag who ought to have his prick nailed to a block of concrete and be left out for the vultures to slowly peck him to death. Even better, a version of Prometheus – each day the vultures peck his balls away, they regenerate over-night so that the process can be repeated the next day.'

'Mum!'

'Well, don't tell me you didn't think the same, Claire.'

'Well, yes, but ... '

'But I'm supposed to be your good old mum and not have thoughts like that? Or not use language like that? Claire, if there's one thing I regret it's that I let them – your father, your grandfather and your grandmother – treat you like a little angel. It was fine when you were young, but not when you were a teenager.'

'Gran's been very good to me.'

'Yes, I know you think she can do no wrong. But I know her better than that – she is my mother, after all. Do you want to know why I married your father? I told your grandmother yesterday. It was because I was always treated as a nuisance. Your uncle Adam was the only important thing. When he turned up with your father your grandmother thought him the bee's knees – after your uncle Adam, of course. So I thought, well, if I can catch him maybe my mother will think better of me. Oh, it wasn't a conscious thought. It was only over the last few years that I even realised that that was what had happened. I never really loved your father. I wish I could say I did, but I didn't.'

'No, you didn't. I remember that quite clearly. But I did. Love him, I mean.'

Jane Green nodded.

'Funny how daughters tend to forgive their fathers anything, and their mothers nothing. Why are we so hard upon our own sex?'

'I don't believe I am. Dad worked all hours to give us a good life. He needed support, you never gave it to him.'

'Ha! Worked all hours? Are you telling me that you really never knew where he had been when he came back late at night? He'd been with whatever latest floozy he'd found. It was like that from day one. Or drinking with the boys from work. At first I tolerated it – god knows why, looking back. Afraid that my mother would say that I was a failed wife, and that there was no wonder Jack needed to find comfort elsewhere, I suppose.'

'I don't believe it.'

'Ask Gail. It took her a while, but she finally twigged what was happening.'

'Gail? I wouldn't trust Gail to give me the right time of the day.'

'I can't say I blame you.'

'What?'

'I said I can't say I blame you. I wasn't aware of what was going on at that supposedly exclusive girls' boarding school you went to – something I agreed to because of your grandfather, another regret I have. But I bumped into one of Gail's chums a year or so ago. We had a drink together. A bit of a mistake, really – I didn't spot the signs that she'd already had a few. Stupid of me. Anyway, it all came out, the bullying, the teasing – she even claimed that she'd been seduced by one of the female teachers. Then she tried to come on to me, would you believe? I told her I wasn't a lesbian and got out of there as soon as I could. I wasn't sure that what she had told me was true, she was obviously three parts off of her trolley. So I made some enquiries. It sounds like it was worse than the stories you hear about boys' public schools.'

'It was.'

'I'm sorry about that. No, really, I am. If I'd known I could have done something about it. But I didn't and it's too late now. But it isn't too late to do something now.'

'I know. And I'm going to do it.'

'I mean something good, Claire.'

'I don't.'

Chapter Twenty-five: A record of the past

'Oooooh! My head,' groaned Valerie as Gail maliciously opened the curtains wide to let in the morning sun. 'Argh, I need a headache tablet. And something for my stomach.'

'Feeling a little queasy, Val?'

'I think maybe I'll just stay in bed this morning,' Valerie moaned, pulling the bedcover over her head. 'Something I ate must have disagreed with me. Can't you close the curtains?'

'Something you drank, more like it. I think this room needs some fresh air. I'll open the windows. Don't want it to end up smelling like the girls' locker room.'

'Don't, please don't. I didn't have that much. Not really.'

'Perhaps someone slipped something into your drink. Someone who doesn't like you very much. I dare say I could think of one or two who might fall into that category.'

A bleary eye peaked out from underneath the bedcover, a hand shielding it from the light.

'You think so? Hey – that story angel-face told. Didn't she say she poisoned the evil friend. You don't think she meant it? That she put something in my drink?'

'Well, Val, that is a possibility. I think you'd better be careful of Claire. I think she might be seriously out to get you.'

'I need to go to the bathroom, I think I'm going to be sick.' She staggered out of the bed, holding a blanket wrapped around her.

'Raw egg's supposed to be good for that,' Gail called after her. 'Bitch,' she added under her breath.

She wandered down towards the kitchen. As she came down the stairs she heard the sound of Lucy's voice accompanying "Jingle Bells" coming from the lounge. She turned, made her way in, and found Robert on the floor next to his daughter. She was singing along with a record player, watching it in fascination.

'Lucy's never seen a record player,' Robert said with an apologetic grin. 'Only CDs and DVDs. We got rid of ours years ago, it was just cluttering up the apartment. Patience's dad is an gadget freak. Out with the new and in with the new. Their LP player disappeared years ago.'

'It's lovely!' exclaimed Lucy. 'Can't we have one, daddy?'

'Honey, I'm not sure you can buy them these days.'

'But it looks so much better than a CD player. It's a lot bigger.'

'We'll see what we can do when we get back,' Robert replied, winking at Gail. 'But you mustn't play the records too much, Lucy, otherwise you'll wear them out. Old things are like that.'

'Like great-great-great-grandad?'

'Er, not quite, no Lucy.'

'Lucy,' said Gail, 'did you know that Valerie loves Christmas carols? I think you should play one whenever she comes into the lounge. Jingle Bells, the Twelve Days of Christmas, Gathering Winter Fuel, that sort of thing.'

Lucy looked at her, a child's suspicion aroused.

'She doesn't like them, does she? You're just saying that because she hates them,' she accused. Gail's lips twitched.

'Okay, you're right, she hates them.'

'Then I am not going to play carols for her,' Lucy said definitely, turning back to the record player as it finished. 'She's not nice. Records are only for nice people.'

Chapter Twenty-six: Brothers and sisters in law

Robert was sitting in the lounge flipping through a magazine when Rebeccah walked in with George in her arms. Lucy had been parted from the record player with the promise of being allowed to help her mother and her grandmother make real biscuits – cookies – in the kitchen.

'So, Rebeccah,' he asked, 'enjoying life within the bosom of your chosen family?'

'With all due respect, Rob, as you're part of the family, they aren't my chosen family. They're Peter's family, and I don't think he was given the option of choice.'

'Very well put, Becky. But don't worry about the all due respect, I feel a stranger here myself.'

'I'm not surprised, after being away for – what, more than twenty years? Twenty five years? Why did you leave, if you don't mind me asking.'

'Not at all. I didn't leave as such – I joined a company which needed someone who could travel. First place was the good old U. S. of A. As the days went by I just began to enjoy it more and more. It wasn't so much a case of making a conscious decision, there just seemed so much to do that the days flew by until I realised how long it had been since I had seen the old sceptered isle.'

She sat down, smoothed sleeping little George's hair and then looked up at Rob.

'Not a conscious decision,' she repeated. He smiled.

'I like to be diplomatic when I can.'

'I suppose being married with two little children make it that little more difficult. A couple of added reasons, as it were.'

'Well, we could hardly fly half way around the world when

they were babies. Personally I didn't think they were old enough now – to travel such a distance. But Patience was right set on it. She reckoned Lucy was old enough, and David too young to notice.'

'Is she still?'

'Still what?'

'Still set on it? Or, to put it another way, does she think she's made the right decision?'

'Well, put it this way, I convinced her beforehand that we should have a flexible itinerary – maybe take the kids to see the sights of London straight after Christmas if things weren't going well, or the kids were bored or whatever. Right now I think she's rather glad of that.'

'And she's such an obedient wife.'

'Ouch.' He grimaced. 'Yes, I don't know why I used that word last night. Almost like the house is haunted by my father, and we end up talking like him. I'll be glad to get away. Just hope Patience forgives me for being such an arsehole.'

Rebeccah looked down at her child.

'I'm trying to convince Peter that we should take little George home straight after Christmas.'

'Well, I'm sure his other relations – your ma and pa – would be awful glad to see him.'

'Yes, I think they would. So long as he wasn't accompanied by myself and Peter.'

'They disapprove of your not being married?'

'They probably give prayers of thanks that we aren't married – Hebrew prayers. You see, Rob, to them Peter is a gentile. They're hoping I'll see sense and get married to a good little Jewish boy. It would be difficult, but Jews have laws for everything. I'm sure there's one covering a lost woman with a child of a gentile returning to the fold. It probably involves a ritual bath or two.'

'Ah, I see we share something.'

'We do?'

'Patience's parents were hoping she would marry a good little Chinese boy. Marrying a white boy – well, apparently the only thing worse would be to marry a Japanese or Korean or something. But I did have a laugh. Know what her dad said to her?'

'Go on.'

'He said that I wasn't even an American, a real American, born in the US like them.'

Rebeccah laughed.

'So much for a land free of prejudice.'

'Prejudice? Yanks can be the most prejudiced people in the world. Patience and I might be accepted in places like New York or the larger cities, but backwoods America still believes in the colour bar, and that includes the Chinese, no matter where they were born.' He smiled bitterly. 'I was on an overnight train the once, by myself, cheap ticket. I found myself in a sleeper cabin with two Chinese boys, real Chinese, could hardly speak a word of English. Very polite. And then the conductor, or whatever he was, offers to get me a cabin by myself – away from, and I quote, "the rice-eaters". The funny thing was that he was black. The conductor.' He sighed. 'Nope, stack them statistics as you will, prejudice ain't gonna go away no time soon.'

'Not to mention rural England. Or perhaps I'm just thinking of your father.'

'Ha. Dad's one of the most blinkered people I've ever met. It was such a joy to watch his face when he realised that this Chink in front of him was my wife. I had mentioned it in my letters, but dad has always had this ability to convince himself of an alternative reality, if I could put it that way.'

Rebeccah looked at him.

'Do you ever wonder if you married Patience as a Chinese to spite your father?'

'Oh, no. I love Patience, end of story. I'd never understood what love really meant until I met her. In my line of work you develop a rather cautious approach to that sort of thing.'

He looked at Rebeccah and grinned.

'However – there's a phrase I heard the other day, apparently from some television show or other. Pissing dad off was a Brucie bonus.'

'And you're hoping to add to the bonus.'

'I sure am.'

Chapter Twenty-Seven: Sisters

Gail tapped softly at Claire's bedroom door.

'Who's there?' asked a drowsy voice.

'It's me, Gail. Can I come in? Please?' There was a silence as Claire considered this plea.

'If you must,' she replied eventually. Gail opened the door and closed it behind her as quietly as she could.

'You okay?' she asked.

'I'm tired. I was trying to have a few minutes' sleep.'

'I know, I'm sorry,' Gail said, sitting down on the bed next to her and stroking her hair. 'Do you mind if I sit here? You can get some sleep and I'll keep an eye on little Sarah.'

'Why should you care?'

'Claire, I know I was a failure as an elder sister. I want to make up for that. Not just because we're sisters, but – well, I never really understood you. I thought you were just a little goody-two-shoes. I was speaking to gran yesterday. She explained how – well, you know, the folks. Their getting divorced. It must have been harder on you than it was on me.'

Claire looked at her.

'Mom says dad was screwing around. Is that true?'

Gail sighed, leaned over and rested her elbows on her knees, looking at little Sarah sleeping.

'Yes, that's true.'

'No-one bothered to tell me. I was just the little baby doll. The little mushroom, more like it, kept in the dark and fed shit.'

Gail stretched, and rubbed her neck.

'Yes,' she said, 'that describes it quite well. All I can say is that I'm sorry. Claire – Claire, I know it's not an excuse, but I –

oh, I don't know. I was young and stupid. What more can I say?'

'How did you feel about it?'

'Dad screwing around?'

'Yes, that's what I was wondering about.'

'I don't know. We used to have long arguments about that sort of thing at school, after lights out. I didn't join in, really. The consensus seemed to be that most men would screw around if given the chance, but there were some who would remain faithful. The Holy Grail of mankind, as it were.'

'And Valerie didn't believe in the Holy Grail.'

'Nope. She thinks everybody screws around, so why shouldn't she get her share?'

'Why were you such friends with her at school?'

'To be honest?'

Claire answered with silence. Gail sighed.

'Because I was thick. Because I turned up at that school looking for a friend to be close to. It was boarding school. I needed a friend. I was feeling lost and alone. She was the first to show that her tits were big enough to hold a pencil under them. It was a big thing for us, for some stupid reason. I've often wondered what boys do in the same way. I've read somewhere that they see who can piss the highest against a wall. I don't know. If the size of our tits or the height boys can piss is a marker of our civilisation ...'

'How high do you reckon Tom could use his thing?'

'Claire!'

'Come off it, Gail, I've seen the way you look at him. Even Sarah doesn't drool as much as you do.'

'He's Hope's boyfriend. He's out of bounds.'

'Gail,' Claire said, closing her eyes and resting on the pillows, 'Hope has only ever had one boyfriend, and that's Peter.'

'Claire! He's her brother!'

'Open your eyes, Gail. Hope's never kept a boyfriend. Why? Because Peter doesn't approve. He never has. She only gets boyfriends so that he can disapprove of them. She hates Rebeccah because she's given birth to the child Hope thinks she should have had.'

'Claire! That's ridiculous.'

'Suit yourself. I'm tired. I'd like to have some sleep now. Will you look after Sarah?'

'Absolutely! Of course! You get some rest.'

'Hope's still a virgin, Gail. You fancy Tom. He's the sort of man I would have wanted. Grab him while you can.'

Claire closed her eyes. But not before turning towards her sister and her child and taking hold of Gail's hand. Even though she had long regarded Claire as something of a doll, Gail was surprised at how thin and small Claire's fingers were. We owe you, she thought. We owe you, and, if it's the last thing I'm going to do, I'm going to pay what I owe.

Even if that price included Tom.

Now why, she asked herself, did I have such a silly thought?

Chapter Twenty-Eight: A hearty lunch

'Where is everyone?' demanded George Browne as he stomped into the dining room and sat down to lunch. 'Not gone to town for some of that Macwhatsits rubbish? Not when I've spent a lot of money on good old-fashioned English grub?'

'Robert and Patience are having lunch in the kitchen, dear, with Peter and Rebeccah and the children – and Claire, of course.'

'What? In the kitchen? What's wrong with the dining room, like the rest of us?'

'The children, my dear. You can't expect them to sit at table like the grownups. There'd be food everywhere. It's easier to clean up in the kitchen.'

'Load of nonsense! Teach 'em manners while they're young. You can tell a gentleman by his table manners, remember that, Philip.'

'Tom,' said Maria-Hope.

'That's what I said, wasn't it? Young Tom. Remember, a gentleman is a gentleman.'

'Now, don't stand on ceremony, tuck in everyone, before it gets cold.'

'Just a second, what about grace? Must say grace before. Family that prays together stays together. Now, heads down. For what we are about to receive, oh Lord ... '

'When did granddad get religion, gran?' whispered Gail to her grandmother.

'He ran out of friends to argue with, Gail, so he decided to take on the big man himself.'

'... make us truly grateful. Amen.'

'Smashing spread, Mrs Browne,' said Tom, eyeing the table and making an exaggerated sound of licking his lips.

'Only done with yours and everybody's help, Tom. I couldn't have done it all on my own, not at my age.'

'This takes me back,' Gail said, spooning mashed potatoes onto her plate. 'I remember the dinners we used to have at your place when I was young, gran. We were bloated by Christmas day, and then managed to stuff Christmas dinner down somehow.'

'A long time ago, Gail.'

'Too long,' grumbled George Browne. 'People rushing around these days, no time for family and relations.'

'Have some more potatoes, Valerie, you're looking a bit peakish.'

'Ah, thank you, Mrs Browne, but no, I think I might have picked up a bug somewhere. I'll just have a little more wine.'

'Claire helped you with lunch, didn't she, gran?' asked Gail innocently.

'She did offer, Gail, but we were more or less finished and little Sarah was demanding to be fed.'

'Ah, I think I will have a few more potatoes in that case,' Valerie decided.

'Best thing for a stomach bug,' George Browne said. 'Plenty to eat, followed by a good few ports and sleep. Sweat it out, that's the trick. A good curry, that's the thing.'

'George! Really. Not at the dinner table. Valerie, are you sure you're okay? You looked a little queasy there.'

'Where's the port, gramps? I'll get a large glass for Valerie.'

'I do not need any port, thank you, Gail,' Valerie replied, adding softly, 'Bitch.'

'What was that?' George Browne called. 'What are you two whispering about? Bad manners, whispering at the dinner table. Still, you always did, you two. Whispering and giggling. Charming, in a way. Schoolgirls always are. It's the age.'

'Is that mutton okay for you, George? You were saying the last lot was hard on your false teeth.'

'Nonsense! I never complain about my grub. Young Tom, ever have army grub when you were – where was it, the Balkans? Yugoslavia?'

'Several times, Mr Browne. The army – the British army – are always friendly to British journalists. Well, most of them, most of the time. The ranks will wind you up and see how you respond. If you show that you can take a joke, if they decide you're okay, they'll do almost anything for you. Come across as pompous or vain and they'll make your life a misery as far as they can. And they really know how to do that.'

'Not the same these days, army grub. When I was in the army we took what we got and were grateful. These days they complain if it's not haute cuisine or whatever French rubbish they prefer. Back when the Hun was sinking our shipping we took what we could get. There was rationing. Bloody Hun sitting comfy in France, just waiting to have a crack at us. But we showed them. Bully beef and biscuits. Eighth army lived on those in North Africa and they showed Rommel a trick or two. Often wished I was with them, but I had my own outfit, and we were proud of what we did.'

'You fought in France, Mr Browne?'

'Let me put it this way, young Tom, out of my platoon of twelve men only three survived.'

'Oh, Christ, not the war again,' muttered Maria-Hope.

'What was that, Hopeless?'

'I was just saying to Tom how much easier it must have been to be a vegetarian during the war, gramps.'

'Vegetarian? Vegetarian? We didn't have any of that bloody

nonsense in those days, young girl. Anyone who even suggested it would have been put down as a pouf, and rightly so. The bloody limp-wristed, animal rights, long-haired – that's what they are. Vegetarian!'

'This broccoli in butter is lovely, Mrs Browne.'

'It is, isn't it, Valerie? It's a new recipe that Claire gave me yesterday.'

Valerie's face turned a shade of greeny-white and she pushed the broccoli to one side.

Chapter Twenty-nine: Walking alone

After lunch George Brown retired to "watch a bit of telly" in the television room. His wife went to the kitchen to put everything in the dishwasher, but was prevented from doing so by the other women. Having kept herself busy hovering around them, checking food supplies, debating whether the kitchen curtains needed washing with the smoke coming from the smokeless fire place, and other little things which gave her purpose while they worked, she went upstairs to have an afternoon nap. Valerie had already retired to sleep off her upset stomach. With the washing up done, Robert and Patience took the children for a walk while most of the others met in the lounge to debate what they should spend the afternoon doing.

'You did that deliberately, didn't you, Maria?' asked Tom as they sat in a group before the fire, Gail holding Sarah and making soft cooing noises at her sleeping face.

'What's that?' asked Maria-Hope.

'Mention vegetarianism when your grandad was about to talk about the war.'

'Grandad didn't start on his war reminiscences, did he?' asked Peter.

'He started, Peter, but Maria here dropped a comment about vegetarians, and he went off at a tangent. I thought he might have something interesting to say.'

'Tom,' said Maria-Hope, 'you don't know how we had to suffer as kids with his talk about the war. The same stories every time. How grandad won the war.'

'I always enjoyed his stories,' Claire said.

'You did, Claire,' said Gail. 'But you only had to suffer them a few times.'

'Oh, I forgot, I was the little baby. Thank you for reminding me.'

'Jesus, Claire! Give me a break. I'm sorry I teased you when we were at school, okay?'

'I think I'll take Sarah back now, Gail.'

'Oh, please, just a few more minutes. She's sleeping so innocently. Please, Claire, don't use her to get back at me.'

'Talking of tormentors, where is Val the voluptuous?' asked Peter.

'Val the what?' asked Maria-Hope.

'Gone for a lie down,' said Gail. 'Thank god.'

'I wonder what Rob and Patience are talking about,' mused Claire. 'They seem very much in love, but, after that comment he made last night about her being disobedient ... I'd have whacked him one.'

'He had a point,' said Peter. 'Admittedly he chose the wrong word, but if he'd asked her not to mention the book he was working on, then she shouldn't have.'

'Probably worried that some other academic will hear about it and jump the gun,' said Tom. 'Get in with his own work first. I've heard of that sort of thing happening. Academics like to pretend that they're pretty harmless, but from what I've heard of their politics ... ruthless bunch, professors.'

'You know,' said Gail, 'if I was married and my husband accused me of being disobedient, I don't think I'd whack him. I'd be too busy laughing. Wouldn't I, little Sarah? Oh, yes I would!'

Claire smiled.

'It was a silly thing to say, wasn't it?' she agreed. 'And Patience looks like one of those wives who just has to give her husband a certain look to keep him in line. She wouldn't even have to mention what he said. Not a word.'

'I shall take that on board, Claire,' said Tom. 'Gail, do you mind if I ask you a personal question?'

'Hmm? Sorry, what was that?' Gail asked, her concentration back on little Sarah who had gripped her finger in her sleep.

'I was wondering why you invited that trollop down – Valerie?'

'A bit of an old-fashioned word,' said Maria-Hope.

'But very fitting,' said Peter.

'Yes, very fitting,' said Maria-Hope.

'So why did you invite her down?' asked Rebeccah.

'Oh. Well. Genetically inherited stupidity, I think. Or maybe not. Maybe I'm an adopted orphan. Anyway, I'd just dumped my boyfriend because it turned out that he was already married, she, Val – well, she'd just been through the same sort of thing. We got together to have a cry over a few drinks. I thought there probably wouldn't be anyone else here, and I wanted company of my own age. I hadn't seen that much of Val over the past few years. I'd forgotten what she was like. I'd forgotten how she can go for anything wearing trousers. And I presumed she drank too much that night to drown her sorrows. I didn't realise that she's two shorts away from being alcoholic. No doubt she'll be at it tonight again, once she's recovered.'

'At the booze, or the trousers?'

'Both, I would imagine.'

'There you go, Tom, there's your chance,' Claire said idly. 'A freebie. Valerie's bed is open to first comers. And second and third comers.'

'Maria!'

'Well, you know how I feel about it. Might as well take it where you can get it.'

'Maria,' said Peter, 'I think you might –'

Tom stood up, his jaw set.

'I think what I'll take is a walk. On my own, if you don't mind.'

Chapter Thirty: Walking out

'Well, that was well managed, Hope,' Gail said mildly, making a face at Sarah. 'Or should I call you Maria, in case you throw something at me? She's a silly girl, your aunt, isn't she? A silly, silly girl. Yes, she is.'

'Oh! Oh, I don't know. I shouldn't have said that to him, he didn't do anything wrong. I just feel so – bitchy. Gail, please go after him, tell him I'm sorry. Tell him I didn't mean it. Tell him – oh, tell him it's just me being a silly woman, whatever he wants to hear.'

'Why don't you tell him yourself?'

'Because we'll just end up having an argument. He'll say something like, if I really loved him I'd agree to marry him. And he knows that I don't want to get married. To anyone.'

'Sounds like you've got your head screwed on the wrong way round. Here, Sarah, go to mummy. Aunty Gail has to perform a mission of mercy. And aunty Gail is about as crap at missions of mercy as anyone could be.'

'Why don't you want to get married to him?' asked Claire as Gail hurried out.

'Claire, it's a principle. People get married, they fall out of love, they get divorced. If you don't get married you're forced to look at your partner every day. Why am I with this man? Because I love him. He might not be perfect, he might often be irritating, but I have made my choice and I am going to stick with it. If you don't get married, you can't get divorced. You have to stick with it.'

'Maria?'

'Yes?'

'I think you're being an arsehole.'

Peter's head jerked back.

'Tom! Tom, wait up,' Gail called breathlessly as she ran along the path after him. He turned around in surprise.

'Gail?'

'Oh, god, you walk far too fast, I'm all out of breath. Let me take your arm.'

'Gail, why are you here?'

'I'm with the UN troops – a peace keeper. See, I'm even wearing blue. Blue denim skirt. I knew I put it on for a reason. Apart from hiding my big backside.'

'Not funny, Gail.'

Gail held on to his arm while she paused for breath.

'Oh, I'm sorry. I forgot, you must have met a lot of them. The UN lot. The ones with the blue berets.'

'Quite a few.'

'Look, Tom, Hope – Maria – asked me to speak to you. She sends you a kiss. Like this.' She put her arms around him and held him tight as she kissed him on the lips. It took him a while to realise what was happening. He forced her away from him.

'Gail, stop it.'

'You didn't enjoy that? Took you a while to decide that, didn't it?'

'Gail, leave me alone. Go back to that friend of yours. The pair of you can seduce someone else, I'm not interested.'

'You don't understand, Tom.'

'I don't understand? You're right there. I'm coming to understand that I don't understand this whole fucked-up family of yours.'

'I meant that you didn't understand me. But I can understand your confusion over this fucked up family, as you put it.

Please, Tom, let me take your arm and we'll walk for a while. Hope – Maria – has asked me to pass on a message.'

'Don't bother coming back, I suppose.'

Gail took her time to recover her breath.

'No, Tom,' she said. 'She's asked for your forgiveness.'

'Ha! Really, Gail, you can do better than that. Maria would no more ask for forgiveness of anybody than she would howl at the moon.'

'I'm serious, Tom. She knows she shouldn't have said what she did. Tom, it's that time of the month, she's trying to cope with the fucked-up family – Tom, if you wanted to you could make her go down on her knees and beg forgiveness.'

'Gail, you haven't been smoking any funny tobacco, have you? Maria go down on her knees? I'll believe in flying pigs before I see that.'

She gripped his arm.

'Tom, Tom, look at me. I mean it. She says she loves you.'

Tom looked at her. She looked down.

'She has a strange way of showing it,' he said.

'Tom.'

'Yes?'

'I know I shouldn't say this, but –'

'What?'

'I've done my duty. I've passed the message on. And I know that what I'm about to say is – wrong. I will hate myself for it ever after. But life is too short.'

'What the hell are you on about?'

'Tom, look at me. Tom, I've told you how Hope – Maria – feels. Actually, I've told you how she says she feels, personally I don't believe she does feel anything for you, but that's another story. But now I'm going to tell you how I feel. If you should ever ask me to marry you I would say yes. I would kiss your feet for doing so. I would be your good little wife and never criticise you. I would happily be your slave. I will cook for you, I will wash for you. Hell, I'll even iron for you.' She paused to take another breath. 'Right, I've passed Hope's – Maria's – message on, and I've passed my own message on. It's up to you to decide. I'm going back to prostrate myself before Claire in the vain hope that she'll forgive me for something that happened years ago.'

He watched as she ran back towards the house.

'Christ Jesus! I do not believe this bloody family.'

He stood there for some time, trying to make up his mind as to whether to return to Maria-Hope. After a few minutes he turned back and walked away.

'The rabbit-warren of Westminster,' he commented to himself, 'sounds rather appealing. At least I know their rules.'

He stopped and looked back again.

"Big backside"?

Not big, womanly. Gail was a real woman where Maria was – to be honest, skinny.

Tom Woods, he said to himself as he stomped forward to nowhere, get a grip on yourself.

If only he and Maria had come in their own cars, separately. He could easily find an excuse to leave. But Maria didn't have a car. She couldn't drive. She was reliant on him.

'Who the fuck is pulling whose strings here?' he asked a tree.

There was a noise in the undergrowth. A snort preceded the appearance of the pig. Tom laughed.

'You just want company, Mr Porker,' he said, scratching the pig's neck.

'Or is it Miss Porker?'

'Just who, as friend Robert the professor might put it, is yanking whose chain here? After all, you might enjoy my scratching your back, but your future lies in becoming sausages.'

'Though it has to be said,' he added after a pause to scratch and think, 'it's a far better future than the one I'm looking at. At least you're likely to be killed humanely.'

Chapter Thirty-one: The stories continue

After dinner that evening they gathered around the fireside in the lounge, George Brown and his wife in armchairs, the others scattered around on the sofas, chairs or on cushions on the carpet.

'You're looking much better, Valerie,' Winifred Browne noted.

'Thank you, Mrs Browne, I think it was one of those twenty-four hour bugs.'

'The sort that can be cured by a hair of the dog, no doubt,' murmured Gail. 'And so far I've seen four hairs disappear.'

'Why are you whispering again, Gail?' demanded George Browne. 'What is wrong with young people today? We were taught to speak correctly and clearly. Enunciation, that sort of thing.'

'Sorry, gramps. I'm feeling a little hoarse.'

'Horses? Too cold for riding. Let's get back to these stories, I enjoy them.'

'George, I think we've had enough of the stories. Claire, Sarah is such a sweet little baby. You wouldn't believe what trouble I had with mine – your mother, Adam and the others. Waking all hours, demanding to be fed.'

'I think she's getting to that stage, gran.'

'Nonsense!' interjected George Browne. 'Nothing like a good yarn of the evening before bed. Robert! You must have picked up some good stories in that place.'

'Well, dad, the rule is that you have to put the names of those who haven't told a story into a hat, and pick out who goes first.'

'What utter rubbish! I shall decide who goes first. Head of the household should choose.'

'I think the hat sounds like a good idea, my dear,' said his wife. 'Though we haven't a hat. What about that bowl? The children have eaten almost all the sweets. Claire, why don't you empty out the last few, and then write everyone's name on a piece of paper. Tom can choose, he'll be – what's the word? – an unbiased spectator. After all, he's already told his story.'

'Load of nonsense,' muttered George Browne, subsiding further into his chair, adopting the air of a man who knows he is right, but can't resist a snooze. 'Head of the household,' he murmured. 'Head of the household.'

'Here, Gail, hold Sarah for a moment,' Claire said, as the others wondered who the "children" were who had eaten all the sweets, since they suspected it had been themselves.

'Oh, yes, please. Hello, Sarah, Aunty Gail is going to sing for you while mummy's busy.'

'I think Patience should choose,' Tom said.

'No, Tom, that wouldn't be fair on Patience.'

'Here you go, Tom. Choose carefully. Choose wisely,' Gail said, leaning towards Tom, holding up the bowl.

'Oh, if I must. Swivel, wivel, tom-cat's piddle. There. The answer is – Gail.'

They looked at each other. Gail shook her head as if to say "No! Not me!" Tom smiled back and winked.

'Tom cat's what?' asked Peter.

'Shush, Peter. It's Gail's turn.'

George Browne startled into a half-waking.

'Gail? What about that friend of hers? Victoria? Valerie? That's the one. Good looking girl, she was. Filled a gym-slip nicely. Large for her age, I always thought. I wonder where she is now.'

'Yes, my dear. Gail? Do you mind?'

'Not at all, Gran. Just give me a few seconds.' Gail looked at Tom and raised a middle finger. "You bastard!" she seemed to be saying.

'Is grandad okay?' whispered Claire to her grandmother.

'He's fine, my dear. It's just age. He tends to fall asleep quite often, forgets things. I wouldn't worry about, just pretend it isn't happening, it embarrasses him.'

'Okay, gran.'

'Come on Gail,' called Robert, 'you've had plenty of time. Give us something like sex in the city.'

Chapter Thirty-Two: Gail's Story

'Well it isn't quite sex in the city, but here goes. Once upon a time, in a land far, far away – sorry, that's corny, I know, but anyway – in a land far, far away, lived a king and queen and their sons. There were one or two daughters, too, but they were more or less unimportant, since it was the sons who would grow up to be king – one of them, anyway. Sort of pre-Nineteen-Sixties stuff.'

'Ah, but Queen Elizabeth came to the throne in Fifty-two,' pointed out George Browne.

'Well, okay grandad, it's way back when.'

'Do let Gail tell her story without interruptions, George.'

'Where was I?'

'King, queen, randy sons and daughters,' suggested Valerie.

'The sons, that's it. There was great rivalry amongst them. Both the sons and daughters – who, again, weren't really that important, but they could have influence if they could get the ear of the king – held themselves high, while doing the dirtiest of low tricks to further their cause.

'The king was a proud man. A bit like King Lear. A man who had sired the most important sons in the land. They fought for his approval, his acknowledgement. But they also looked forward to his death, when one of them would become king. But he was a strong man, in health and opinions, and while he lived they pursued their pleasures and bided their time.

'They had families, at least the sons did, the daughters weren't married. Sons, daughters, nieces, nephews. They also had perversions – but since they were so important, these were regarded as mere hobbies. A peasant's daughter interfered with. Who cares? A peasant son, golden locks about his face –

it was to the peasant family's honour that a young prince should favour him so.'

'I don't like that, young Gail. Perversions. Not good for a Christmas story. Raping peasant girls, if you have to, but not perversions.'

'Okay, granddad, not perversions then. They just tended to rape the peasant girls on a regular basis. Your normal red-blooded young prince type people. So, where was I? Ah, yes. 'So one day a young man rides into town.'

'On his trusty steed? A white steed? With his standard erect?'

'No, it was a bloody red Harley Davidson, Valerie, do you mind?'

'Sorry. I'll just concentrate on my drink, shall I?'

'You do that.'

'I need a top up, anyway.'

'A young man no-one had ever seen before. He rides slowly, straight towards the castle, looking neither left or right. But even though he does not look at the field-hands or the villagers, he sees everything. He sees the man hanging from the tree, the man who had dared to try to stop one of the princes from interfering with his daughter. He sees the wife of the man, too afraid to cut his body down. He sees the cripple, the boy whose leg was broken as the princes raced their horses through the village streets. He sees the poor villagers, starved and in rags, forced to work the king's fields for what few scraps he gives them.

'The villagers are amazed by this stranger, for he rides straight into the castle, without even asking permission. The castle guards are also stunned, they don't know what to do, he just rides right past them as if they weren't there. They run after him. He gets off his horse and orders one to announce him to the king. Prince Herbert of the kingdom of Night. The guard rushes off to tell the king, for he knows of the kingdom of Night; the king of Night is the oldest sworn enemy of the king of Day – that's the first king, by the way.

'The king of Day comes down into the courtyard, with his sons at his side, all of them carrying swords, backed up by a platoon of guards. Fronted, more like it. The platoon are in front. Anyway, the king demands to know how the prince of Night can have the temerity to ride into his castle – does he not know that his father is the king's sworn enemy?

'Of course, replied the prince of Night. That is exactly why he has come. His father has recently died, and he – the prince – has come to see if the rift could be healed. It was his father's dying wish that this should be done. And to show that he is serious, and to seal the pact, the prince has come to request the hand of one of the daughters of the king of Day – that they should be wed on the same day that he is crowned king of Night.

'At first the king of Day thinks it a joke. He can take them all, he says in an aside to his sons, he doesn't have to marry them. Just so long as he doesn't send them back when he's finished with them. And then he realises that the prince is in earnest, and that this is a perfect opportunity to revenge himself on the old king of Night; even though the king might be dead, revenge on the king's son will be just as sweet.

'So he tells the prince of Night that it would be a great hardship to lose one of his lovely daughters, but that, if it would help heal the generations-long rift between them, he is prepared to do so. The prince of Night will choose his bride. However, the prince must first prove himself. There is a lioness in the mountains which preys on the villagers. It is not only the largest lioness ever seen, but also the cleverest – it has escaped every trap made for it, and avoided every hunting party sent after it. If the prince of Night can catch the lioness, he may choose whichever of the king's daughters he wishes.

'Now there is a lioness in the mountains, and it is a dangerous beast, but the real reason it has not been caught is that the king's sons are too afraid of it. The only thing they have ever done in the least way to capture it, if it can be called that, is to tie a villager to a stake and then watch from safety as the lioness killed and ate the villager.

'The following morning the prince of Night rides out to face the lioness, while the king and his sons make merry in the castle, making jokes about many scraps will be left of the prince when the lioness has finished with him. But the king's daughters wanted the prince of Night to succeed, since it will mean a way out of the castle for one of them. Secretly they agree that whoever is chosen will ask that her sisters accompany her as maids of honour, thus freeing them from the overbearing atmosphere of the castle of the king of the Day.

'That afternoon the prince of the Night returned with the mountain lioness in a cage. The king and his sons were incredulous, gobsmacked. The prince of the Night demanded that the king keep his promise. The king had no option but to call for his daughters, and the prince of the Night chose the youngest and fairest daughter. The king congratulated him on his choice, and then sent his daughters out, telling them to give the kitchen orders to prepare a banquet. He told the prince of Night that there was one thing he must request concerning his daughter. It was the custom that she should henceforth be fully veiled and her face not seen until she stood next to her husband to be at the wedding altar. The prince agreed to this, as they had much the same custom where he came from.

'The king's sons were much appalled at all of this. While their sisters meant nothing to them, they hated the idea of the prince of Night marrying one of their own. Better that they should be dead rather than be enjoyed by the prince of Night. When the prince of Night retired to his bedchamber they remonstrated with their father. He laughed and asked them if they thought he was too old and losing his marbles.

"'Send someone to fetch the village idiot," he said. "No, better, go yourselves. Hold him overnight. Tomorrow he will be dressed in the finest wedding garments, and a thick silk veil to cover his good looks. He will be told to hold his tongue if he wishes his mother to live. Until the prince of Night unveils his bride at the wedding altar, and then he may laugh with all the rest. In fact, sew up his lips so that he cannot speak."

'The brothers thought this an excellent plan. But, they said, would not their sisters object?

'No matter, said the king. Lock them up until the prince of Night has gone.

'And when the prince discovers the trick, they asked, will he not return with all his knights?

'Of course he will. But it will take him two weeks to return to his castle to discover the bride we have given him. Another week to gather his forces, and two more to return. In that time we will have gathered all our loyal knights and those who can be bought. The castle will be stocked for a siege. We can sit within the walls and laugh at him. He will starve outside, and then we will attack him.

'The next morning the prince of Night departed with what he thought was his bride. The king explained that the other princesses were in mourning at the loss of their sister – an ancient tradition, he explained. Once the prince was well away the king sent out soldiers to keep watch on the approaching roads so that he could hear of the arrival of the knights he had ordered to join them, and also of the return of the prince of Night when he discovered how he had been fooled. The king and his sons then set out to enjoy a hunt, since there would be little opportunity once the siege began.

'The princesses escaped from the room they had been locked in by convincing a maid that it was a game the princes were playing. Once free they carried out a plan they had agreed on during the night. They told their menservants that the cage holding the lioness was not strong enough, and that the animal should be released into the strongest room in the castle, the banqueting hall, and that the solid oak doors must be locked on it. The men-servants feared to do this, but the king and princes were out hunting, and the cage did appear to be falling apart as the angry beast tried to break free. So they dragged the cage to the doors of the banqueting hall, threw a haunch of venison inside, and slammed the doors on the lioness once the cage door was opened and it chased after the meat.

'Out in the fields the king and princes were startled by the appearance of one of the lookouts coming racing towards them. He shouted that the prince of Night was fifteen minutes away, accompanied by over a hundred knights, all wearing battle armour, accompanied by siege engines. The king and princes galloped back to the castle, calling for the drawbridge to be taken up and the castle prepared for siege. The eldest son pointed out that the castle was not yet siege-worthy, that they could not hope to hold out for long. The king ordered his soldiers to the battlements, and said, the soldiers must hold them as long as they can, we will take our position in the strongest room of the castle – make haste to the banqueting hall!

'And so they rushed to the doors of the banqueting hall, unbolted them, ran inside, and bolted the doors from the inside.

'There was silence for two full minutes, two long and lonely minutes, as the princesses stood outside listening, having also bolted the doors from the outside.

'And a roar! Another roar! A scream, a scrabbling, a scrabbling at the door, pleas to let them out, another scream, a whimper, a plea ... and then silence, silence apart from the low panting of the lioness.

'A soldier came down from the ramparts, fear in his eyes. My madam, he said to the eldest of the princesses, the prince of Night is demanding our surrender, and I can find the king nowhere.

'Fear not, replied the eldest princess, the king has made his final meal. Come, she said to the youngest and fairest princess, let us go to parley with your husband-to-be.

'And so they ascended to the ramparts and the eldest princess called down to the prince of the Night, Prince, your enemy is dead, and your wife awaits your presence. We give our word that we had no part in what happened. Give your word that no harm will come to us.

'Dead? asked the prince of Night. What do you mean, dead?

'Popped his clogs. Kicked the bucket. We are all free now. You are free to claim your wife.

'Claim my wife? asked the prince of the Night scornfully. You do not think I ever really intended to marry one of you?

'But you asked our father ...

'That? That was a trick you foolish woman. You don't think that I would ever want to marry one of you, do you? I knew he would set me a challenge. My spies told me the lioness would be the challenge most likely. The lioness I returned with was one my soldiers had captured two weeks ago and carefully starved. And I knew that when I had met his challenge he would still try to trick me. It gave me the excuse I needed to attack. My knights were awaiting me less than a day's ride away. When your father insisted on the veil I knew what he was going to do. Now, lower the drawbridge so that I may enter and see for my own eyes that my enemy is dead.

'The elder princesses whispered amongst themselves, the youngest in tears. Finally the oldest said to the prince of Night: You may enter with one page to assist you. After that, never darken our lands again.

'The prince laughed mockingly. I intend to take this country, woman. You cannot resist. My siege engines will conquer you within a fortnight. However, I will see my enemy's dead body before you place him upon his burning bier. Let myself and my page enter, and I will conquer the castle later.

'The drawbridge was lowered to admit the two. The sisters led them to the banqueting hall.

'Hold, cried the prince of Night, I sense a trick. Let me look before entering. He opened the viewing grill in the door and gasped.

'God's bodkins, they have truthfully been ripped apart, he said in a mixture of awe and approval. He unbolted the door and strode in. Behind him the princesses softly closed the door and silently bolted it.

'Let us see if he can tame the lioness in truth this time, said the eldest princess.

'There was silence from the hall. And then a scream. And then more screaming. And more. Until, at last, again, silence.

'Keep away from me, cried the page, drawing his dagger, backing away from the women. You have tricked the prince.

'See for yourself, page, your prince has tricked himself, said the eldest princess. Look through the grill.

'The page nervously approached the grill in the door, keeping one eye on the women, his dagger pointing all the time at them. When he looked into the banqueting hall he gasped and pulled back.

'Now, if you have feasted your eyes sufficiently, said the eldest sister, go tell your countrymen what happens to those who trifle with the princesses of the Day.

'The drawbridge was lowered to allow the page to flee and inform his fellow countrymen that their prince was dead, killed by the lioness he had pretended to have captured.

'And from that day the land of the Day was renamed the land of the Moon, and ruled over wisely by the princesses. And every week the day that the king had died was celebrated with an Anne Summers party.'

Chapter Thirty-three: Bedtime

'Anne Summers party?' asked George Browne, jerking awake from a half-sleep. 'Some ancient Greek tradition?'

'It's sorta like a Tupperware party, grandad.'

'Tupperware? Huh! Plastic rubbish. What you need is a good old-fashioned pantry like the one we have here. Pre-dates fridges, you know. Cheaper, too. In the old days ...'

'I think it's time for bed,' said Winifred Browne.

'I'm a bit tired myself,' decided George Browne, standing up. 'Don't stay up too late now, you youngsters.'

'Good night all, sleep well.'

'Night, gran, night grandad.'

'Good story, Gail,' said Robert, 'but I'm not sure about the end – what happened to the other knights – outside the castle? Why didn't they besiege the castle?'

'They were leaderless. They cursed the country where their prince had died. They waited only long enough to recover his body and then buggered off to bury him in his own land.'

'That makes sense,' nodded Robert. 'One charismatic leader dies, the entire group split up. Especially in feudal systems.'

'What happened to the evil friend? Why wasn't there one?'

'You can't be in every story, Val.'

'But I want to be! I want to be!'

'Have another drink, Val.'

'So what was the moral of the story?' asked Peter.

'Moral?' asked Gail. 'I don't know if it had one. Do stories always have to have a moral to them?'

'All stories have a moral,' Peter said.

'Don't mess with the princesses of the moon, 'cause they can be right bitches,' said Claire.

'Claire!'

Claire shrugged.

'I liked it. Especially the lioness. Male domination reaps death via the wild instrument they thought they had captured.'

'That's a bit deep for the night before Christmas Eve, isn't it?' asked Tom.

'Better take these glasses to the kitchen,' Maria-Hope said, standing up. Tom stood up next to her and squeezed her waist gently.

'And then to bed, my love,' he said.

'Jesus, stop bloody groping me, Tom,' she exclaimed. 'What is it with you?' He backed off in surprise.

'I'll give you a hand,' Gail said. 'And then it's bedtime for me too. Coming, Valerie?'

'Not yet. I think I'll have one for the road. Anyone want to join me?' There were no offers. She shrugged. 'I shall sit here in silent solitude then. Good night all.'

They said their goodnights, put the glasses in the kitchen and made their way upstairs.

Chapter Thirty-Four: Sleeping apart

'I think I'll take the room at the end of the corridor,' Tom said to Maria-Hope once they were in their bedroom.

'What?'

'Well, you're obviously pissed off with me for some reason. Ever since we got here you've been having a go at me. I can handle burnt bacon, but that shot about groping – sorry, but I'm not putting up with that.'

'Tom, stop being silly.'

'You can call it being silly if you like. It strikes me that you take after your grandfather, wanting to rule the roost. Well, I'm not having it. I don't expect you to treat me as the lord of the manor, but I'm damned if I'm going to be hen-pecked. It's your choice, Maria. You can come to my room if you want me back. I'm not going to force myself on you. And if you do, never, ever accuse me of groping you again because, if you do, it won't be a grope you'll get, it'll be a bloody good slap.'

She watched in fury as he walked out, closing the door behind him. Then she flung herself onto the bed and cried.

Valerie sat on the couch sipping her drink, watching the fire die down. She was still there an hour later when Robert came down in his pyjamas and dressing gown.

'Can't sleep?' she asked, her voice slightly slurred.

'Still working to a different time-zone I reckon,' he said, pouring himself a drink. 'Lucy and little Davie are fast, though, don't know how they manage it. I promised Patience I'd get a drink for her too.' He took a sip of whisky and began pouring another drink. 'Though, having said that, about three seconds after we fall asleep Lucy or little Davie will wake up and decide that it's time to play.'

'I've always thought it must be hard on a man with young kids. Most women I know lose interest in fucking after they've had kids.'

Robert smiled thinly at her.

'And that's why you decided to stay up. To see if anyone was interested in a quick bang.'

'And you came down to get in first.'

'No, thanks, Val. I'm strictly a one-woman man, and Patience is that woman.'

'Oh, come off it, Rob. I know what men are like.'

'I don't think you do,' he replied, picking up the two drinks and moving toward the door.

'Well, I think I might go watch television in the television room. There's a nice thick carpet in there. So if you happen to need to come down again for anything you'll know where I am.'

'Somewhere,' he murmured to himself as he left the room, 'fast asleep between here and the television room. Unless you manage to bounce off the walls into somewhere else. The cupboard under the stairs with the dodgy electricity board for preference.'

The door to Tom's new room opened and a white-clad figure flitted inside before closing it and locking it. The figure moved across the room and slipped into Tom's bed.

'Maria?' he asked.

'No, it's me,' said Gail, giggling.

'Jesus, Gail, what are you doing here?'

'Trying to get warm, that room is bloody freezing. Val promised to put the heaters on after supper, but I think she forgot. Or was too pissed to remember.'

'Bloody hell, Gail, Maria might turn up at any moment.'

'She won't. She's too proud. Me, on the other hand, well, I'd never accuse you of groping me. And I wouldn't burn your bacon either. Actually I can make a mean bacon butty. And my chicken in white wine sauce is highly recommended. Or, if you're more a red-meat man, I know a good recipe for marinating fillet steaks for a barbecue.'

'You were eavesdropping.'

'I was not eavesdropping. You were almost shouting.'

'Shouting? I don't shout.'

Gail giggled again.

'Keep it down, Tom, someone might hear you.'

She cuddled closer and put her head on his shoulder.

'Gail, what the hell are you doing? Someone could find us here.'

'Put your arm around me. That's better. Just for a few minutes until I stop freezing. You feel as if you could do with some warming up too.'

'Gail –'

'Stop worrying, Tom. I'm wearing my winter pyjamas, my towelling dressing gown and the thickest socks I have. By the feel of things you've also got your pyjamas on, plus socks and a jumper. I don't think we're quite dressed for a spot of unbridled lust. More's the pity.'

'It's cold in here. I switched the oil heaters on, but they're taking a while.'

'It's getting a little warmer.'

He sighed.

'Gail, what are you really doing here?'

'Looking for some warmth and some gossip. Hope doesn't seem to have changed. In fact she seems more frigid than ever.'

'She's just in a bad mood for some reason.'

'Oh, Tom, really, she's been treating you like shit. She doesn't deserve you.'

'Gail, leave it off. Maria's just in a strop, she isn't normally like this.'

'No? I've known her a lot longer than you, Tom. She's always been a moody little bitch. What you're getting from her now is what you're going to have to live with for the rest of your life if you're not careful.'

She yawned, put an arm across his chest and one leg across his thigh.

'Gail! Now stop that.'

'How long have you being going out with her?' she asked sleepily.

'About three months now.'

'I bet you and she haven't done it yet.'

'Gail! That's none of your business.'

'It might be.'

'How do you mean?'

'I don't know. Things happen. Just say, for instance, that you and her broke up, and you were looking for someone else, and we just happened to bump into each other in London, and decided to give it a try.'

Tom sighed.

'Won't Valerie wonder where you are?'

'Val hasn't gone to bed. She's probably passed out in the lounge. Too pissed to mount the stairs.' She giggled. 'Someone else will have to do the mounting instead.'

Tom closed his eyes. Then he opened them and looked up into the darkness. He wondered how on earth he was going to convince Gail to go back to her bedroom. He hadn't realised just how drunk she must be, though he hadn't noticed her putting the stuff away like Valerie had done.

'Gail,' he began. He tried to look down at her face. While he couldn't see clearly, he could feel one thing clearly. Gail was fast asleep.

'Oh for Christ's sake!' he muttered.

He looked at the ceiling and pulled her closer to make both of them both comfortable.

'Well,' he said to himself, 'I might as well get a decent night's kip myself. Unless this is all a dream and I'll wake up on my own. A dream of a nightmare.' He sighed and kissed the top of Gail's head. 'Sweet dreams, strange one.'

Down in the television room Valerie was stretched out on the couch, eyes closed. The light was off, but the television was on, flickering light across the room. Someone entered the room.

'Thought you'd be back,' she murmured without opening her eyes.

A hand touched her.

'That's nice,' she said.

Chapter Thirty-five: Saturday, Christmas Eve

'Morning, Hope,' Gail said as she walked into the kitchen.

'Morning,' replied Maria-Hope, sitting at the table, wearing her nightgown, eating muesli.

'Are you the only one up?'

'Guess so.'

'Tom still in bed?'

'Guess so.' Maria-Hope put her spoon down and wiped her mouth with the back of her hand. 'I had to kick him out of the bedroom last night. He'd had a few drinks too many and was getting frisky, so I sent him to sleep in the end bedroom.'

Gail sat down with a cup of coffee.

'I see.'

'The thing is – well, Tom and I aren't actually sleeping together. We haven't reached that stage. I just agreed that we would share a bedroom because I thought everyone else was coming, and all the rooms would be full.'

'I see.'

They sat in silence for a few moments.

'Gran said she wouldn't mind a hand putting up the decorations in the lounge,' Maria-Hope said, standing up. 'I'm going to have a bath and give a hand afterwards.'

Gail watched her leave. She tapped the side of her forehead with a finger. Then she frowned. From the back, even wearing a figure-less dressing gown, it could be seen that Maria-Hope had a slim body.

Then she finished her coffee and wandered through to the lounge. Tom was standing staring out of the window. She stopped and watched him. After a while she slipped in quietly until she was just behind him.

'Boo!' she said in a whisper. He jumped and turned around.

'Jesus, Gail! Don't do that.'

'Sorry. I couldn't resist it. You looked so thoughtful standing there. And much more relaxed, if you know what I mean.'

'Yes, well –'

'But you haven't had breakfast.'

'Well –'

'Not feeling guilty, are we? Little Tommy's feeling all guilty-wuilty.'

'Gail –'

'Or is it the thought of burnt bacon and eggs you can't face? Horrible, charred bacon and leathery eggs, covered in too much oil. Yuk!'

'You're not taking things very seriously, Gail. I'm trying to decide whether I should stay or not.'

'I love it when you say my name. You make me feel all girly inside.'

He shook his head and looked at her with a rueful smile.

'I think I know why your grandad called you his favourite grand-daughter. I'll bet you used to simper at him like that.'

'I'm quite happy to simper if you want, Tom. Simper, simper. How's that?'

He shook his head and rubbed his jaw.

'Gail –'

'Tell you what, let's pretend we're ten again. I'll go hide and you come looking for me. I'll be hiding in the cupboard under the stairs, by the way.'

Gail, don't be –' he started as she turned and skipped towards the door. She stopped.

'Damn,' she said, 'I can hear grandad's voice. Quick, let's pretend to be doing something with the decorations. Where are they?'

'There's a box there. Looks like it might be a Christmas tree. I'll get it out.'

They rushed to the box and began opening it. Tom paused and looked at her.

'Now why are we acting as if we'd done something wrong? Pretending to be busy in case your granddad walks in? We could just have been having a polite conversation about the weather. It's not as if we had anything to be guilty about.'

She leaned across and gave him a slow kiss on the lips.

'Now you do,' she said.

Chapter Thirty-six: The Ghost

'Hello? Mrs Caxton? George Browne here,' the voice boomed from the passage. 'That lazy laggard of yours, the boy supposed to deliver the newspapers. Well he hasn't.'

'Cancelled the order? Nonsense! Of course we haven't cancelled the order.'

'My wife? Ridiculous! Crossed wires. I've always taken the Times and I have no intention of stopping now. Re-instate the order. Immediately.'

'Yes, the grandchildren are all down for Christmas. And my son, Robert. He's a professor in America, you know. Very smart university. He's very highly regarded over there, one of the top men in his field. And the grandchildren are doing extremely well, too. Gail's ... Sorry? Oh, you have to serve a customer. Very well, don't forget about the Times.'

As he put the phone down his wife entered the hall carrying a box of decorations.

'That Mrs Caxton is losing it in her old age. Seems to think you cancelled the Times.'

'I did, George, just as you asked.'

'Don't be ridiculous, Winifred, why would I want the Times cancelled? I've had the Times every day for the past forty years at least. Apart from the strikes in the Eighties of course.'

'You said that you'd be quite happy to walk down to the news agent to pick up a copy if you felt that way.'

'In this weather? It's freezing out there. Speaking of which, where are the youngsters? Gone out, I suppose.'

'They're mostly in the lounge. They're going to help me put up the decorations.'

'Are they now? Well, that'll make a change, them helping out.'

'And you'll be doing the same?'

'Of course, naturally. After I've taken a stroll down to the news agent. I need the exercise, you know.'

She watched him walk upstairs to get his coat. Lucy appeared alongside.

'I saw a ghost last night,' she informed her grandmother.

'A ghost, Lucy?' her grandmother asked, putting her reading spectacles on and checking another list. 'I don't think we have ghosts here, my dear. Not real ones, anyway.'

'I did, nan! It was a real ghost. She was wearing white. All white. And she walked through the wall.'

Lucy paused to reconcile her imagination with what she had seen.

'She looked just like Aunty Gail. But older. Four hundred years older. You know, the way Aunty Gail would have looked in those days.'

'My goodness,' said her grandmother. 'In that case you must be right. Well, fancy that, a real ghost.'

Chapter Thirty-seven: Decking the Halls

'Ye gods!' exclaimed Gail as Tom pulled an artificial Christmas tree from the old cardboard box. 'I recognise that tree. They must have had it for over twenty years.'

'Twenty years?' asked Tom, tentatively pulling at a wire branch covered with shiny green tinsel. 'I've heard of quality lasting, but twenty years is a good run for a Christmas tree.'

'It's older than that, Tom,' Winifred Browne said as she came into the lounge. 'I think we bought it just before Gail was born.' She looked around. 'I thought all the others were in here with you.'

'Let me take that box, gran.'

'Thank you, Gail, it really isn't very heavy. Just all the old decorations. You probably remember some of them.'

Gail took the box, opened it and began taking decorations out.

'Oh, wow! I remember this angel. I thought it was a doll. I was about six, and I couldn't understand why such a pretty little doll had been stuck on top of the tree. I just wanted to take it down and play with it.'

'Yes, we have had that since, well, even longer than the tree.'

'Very green, Mrs Browne. The tree, I mean.'

'Yes, I suppose it is. But it is meant to be green, isn't it? Although I remember seeing some that were white. I thought it rather strange.'

'No, I meant as in – well, environmentally friendly. Not buying a new Christmas tree and throwing it away every year.'

'Oh, I see what you mean. Well, I can't say that we ever considered that aspect of it. Gail's grandfather thought a new tree every year a waste of money, and I was happy enough not to have to clean up underneath it every day of the season. I've never really understood the attraction of a real tree. They seem so messy.'

'I bought my parents a little tree a couple of years ago,' Tom said as he straightened out the branches on the tree. 'A little artificial one. It's about a foot high, sits on the mantelpiece quite comfortably, with miniature balls and lights what have you fixed in place. I think they were quite glad to have the excuse of not putting up a proper tree. They don't really have the room for it, anyway.'

'A miniature tree? What a good idea,' said Winifred Browne. 'The last few years we haven't really bothered with anything. But then we did celebrate Christmas more or less on our own. This is the first year that all the family will be together in ages, and it's so nice to have a tree for the children.'

'Which children would that be, Mrs Browne?'

'I'm sorry, Tom, I don't think I understand.'

'I was wondering whether you meant the toddlers or the children like Gail here.'

Gail stuck out her tongue at him. Her grandmother smiled.

'Yes, I see what you mean,' she said. 'You know, it's strange. I always think of my children as they were when they were babies. It seems easier to think of your grandchildren as grown up. I wonder why that is.'

'Here's a red one, Uncle Tom!' cried Lucy, holding out a bauble. The house was full of the sounds of people putting up decorations. Tom and Gail had found themselves in charge of the Christmas tree. Young Lucy had appointed herself their assistant, after making sure that the record player was switched on and playing Christmas carols. It was currently playing Joy To The World.

'That's a lovely red one, Lucy. Where do you think we should put it? Next to the blue one? Or down here, below the silver one?'

Lucy gave the tree the critical eye of a six-year-old.

'Next to the blue one, Uncle Tom,' she decided. There was a laugh from Robert on a pair of steps, hanging up a streamer.

'You won't have another moment's peace, Uncle Tom,' he said. 'I think Lucy has decided that she likes you.'

'I do like him,' said Lucy, delving back into the box Gail was holding on her lap.

'And I like Lucy,' said Tom. 'Best Christmas tree decorating assistant I ever had.'

Maria-Hope was sitting on the couch at the other end of the room, sorting streamers. She was watching and listening.

'I think I'll see if Peter needs any help,' she said, throwing down the streamers and stomping out. Robert raised his eyebrows to Tom. Tom shrugged.

'Lucy saw a ghost last night,' Robert said, returning his attention to a wandering streamer. 'Didn't you Lucy?'

Lucy gave her father the kind of look only a six-year-old can give an errant father.

'It was a real ghost,' she said to Tom, deciding that he was more likely to understand.

'Oh? What did it look like?'

'It was a lady. A lady all in white. I needed to go to the bathroom, and I peeked out the door. That's when I saw her. All dressed in white. She was beautiful.'

Tom cast a glance at Gail who had her head down, studying a tangle of tinsel, her hair covering her eyes.

'Did she waft?' Tom asked Lucy, his mouth twitching.

'Waft?'

'Er, waft? Float? Glide along?'

Lucy nodded certainty.

'Yes, that's it, she glided. Just like real ghosts do.'

'Did she have a – an unusually large derriere?'

'Derr – I don't understand.'

'A big backside,' said Robert.

'Oh, no, she was lovely!'

'Elegant?' asked Tom.

'Oh, yes! She was very elegant.'

'Well, then it couldn't have been who I was thinking of,' Tom said, cheeks sucked in.

'Dad's bloody fairy-tale books,' muttered Robert. 'The elegant Lady Pig-face-Smythe-Pom-Pom. Toodle Poo. Died of a broken heart fourteen hundred years ago.'

'She was not a pig-face!' exclaimed Lucy turning to her father. Gail took the chance to throw a ball of tinsel at Tom. 'Daddy, you didn't even see her!'

'What did she look like?' asked Tom. Lucy frowned and shrugged, concentrating on another bauble.

'I didn't see her face,' she admitted. 'But she had lovely hair. Almost like – well, the colour of leaves in the fall.'

Gail returned to her deep contemplation of the box of decorations.

'Now if you'd said blonde hair, we'd have known who the culprit was,' Robert said. 'On her way to the bathroom, not so much wafting as racing. Or stumbling, more like it.'

'Dad doesn't believe me,' Lucy explained to Tom. 'He's like that. He thinks I'm just a little girl.'

Tom held up a hand, a gesture to give him time to think how to explain to Lucy that she was a little girl. It failed. He held up his other hand, index finger pointing at the ceiling. Then his first hand came out, turning in circles as if attempting to draw in the great mysteries of life in a single movement.

'Tell you what,' said Robert stepping down from the ladder, 'it's a simple matter of deduction. Find out who popped out to the loo at the time, and that's your ghost.'

'She didn't go into the – loo,' cried Lucy. 'The bathroom. She walked through the wall before then. Before the end of the corridor. Anyway, real ghosts don't go to the bathroom. They don't need to.'

'Ghosts are always a problem, Lucy,' said Tom. 'they never appear in daylight, for a start. But, I tell you what, I'll keep an extra eye out tonight, how's that?'

Lucy considered this with the thoughtful eyes of a child who knows that the only thing more unreliable than ghosts is her father, but that an uncle-type man like Tom would most likely understand.

'You will?' she asked.

'Lucy, after what you've told us, I think we all will. But we'll have to wait until midnight.'

Lucy nodded and returned her attention to the tree.

'Oh, Lucy! Here's a problem,,' Gail said, holding out a white-and-pink length of tinsel. 'You know, Lucy, I remember this one from when I wasn't very much older than you. I always felt sorry for it. All the others are gold or silver, but there's just this one little thing of pink and white. Poor little thing.'

Lucy regarded the lonely tinsel.

'It needs a special place,' she said. Gail nodded.

'Where do you think?'

Lucy looked at the tree, and then back at the tinsel.

'Around the bottom,' she said, taking the tinsel, kneeling down, and weaving it slowly around the bottom of the tree, her tongue sticking out in concentration.

'That's exactly where I used to put it,' said Gail.

'And I used to demand that it went on top,' said a voice from the doorway. They turned to find Claire standing there with little Sarah in her arms. Gail pushed the box to one side, jumped up and went over to them.

'Oh, little Sarah!' she cooed. 'Oh, she's asleep. She likes her sleep. Oh! She's so cute!'

'She likes her feed,' said Claire, entering the lounge and sitting on the couch, Gail following. 'My boobs are getting bloody sore with feeding her.'

The two men suddenly found renewed interest in their decorations. Lucy looked at the mother and child with interest.

'That's what mummy says about David,' she revealed. 'But he's just a baby. Babies do that. They make mummy's boobs big.'

For some reason Tom and Robert found themselves giving in to the urge to mutter Christmas carols to themselves.

'We three Kings of Orient are,' sang Robert softly.

'One in a taxi, one in a car,' joined in Tom.

'One on a scooter, beeping his hooter!'

'Following yonder star.'

'Those aren't the right words!' Lucy exclaimed, folding her arms and stamping a foot.

'We three kings of Leicester Square,' sang Tom, 'selling ladies underwear, so fantastic, no elastic, only tuppence a pair.'

'Good King Wenceslas looked out,' replied Robert, 'in his pink pyjamas, sliding down the banisters, eating bad bananas! Hey!'

'Ah, so this is where the crèche is,' said Patience from the doorway, David in her arms. 'I see we have more children than I thought, though.' She looked at Claire on the couch, Gail leaning over her little niece. 'I wish I had a sister to look after my little ones.'

'Come sit with us,' said Claire. 'It's so much fun watching the hunter-gatherers putting up the Christmas decorations. Though I have to admit they could do with some singing lessons.'

'Thanks. I could do with a bit of rest. David and I seem to be on different time-lines at the moment. He's always awake when I'm ready for some sleep.'

'That's a bit of a nuisance,' said Robert.

'I am sorry, Bobby,' Patience said, sitting down next to Gail and Sarah. 'I shall try to do better next time.'

'I didn't mean it that way, sweetness. I was just thinking that a pre-lunch stroll down to the village and a small amount of quaffing of traditional festive beverages might be a good idea. But not if you don't feel up to it.'

Patience smiled.

'I could probably find the energy for that,' she said. 'But will they allow babies and children in?'

'I'm sure they will. Especially when we happen to let fall that we're all the way over from the You-nited States of America. And that we'll only be staying for just the one quaff. By the time the second comes – presuming the children have been quiet – they won't even think about it.'

'Sounds like a good idea to me,' said Tom. 'An excellent idea, in fact. Very traditional.

'I hope you two aren't planning on a drinking binge on Christmas Eve,' said Gail.

'A pint or two hardly qualifies as a drinking binge,' said Tom.

Gail looked from one to the other.

'Well, I wouldn't mind a stroll and a drink,' she said. 'But we'll have to be back in time to help gran with lunch.'

'Plenty of time,' said Robert. 'The decorations are more or less done. We'll just quickly get the lights on the tree while you ladies get your coats. Won't take long.'

'We should ask the others if they want to come along,' Patience suggested. There was a pause while everyone waited for someone else to say, "Well, I suppose we really should." Or preferably find a good reason not to.

'I'll go ask them,' Gail said eventually, reluctantly leaving for the kitchen.

Putting the lights up did not take long, even though delayed by Lucy's critical eye, first with folded arms, and then struggling against her mother's attempts to get her into her coat while keeping an eye on the hunter-gatherers. Eventually Robert stood back while Tom leaned over and switched the lights on.

'Here we go!' he cried.

There was a crinkling sound, little stars of light erupted, travelling along the chain, a fizzing sound, a "pop", and the lights went out with the smell of something burning.

Robert scratched his head.

'I thought those wires looked a bit old,' he mused.

Lucy frowned. Had it been her father who had switched the lights on she would undoubtedly have had something to say. Uncle Tom was above reproach.

'We can't have a Christmas tree without lights, Daddy.'

'Don't suppose there's a place in the village that sells Christmas tree lights,' Rob wondered.

'There's one place that will know,' said Tom. 'The pub. Best place to look for information.'

'Get your coat, Tom, we're on a mission.'

He paused.

'But before that, turn that switch off. It might look all shorted out, but those things are dangerous.'

'No other takers,' Gail said, appearing in the doorway muffled up for the winter air, carrying Tom's coat. There was almost a collective sigh of relief.

'Daddy, we are going to have lights on the Christmas tree, aren't we?' insisted Lucy, looking out from underneath the hood of her coat with the air of a six-year-old master-artist who fears her plans will be ruined by the Barbarians.

'Darling, we're sure going to try our darndest.'

The women looked at each other. It was almost as if they were saying "Once you get to the pub? Fat chance."

"Maybe we should light some candles instead?" suggested Claire.

'It's a possibility,' said Robert. 'An olde-worlde Christmas. Going back to the days of Dickens. Bob Cratchitt and Tiny Tim.'

'I don't want candles, I want lights,' decided Lucy. 'It isn't Christmas without lights.'

'Lucy,' said Tom, 'if we can find Christmas tree lights we will. That's a promise.'

Rob shook his head slowly and tapped the side of his forehead.

Chapter Thirty-eight: Boys will be boys

'I'm just going to pop into the post office over there quickly,' said Tom, nodding at a little shop as they arrived in the little village. Alongside the red and yellow "Post Office" sign there was faded dark-blue sign saying "General Stores". 'Just a pity I didn't bring my camera along. The government are hell bent on closing little post offices like that, there won't be any left in a few years. Shan't be a tick.'

'I'll come with you,' said Gail. 'I need some notepaper and envelopes.'

'Notepaper and envelopes,' noted Robert as the two disappeared into the post office. 'Fancy that, and in this digital day and electronic age. I thought I was the only one left who still wrote letters. And those mainly to mom.'

'You write to me every night you're away on a lecture circuit,' said Patience.

'I told you, that's because sitting in a hotel room doing nothing bores me to insanity.'

'Bobby is as close to being the perfect man as I've ever found,' Patience told Claire. 'But I don't think I'll ever be able to get him to admit that romantic side. Even though he's got his laptop and an Internet connection he still writes me little love poems.'

'Aren't we going into the pub?' asked Lucy.

When they entered the pub it was just after opening time and still quiet, with only one red-faced and blue-veined aficionado sitting on a stool at the bar, close to an open log fire. Robert established the order before the others went to a large table.

'Morning, sir,' said the landlord behind the bar as he began pulling a pint. 'A fine morning it is.'

'It is that,' said Robert. He gave the order.

'From the Manor, are you, sir?'

'Yes, we are. Say, do you know if there's anywhere around here we can buy Christmas tree lights? The set we put up this morning kind of fused on us.'

The landlord nodded.

'It's the electrics in that old place, sir,' he said. 'The electrician doing the work told me all about it. Old cabling. Dangerous stuff. Pre-war, some of it.'

'No, in this case it was the lights that were the problem. There isn't a little shop around here that might sell lights? You know, Christmas tree lights?'

The landlord pondered this, pouring a glass of wine.

'Think you'll have to go to town for that,' he decided finally.

'Used to be Mrs Stove's old place,' offered the man at the end of the bar. 'Sell everything, she did.' He nodded several slow times to emphasize his point.

Robert smiled the smile of someone who had encountered such conversation before. It would be the last sixty years of the village recounted in slow motion. And with a grinding and determined debate over whether Mrs Stove's little shop had closed in sixty-four or sixty-five. Had he been on his own, and had the time, he might have enjoyed it, but right then he wasn't in a mood to face it.

'Ah, well. Thanks anyway. Have to get to town after this drink, then.'

'Of course she closed her place – must be ten years ago.'

'Twelve, I think,' said the landlord. 'Ye-es, pretty sure it was twelve, Samuel.'

'That's very kind of you,' said Robert as Samuel geared himself up to answer this criticism. 'Must get these drinks over there, my patient gets diabetic fits if she doesn't have regular treatments of orange juice.'

He managed to retreat while the two men in front and behind the bar were trying to digest the statement. As he sat down Tom and Gail entered, Tom carrying a large plastic bag. Robert stood up again and came up to them.

'My round. What's your poison,' he asked.

'Gail?'

'A glass of white wine, I think. Dry, if they have it.'

'We serve dry white wine,' said the landlord, in a manner suggesting both pride in the accomplishment and regret that anyone should actually want the stuff.

'I'll have a – let's see, a pint of your best bitter,' Tom said.

The landlord nodded and began pouring.

'You're also from the house, then,' he said.

Tom looked at Robert. Robert raised his eyes and tapped his nose slightly, as if to say, yes, one of them.

'Got out of prison two days ago,' Tom said, taking his pint from the landlord and enjoying a deep sip. 'God, you don't know how good that tastes. Better join the women-folk, though.'

'Haven't had one of them in an age either,' he added, causing Robert to splutter.

The landlord and the drinker at the bar navigated towards each other as if molecules in some slow but magnetically unstoppable flow.

'Jail, eh?'

'I knew there was something going on there. Something funny about the old man. Calls himself Mr Browne. Well, we all know what that means.'

They both nodded, almost imperceptibly.

'Has an E on the end, he says. Browne. With an E. Bet he wasn't born with that. The E.'

'Had an American accent, the older one.'

'The Cosa Nostra. Family. Babies all over the place. Hot blooded people. Better not to show any interest. Especially towards the women. They'll be carrying knives.'

'The women?'

'Them too.'

They nodded again.

'Hear what that one said about women? Shameful.'

'It's lust. It's all that sun.'

'Won't get through Christmas without the police being called in. Someone's going to be shot.'

'People like that don't call the police. Never.'

'Cheers,' said Tom. The others raised their glasses, echoed the toast and drank. 'And guess what I have in this bag?'

'Something for the weekend?' asked Robert, causing several of the others to choke on their drinks.

'What's that mean, dad?' asked Lucy. 'For the weekend? You mean for this weekend? For Christmas?'

'Ask your mom, honey. She'll explain.'

'Mom?'

'I don't know, darling. Why don't you ask your dad. He seems to know.'

Lucy pouted. Robert laughed and ruffled her hair.

'Just teasing, darling. Go on, Tom, what is in the bag?'

Tom took out his purchase.

'Christmas lights!' exclaimed Lucy, clapping her hands and then demanding the box to inspect.

'It was a long shot,' said Tom, 'but these old village post offices often sell all types of things. It seemed worth a go. Either that or drive into town. And I didn't fancy doing that after a couple of pints. And they were pretty cheap. Well, as far as I know. I don't often buy Christmas lights, but these had a discount sticker on.'

'I think that was very clever,' said Gail. 'Don't you, Lucy?'

'Oh, yes, it was! I would never have thought of that.'

'Nor would the landlord and local bar-propper,' noted Robert. 'They assured us that the town was the only place to find such luxury items.'

'In America we drive everywhere, or catch taxis,' Lucy informed Tom. 'I like England. You can walk wherever you want to. That's too dangerous in America.'

Tom looked at Robert. Robert sighed.

'Well, honey,' he said, rubbing an eyelid, 'there are plenty of little towns in America where people do walk everywhere, just like here. Remember that place we went to last summer?'

'That was in Canada, daddy.'

Robert's mouth twitched.

'Honey, would you like to try some English pub food? They have something called pork scratchings. I tell you what, I'll give you the money and you go buy a packet. How's that?'

That was eminently okay, despite her mother's warning of not too much before lunch. Lucy went off to the bar with all the assuredness of a child in foreign territory who knows the natives are all friendly.

'Bribery and corruption, eh?' said Tom.

'When you have kids, Tom, you'll realise that a little bribery goes a long way.'

'So long as it doesn't get to the corruption stage,' said Patience. 'Fortunately Lucy isn't that way inclined. She knows when to stop.'

'Takes after her father,' said Rob. Patience gave him a look.

Tom leaned back, took a deep pull on his pint, and sighed in enjoyment and relaxation. He looked at the blazing fire.

'Like a different world, compared to London,' he said. 'Ye Olde Englande. You can almost imagine the nuns cycling to work in the morning mist, and the sound of leather upon willow as the local cricket team play in the hazy summer evening.'

Robert looked at him and smiled.

'Tom, you a journalist or a poet?' he asked. Tom shrugged. He stared out of the window.

'You ever live around here?' he asked.

'Not to my memory.'

'Only, your father – he makes things sound as if he grew up around here.'

'News to me too, Tom.'

'So why didn't the others want to come? To the pub.' Patience asked Gail. 'Apart from the obvious reason?'

'Grandad's asleep in the television room, as usual. I don't think it's gran's sort of thing, the pub. Rebeccah looked as if she would have liked to come, but Peter said no. I don't understand him. He used to have a religious streak in him, but the last time I saw him I thought he had got over it. Now it seems worse than ever. I was afraid he was going to give me a lecture about the evils of drink.'

'And Hope? Maria?'

'Oh, she was sitting in the kitchen looking at the knives as if thinking about how she could use them on Val. Who isn't out of bed yet, as per usual.'

'I was thinking about that,' said Claire. 'She was talking about pushing Valerie off a cliff yesterday. I said I'd help if she got Valerie and the cliff together, but otherwise she wasn't worth the effort.'

'Got that right in one,' commented Robert.

'But it isn't just that,' Claire continued. 'If you think about it, it would be easy enough to push Valerie over the banister at the top of the stairs when she comes up pissed at night. Or even just trip her and give a helpful nudge. Pure accident. Valerie ends up at the bottom of the stairs with a broken neck, a terrible accident, no-one to blame.'

The others looked at her.

'Oh, I'm not thinking about doing it. That's my point. We don't need to look for anything exotic, we don't need a cliff, there are any number of ways to get at her in the house, if Hope really wanted to. But she isn't doing that.'

'You mean she likes the idea, but hasn't got the guts to do it?' asked Robert.

'Something like that.'

'What about you? I thought you had a grudge against her? Val, I mean.'

Claire gave a thin smile.

'I'm too busy looking after little Sarah here,' she said. 'And mum and I seem to be getting on in a way we never did before. Oh, if I get the chance to put something nasty in Valerie's gin I'll take it, but I'm not going to go out of my way to do it.'

'And would she notice the difference?' asked Gail. 'Her life seems to consist of two stages, being drunk or having a hangover.'

'I dare you to suggest the idea of tripping up Valerie on the stairs to Hope,' said Robert, winking at Claire. 'Just to see if she actually does it.'

'Bobby! Stop that!'

'Ah, well,' Tom said as Lucy returned bearing both pork scratchings and the correct change, which, as she pointed out, she had counted in English money, 'Ours not to wonder why, ours but to accept the ambience and enjoy ourselves.'

'That man says that the big house was a place where mad people were kept,' Lucy said as she daintily lifted herself onto the seat next to her mother in a manner of a little girl who was old enough and big enough to do so herself. She handed the packet to her mother to be opened. 'He called it a lunar tick a-sigh-lem.'

'A lunatic asylum?' asked Tom. 'No change there, then.' Gail stuck an elbow in his side, and he choked on the sip of bitter he was taking.

'Was it, daddy?' asked Lucy. 'Was it a mad house? Full of murderers, and dangerous people? The man said they buried bodies in the garden. All over the garden. He said they made the beans grow better.'

'I doubt it, honey,' her father replied. 'That's the sort of thing locals tell to strangers to make them frightened. You know, ghosts and things.'

Lucy frowned at her father and pouted.

'I did see a ghost!' she insisted.

'Here you are, Lucy,' her mother said, handing her the opened bag of pork scratchings.

Lucy shared her pork scratchings with everyone. She decided, on reflection, that they were "interesting". It was while they were nodding their agreement that she returned her attention to the Christmas lights in front of her.

'They've even got a proper plug!' she announced.

The others took a closer look. It was an American plug.

'Not to worry, Tom,' chuckled Robert as Tom frowned at the lights in the manner of a deposed hero. 'We've brought a couple of converters with us.'

Tom and Robert led the expedition home, as befitted the hunter-gatherers of the tribe. Robert was carrying Lucy on his back.

'You're very quiet,' Patience mentioned to Gail as they and Claire followed the men, David asleep in Patience's arms. She didn't add "You've been deliberately not looking at Tom the whole time."

'Sorry. I didn't mean to be rude. I think I'm a little tired, really. I've been through a hectic time recently. Emotionally, that is. It makes you wish you'd taken up mountain climbing, or something. Much less stress. And you get to sleep better afterwards.'

Patience smiled.

'It does sound better. If I ever had the urge or energy to go mountain climbing.'

'Don't you ever want to scream and shout? Just let it all hang out?' asked Claire.

'On a regular basis. Unfortunately I wasn't brought up that way. Maybe, after the kids grow up, I'll have a quiet nervous breakdown somewhere peaceful.'

'I'd rather have a very loud one somewhere extremely noisy,' said Gail.

Patience smiled again.

'Send me a postcard,' she said. 'I'll join you. I've always wanted to try something like Thelma and Louise.'

'I finally remembered,' said Claire.

'What's that?'

'Jingle Bells,' she sang in a low voice, 'Batman smells, Robin flew away, Father Christmas lost his knickers, on the motorway.'

'I wasn't a good little girl every day at boarding school,' she added.

They returned to find the Christmas tree in the lounge

sparkling with little lights, Winifred Browne thoughtfully checking the mantelpiece for dust.

'Mom!' said Robert, 'those lights are dangerous. They short-circuited when we put them up. Tom here has bought a new set from the village shop. They need an adaptor plug, but we've got a couple.'

Mrs Browne blinked.

'Oh, there's nothing to worry about, Robert. It's my fault, I'm afraid. I'd forgotten about the old lights, I should have thrown them away. These are new ones I bought last week. They have a special connection of some sort which stops them burning the place down if something goes wrong. A trip switch, or something like that. Anyway, Peter and Hope put them up for me.'

There was a mocking smile on Robert's face as he turned to Tom.

'Well, Tom, my son, looks like you got rooked coming and going.'

Tom was trying to hide an irritated frown. He turned to Robert.

'There you go,' he said, handing the box over, 'compliments of the season. At least you won't need an adaptor to make them work in America. And they'll remind little Lucy every year of the wonderful time she's had here.'

'Oh, yes!' exclaimed Lucy. 'Thank you, Uncle Tom.'

'Cheap shot,' murmured Robert, 'using a man's kids against him.'

'Ah, but Rob, I'm an utterly ruthless person when you get to know me.'

Robert nodded.

'Now that I can believe. But I must warn you, I've been known to be ruthless myself.'

'What are you talking about, daddy?' asked Lucy.

'Oh, just saying that it's time I helped your gran in the kitchen with lunch, honey.'

'That's alright, Robert,' said his mother. 'Peter and Hope have already helped me with everything. It just needs cooking now. The meat's already on, and the potatoes are roasting. Lunch should be ready in about an hour or so.'

Tom tutted.

'You've let the side down, Rob. Promising to help your mother with lunch and then disappearing down the pub. You're a feminist example of the typical male.'

Robert smiled thinly and broadly at him.

'I'll make up for it, shall I? I'll do the dishes.'

'Oh, don't worry about that, Robert,' said his mother, 'the dishwasher can cope. I don't know what I would do without it. Now, come along, I think it's time for a pre-lunch drink. In the kitchen, I think. I must say that I far prefer the kitchen to the lounge during the day.'

Tom and Robert jostled each other as they tried to leave through the doorway at the same time, following the women.

'I used to play American football,' said Robert. 'Did I ever mention that?'

'I'm surprised they allowed you to, at your age,' said Tom. 'Which little-junior league was it?'

'Tom!' called Gail. They looked forward to find both Patience and Gail looking back at them. Patience had the inscrutable look of a wife who knows her husband extremely well, and just hoped he might grow up at some stage. Gail was frowning.

'Nothing,' Gail said, and turned back towards the kitchen, walking fast.

'Wimmen!' muttered Robert.

'Speak for yourself.'

'No, Tom, I think I'm speaking for both of us. Though you might not realise that yet.'

'I don't have a wife and two kids.'

'Send me an e-mail when you do. I'll fly anywhere in the world to see that.'

'You just want the last word before we get to the kitchen.'

'So do you. And you ain't got it.'

'Yes, I have.'

'No, you haven't.'

'So, what does everyone want to drink?' asked Winifred Browne as they entered the kitchen. Peter and Maria-Hope did not look up at their entrance. Rebeccah did. She smiled.

'You two remind me of a picture from one of those books by Richmal Crompton,' she said. 'The William books. All you need are shorts and caps. With a touch of mud.'

Tom and Robert looked at each other. Then back at Rebeccah.

'We can do mud,' said Robert. 'Can't we, Tom?'

'I was trained in mud, Rob. Trained in it.'

'Brought up in it, more like,' said Maria-Hope before flouncing out of the kitchen.

'If you ever marry one of my nieces,' Robert said in a stage whisper to Tom, 'for Christ's sake make sure it isn't that one.'

Tom's mouth twitched. He turned to Robert with a retort on his lips. As he did so he realised that all the women had heard Robert's comment and were waiting to hear his reply. He was particularly aware of Gail's look.

His eyes lighted on Lucy's. She seemed fascinated.

'Lucy,' he said, 'your father is a very, very naughty man, and very, very naughty men come to a sticky end.'

Robert laughed.

'Only in the movies, Tom, only in the movies,' he said.

Chapter Thirty-nine: Grandad's acting strange

'For what we are about to receive, may we be truly thankful.'

There was a chorus of amens from the group who were learning the rules. Valerie took a draught of wine and shivered.

'Still suffering, Valerie?' asked George Browne. 'We'll have to get the doctor in soon.'

'It's okay, Mr Browne. I'm fine. Just one of those things.'

'Ah, yes, well, you're looking a bit peaky. Get some grub into you, that'll sort it out.'

There had been a subtle re-alignment of seating positions. Maria-Hope was now next to Peter, who had decided to join the table, leaving Rebeccah in the kitchen with little George. Robert had been ordered by Patience to attend in the dining room while she looked after the children in the kitchen with Claire. Tom and Gail found themselves sitting alongside each other.

'I know you youngsters think I'm old-fashioned and foolish,' George Browne said, spooning potatoes onto his plate. 'But there's one thing it always comes down to: food. The trouble with the modern generation – at least that's what I believe they're called these days – is that they have it too easy. Never felt hungry in their life. That's what separates the men from the boys, hunger. Now your grandmother and I – well, there was a time when the most impressive gift I could give to her was a banana.'

He looked at Tom.

'Not your grandmother, of course, Phillip.'

'Tom,' said Gail.

'Eh?'

'His name's Tom. You called him Phillip.'

'Nonsense, my dear, you weren't listening properly. Anyway, the point stands. You, my boy, have never looked at young Gail here and thought that a banana would show that you love her. Not like your grandmother and myself. In fact, it wasn't a banana, it was an orange. Remember that, eh, Winifred, that orange?' He chuckled. 'Almost got thrown into the glass house for that orange.'

A few glances were exchanged. Maria-Hope kept her reddening face concentrated on her plate.

'Things were different in those days,' said Winifred Browne. 'I don't expect the youngsters to understand, of course. During the war there were so many shortages. I suppose, looking back, you could say things were hard. But we coped, we coped. Didn't we, George?'

George Browne nodded enthusiastically. Sweat was beginning to form on his brow. His eyes were wide as he attacked his food.

'Needs a little more salt,' he said, spraying salt across his food.

'Not too much, George. But – George, not too much, now – the story of the orange is quite interesting. Well, not to everyone, of course, but, well – different times, different times.'

'Mom,' whispered Robert, nodding towards his father, 'is everything okay?'

Winifred Browne managed to communicate the positive in a negative shrug of her shoulders and a nod of her head.

'Everything was rationed in those days,' she said. 'You brought me an orange, didn't you, George? Oranges were almost like gold, weren't they, George?'

'About time you married her, Philip,' said George Browne, turning to Tom. 'Do the decent thing. I don't care what they say these days, there's still the decent thing. Gail's always been a good girl. She'll make you a good wife. Where's the Cranberry sauce?'

He was breathing hard, looking around him blindly. The others, apart from Winifred Browne, looked on with open mouths. She carefully laid down her knife and fork.

'That was a wonderful lunch,' she said. 'But I do feel that I could do with a lie-down. Will you help me upstairs, George?'

'Of course, my dear, of course,' George Browne said as Tom and Gail stood up to help him. Each took an arm.

'Tom is not going out with Gail!' exclaimed Peter. 'He is going out with Maria.'

'Maria?' coughed George Browne as Tom and Gail guided him towards the door. 'Don't tell me we've got a Spaniard in the house now. Might as well call it the United Nations and invite the Chinese over. Bloody Russians, too.' He laughed, which turned into a choke. 'Russians think they're going to invade Europe? We'll soon show them what! They'll find out what an Englishman is made of. The Germans – the Germans –'

'Yes, George, now, please, help me upstairs.'

'Maria! Hope, as you insist on calling her,' said Peter, standing up, ignoring Winifred Browne's waving hand.

George Browne paused and wheezed.

'Hope? And Phillip? Don't be ridiculous. Why would he want to go out with her? Why would anyone want to go out with her? Silly girl takes after her brother. That priest, you know.'

He gasped again.

'Died too young. Phillip. Died –'

'George, please, my ankles. You know what the doctor said about resting my arthritis.'

'Yes, my dear. Sorry, Win. Where are we? Philip. He died,

didn't he?'

'He did, George. Now I need a lie-down.'

'Of course, my dear. Come. Let me take your hand. You really must learn to take it easy, my darling. We aren't – we aren't as young as we used to be. Still – knew more – knew more about – about bloody life than – than they do. Hopeless! Really!'

Those remaining looked at each other in silence as George Browne was escorted upstairs, apart from Robert who was looking at the table with a darkening realisation.

'I'm sorry about that,' Winifred Browne said, re-entering the dining room with Tom and Gail. 'Your grandfather is very tired. He's had a turn. Nothing to worry about, it happens every few months. He's gone to sleep now. I'm sure he'll be fine in the evening. Please, carry on with lunch.'

Peter looked at the knife and fork on his plate as if wishing he were holding them so that he could throw them down in a clatter.

Tom looked at Robert. Robert's mouth was open, looking at his mother as if he wanted to ask a question, but couldn't get the words right.

'Gran,' said Gail, 'if there's anything we can do ...'

'Just carry on as usual, my dear. Just carry on as usual. He won't remember it. He'll be fine after a little lie down.'

Robert slowly put his knife and fork down.

'Mom, I know I've been away a long time ... But you never mentioned ... '

'I know, dear, I know. It's not the sort of thing you do mention.'

'Gran, shouldn't we call a doctor?'

'I've already done that, Gail. He'll be here in a short while.

But I'm sure your grandfather will be fine, he's had that kind of attack before a few times, he's always much better after some rest. It's just the excitement that gets to him.'

'Mom, it looks pretty serious.'

'Robert, when you've lived as long as us you realise that everything is serious. And the best thing we can all do is to carry on and pretend that things are normal. Or not pretend, no, that isn't the right word. Everything is normal. Now let's not let the food go cold. There are people starving in India, you know.'

'Gran,' asked Gail after a pause, 'who was Phillip?'

'Phillip would have been your oldest uncle, Gail, had he lived. He died at two months old. Could someone pass me the butter? I can't seem to see it.'

Chapter Forty: Gail and Tom go for a stroll

It was mid-afternoon with an hour or so of sunlight left. The decorations had been completed, muttered discussion of George Browne's "turn" had been approached and abandoned. A group of them sat or stood in the lounge.

'Anyone fancy a walk?' asked Tom. Maria-Hope glared at him.

'Why don't you go for a walk on your own,' she suggested. 'Maybe you'll meet some slut also on her own just begging for it?'

'Maria, what the hell are you on about?'

'Oh, for fuck's sake. Fuck off, Tom. Go for your little walk.'

'I'll come,' Gail said, springing from her stool. 'Give me thirty seconds to get my coat.'

'Make sure you don't let him get too close, Gail,' Maria-Hope said. 'You don't want to know where he's been. I do.'

Tom shook his head, then tapped a finger against his forehead. He walked out of the lounge.

'What's wrong?' Claire asked, looking at Maria-Hope.

'I'm going to get that bitch.'

'Valerie?'

'Who else? She's been after Tom ever since we arrived. Not that he's put her off, that sort never do. But I'm not going to stand for it.'

Claire looked down at Sarah. For once the child was awake. She laughed back at her mother.

'Funny, really,' Claire said. 'I just can't be bothered with Valerie anymore. She isn't worth the effort.'

Maria-Hope stared at her.

'You can't mean that. After all that she's done? I mean, look at her, even now. She deserves all that she's going to get.'

'Oh, I don't mean that, if the chance came up to shove her over a cliff, I wouldn't take it. I just can't be bothered spending energy on arranging for her and a cliff to meet each other. Life moves on.'

Maria-Hope hugged her knees and looked into the fire.

'Don't worry, I'll arrange the cliff.'

Claire looked at her cousin. She remembered the conversation in the pub. She wondered if she should mention the bannister at the top of the stairs.

Tom watched as Gail skipped ahead, pretending to hide behind a tree.

'Don't you wish it was summer?' she asked. 'Just think, warm summer evenings, I'd be wearing a skimpy dress, you'd have shorts and a loose shirt, and who knows what might happen.'

'Gail, about last night –'

'You know, I bet that you're a good lover. I can tell,' she said, leaving the protection of the tree, rejoining him and taking his hand. 'Not that I've had all that much experience,' she added hastily. 'Call it a woman's intuition.'

'Gail –'

'No, please don't,' she begged, looking at him with pleading eyes. 'I know you'll go back to sad old Hope. Let's just pretend for a moment, can we? Claire has almost forgiven me. It's Valerie she's after. My little sister and I are almost pals, the way it should be. The way it should always have been. But it wasn't. But now that's over, it's in the past. I have a gorgeous little niece. She is so cute! And I have a handsome lover. Well, let's pretend I do. That's you, by the way. Tom! Can't we just pretend for a short time that it's real? I know that after Christmas you and Hope will go away together and

I'll be on my own again, but please, darling, just for a short while? A Christmas fairy tale. Go on, call me darling. Pretend you mean it. After all, this is the season for fairy tales. Please, please call me darling?'

He stopped and looked into her eyes. Then he tried to look away.

'I don't understand you,' he said. 'On the one hand you're doing everything you can to placate Claire, yet you're quite happy to go behind Maria's back and – well, take me away from her.'

'I don't understand you, darling,' she corrected.

Tom looked at her again. She was nervously fiddling with the buttons on his coat, looking down at them one moment, and then up at him the next. He noticed that she'd spent the seconds in getting her coat also applying some mascara.

'I don't understand you, darling,' he conceded. She smiled widely and threw her arms around him.

'Put your hands on my backside,' she said. 'Good, now squeeze darling. Mmm, that feels good. Do you like it?'

'It's, ah, interesting.'

She pulled back from him, looking into his eyes and laughing.

'Come, Tom my love, let's walk in case anyone sees us.'

She took his unresisting hand in hers and skipped alongside him as they continued their walk.

'I feel almost like a little girl again. No worries, no job to worry about, back at nan's place, just having fun.'

Tom grimaced.

'I suppose we all want that from time to time,' he said. 'But we have to face up to facts.'

'Doan wanna!' exclaimed Gail. 'Lalalalala! Not Listening!'

Tom turned amazed eyes on her. She looked down and then back up again.

'Tom, you want to know why I'm desperate to get into get into Claire's good books while quite happy to try to steal you from Hope? It's simple, really. I don't owe Hope anything. She was in love with this boy called Duncan once, and Val deliberately made a move on him. She wasn't really interested in him, he was a bit of a goofball. He and Hope probably would have made a good couple, which is probably what pissed Val off. But Claire – she's my younger sister. I should have protected her. Instead I let Val lead me on in teasing her. Let's be honest. Bullying is the word. Grandad enjoys bullying people, perhaps I got it from him. But I really was more like my grandmother. That's the worst of your teenage years, you spend the whole time trying to fit into a picture of what your friends think you ought to be. And the silly thing is, they're playing the same game. None of you really knows what you really want to be. You just need one person who knows where they're going and the others will follow like good little soldiers. Bloody stupid little robots. Vicious little robots. Tom, people think men can be cruel. Women can be far worse, far more subtle.'

'I still don't understand. Why you feel such a difference about Maria – Hope – and Claire.'

Gail shrugged.

'Maybe because I think Hope's a lost cause and Claire is worth saving,' she said. 'Well, saving isn't the right word, but you know what I mean.'

She looked up at him.

'Darling, kiss me, please,' she asked.

'What?'

'Don't spoil my fairy tale. Please, darling?'

He kissed her, reluctantly at first.

'Mmm, that was nice,' she said, leaning against him. 'Squeeze me, please, darling.' He did and she giggled. 'I don't suppose, should we find a secluded nook, that there's any chance for nookie?'

'Is that all you think of?'

'You seemed to be thinking about it in your sleep this morning, when I left you. I almost stayed to see what would happen.'

'Why didn't you?'

She folded her arms and walked on.

'I don't know. I suppose I thought you might hate me if I took advantage of you.'

Tom's eyebrows rose.

'Well, that's an interesting concept. A woman taking advantage of a man. It's normally the other way around.'

'Women take advantage of men all the time. Not all women, and many men do take advantage of women, of course, but blaming it all on men alone – well, that's another way of taking advantage, if you see what I mean.'

Tom pulled his ear and looked at her.

'You have to be the strangest woman I have ever met,' he said.

'Don't be silly, Tom, you're going out with Hopeless. She's by far the strangest woman around here. If she's actually a woman. I wonder sometimes.'

Tom scowled and looked at the ground.

'Somehow I wonder if I am still going out with Hope. Her attitude seems to suggest not.'

'Oh, come on, Tom. I'm sure she's done this to you before. Gone all moody and treated you like shit. Then suddenly it's all love and light again as if nothing had happened.'

'Well, yes, I've just presumed that it was – that time of the month. But it's never been this bad before.'

'Let's go have a look at that spinney. Maybe we could get some firewood together and build a little fire. It's a bit chilly in the open.'

Tom followed her into the wood. They came to a small area hemmed in by trees and brambles.

'Perfect,' said Gail. She opened her handbag and took out a large folded square of silvery material. 'Apparently this is the stuff used by NASA. Guaranteed to keep you warm in sub-zero temperatures.'

'You had this all planned, didn't you?' he said as she sat down. She held a hand up to him. He took it, apparently unwillingly. She pulled him down and kissed him on the lips.

'No, Tom, my darling. But I thought it better to be prepared. Which I shan't be when you have your wicked way with me.'

'I'm sorry, I don't understand.'

'I'm not on the pill, Tom. Not at the moment. So if any of your sperm want to say hello to any of my eggs there's not much I can do about it.'

'Gail!'

'Oh, Tom, who cares? You're going to leave me and go back to bloody Hopeless anyway. If I get pregnant Claire and I can spend our time looking after our babies and exchanging complaints about the men who left us.'

'Gail, now stop it, you're being silly.'

She pulled her arms away and turned her back to him. He realised that she was crying.

'Oh, Christ,' he muttered. 'Look, Gail, be sensible.'

'Why? Here I am, throwing myself at you, and you don't even want to know. Do you know how that makes me feel?'

'Well –'

'Like a cheap little slut, that's how.'

'But, Gail –'

'And I'm not a cheap little slut. I've never thrown myself at a man before. Ever!'

'Look, Gail –'

'Oh, just go away, will you? Leave me here, I'll get over it.'

Tom put a hand over his face, rubbed his eyes and squeezed his temples. He paused, looked at his hand. Then he chuckled.

'You find it amusing, do you? Go on, have a good laugh. Yes, have a good laugh. You can e-mail your friends about me when you get back. Silly bitch was so desperate she – she –'

'I've just realised. The first day, when Maria was explaining our living arrangements to me, I did exactly the same thing I've just done. Tried to stop myself getting a headache.'

She turned back to him, concerned.

'Are you okay? I've got some aspirin with me.'

'No, no, I'm fine. I just don't seem to be cut out for handling women. Maybe I should become a monk. Or just settle for bachelor status.'

She held out a hand to his cheek.

'Oh, Tom, you aren't trying to tell me something, are you?'

'Such as?'

'Well, you aren't a closet gay, are you?'

He laughed.

'No, I'm pretty sure I'm not that. I've never had a problem relationship before I met Maria. And now you.'

She put a finger under his chin and gently turned his face towards hers.

'But you never got married,' she said. 'Even with these problem-less relationships. Why not?'

He shrugged.

'It was the job. I'd have to go off on an assignment, I'd come back, and the girl had got bored and found someone else.'

'Sounds like a pretty feeble excuse. I'd have waited for you.'

'Would you?'

She leaned forward, put her hand behind his neck and pulled him close, kissing him gently.

'I will now. I'll wait six months for you. If you're still going out with Hopeless after that I'll give up on you. How's that for a promise?'

'It might not take six months for Hope and me to break up, the way things are going.'

'How about six minutes?'

'Perhaps decorum might require us not to be so close,' suggested Tom as they approached the house, Gail holding his arm and leaning on him.

'Decorum be fucked, my sweet,' she said and giggled. 'Whoops, there's a pun in there somewhere. Tell you what, I've sprained my ankle and you're helping me walk.'

'Oh, good, the old sprained ankle ruse, the one that went out in concert hall about two hundred years ago.'

'Jesus, Tom, lighten up. If I'd known you were going to be such hard work –'

'Yes?'

'Nothing, my darling. But I'm telling you, if I ever really, definitely, absolutely get you into my hands you will pay for that.'

'Which bit?'

'Oh, never mind. What's this car doing coming up the drive?'

'Police. Now you can clutch at me in fear. What? A police car? Why, it would scare any normal person. Perfectly normal reaction.'

'Stop being silly, Tom,' she said, clutching his arm. 'Why are the police here? What do they want?'

Two uniformed officers got out of the police car.

'Good evening. Is Miss Claire Green here?'

'Yes. Is there a problem, officer?' asked Tom.

'I'm afraid we have some bad news for her. Could we come in?'

'Yes, yes, of course. Come through to the lounge. I think it's empty. Everyone's either having a siesta or has gone out for a walk or something. Gail, any idea where Claire is?'

'No more than you might do, darling. Upstairs, I would think.'

'Be a love and ask her to come down.'

'Any specific reason or shall I just say that the rozzers are looking for her?'

'Gail! Just tell her to come downstairs. Sorry, officers, this way. Gail – Miss Green – the other Miss Green – can be quite flippant at times.'

Chapter Forty-one: A visit from the police

'Miss Claire Green? I'm afraid we're here to tell you that your mother has been taken to hospital. She was involved in a road accident. Drink driving, I'm afraid. Apparently a combination of that and failed brakes.'

'Mum? How – how is she? What happened?'

'We don't really know, Miss Green. We were called on the radio and asked to let you know.'

Claire stood and looked at the officer, her mouth opening and closing without saying anything. She held little Sarah tightly, causing the baby to wake and cry.

'Come on, Claire,' Tom said, 'I'll drive you there.'

'I'm coming with,' Gail put in. 'She's my mother too.'

'I just need to grab a clean pair of trousers. These got snagged on a bush.'

'Me too.'

The police officer driving exhaled a sigh of relief as they left.

'That wasn't as bad as I thought it would be,' he said. 'I've seen some bad ones. Relatives go berserk, screaming and shouting and such. You wouldn't believe what I've seen. Even blame you for it.'

'Right bummer on Christmas Eve,' agreed the other. 'Must say, I felt sorry for her. She looked all of about fifteen, and with a little baby in her arms.'

'Yeah, that was a bit strange.'

'Strange?'

'Well, you know the estate. Single mums all over the place. Not a penny between them. Chavs, one and all. Scum, really, when you come to think about it. But that lot – well, they must be upper class, living in a place like that. She looked like a single mum, but she didn't sound like one.'

'Didn't sound upper class neither.'

'No, you're right there. Sounded quite normal. Strange, that.'

'Her sister looked well fit, though. I could swear that she and that bloke with her – well, you know, there was something about them I couldn't place. I reckon they'd just being doing it, know what I mean?'

'Listen, son,' said the first man to someone at least two years his junior, 'in this job you don't think those thoughts. Not when the well-fit bird is obviously a member of the aristocracy or something. Next thing you know her uncle is a member of the House of Lords or something, and your career is on the line. Trust me, just think, we've got one hour of shift to finish, and then it's off down the pub and a couple of pints to get into the mood for Christmas.'

'Okay for you. I'm shifted for tomorrow afternoon.'

'Yeah, well. You're single. It happens. And you've got the New Year off. More likely to score on the New Year, aren't you?'

The other young officer contemplated this with pessimism. Somehow the reply to the question "What do you do then, sexy?", in the middle of an illegal rave, being "I'm a police officer" had yet to go down well. The first and last time he'd done it had cleared the barn.

'Trouble is,' he said, 'most of the birds you meet at New Year are like, well, sixteen, or even younger. I mean, they look okay, well, some of 'em, but they ain't got any brains. And most of 'em are pissed. You can't have a proper conversation with them.'

His partner glanced at him and shook his head.

Gail and Claire sat in the back as Tom drove, Claire holding Sarah, once again asleep in her mother's arms, Gail with an arm around her sister. No-one spoke until they came to the hospital.

'I'll drop you off here and find somewhere to park,' Tom said as they reached the entrance to the Accident and Emergency doors.

'Hold Sarah for me, just for a few minutes,' Claire said, putting the baby into Tom's arms.

'But –' he started. The others ran into the hospital.

'Can't park here, mate,' a porter said, appearing at the side of the car. Tom looked from him to Sarah to the steering wheel in front of him.

'I'm not sure I know how to drive with a baby in my arms,' he said. The porter chuckled.

'Haven't heard that one before. But you'd better get moving before the security boys get here. It's a hundred pound fine, and that's before they start clamping you. And they don't seem to know it's Christmas.'

Tom looked down at Sarah and sighed.

'Women!' he muttered. Sarah giggled back as Tom began to drive slowly towards the car park in first gear, the baby in his left arm. 'Just one thing, little Sarah, please, please, please do not suddenly decide that you need your nappy changing.'

Inside Accident and Emergency Claire and Gail had reached reception.

'Nurse, I'm Claire Green. My mother's been brought here. Where is she? How is she?'

The nurse paused in re-arranging some folders.

'Ah, let me page Doctor Hillman.'

'But how is she?'

'You haven't been told?'

'No, of course we haven't. How is she?'

'Well, as the doctors no doubt told you, when someone is that frail they can go any time.'

'Frail?'

'Claire? Gail? What are you doing here?' asked a voice behind them.

'Mum!' exclaimed Gail and Claire together as they turned around. Jane Green stood there, one arm in a sling, leaning on a crutch.

'Nothing's happened to Sarah, has it?' asked their mother. 'What's wrong? What's happened? Where is Sarah?'

'No, Sarah's fine,' said Claire, looking towards the entrance door. 'Tom's got her. He should be here any second.'

'The police told us that you'd been injured in a traffic accident,' Gail said. 'What happened, mum?'

'Well, thank god for that. Yes, it was an accident, but it was only a few scratches. A stupid idiot in a white van came flying through a red light. Caught my car at the front and sent it spinning, and carried on into one of the traffic lights. Then he staggered out of his van as if he'd spent the entire day in the pub. Smelt like it, too. When I got here I asked if someone could get a message to you to let you know I'd be a little late. I didn't realise they'd send the police around.'

'Um, excuse me, Miss Green?' said the nurse.

'Yes?' said Claire and Gail.

'I think there might have been a little confusion. Your mother isn't Mrs Emily Greene? With an E at the end?'

'No, this is our mother, Mrs Jane Green. Without an E at the end.'

'Ah, sorry about that. Mrs Greene – the one with the extra E – was admitted this afternoon after slipping on an icy pavement. She didn't make it.'

The girls and their mother looked at each other. Then Jane Green put her good arm around Claire.

'You had me worried there,' she said. 'The only reason I could think for your being here was Sarah. I almost had a heart attack when I saw you.'

'You had us worried, mum.'

'And there she is now,' Jane Green said as the doors opened and Tom walked in slowly, cuddling Sarah and talking to her. 'Funny things, men. I'll bet he never flinched in the Balkans as the bombs were flying overhead, but look at him with a baby. Scared out of his wits.'

The other two smiled and Claire relieved him of the baby.

'Hello, Mrs Green. We were a little worried about you. What happened?'

'Let's find somewhere to have some coffee. Not here, though, hospitals make me nervous. Especially accident and emergency. You wouldn't believe what they brought in while I was waiting to be seen. Oh, and it's Jane, not Mrs Green. I might be a grandmother, I certainly don't feel like one.'

'I was lucky,' Jane Green said once they had found a tea shop open and had ordered. 'They only took three hours to see me. Apparently that's pretty fast for a sprained wrist and a sprained ankle.'

'Sounds like you were lucky not to have had worse.'

'Oh, not really, Tom. I've driven all over Europe. You learn to predict what other drivers will do. I had a feeling that that van driver was going to jump the lights. I should have waited, I suppose, but there was an idiot behind me blowing his hooter. A man, of course.'

'Ah,' said Tom. Jane Green laughed.

'Sorry, Tom. I'm just not feeling charitable towards the male sex at the moment.'

'What happened to the van driver?'

'After he'd clipped my bonnet he drove into the traffic lights. I think he was trying to get away. At first he accused me of jumping the lights, then he claimed that he had brake failure.' She sighed. 'It's a real nuisance. The car's going to need quite a bit of work before I can use it again, the front right side is sticking to the wheel. And even if I could find a replacement I can't drive with this hand. I don't know how I managed to pull it so badly, but it's bloody painful when I try to use it.'

'Well, I don't mind giving you a lift when you want to go somewhere,' said Tom. 'It would be good to get out of the house more. It's too easy to sit around in the warmth, overeating and doing very little.'

'And I've got my car as well, mum,' said Gail. 'So give a shout whenever you need to go somewhere. You'll just have to dress up warmly, the heating went wonky on our way down.'

'You could stay with us, mum,' said Claire. 'There's plenty of space. We could look after you.'

'Now that does sound appealing,' Jane Green said with a smile. 'But not with your grandparents. I know it's the season of goodwill to all, but I'd be having a flaming row with them very quickly if I was actually staying there.'

She turned to Tom.

'You might have noticed that we tend to be a rather dysfunctional family, Tom.'

Tom's mouth opened and closed a few times.

'Er, probably not more than most.'

'Liar. Why do you think Rob disappeared for twenty-five years? Why do you think Peter refuses to get married to Rebeccah? As for Hope – well, I don't want to hurt your feelings, but she could do with a psychologist on permanent call.'

Tom raised his eyebrows, rubbed them, and then sipped his tea.

'I just thank the heavens my daughters are normal.'

'Well, thanks, mum,' said Gail. Jane Green laughed.

'Well, you are, everything taken into account. Considering your father and I messed up more than most. But that's all behind us.'

'What do you think of Valerie?' asked Claire. Jane Green turned to her, a sardonic smile on her lips.

'She's another who could do with some psychological help. She has a certain self-destructive urge. The trouble is she's intent on taking others with. I'd keep well clear of her if I were you.'

'She's a downright little bitch who deserves everything coming to her,' said Claire.

'Well, that's another way of looking at it,' said Jane Green. 'But I wouldn't worry about her. She's going to end up doing a lot worse to herself than anything you could dream up. And the worst is that she'll end up realising it. One day. One day when she's all on her own and she has no-one left. And she can't attract any men for a one-night stand.'

'I actually feel a bit sorry for her – when she's not around,' said Gail. 'When she is I just feel like slapping her.'

'Well, enough of her. I think we're embarrassing Tom here. And, Tom, I think I will take you up on your offer to play the knight gallant to a crippled old woman. There's a mother and baby's shop I'd like to visit. I want to ooh and ahh over clothes for my little grand-daughter.'

'Ooh, me too,' said Gail.

'Sarah's got enough clothes,' Claire snapped.

'Oh, darling, this is shopping we're talking about, not buying. And woe to any sales assistant who asks us if we need assistance. We'll drive them potty and then walk out without so much as a bib.'

Tom looked as if, given the choice, and no other choice, he would have preferred to discuss Valerie.

'Where have you been all afternoon?' asked Maria-Hope, finding Tom in the lounge.

'Ferrying your Aunt Jane around. You heard that she was in an accident?'

'Couldn't Gail have done that? She's got her own car.'

'It's just the way things turned out. I took Claire and Gail to the hospital, and after that they wanted to do some shopping for little Sarah. I could hardly refuse. Even if we did spend three hours there and bought absolutely nothing.'

'Valerie didn't go with you?'

'I haven't a clue where Valerie is.'

Maria-Hope scowled at him.

'Peter and I went for a walk,' she said.

Tom nodded and tried to think of something to say. Some polite conversation.

Maria-Hope stomped out before he could come up with anything.

He watched her leave, wondering why on earth he bothered to stay. He could be back in his own flat in London in less than two hours, depending on traffic.

Winifred Browne wandered in with a list.

'Mrs Browne,' Tom said, interrupting the words with a cough, 'er, would you think it very rude of me if I had to leave – an unforeseen emergency.'

Winifred Browne smiled at him.

'Of course not, Tom,' she said. 'But it's rather like suicide, isn't it?'

'Er, suicide?'

'Yes. You never get to know the final outcome, do you? How the story ends.'

Tom opened and closed his mouth a few times.

'And, all in all, I think you're doing far too well to think of suicide,' Winifred Browne said. 'I think you should stay and see what happens,' she added as she left the room.

Chapter Forty-two: Nice little orphans

That evening they were all in the lounge again, the grandparents in their comfortable armchairs while the others were ranged around the room in various poses of post-dinner relaxation. Dinner had started with a nervous silence and discreet glances at George Browne, but it had soon become obvious that he had no memory of anything untoward. His lie-down appeared to have made him more sprightly, if anything.

'Robert, my boy, your turn to give us a story,' he now called. 'At least you should be able to give us a good one. None of this lesbian nonsense, mind. A good old-fashioned moral fable, where the men are men and the women are women.'

'And the sheep nervous.'

'What was that, Gail?'

'Nothing, granddad, just wondered if anyone's glass needed topping up before uncle Rob starts.'

'Good girl, good girl, nice to see you being domestic for a change, haven't succumbed totally to this Marxist-feminist nonsense. But then you always were a good girl. Come now, Robert. Let's have a story for the festive season. A bit like Dickens. Something with the Artful Dodger in. If you can remember that far back, when you were still an Englishman.'

'The Artful Dodger, eh dad?'

'Exactly. And a few little orphans thrown in.'

'Oh, nice little orphans,' said his mother, checking her knitting. 'And don't let them come to any harm, I hate it when children get hurt.'

'I'll try to give it a happy ending, mom. Can't promise anything, mind.'

Chapter Forty-three: Rob's story

'Well, since it is Christmas, I'll start my story two days before Christmas. Winter. Cold, wet and bleak.'

'Gas lamps,' prompted his father.

'No, dad, this is set in modern day times. Let's say this all happened this year. In London.'

'So it doesn't get to Christmas?' asked Valerie. 'Cause it can't, cause Christmas hasn't come.'

'Think of it as what might be. Christmas to come, as it were.'

'Good, good, like it my boy. Very Dickens. Tale of Two Cities. Good stuff.'

'Isn't that A Christmas Carol, grandad?'

'Well, that's what I said, wasn't it? Really, Peter, you should pay more attention. Carry on, Robert.'

'I think we should all stop interrupting Robert,' his mother said, 'or he'll never have time to finish.'

'Good point, Win. Everybody stop interrupting Robert right now.'

Robert looked around the room, a wry smile on his face.

'Right, this Christmas. It all began a day ago – well, it all began many years ago, but yesterday is when the problems came to a head. There's this woman, a girl, really, you see – let's call her Marigold. Her parents were old fashioned, her mother was almost fifty when Marigold appeared, her father already retired. They were completely amazed when they found out they were to have a child, since the doctors had long ago told them it couldn't happen. They did their best for the child, but they weren't rich, they hadn't expected to have a daughter to look after, and simply they were totally at a loss as to how to raise a baby girl. Now, when she was about five her father died. He'd been in failing health for some time and –'

'Not so failing as to give his wife one,' chuckled George Browne.

'George! Really! Robert, never mind him, do go on.'

'He'd been in failing health for some time but not so bad as he couldn't manage a leg-over at Christmas,' continued Robert. There were several titters. His mother pursed her mouth and shook her head at her knitting.

'Her mother continued to look after her as much as she could, but she wasn't well either. The mother received a reduced pension from the company her husband had worked at for thirty-five years, but it was a struggle to pay for the basics in life. And it was a struggle for young Marigold. At school the other pupils teased her about her name. She began to call herself Mary rather than Marigold, but it made no difference. All the other young boys and girls had young mothers and fathers, she was different. And when children see someone as different they see them as a target.'

'You don't have to be different to be seen as a target,' Claire said. 'You just have to be seen as being weak.'

'Oh fucking misery,' declared Valerie. 'Here we go again.'

'Shut up, Val,' Gail said. 'Go on with the story, uncle Rob.'

'She didn't do well at school – in her studies, I mean. Not surprising, really. No money, no extra lessons, unable to concentrate because she was always hungry and the others continually teased her. Her clothes all came from charity shops, they never quite fit her properly.'

'I know this one,' said Val. 'It's Carrie. Has her period in the showers and freaks out.'

'Val, will you shut up?'

'She wouldn't know how to. The only part of her bigger than her mouth is her –'

'Now, now children,' said Winifred Browne. 'Let Robert carry on with his story.'

'And then, when she was fifteen, she realised that her mother was acting strangely. She would forget things. Sometimes she asked Mary who she was. Mary couldn't understand it. She had never heard of Alsheimers. Over the next three years things got worse. All Mary understood was that her mother was ill, and she had to look after her. She would have asked for help, but she had no friends. The other girls at school would have taunted her, look, look, it's Marigold with the mad mother! There was one boy she secretly loved. She knew he could never love her, he was always surrounded by other girls, all much better looking than her, and much brighter too. But, when she was almost seventeen, and she came home to find her mother missing, yet again, after she had found her and brought her home she knew she had no choice but to ask for help. And so she went to the boy and tried to beg his help. He suggested they go to his parents' home. She agreed, unwilling, but desperate, not knowing that his parents were away on holiday. She thought he was going to listen to her and help her. She had never had alcohol before, but he told her it would help her relax. She kept trying to explain herself, becoming more and more confused as she drank.

'Nine months later the baby was born. By then her mother was dead. Her appeals to the young man's parents were scorned, with the threat of the police if she came back. That terrified her, she'd always been afraid of the police, anyone in authority. But, somehow, with the help of strangers who appeared only interested in ticking off notes on their clipboards, she managed to bury her mother and give birth. And then she was on her own. Eighteen, jobless, moneyless, a helpless little girl to look after, unschooled in the ways of the world, with hardly the education to get a job flipping burgers, never mind what to do with the little daughter she loved so much.

'Because she did love her daughter. Her daughter relied on her. Her daughter was the only being in the world who might actually love her back. She understood that her parents had done everything they could to look after her. And now she had a new-born babe that was her responsibility. She named her Nell, because she remembered the name from a story she had heard at school, and thought that the Little Nell in that story had grown up to marry a rich young man. She didn't realise that she had got the story wrong.'

'Why didn't she go on the dole, uncle Rob?' asked Claire.

'Ah, that's part of the point, you see, Claire. Her parents were old working-class types, they saw the dole as a sign of failure, of disgrace. The only thing she knew about the dole was that it was a bad thing. Nobody had ever bothered to explain things to her.'

'Sounds like a total wet to me,' said Valerie.

'I've always thought alcoholics were thin,' Claire commented. 'You seem to have become fat and bloated. Carry on, uncle Robert.'

'Er, right. Okay. Five years passed. Five years in which a penny found in the street was God's sign to her that he would look after her, that, however bad things might become, He would be there. She took to begging in the street during the winter, sitting in a thin frock with an equally thin coat and a sign saying "Please help". Some passers by tossed her the occasional coin. Some coming out of a pub would throw her their change. Others would laugh and kick at her to impress their friends. Other beggars threatened her. The police told her to move on, often. But she survived. And her daughter survived.

'Then, a week or two before Christmas a young man stopped and asked her why she was begging. He was drunk, she could see, but not like the others. It was as if he really wanted to know. And so she said, Sir, I have a young daughter. Please help. I cannot get a job unless she can go to nursery school, and I have no money to pay them. Please help me, please help me, sir.

'He staggered back, being pretty darn tipsy and confused.

'"What, he asked, aren't you getting enough from the social?" She looked back in fear.

'"Please don't tell them", she pleaded. "They will take my daughter from me."

'He shook his head in confusion, and went down on his knees to inspect her from closer range.

'"God, Jeremy, called one of his friends, you really must be desperate. Don't pay her more than a fiver. And remember to wear a thing."

'They moved on, laughing, while Jeremy continued to inspect Mary on his knees through thick glasses.

'"Ah'm a shoshul worker", he said, fumbling in his pockets. "Ah've got me name somewhere, no, no, shomewhere."

'Mary stood up, terrified. Please, sir, I can look after her, she pleaded. But Jeremy the social worker was trying to find the pen he had dropped. Mary fled.

'She avoided that spot for a week, but was forced to return, as the professional beggars drove her away from other spots. She was sitting with her begging cap, face cast downwards, praying that someone might be generous enough to give her just enough money that she might be able to return to her daughter for the evening. Just then a voice said, "It's you! I recognise you."

'Unwillingly she raised her head. She expected to see a police officer who might – one of her great fears – lock her up for the night. But instead it was the young man from the week before. "I knew I hadn't imagined it, the young man said. Now, tell me what you know about the social."

"'Please, sir," she begged, "I don't want no trouble. I just need some money for me daughter. Please, sir, please leave me alone."

"'Never heard of Single Mother's Allowance, then, eh?" he asked roughly.

'I haven't done anything wrong, sir. I've never asked for – for that – what you said.

'He looked at her in disbelief.

'You've never heard of Single Mother's Allowance? he asked.

'Please, sir, let me go and I promise not to beg here ever anymore.

'Where's your daughter? he asked.

'She's at home, sir. Please let me go.

'No, I don't think I will. Not until you show me where you live. I might not be at work, that doesn't mean I'm not on duty.

'She pleaded as much as she could, but she was hungry, cold and sick. In the end she gave up and took him to the basement bed-sit where she and her daughter lived. Her daughter, going on six, stared in mute surprise at this semi-drunk man who had appeared. He went on a knee to say hello to her, but that only drove her into the corner of the room.

'This is it? he roared, standing up, looking around the room. This is where you and your daughter live?

'It's all we can afford, she said. But we – we get by.

'He looked around.

'Where's the paperwork? he demanded.

'Paperwork?

'From Social Security. We love paperwork. There must be some.

'Please, sir, it's just me and my Mary. We don't bother no-one. We're getting along. I'll be able to get a job when she's older. She's very bright for her age.

'Jeremy looked at her.

'You really don't understand, he said. You really are afraid of the social, aren't you?

'I ain't done nothing wrong, she said, both afraid and angry. I ain't asked for nothing, just to be left alone with Mary. And this is my home, Mr Clever, and now Mary and me want you to leave.

'He looked at her in amazement. He scratched his head and looked at little Mary in the corner.

'Talk about falling between the stools, he said.

'She hasn't fallen between anything, Mary said. You can't get us that way, I take good care of her. She never has bruises or nothing.

'Jeremy patted his pockets and came out with a pack of cigarettes. He was about to light one when he looked at little Mary in her corner.

'Perhaps not, he said. He turned to Mary. Look, Miss – what is your name?

'None of your business, she replied. He smiled.

'Okay, Miss None-of-your-business, for your information the social are there to help people like yourself, not take your daughter away. You obviously don't realise it, but you could be getting at least fifty quid a week.

'She laughed. She had been offered a hundred quid a week to go on the game. She might not know much, but she knew about that. Here was he offering her half that.

'I'm serious, Miss None-of-your-business. Look, he said, patting his pockets and rummaging through them, I don't get paid a lot, and hopefully I can claim this on some sort of expenses which we don't have, but – ah, I knew I had one. Here we go, what would you do for this? he asked, holding out a ten-pound note.

'She looked greedily at the note. Ten pounds was a fortune to her. It would buy a lot of food for her daughter. She was desperate. It reminded her of the desperation she had felt when going to see the young man who had raped her and given her her darling daughter. All she had to do was let the young man take her. She turned away.

'I'm not like that, she said. I don't do tricks.

'I'm not asking you to do bloody tricks, he answered angrily, furious, I'm trying to help you, for fuck's sake.

'Language, dear,' his mother said mildly.

'Sort of language he would have used,' George Browne muttered, having woken up long enough to hear the exchange. 'I would have used the same with the stupid girl. Sometimes you have to, you know.'

'I wouldn't have said she was stupid,' Claire said. 'She's obviously managed to look after her daughter without ever having a decent education.'

'Poor little thing,' Mrs Browne said. 'Trying to hide in the corner from the strange man.'

'Carry on, Uncle Robert, did he get to have his evil way with her? Good looking, was she?'

'Give her big tits, Rob,' called Valerie. 'She's got no brain so she might as well have big tits.'

'Oh, do shut up Val. Go on, Uncle Rob.'

'Okay, so where was I? Ah, yes. Mary was confused. The young man was offering her money, but said he didn't want her for that.

'What do I have to do? she asked him.

'Take the money and buy yourself and your daughter some food, he said. She held back. Finally he put the ten pound note on the bed. I'll be back,' he said. For now, treat yourself to something.

'She stood for some time after he had left, looking at the ten pound note. It was not hers, she knew that. The young man had said he would return. When he did he would want it back. If she didn't have it he might call the police. He would call the police. But he had left it there. She could tell them that. But would they believe her or him?

'Finally her daughter made her mind up for her.

'Mummy, she said, I'm hungry.

'Oh, poor little mite!' exclaimed Robert's mother. 'Can't her mother win the lottery or something?'

'Sorry, mom, not in this story. Anyway, Mary and her daughter went to a local corner shop which was more expensive than the shops she normally went to, but it was open almost all hours. She bought a small loaf of bread and the cheapest tin of pilchards she could find. As an act of defiance, or celebration, she also bought some margarine. And then, almost laughing, hysterically, frightening the old man behind the counter, she added a small bag of sweets for her daughter, something she had always wished she could do, but could never afford. And then they went home to feast.

'The following day was a Sunday. Mary hardly ever went out on a Sunday. Sunday was the day for washing the few spare clothes they had, cleaning as best she could the little bedroom and bathroom, telling her daughter stories to make up for not having a television. And then there was a knock at the door.

'She made a sign to her daughter to be quiet, took her in her arms and held her as they sat behind the bed, out of sight. She knew it would be the young man coming to get his money. And it was. "Miss None-of-your-business, he called, I know you're in there, open the door." But she and her terrified little daughter stayed hidden. The man knocked again, and again and again, but they stayed silent. Finally they heard him go away.

She looked around her. She wanted, desperately, desperately, to protect her little baby. Her eyes locked on to the cheap kitchen knife she had once found dropped, or thrown away.

'Can we go to the park? asked her daughter. It was one treat she could give her. Even though it was cold and bleak, winter, the grass dead and the trees bare, at least the air was fresher than in the damp little bed sit. And so they put on as many clothes as they had and went out. They had not got past the front gate before the young man stepped out.

'Now, Miss None-of-your-business, stop being silly, he said as they shrank back from him. Come, let's go inside. There are some papers I want you to sign.

'She trembled as he took her thin arm and pulled her back into the bed sit. Her daughter clung to her, terrified. He sat Mary on the bed, sat next to her and put his briefcase on his lap.

'First, he said, opening it, here's a bar of chocolate for your daughter, and one for you. You obviously don't eat properly, so the sugar should do you some good.

'We don't want it, Mary said desperately. We don't want anything.

'I think your daughter does want it, he said, judging by the look in her eyes.

'Mary looked at little Nell. Her eyes were wide open, staring at the bar of chocolate the young man was holding out to her.

Little Nell looked up at her mother, pleading.

'What do you want for it?' Mary asked.

'Your name, Miss None-of-your-business. That'll do for a start.

'Mary, said Mary unwillingly.

'There you go, that was easy, wasn't it? And now you, little girl, can take your chocolate. Go on.

'Nell looked at her mother for permission. Mary nodded briefly. She felt tired, so very tired, too tired to stand up to the man in the thick glasses.

'And don't forget yours, Mary, he said, pressing the other bar of chocolate into her hand. Now, down to the paperwork.

'It took a great deal of patience on the part of the young man to get the information he needed. Mary did not know what her National Insurance number was, but he was sure he could find that out. It was when he mentioned the word dole that she became really agitated.

'No! she cried, I'm not going on the dole. I'm not going to let them take my daughter away from me.

'Why would they take your little chocolate lips away? he asked, puzzled, looking at little Mary who was licking her lips of the remains of any chocolate bar she could find..

'If you go on the dole they take your children away. That's what they said at school.

'He shook his head in disbelief.

'Mary, no one is going to take your daughter away. Maybe they did that sort of thing a hundred years ago, not these days. Anyway, I'll give you my telephone number, and if anyone tries anything you give me a call and I'll come around and beat them up, how's that?

'That made Mary laugh. He was such a small young man, with such thick glasses that the thought of him trying to beat anyone up tickled her.

'When he left Mary was very confused. He had talked of money that she could get from the unemployment agency, of grants that would mean she wouldn't have to beg anymore, money that would buy clothes for Little Nell, food, Little Nell could go to school for free, she could have little friends. It all sounded like a fairy story, too good to be true. But the young man – Jeremy, he said his name was – had promised to be there the following morning at ten to take her and Little Nell to the office where he worked, and he would see that everything was done properly, and she would be able to get the money he promised.

'The next morning she made sure that she and Little Nell were carefully washed and clean, wearing the best clothes they had. Ten o'clock came, and her nerves were all over the place. She wished she had some make-up, even just some lipstick to make herself attractive for Jeremy.

'Half ten came and went. Eleven. Twelve. No Jeremy. Isn't the chocolate man coming? asked Little Nell. By the time winter darkness came Mary had to admit to herself that Jeremy wasn't coming. For less than a day she had lived in the hope that there might be a little happiness in her life. Now she knew there would be none. Jeremy had promised so much. No doubt he had only done so in the hope that she would sleep with him. She wished she had. But then he would have disappeared just the same, having got what he wanted. It was a cruel, cruel world. For a moment she wished she had never had Little Nell, for what was there in life for her little baby to look forward to?

'And then it seemed that God had heard the dreadful wish she now wished she hadn't had, for Little Nell grew ill. Lack of proper food, the winter cold, a damp bed sit, thin clothing, all conspired against her. Mary grew more and more fearful. She wrapped her child as warmly as she could. She couldn't go out to work or to beg. With no money she felt forced to steal, leaving the bed-sit for an hour each day to shoplift what she could, twice almost being caught. But even the little food she stole did not help Little Nell, and by Christmas Eve she was too weak to drink the thin soup Mary made for her.'

'Oh, don't let her die, Robert,' pleaded his mother.

'What?' asked George Browne, waking up for a second. 'Little Nell always dies. Everyone knows that.'

'Well, I don't see why this Little Nell should,' his wife said. But George Browne had gone back to sleep.

'Should've given that smarmy little Jeremy his leg-over,' muttered Valerie.

'Shush!' said Gail. 'Go on, Uncle Robert.'

'So, Christmas Eve dawned, and Little Nell, pale, thin and weak, could hardly breathe. Mary was desperate. She knew her daughter needed medicine. She didn't know what kind of medicine. But there was a chemist's nearby. She had managed to steal food for her daughter, surely she could steal medicine? Any medicine was better than none.

'She hurried to the chemist's. There weren't many customers, which made it harder to shoplift. She pretended to be browsing, keeping an eye on the man behind the counter. While he was busy with a woman trying some perfume she slipped a bottle of tablets into her bag. And then another, of a different kind. And another, and another. Once she had six she walked towards the door, as if she hadn't found what she was looking for and was leaving. As she stepped outside she felt a hand grab her arm.

'Thought you could steal and get away with it? asked a big man, holding her roughly. You kids! Well, you'll be spending

Christmas in jail if I have anything to do with it.

'No, please, Mary begged, please let me go. I only wanted some medicine for my daughter. She's ill, she's very ill.

'The man laughed scornfully, dragging her back into the shop, telling his assistant to call the police, ignoring her begging. When she wouldn't stop he cuffed her around the head and threatened to do worse if she carried on. She sat on a chair, crying. Now she had no medicine for her Little Nell, and Little Nell would not even have her mother to comfort her.

'The police came and took her away, putting her in a cell. She confessed that she had tried to steal, and begged them to let her go. She could not tell them about Little Nell, for surely they would take her away. Her heart was broken. Little Nell would surely die now, if she was not already dead, all alone in a pitiful, damp little basement bed-sit.

'Perhaps, thought Mary, it was better this way. Better that she and Little Nell should die. Perhaps there was a heaven after life. If not it would matter little. She took the belt from her waist, made a loop and hung it from the door of the cell. She closed her eyes, asked Little Nell for forgiveness, and put her neck into it. With tears streaming down her face she let her knees buckle and the belt tightened around her throat. She forced herself to keep her hands away until the darkness came.'

Robert paused and took a sip from his glass.

'That's it? Mary commits suicide and leaves her daughter to die alone? Suicide is a sin, you know.'

'Just a sec, Peter, just lubricating the throat muscles. All this talking has given me quite a thirst.'

'I know,' said Valerie. 'Jeremy turns up, finds Little Nell, rushes her to the hospital, and then races to the police station where they find Mary just in the nick of time.'

'How would he know she's been arrested?' asked Gail. 'Anyway, Little Nell is hardly going to get up from her sickbed to answer the door.'

'Shush, you two, let Robert finish.'

'Mary wakes up to find herself in a bed in a white room. White walls, white ceiling, white sheets. She wonders whether this is heaven. She turns her head and finds Jeremy in a wheelchair next to her.

'You are a silly, silly girl, he says, having noticed that she's awake.

'Where am I? she asks.

'You're in hospital. You've given everyone a huge fright, especially the police lot. They get into a lot of trouble when they let someone top themselves in one of their cells. It's bad manners, anyway.

'Nell! exclaimed Mary, trying to sit up, I must go to Nell. Jeremy stretched from his wheelchair and tried to push her down.

'Nell's fine, he said. She's in a room nearby, being pumped with penicillin and antibiotics and god knows what else. Her fever's stabilised and she's sleeping. The doctors reckon she'll be well enough to go home before the New Year.

'I must see her, insisted Mary, shaking off Jeremy's hand.

'Oh, very well, then, said Jeremy. God, you are a handful. You can push me. I'll show you where she is.

'Mary looked at him, as if only now realising that he was in a wheelchair.

'What happened? she asked.

'Push,' he said, and I'll tell you.

'As she pushed him in the direction he told her to he explained.

'You won't believe this, but I got hit by a bus. Monday

morning I'm on my way over to your place, crossed a road without paying enough attention, next thing, whammo. I don't remember too much after that, until I woke up with an arm and a leg in plaster and funny tubes coming out of various places. Anyway, I'm a fast healer, and I hate hospitals, so I decided I would be out of here for Christmas. And I wanted to see you and Little Nell. I was just ready to wheel myself out when you turned up on a stretcher, cops and nurses running all over the place, shouting and panicking because they thought you weren't going to make it. Soon as I saw you I realised Little Nell would be on her own. No way I was going to make it down those steps to your place, or not very quickly at any rate. So I grabbed a passing copper – literally, I grabbed his jacket by the coat tails, he wasn't very impressed – and told him that Little Nell would be on her own. He was already shit-scared by the thought that they'd let a young woman commit suicide, if it was found out that the young woman's daughter was also left alone they'd really be for the high jump. That was when I found out that you'd been arrested for shoplifting. The copper turned to his mate and said something about the chemist saying that you'd claimed you wanted the medicine for your sick daughter. So off they went, broke into your place, found Little Nell almost dead, and raced her back here. She's in here.

'He leaned forward to open the door they had arrived at and they went in. Mary sobbed at the sight of Little Nell, deathly pale, but sleeping and breathing normally. She held her little hand and cried.

'Funny, that, Jeremy said. If you hadn't tried to top yourself you wouldn't have been brought here, I wouldn't have recognised you, and Little Nell wouldn't have been rescued.'

'This is where she falls in love with him, isn't it?' asked Gail.

'I don't see why not,' said Robert. 'Trouble is, we don't know, because that's all that's happened to date.'

'You mean it's a true story?'

'Well, not quite. I picked up a newspaper before we left the States and read an article about a girl who had been arrested for shoplifting, and didn't tell the cops that her little girl was on her own at home because she was worried they'd take her daughter away. So I based my yarn on that.'

'Well I think Mary and Jeremy fall in love, get married and live happily ever after with Little Nell,' Mrs Browne said, standing up. 'And on that happy note I think I shall go to bed.'

'Eh?' asked George Browne, waking up. 'Yes, you're right, time for bed. Pity about Little Nell. But she always dies, can't be helped.'

'Goodnight all,' Mrs Browne said, and was met with a chorus of "Night, gran".

'Going to sleep on your own again?' Maria-Hope asked Tom.

'Yup. I could do with a good night's kip. It's been a long day.'

'You might want to lock the door. In case someone sleep-walks into your room.'

'I'll do that. Night Maria, see you tomorrow.'

Claire looked at Robert and Patience after the others had left.

'Little Nell doesn't have to die,' she said. 'That's the point of the story, isn't it?'

Rob nodded.

'No, Claire. Little Nell doesn't have to die. Not anymore. Not if others want her to live.'

Chapter Forty-four: A trip upstairs

Tom lay in his bed and stared at the ceiling. He could just make its outline in the darkness. He had switched the oil heaters on early enough to make the room snug, and had expected to fall asleep quite easily. But sleep wasn't coming. Being honest with himself, he knew that sleep wasn't coming because he was expecting someone else to call, and Gail hadn't turned up.

Whether he was hoping that she would was another question. He wasn't sure about that.

He threw the blankets off, got out of bed and put his dressing gown on. It was time for a visit to the loo. At least it would give him something to do other than stare at the ceiling and avoid the answer he knew to be the correct one. He was hoping that Gail would slip into his bed. After what had happened that afternoon it would be perverse of the woman not to. He slipped a pencil torch into the dressing gown pocket. He had no wish to choose between switching lights on and waking everybody up, or bumping into walls in the darkness and waking everybody up.

As he stepped into the corridor and quietly closed his bedroom door another figure appeared next to him carrying a flashlight.

'Not going sleepwalking, are you Tom?' asked Robert softly.

'I hope not. I'm pretty sure I'm awake.' He grimaced. 'Ever had one of those nights when you dream the whole night that you're awake? And end up waking, feeling that you haven't had a minute's sleep?'

'Not since I got married, Tom. Plenty times before then, mind you.'

'So you're recommending marriage as a cure for sleepless nights?'

Robert chuckled softly.

'I'd recommend marriage as a cure for sleepless nights, but I sure as hell wouldn't recommend having children for the same reason. I've been tasked by Lucy to check out all spectres.'

'Ghosts?'

'Yup. She won't take my word that they don't exist. Apparently all English castles have ghosts. And this, according to my little daughter, is close enough to a castle to have ghosts. Especially as it has been a lunar tick a-sigh-lem in the past. Dead bodies all over the grounds. I promised to make sure that they had all gone to sleep.'

'Ghosts go to sleep? I thought they never did.'

'Yeah, well, it's amazing what a six-year-old child's imagination can't come up with.'

'Can come up with.'

'You correcting my grammar, Tom?'

'Yes, as it happens.'

Robert grinned.

'Glad you aren't in my class.'

'You'll have to check upstairs, you know. Beyond the locked door. And who knows what lies beyond the locked door? Where the old servant quarters lie.'

'Trouble is, it's locked.'

'We could check.'

Robert nodded and they moved towards the door to the staircase which led up to the old servants' quarters. The key was in the lock. Robert turned it. It turned silently. He tried the handle. The door opened silently.

'Spooky,' he noted. 'Isn't it supposed to creak?'

'Not with half a can of WD40 on the hinges,' Tom said, flashing his torch on the stains.

'Well, I wonder who did that. Mom, because she found it irritating, or the builders for the same reason.'

'Builders, I reckon,' said Tom, moving quickly up the narrow stairs. 'I can't see your mum getting that upset about it. Let's see what the forbidden zone holds.'

'She wouldn't get upset,' said Robert, following, 'she'd just quietly drown those hinges into submission. She'd shake her head sadly and then drown them.'

The staircase led up to a corridor which went towards the middle of the building before turning left and running its length. Open doors showed the interiors of various sized rooms as Tom and Robert walked quietly along the wooden floor. In the light of their torches the forbidden zone appeared to hold a great deal of builders' requirements. Bags of sand or plaster, a shovel, buckets, an upright trowel which some infuriated builder had thrown into the floor, its point stuck fast.

'Looks like a lot of partitions have been knocked out,' noted Tom as he played his torch along a ceiling and down a wall. 'Must have been divided up into smaller rooms at some stage.'

'Ceilings are a lot lower than downstairs.'

'Nor as ornate. Presumably the servants didn't need as much headroom.'

'If memory serves me correctly, servants were almost always single. If a maid got married she had to move out and live with her husband. I guess that meant they'd live two or three to a room.'

'Must have been a shitty life. First up to light the fires and get the water on the go. Not a lot of space, but their uniforms had to be pressed and starched. I can imagine damp clothes hanging on clothes-lines strung across the rooms. In the winter, anyway. Sort of life my grandparents must have lived. Or possibly great-grandparents.'

Robert glanced at him.

'Better check every nook and cranny,' he said. 'Lucy will know if I haven't. And then she'll demand to look for herself. And this doesn't look like the safest kiddies' playground I've ever seen.'

'So, Tom,' he continued as they made their careful way in a room piled with boxes, presumably those things the Brownes had yet to unpack, 'what do you reckon to this whole servant idea?'

'How do you mean?'

'Well, you said your parents were working class – I guess somewhere in your ancestry you would have had servants and such in your family.'

Tom shrugged.

'I'm a child of Thatcher, Rob. I grew up with the idea that it's up to the individual to make something of life. Left all that working class anger behind me. It would have been angst, but we couldn't afford it. You know, foreign imports, like.'

'Sounds more like you're a child of New Labour. Or are we all Thatcherites now? Fuck!'

'What's wrong?'

'Stepped on a bloody nail. Just a second.'

Both torches played on his foot as he took his shoe off.

'No blood, anyway,' said Robert. 'Well, mom did warn us about playing up here.'

'You're going to have to think up a better story for Lucy. "Sorry, darling, no ghosts but daddy did step on a nail" just won't be good enough.'

'I hate it when that happens,' Robert said, limping as he led the way into the next room. 'Hurts like hell but there's nothing to show for it.'

'Aha! Now here's something.' Tom leaned around a pile of boxes. He grunted as he pulled something out. A framed portrait of a man in uniform.

'Well, now that's interesting. First World War, I'd say.'

'Must have been here when your folks moved in. Looks like it's been in the attic for the last fifty years. At least.'

'"Sir Edward"' Robert said, reading the inscription. 'Wish they'd been a bit more explicit. Sir Edward who?'

'I suppose in those days you were supposed to have known.'

'1915, I'd say,' said Robert. 'Judging by the uniform.'

'Late 1915, more like 1916 or 1917. Khaki uniform. If it had been earlier he would have been wearing whatever fancy uniforms they had for strolling around Mayfair. Feathers in the hat, that sort of thing.'

Robert nodded.

'Guess you're right. Well, Sir Edward, you're an old anachronism, aren't you? But you have to love that moustache. People in those days were serious about their moustaches.'

Tom shoved the portrait back behind the boxes.

'So, Rob, why did you really go to the States? Leave Merry Old England just as it was about to enter its heyday?'

Robert watched him play his torch idly over the room.

'You're an only child, aren't you, Tom?'

'Yes. Yes, I am.'

'Well, I grew up with an older brother who was expected to be the success of the family, and an older sister who was expected to be the perfect woman. There didn't seem to be a role for me, so I decided to get out and find some fresh air to breathe. Any air to breathe.'

'Must be strange to be back after all those years.'

'It was at first. Now – well, it doesn't seem to matter much anymore.'

'That's a bummer.'

'A bummer?'

'It means we're totally out of ghosts. You have no ghost to lay, and we haven't found one around here, not even tucked up for the night. What are you going to tell Lucy?'

'I'll tell her the truth. That it's dusty and dirty as hell, and her daddy stepped on a nail. And that we'll go to a real castle next week, one that really does have ghosts.'

'It was Christmas Eve, and nothing stirred in the house, not even a mouse.'

Tom paused, and added: 'A fruitless search for things that go bonk in the night.'

There was silence for a few moments.

'You thinking what I'm thinking, Tom?' Robert asked, very softly.

'You mean that we're a couple of arseholes?' Tom replied, as quietly.

'Uh-huh. We're a couple of assholes who left a key in a lock to the only door that will let us out of here. And on the other side of that door are a number of people who are childish enough to think it a pretty good trick to lock the door on us. Apart from my mom, who might just happen by and think that she forgot to lock it.'

'Sshh! Did you hear something?'

Robert listened.

'No. Don't think so.'

'Well, you're going to hear something now. Me legging it.'

It took Robert a few seconds to realise what Tom had meant,

a few seconds in which Tom was out of the room and on his way down the stairs. Robert followed him with impressive speed.

'Thought you might have got the idea of locking me in there yourself,' he whispered in a hoarse voice once they were out on the landing and safe.

'It did cross my mind,' Tom replied in as hoarse a voice.

'What stopped you?'

'The idea of things going bonk in the night.'

'What?'

'I had this awful image of locking the door on you and turning to find Valerie looking at me. You know, with a certain kind of look.'

'Mrs Count Dracula?'

'Yup. That's the sort of thing.'

Robert breathed out. He turned the key in the lock and put it into the pocket of his dressing gown.

'I've had enough for the night. I'm off to bed. I'd lock your door if I were you.'

'I fully intend to.'

Robert nodded a good-night and left to see whether Lucy was still awake, or whether he could postpone his explanations about ghosts until the morrow. Tom watched him go.

He entered his room, trying to decide. He could lock his door, which would deny Gail access. He could leave it unlocked, which would permit either Maria or Valerie access.

Sod it, he thought, throwing his dressing gown on the bed and climbing under the bed clothes, if Maria or Valerie turned up he would just boot them out.

Then he got up again and locked the door. The way things were going Valerie would turn up first, and before he had time to boot her out, Maria would turn up, and then he would be standing there trying to explain things to Maria. She wouldn't believe him, he wouldn't care if she did, and the entire household would be roused to join in the fun. He could do without that.

Anyway, Gail, on finding the door locked, would knock quietly, wouldn't she?

And he'd hear the knock, wouldn't he?

Shit, he'd learnt to wake up to the sound of the soft wings of a mortar, a knock would be no problem.

With this comforting thought he fell asleep until the dawn of Christmas Day.

Chapter Forty-five: Sunday, Christmas Day

'Good morning, Gail,' Tom said, entering the kitchen, rubbing his hands. 'Excellent, a lit fire, it's a bit parky upstairs.'

Gail turned from the window she had been looking out, watching snow-flakes fall in the darkness.

'Good night's sleep?' she asked.

'An excellent night's sleep. I was fagged out from all the excitement yesterday.'

She came up to the fire and stood next to him.

'I would have popped in to kiss you goodnight, but Valerie actually made it to her own bed for a change. If she woke up and noticed my bed was empty she might have put two and two together. Actually, it doesn't matter what she would have put together, she would have mouthed off about it and others would have done their own arithmetic. I'm sorry, Tom. I really wanted to come to you.'

'Just as well. I like an uncomplicated life. I think it's better we just leave it and enjoy Christmas. Anyway, you wouldn't have found me there. Rob and I went ghost busting.'

'Ghost busting?'

'I popped out to go to the loo. Rob was under orders from Lucy to find the ghost. We popped up into the servants' quarters. We didn't find anything, but Rob stepped on a nail.'

'Rob stepped on a nail?'

'Yup. If you see him limping this morning, pretend you don't know why.'

She looked at him. Then she gave him a quick hug.

'You might be right,' she said. 'About an uncomplicated life. I was thinking of making some breakfast. Fancy anything?'

'That's okay, I'll probably just have a couple of slices of toast.'

'You'll have a proper breakfast, my boy. Eggs and bacon. Now sit down while I get you some coffee.'

He turned and looked at her as she switched the kettle on and busied herself with a pan. Before he could say anything Claire walked in with Sarah. She yawned and sat down.

'Nice life being a baby,' she said. 'You wake up mummy for a feed and then go back to sleep. I just wish mummy could do the same.'

'Hungry, Claire? I was just about to make some breakfast.'

Claire looked from her to Tom.

'I could do with a strong cup of coffee to start with. Making breakfast for Tom? He's the lucky one, isn't he? If Hope isn't around to look after him some other woman will jump in.'

'I think I will just stick to a couple of slices of toast,' Tom decided.

'Oh, don't mind me, Tom, I didn't mean anything. Just tired, that's all.'

'You could make yourself useful, Tom,' Gail said, bringing a couple of mugs to the table. 'Hold Sarah while Claire relaxes with her coffee.'

'Er, yes, okay,' Tom said, taking the baby and sitting down awkwardly opposite Claire. Claire gave him an evil smile as she sipped her coffee.

'I do like to see a man holding the baby. It makes such a change.'

'Morning,' said Maria-Hope, coming into the kitchen, yawning. 'Everybody's up bright and early.'

'No, up, maybe, certainly not bright,' yawned Claire. 'Except these two. All happy and chirpy and washed and dressed and looking disgustingly cheerful. It shouldn't be allowed before sunrise. Unless it is sunrise. Is it?'

'Officially, yes,' said Gail. 'But the storm clouds are hiding it.'

'Storm clouds?'

'Well, clouds. They look a bit dreary, but if we're lucky they'll turn into real snow this time.'

'Little Sarah's asleep,' noted Tom. 'But she does look very cheerful. At least I think she looks cheerful. If that scrunched-up little smile means anything.'

'Valerie not up?' asked Maria-Hope.

'Can't see her being up much before noon, as usual.'

'I think we'd better enjoy the peace and quiet,' said Tom. 'Any minute now Lucy will be down to open her presents.'

'And she'll want to show every one of them to her favourite Uncle Tom.'

'That explains it,' said Gail. 'I noticed Uncle Rob likes you, Tom. Now I know why. You keep little Lucy amused.'

'Everyone likes Tom,' Claire said, leaning her elbows on the table and giving him another evil smile. 'Gran thinks he's the bees' knees, and even mum likes him. I'd be careful, Tom, I think mum might fancy you.'

Tom looked around him. Maria-Hope was scowling at him. Gail was looking at him, chuckling at his embarrassment.

'When's your grandfather getting up?' he asked. 'I'm beginning to think I prefer his having a go at everyone. It makes me feel safer.'

'You are three months, going on four,' Tom crooned to Sarah as he sat in the lounge holding her, 'dum-dee dum, dee-dee dum. Something and something, and something I can't re-mem-ber, but that doesn't matter, cause you can't under-staand.'

'Oh, she's so sweet,' Gail said, sitting down next to him. They had finished breakfast. Gail and Claire had done the washing up, and then Claire and Maria-Hope had gone back upstairs to each have a long bath. The kitchen had been taken over by Rebeccah, Rob, Patience and their children. The children were under orders to have a proper breakfast before opening their presents. They were following the orders at indigestion-inducing speed.

'Know what I really like about little Sarah, apart from the fact that she absolutely the cutest thing in the world, and my niece?'

'No, tell me.'

'It gives me the perfect excuse to cuddle up to you without making anyone in the slightest suspicious.'

Tom sighed and looked at little Sarah.

'Know what I'd like?'

'What's that?'

'The perfect excuse to get out of here before I really get into hot water.'

'You can't do that, you promised to ferry mum around, remember?'

'Oh, god, yes! Damn, I'd forgotten about that.'

'And we have to collect her for lunch. She can't drive over here, now can she?'

'We?'

'Well, I'm certainly coming with you. She is my mum, after all.'

Tom thought about this.

'Claire will want to come too.'

Gail laughed and kissed him on the cheek.

'You poor thing. Wanting Claire as your bodyguard. It must be terrible.'

'Actually I was thinking more of little Sarah here. She makes a much better bodyguard. Don't you, you little sweetie? Oh, yes, you do, you do, don't you?'

He paused.

'I think her nappy might need changing,' he said.

'We're going to early service,' Winifred Browne said, appearing in the lounge doorway with Peter and Maria-Hope behind her. Claire had retrieved little Sarah and changed her nappy and was sitting with Tom and Gail. 'We should be back in an hour and a half or so. You don't need anything, do you? There are some corner shops in town which open today. I think they're Turkish or something.'

'No, gran, we're okay,' said Gail. 'We've got to be off soon to fetch mum.'

'Oh, dear, I forgot to ask her whether she wanted to attend service. Still, I'm sure there are churches in town. Of course there are, I meant that she'd need to know what time the services are held. Well, I'll see you all later. Drive carefully, Tom.'

'Will do, Mrs Browne,' Tom replied. Mrs Browne and the other two left, each giving Tom a different look. Peter's was a sneer. Maria-Hope's was filthy. He noticed that she was wearing her silver crucifix outside of her clothes.

'Now I know how the average Irish Catholic bloke feels,' muttered Tom. 'Your gran, fine, no problem. But Peter and Maria make me want to go hide in the pub with a pint until it's all over.'

'Ah, but sure, Thomas,' said Gail, leaning towards him, fluttering her eyelids and adopting a mock-Irish accent, 'did you not know that ex-convent girls are the randiest of them all?'

'You aren't an ex-convent girl.'

'I'm ex-boarding school. Pretty much the same.'

'You wouldn't take advantage of a man holding a baby, would you?'

'You aren't holding a baby at the moment.'

'Claire, can I borrow Sarah for a few moments?'

'Sorry, Tom, sometimes you have to fight your own battles.'

Tom stood up and headed for the door.

'Time we were collecting your mother, I think. I'll go grab my coat.'

'Coward!' called Gail after him.

'It's a wonderful coat,' he called back. 'It's saved my life before.'

Chapter Forty-six: A little deception

Jane Green was waiting in the hotel restaurant when Tom, Gail, Claire and little Sarah arrived.

'You're early, I've just ordered a pot of tea. I'll get them to bring some more cups.'

'It was the traffic, Mrs Green,' Tom said. 'There wasn't any.'

'Sit down, sit down. How's my lovely little grand-daughter?'

'Your lovely grand-daughter is busy bewitching everyone who looks at her,' said Claire, sitting down. 'Even Tom was baby-sitting her this morning while I had a bath.'

'Oh, sweet little thing! Can I hold her, Claire?'

'Of course, mummy. Here you go.'

'Hello, sweet little Sarah. It's your nan. Recognise your nan, do you?' She frowned and laughed. 'Not while you're sleeping, you won't.'

'She was wide-awake on the way over. She seems to like travelling in a car. As soon as Tom parked she dozed off again.'

'Oh, that reminds me. I need to get my handbag from my room. Tom, you wouldn't be a darling for me and get it? Here's the key, room twenty-three, it's on the first floor. Why, I don't know. You'd think it should be on the second floor. Actually, Gail, you'd better go with Tom. Men aren't that good at recognising handbags.'

Tom's eyebrows raised slightly as the key was passed over. Gail blinked.

'I think I know what a handbag is,' Tom said, 'but probably best to be on the safe side. Come on, Gail.'

'She was trying to get rid of us,' Gail said as they walked up the stairs to the first floor. 'What the hell is she playing at?'

'Pretty obvious when you think about it.'

'Oh, really? Well, I must be pretty dumb, then. She wants to be alone with Claire? Why?'

'No, she wants Claire alone with her. Think about it. What day is it?'

'Is that a trick question, oh genius journalist?'

'Nope.'

'It's Christmas Day, then.'

'Correct. And what happens on Christmas Day?'

Gail considered this as they walked along the corridor.

'People eat too much and drink too much?'

'Really, Gail, you are being obtuse. What did we do yesterday?'

'Not as much as we could. You aren't suggesting we – well, not in mum's hotel room.'

'Gail! You do have a one-track mind. What did we do when we went into town?'

'We bought some presents for little Sarah without Claire realising – You don't mean ...'

'Precisely. Your mum isn't likely to forget to buy a present for her new grand-daughter, is she? And,' he said as he opened the door to number twenty-three, 'it's on the right-hand side, wrapped in gold-coloured paper. She wants us to take it out to the car without Claire seeing it.'

Gail stopped as they entered and saw a large present wrapped in gold-coloured paper leaning against the wall on the right-hand side.

'How the hell did you know that?'

Tom grinned and showed her a piece of paper in his hand.

'She palmed this to me along with the key,' he said.

'Tom Woods, you are the most devious ... Well, really!' She

pushed him in simulated anger. Caught off balance he tumbled on to the bed. She stepped over and sat on top of him, holding his arms down. 'You are a naughty boy! A very naughty boy.'

'Gail, do you mind? The door's open.'

She sprang off, closed the door, and resumed her position on top of him.

'Now, Mr Woods, you are me a forfeit.'

'A forfeit?'

'Yes, for cheating. Pretending to be psychic, or whatever. And as a forfeit ... let me see, now ... yes, I think you owe me a kiss.'

'A kiss?'

'Yes, like this.' She leaned down and kissed him slowly.

They looked at each other.

'Better get little Sarah's present down to the car,' Tom said.

'I suppose so.'

'You'll have to get off me first.'

'I suppose so.'

Gail sighed and stepped off him, smoothing down her dress. He stood up slowly and looked at the present.

'Better get it down to the car,' he repeated.

'I suppose so.'

'Gail?'

'Yes?'

'We shouldn't be doing that sort of thing.'

'Why not?'

'Better get the present to the car before Claire starts wondering where we are. And your mum.'

'You get the present. I'll walk ahead in case Claire's come looking for us.'

'Don't forget your mother's handbag.'

'Oh, Christ, yes!'

Gail looked around the room. She searched all the cupboards. 'Now that's strange,' she said. 'There isn't a handbag anywhere.'

'Looks like she forgot to forget it.'

Chapter Forty-seven: It's here after all

'Mum, your handbag's on the seat next to you,' noticed Claire. 'Is it? Oh, silly me. I find myself doing things like that these days. Forgetting where I've put things. It's part of growing old. Or so I'm told. It's a sort of contradiction, really. If you can't remember what you've forgot – well, you can't remember it, can you?'

Claire looked at her mother suspiciously.

'You did that on purpose, didn't you?'

'On purpose? Why should I do that?'

'Mum, please, I'm not ten years old. You wanted to give Gail and Tom an excuse to be on their own. Even I can see that she's head over heels in love with him.'

'Ah, well, yes ... I did think that there was something between them. And he is a very nice young man.'

'Mum! Really! I never thought of you as an old romantic.'

Jane Green smiled at her daughter.

'It's the curse of our family, ending up with the wrong man all the time. I was hoping at least one of us could escape that curse.'

Claire sighed and sipped her coffee. She looked at little Sarah. 'It would be nice. For once.'

They were interrupted by the entrance of Tom and Gail.

'Sorry, Mrs Green, we hunted all over and couldn't find it.'

'Oh, Tom, I am sorry. I had it here all along.'

'I was going to go up and tell you,' said Claire, smiling at them. 'But I didn't want to interrupt you.'

Tom blushed. Gail counted her fingernails.

'We'd better get going,' said Jane Green. 'We should be in time to help with the final stages of preparation of the grand lunch, and to partake in some pre-lunch witty repartee.'

'And maybe afterwards have a game of hide and seek. Tom could find a small cupboard to hide away in while we all look for him. Of course, we'd have to squeeze in tight next to him when we find him.'

Tom gave a weak smile. If he was going to hide anywhere it would be in Maria-Hope's bedroom. No-one would ever look for him there.

Apart from Maria, who might retire there to mope. Or have a headache.

No, it would have to be the attic. Or the beetroot patch.

Or the spinney.

He wondered where the vicar's pig's sty was.

Claire was sent indoors with little Sarah to the warmth of the kitchen as soon as they arrived at Maid's Manor. Tom was deputed to scurry into the lounge afterwards with the present. He found that he had to add it to a large pile all with tags bearing the name "Sarah".

Chapter Forty-eight: A surprise for Claire

'Everyone here?' asked Winifred Browne in the kitchen. 'Jane, you haven't a drink. And Gail and Sarah and Tom. We've been waiting for you to start with the old tradition.'

'Old tradition?' asked Peter.

'Come, Jane, what will you have? A sherry?'

'A sherry sounds fine, mum.'

'Good, good. Tom? A glass of wine, isn't it?'

'I'll get it, gran,' said Gail. 'Tom and I share the same taste in wine, which is why his is the only drink I ever remember.'

'So that's the reason,' murmured Claire.

'What do you want, sis?' asked Gail.

'Oh, same as you and Tom.'

'Now, here's to us all,' said Winifred Browne. 'Cheers.'

There was a muted response of "cheers" from all present, and they each took a delicate sip of their drinks.

'And now, according to tradition, we all traipse through to the lounge,' said Winifred Browne. 'Come on, everyone through to the lounge. The fire's been lit for a while and it's nice and warm.'

'Tradition?' asked Peter. 'I don't remember this.'

'Do shut up, Peter,' said Gail.

Claire found herself at the back of the line, somehow delayed by Tom who insisted on giving her a hand with little Sarah, and Robert, who turned out to be strangely in the way. When she entered the lounge with Sarah in her arms and Tom behind her it was to find the others lined up in two rows leading to the Christmas tree with presents piled up before it.

'We agreed to break the no-presents rule for the kids,' said Robert. 'And little Sarah is the youngest, so we kinda broke the rules more for her.'

Claire's eyes filled with tears as she realised what was happening.

'No, please,' she said, 'I can look after her, I mean, well, it's very kind, but really, you see ...'

Tom put an arm around her.

'Typical,' he said, looking down at little Sarah, 'we go to all this trouble and she falls asleep. In future, whenever we buy little Sarah a present we'll have to open them while driving in a car if she's going to take any notice. In the mean-time mummy is going to have to open her little baby's presents. You are horribly ungrateful, little Sarah, and I hope I get to remind you of this in years to come.'

Claire blinked her thanks at Tom as he led her to the presents.

'No names, no pack drill, as they say,' Tom said. 'These are just presents to the little one from all of us. I'm a stranger, as it were, so I'll look after little Sarah while you open them.'

There was a wondering light in Claire's eyes as she let Tom take little Sarah. She tentatively took hold of a large gold-coloured present and began to unwrap it. It revealed a little baby's crib on rockers, assembled.

'This is from you, mum, isn't it?' she asked, looking at it.

'They're all from all of us, my darling.'

Claire stretched out a thin hand and touched some of the other presents.

'Baby blankets,' she said, choosing one. She ripped open the packaging and baby blankets fell out.

'I don't know much about babies,' said Tom, 'but looking at the crib, the blankets and little Sarah, I'd say they're a perfect fit. My photographer's eye, you see.'

Claire carefully placed the blankets in the crib. Then she rocked it. She looked at her mother. And then at her mother's wrist. Jane Green tried to hide her wrist behind her other arm. 'They come fully assembled these days,' she said.

'Liar,' said Claire. She looked at Tom. 'Give Sarah to me.' Tom handed over the sleeping infant. 'Mum, could you help me tuck her in?' she asked as she laid Sarah on the blankets. 'I'm feeling a little tired.'

Jane Green knelt on the crib next to her daughter and gently laid a blanket over her grand-daughter. She stroked Claire's hair.

'Why don't we open the rest of the presents?' she suggested. 'Then you can have a snooze until lunchtime.'

'Can I borrow Tom to snooze against?' Claire asked Gail. She tucked herself up into Tom's arms. 'You will look after my little Sarah while I'm asleep, won't you, Tom?'

'Er, of course,' he replied, looking down at her, and then around at the others in a plea for help. The plea was met by frowns of anger from Maria-Hope and Peter. Everyone else tried to hide their smiles.

Chapter Forty-nine: Christmas Lunch

'Well, now this is more like it,' said George Browne at the head of the table, rubbing his hands. 'The whole family together for Christmas lunch. Or most of us. The ones who matter.'

Everyone was there. Lucy was proudly sitting on three cushions to bring her up to sufficient height to eat at the table. Sarah was asleep in her new crib behind Claire. Jane Green sat between Claire and Gail. Tom was next to Gail. Next to Tom was Robert, then, opposite George Browne, his wife, then Patience, Maria-Hope opposite Tom, Peter and Rebeccah.

'To Christmas,' said Robert, raising his glass. "To Christmas," everyone echoed.

'Such a pity Adam and Susan couldn't make it,' said Winifred Browne. 'Anyway, tuck in, everyone.'

'Next year,' said George Browne. 'He'll be here next year. Soon as he hears what he's missed out on this year. One of the best Christmases I can remember, this. That's what makes the difference, being with your family.'

The others observed him covertly but carefully, checking for any signs of another "turn". He appeared to be perfectly normal.

'Who knows where we'll all be in a year's time?' said Gail.

'Prediction time,' cried Robert, serving himself some broccoli in butter sauce. 'Everyone has to make a prediction.'

'Another American custom, my boy?'

'Nope, dad, I just thought it might be a fun thing to do.'

'Superstition,' said Peter.

'No, Pete, just a bit of fun.'

'Well, go on my boy, you start.'

'Me, dad? Okay.' He paused. 'I predict that, in a year's time ... Tom will be married.'

There was a silence as people looked with raised eyebrows from Robert to Tom.

'Why Tom?' asked Rebeccah. Robert grinned at her.

'Because he has the mark of a cursed man on his face,' he said.

'Really, Bobby!'

'Just joking, my love. No, Tom, I think you're the marrying type. And my guess is that you're about ready to settle down. Oh, and you'd be too happy as a bachelor for women to tolerate.'

'Very true, my boy,' said George Browne, 'very true. Women don't like men to be bachelors. Your turn, now, Tom.'

'My turn?'

'A prediction, Tom, a prediction. Come, come, it's just a game. Can't be that hard. Better than crackers, you know. Those silly things in crackers. This is a lovely wine, Win. I don't remember having something so fine since – well, for years.'

'Er – well, I don't know,' said Tom, with a nervous look at George Browne enjoying his wine. 'Um, well – okay, I predict I'll be a year older by next Christmas.'

'That's cheating!' exclaimed Gail. 'Come on, Tom, you'll have to do better than that.'

'Yes, come on Uncle Tom!' cried Lucy.

'Very well,' said Tom, looking at her and smiling. 'I predict that you will have a new little sister by next Christmas.'

'Oh, wow!' cried Lucy, trying to clap her hands together while still holding a knife and fork.

'Careful, Lucy,' her mother said, disentangling her daughter's hands from the cutlery.

'Is that true, mommy? Am I going to have a little sister next year?'

'You'd better ask your daddy, darling.'

Lucy turned her attention on her father.

'Well, daddy? Will I?'

The others laughed.

'Tom got you there, Robert, my boy,' said his father, sipping at his wine and raising his eyebrows at his son. 'That'll teach you.'

'I don't know, honey,' Robert smiled at Lucy. 'It's just a fun little prediction. Your go now.'

'Me, daddy?'

'Oh, yes, everybody gets a go. Everybody.'

Lucy looked at him and then screwed her eyes up.

'I predict,' she announced, 'I predict that Uncle Tom and Aunty Gail will fall in love and get married and have lots of little children and live in a castle just like the prince and the princess.'

There was a silence around the table. Lucy opened her eyes and beamed at Tom and Gail. Gail went beetroot red. Tom coughed on a mouthful of lamb with mint sauce.

'Ha!' exclaimed George Browne. 'Looks like that's you done for, Tom. Gail, you're next.'

'I, ah – me?'

'Come along, girl. What's your prediction for next year?'

'Well, er -'

'Come on, Gail,' muttered Tom, 'stop shilly-shallying. Get on with it, girl.'

'I predict that – that Val will find a job with an Italian company and move to Rome.'

'Me? Rome? I like that idea. All those gorgeous Italian men.'

'Your turn, Val.'

'Okay. I predict that Peter will take holy orders and become a priest. Or vicar, or whatever they're called these days.'

This was met by a silence from everybody but one.

'You'd have to get married, first, Peter,' said his grandfather. 'Church doesn't hold with their vicars living in sin. They might allow gay priests and women priests these days, but not unmarried fathers. Technical point, but there you go.'

'A lot of nonsense,' said Peter. 'Absolute nonsense.'

'Course it is, Pete,' Robert laughed. 'That's the whole point. The more outlandish the better. Come on, your turn.'

'I really haven't any predictions to make. Predictions go against my faith.'

'Oh, go on, Peter, make something up.'

'No, thank you, I'm not interested.'

'Come on, then, Hope,' called George Browne. 'You give us a prediction. Your brother obviously has no imagination.'

Maria-Hope looked at him and then turned to her grandmother.

'Okay. I predict that gran will win the lottery and go on an around-the-world cruise.'

'Oh, thank you, darling, that's a very kind thought.'

'Damned if I'm going to go on any cruise around the world. Seen enough of it as it is. Anyway, cruises these days are for boring old people who like getting dressed up. In my day it was young people having the holiday of a lifetime before settling down. These days it's just a bunch of old fools.'

'I think that makes it your go, gran,' said Claire.

'My go? Oh, dear, I don't know what to say.'

'Say anything, gran, go on.'

'Well. Well, I predict that Jane will buy a little cottage in the country for herself and Claire and little Sarah. With a thatched roof and a rose garden.'

'Thornless roses,' said Jane Green. 'The last time I was in a rose garden I caught my favourite frock on a thorn and tore a deep hole in it.'

'Your turn, Jane, my girl.'

Jane Green looked at her father. She picked up her glass of wine, took a sip, and smiled at him.

'Okay, dad. I predict that you'll start a vegetable garden in the spring.'

'A vegetable garden? Strange prediction. Then again, considering the rubbish the supermarkets sell these days, it's not a bad idea. You know, I might well do that.'

'What about you, Claire? What's your prediction?'

Claire put her knife and fork down and thought for a moment.

'I predict that, this time next year, there will be three more babies here for Christmas.'

'Three more? Who's going to have them?'

'I don't know. I just thought of the figure three.'

'Well,' said Robert, 'apparently Patience and I have some work to do. Pete, I reckon you and Becky must be another couple. So who's going to be the third couple?'

Peter scowled.

'Unless you and Patience have triplets,' suggested Tom. Robert laughed.

'Nice one, Tom. Dad, you haven't made a prediction.'

'Me? Ah, yes. Let me see. Hmmm.' He raised his wine glass and took a sip. 'Very well, I predict that young Claire here will meet a very nice young man, fall in love, and get married. How's that, then?'

'That does sound nice,' said Winifred Brown. 'How is everyone doing? Nearly ready for dessert?'

'I'll get them,' said Claire, standing up.

'I'll give you a hand,' said Gail, following.

'That is interesting,' Robert said as the girls left, 'all the predictions were about falling in love, getting married, having babies, families, that sort of thing. Nothing about which team will win the cup next year, or who will be prime minister, or whether a Brit might finally win Wimbledon.'

'That's because family is the most important thing, my boy. Say what you like, all these celebrities making money, partying until who knows when, politicians climbing the greasy pole, you name it, when it comes down to it family is the only thing you can rely on.'

'That was a bit cruel of grandad,' Gail said in the kitchen.

'How do you mean?'

'The bit about you meeting someone and falling in love. Getting married. I mean, so soon after – you know.'

'I would say thoughtless rather than cruel. And I think he really means it – Grandad. And I don't see why it shouldn't happen. Other people fall in love and get married.'

Gail looked at her.

'I think you should have been the one to be named Hope, Claire.'

'You mean Hopeless.'

'No, I mean Hope. If I were you I'd be spitting fire at any man I came across. I certainly wouldn't be thinking about falling in love again.'

'Maybe it's because I've had a chance to recover a bit. Not have to look after Sarah all on my own. Not have to live on whatever scraps I can be arsed cooking for myself. Be able to lie in bed knowing that people are just a few feet away if I need any help, people that I know.'

Gail nodded as her sister watched her.

'It has been good to get away. Even with grandad and Val. And Pete walking around like an end-of-the-world prophet.'

'And with Tom.'

'Tom?'

'The one you fancy like all hell.'

Gail concentrated on the trifle she was taking out of the fridge, trying not to drop it, trying to let her hair hide her blushing cheeks.

'Why should I fancy Tom?'

'Oh, please, Gail, I'm not a ten-year-old. I saw the way you turned red when Lucy predicted that you and Tom would get married. I was wondering if there was something going on between you two. That just confirmed it.'

The two sisters looked at each other.

'Okay,' said Gail, 'if you want to know it was love at first sight. I swear my knees went wobbly. I've never had that sort of thing happen before. I really do want him so much it hurts. It does, it really does.'

'Well, there you are. Go for it.'

'Go for it?'

'You say that you're in love with him. Hopeless sure as hell isn't. So, go for it.'

Gail sighed and put the bowl down on the counter.

'The thing is, I'm not sure he feels the same way.'

'Oh, I'm pretty sure he does.'

'How do you know?'

'I could tell by the way he choked on his lamb. That lamb was really nicely done. A man doesn't choke on his food unless he's serious about something.'

'I wish,' Gail sighed. 'Tom is it. Tom is the man I've looked for all my life. Unfortunately he's going out with Hopeless.

And he will continue going out with Hopeless. Why, I don't know. Who can ever know?'

She formed her hand into a fist.

'Why, Claire? Why? Why does a man like Tom end up being dragged around like a poodle by someone like shit-face?'

Chapter Fifty: Ave Maria

'It's almost time for the Queen's speech,' George Browne said. 'If anyone wants me I'll be in the television room.'

'I think I'm going to take a walk,' Robert said, standing up and stretching. 'If I don't get a bit of exercise now I'll never be able to move again.'

'Daddy, daddy, I wanna watch the queen.'

'And mightily bored you'll be,' muttered Tom. He stood up. 'I think I'm also up for a stroll.'

'I'll sit with Lucy and Davie,' said Patience. 'You two go for a walk.'

'Well, if Lucy wants to sit with her nan you can all go for a walk,' said Winifred Browne. 'Are you happy with that, Lucy?'

'Oh, yes! Just so as I can watch the queen.'

'Turncoat,' muttered Robert. 'Looks like I'm bringing up a monarchist.'

'Well, I wouldn't mind a stroll myself,' said Gail. 'Where are the others?'

'Jane and Claire are upstairs with Sarah. Claire said something about a siesta, and I think Jane is trying to rest. Peter and Becky and Hope are in the kitchen playing cards.'

'Well,' murmured Robert, 'let's get going before the preacher and Ave Maria decide they fancy joining us.'

They quickly got their coats and slipped out, each wearing different degrees of embarrassed shame at leaving the others.

Chapter Fifty-one: Lucy knows all

'Well, I was surprised,' said Tom as they strolled along the riverbank. 'I was rather dreading an explosion of some kind.'

'You're not the only one, Tom,' replied Robert. 'I was just waiting for dad to say something stupid. He normally manages even when he isn't trying.'

'I think you two deserve gold stars,' Patience said, putting her arm through her husband's. 'That prediction game with you two trying to beat each other kept everyone happy.'

'I wasn't trying to beat anyone,' said Tom.

'It's a man thing,' Gail said, putting her arm through Tom's. 'They're competitive even when they're not even trying.'

'It was just a bit of fun,' said Robert. 'Though you can tell a lot about people when they're having fun.'

'Oh? Such as what?'

'Well, Gail, take your prediction for Valerie. You said she'd move to Rome. That tells me you want her far away, but don't wish her any harm. That tells me that you're a kind and loveable person who can still recognise a nasty little tart.'

'Ah, well, Robert, that's one interpretation, but I'm afraid you're quite wrong there.'

'I am, Tom? And what, do tell, is the correct interpretation?'

'That Gail just hates Italians, especially the ones in Rome.'

'Tom!'

'Only kidding, Gail.'

'It's interesting, though, wondering where everyone will be and what they'll be doing in a year's time. I can't see us being here next Christmas. Travelling that distance with two kids will keep us going for a few years at least. And Patience's folks will demand that we go around to theirs next year.'

'Do they celebrate Christmas?'

'Oh, yes, big time. They're Christian, Chinese, and very confused.'

'You have a lot to put up with, Patience. What made you decide to marry Uncle Robert?'

'He's right, my parents are confused. As for Bobby, well, I think he must have spiked my tea. I can't imagine any other reason I would have agreed to marry him.'

Robert gave her a squeeze and they walked on in silence for a while.

'So who do you think made the most accurate prediction?' asked Gail.

'Lucy,' said Patience.

Chapter Fifty-two: Making up

'I'd better be off,' Jane Green said, looking out of the window. 'Tom's promised to drive me back to the hotel, and it'll be getting dark soon.'

'I wish you would stay,' said Claire. 'We could share a room, there's one along the corridor with two beds.'

Jane Green sat on the bed, kissed her and stroked her blonde hair.

'Maybe tomorrow, my sweet. I haven't got anything with me at the moment.' She smiled. 'It must be the spirit of Christmas. I swore blood I would never sleep here.'

'You could get your things and come back with Tom, mum. You have to go back either way.'

Her mother smiled at her again.

'We should have named you Florence. After that girl in one of Dickens' books. She was very sweet and forgiving.'

'I don't want to be sweet and forgiving.'

'I'm not sure you can avoid it, my darling. Okay, just because you're here, I'll have a word with your gran. If she's happy I'll come back tonight.'

'Just because of me? What about Gail?'

'Gail doesn't have a three-month-old baby to look after. Though I rather doubt that that situation will continue for very long.'

The two looked at other and grinned conspiratorially. And then they hugged each other.

Chapter Fifty-three: Christmas Night

'Well, I think that this has been the best Christmas for many a year,' said George Browne in his armchair next to the fire. 'And God bless us every one.'

'God bless us every one,' murmured the others.

'Good Queen's speech, dad?' asked Robert.

'Excellent, my boy, excellent. I tell you something, we're lucky to have her. I hope she goes on forever. She might have a fool for a son, and wastrels as grandchildren, but she is a living example of what made Britain great. I certainly hope I never live to see the day that idiot boy of hers becomes king. Oh, it has to happen, I grant you, I just never want to be alive to see it.'

'Great-great-great-grandad slept all through it!' accused Lucy.

'No, I did not, I just listened with my eyes closed, young girl.'

'Oh, yes you did!' chorused Gail and Tom. They looked at other and blushed.

'What? Ganging up on me, you little scoundrels? I'll teach you. Oh, no, I did not!'

'Oh, yes you did!' chorused everyone. George Browne chuckled.

'We must go and see a panto,' he said. 'Next year. You've never been to panto, have you, little Lucy?'

'She hasn't,' said Robert, stroking his daughter's head. 'I should have thought of that. We could have stayed in London a couple of days before coming here. Well, as you say, we'll do it next year. I haven't seen one since I was about ten.'

'What's a panto, dad?' asked Lucy.

'Ah, well, it's difficult to describe, honey. Big men get dressed up as ugly sisters, and the male and female leads are good looking young women. Every so often the kids in the audience get to shout "He's behind you!" '

'Why do they do that, dad?'

'Good question. I don't know. It's just one of those silly things people enjoy doing, I suppose.'

'Why don't you put on a pantomime for the children tomorrow night?' suggested Winifred Browne. 'I know it won't be professional, but I'm sure you could make up costumes from something.'

'Tom and Uncle Robert could be the two ugly sisters,' said Gail.

Robert winked at Tom.

'And if we're the two nasty, ugly, terrible sisters, maybe we rewrite the script a bit.'

'I think Claire would have to be Cinderella,' said Winifred Browne. 'And Gail would have to be Prince Charming.'

'I think I know where I come in,' muttered Valerie. 'Okay,' she said, 'I know, I know, I'm the wicked step-mother.'

'Well if the ugly sisters are going to rewrite the script I think we girls should stick together and write our own,' said Gail.

'Including the wicked step-mother?' asked Valerie.

'Including the wicked step-mother.'

'Sounds like a date to me,' said Robert. 'I'm in.'

'Sounds bloody crazy to me,' said Tom. 'Do you know how outnumbered we are?'

'Only in numbers, Tom, only in numbers.'

'Yes, well, that's what outnumbered usually means.'

'Outnumbered, Tom, but not out-foxed.'

'That's settled, then,' said Gail. 'The girls will meet in the East wing tomorrow to decide their strategy. The boys can meet in the West wing.'

'Silly nonsense,' muttered Peter.

'You could be right, Pete. Anyway, let's keep our secrets until the witching hour. It's time for another story. How about you, dad?'

'Ah, my boy, I could tell you many a story. Tomorrow, maybe. Yes, tomorrow, after your pantomime. A story of heroics. Of derring-do. Buchanan, that sort of thing.'

'You must have a story, Val.'

'Not one that can be told in front of the children,' murmured Gail.

'I've never been able to tell stories,' Valerie said. 'I don't know how people do.'

'Oh, come on Val,' said Rob. 'Anyone can make up a story.'

Valerie shrugged her shoulders. She thought for a few moments.

'Okay, then. Once upon a time there was a happily married young couple named Sammy and Sally. One day Sally came to Sammy and said, darling I'm pregnant. Sammy was very happy but also very worried because he knew nothing about babies. But nine months passed and the baby was born without any complications. It was a little girl, who they named Judith. Judith grew up a very happy little girl in a very happy family. Now, next door there was a little boy called Jake, and as they grew up Judith and Jake played together. They went to school together, went to university together, and realised that they were in love. So they got married. One day Judith came to Jake and said, darling I'm pregnant. So they had a little baby called Sammy and lived happily ever after.'

'That's it?'

'Well, I told you I'm no good at stories.'

'Oh, come on, Valerie, surely you can come up with a better story than that. Even if it's based on one you read once.

'Even if it's based on someone you shagged once,' murmured

Gail. 'Must be plenty of choices there.'

'Okay, okay. You want a story of doomed love, then? Or unrequited love?'

'It doesn't have to be a love story, Val.'

'No,' muttered Claire, 'it could be a hate story.'

Chapter Fifty-four: Valerie's story

'Okay. Let me see. Okay, once upon a time there was a rich and beautiful queen. She reigned over a huge country, all the way to the sea. And the islands. She knew that she would have to get married one day. She wasn't in a hurry because she quite enjoyed being queen on her own. And anyway, none of the men she met seemed worth it. But her advisors kept on at her. You will have to choose a husband soon, they said, the people demand it. She didn't want to, but still they kept going on at her. Then one day a man came to the capital where her palace was, a man from one of the islands. He was the son of a minor aristocrat, nothing special, but of high enough rank. She thought he looked cute. And so she decided, very well, she'll marry him. And so she announced her decision to her advisors.

'It turned out that the man was already married. But that wasn't a problem, because his wife wasn't a member of royalty, and under the law that meant that they weren't really married. So the queen's chief minister went to the man and told him that the queen had chosen him for a husband. Now the queen hadn't been told about the man's wife, her people thought her word was law, so they didn't need to worry about such things. And the man thought, well, to marry the queen, that would be a big step up. So he went home to his island, told his wife what had happened, packed his bags, and left for the capital.

'But his wife was a very jealous woman. When he had gone she put all his things, including his famous war shield, in a pile. She got their children together, and before they set off for her father's island, she lit the pile.

291

'When the man arrived at the palace he announced that he had left his wife to come to be king. And the queen said, I didn't know you were already married. No, that's silly, go back to your wife. And so he returned to his island, to find his house in ashes, his wife and children gone.

'And the queen announced that she would never formally marry. She would remain queen without a king. She might take a consort from time to time, but they would never be king. And, well, it all worked out pretty well. The people thought it a good idea, and the advisors were told to shut up or they'd be fed to the palace dogs. And they all lived happily ever after.'

'How many children did the man have?' asked Robert.

'Two, why?'

'Thought so. Medea from the queen's side, as it were.'

'Well, yeah, sort of. I always thought her husband was a right shit. I never could understand why she would want to kill her kids.'

'Husband deserved all he got,' noted George Browne. 'I like that one, Val. Come-uppance, that's what it is. Man deserts his loyal wife when he thinks he's got a chance for something better, loses everything. Very good.'

'What about you, Jane?'

'Me?'

'A story. Come on, we've each given a story.'

Chapter Fifty-five: Jane's Story

'A story. Well ... let me think ... You know, there is a story I've often thought about. Not quite Charles Dickens, though.'

'Come on, Jane,' said Robert, his eyes twinkling in the firelight, 'I've always wondered what sort of story my older sis would like.'

'Oh, I'm not sure it's a question of liking it. Just something that stuck in my mind once.'

'Come along, then, Jane. Come on, the children will be falling asleep before you get started.'

'Okay, dad, okay. Well, my story starts in France in – well, the 1820s, I suppose. There was this young girl – woman – called Fantine. She was a lovely young woman, but very inexperienced. Very young and naive. She got in with a group of young noblemen and fell in love with one of them. She thought it would end up in marriage, but one day the young noblemen, having had their sport, simply upped and left. It was then that Fantine discovered that she was pregnant, and a few months later gave birth to a daughter, Cosette.'

'Foul! I declare a foul!' cried Robert. 'That's Victor Hugo's Les Miserables.'

'Les Miserables?' asked Gail. 'I love that musical.'

'Well, it isn't exactly Les Miserables, but that is where I got the idea from.'

'How different is it?'

'Well, I think it's quite different.'

'Very well, then, continue. Does Fantine leave Cosette with the bar-keeper and his wife?'

'Oh, yes. And she goes off to the city, gets a cheaply-paid job, and sends all the money she can to the inn-keeper and his wife to pay for Cosette. And they, of course, are diddling her. They're treating little Cosette as child-labour, slave-labour, feeding her on scraps and clothing her in rags, while demanding more and more money from Fantine under pretence of having to pay for doctors' bills. Making Cosette sleep in a hole next to the pigsty, beating her every day, that sort of thing. Anyway, a letter arrives at the place Fantine is working, her secret gets out, and she's fired from her job – not, of course, because she has a child, but because she refused to sleep with the foreman. So she's thrown out on the streets, tries to beg for a living, sells her hair for a few francs, and is facing a life as a prostitute merely to earn enough to stay alive.

'And then, one day, she notices an advert for a maid. This is very strange, since maids are normally taken on by reference, and no-one who could afford a maid would advertise in such a way. Anyway, it's her last chance before the gutter, she steals some decent clothes, makes herself as presentable as possible, and goes to the address. It's a tall, gloomy house. Most of the windows are shuttered, it's grey, it needs attention, it's almost as if it were a place to die in.

'She reminds herself that this is all that stands between her and a life on the streets, with no-one left to care for little Cosette. She knocks on the door. It opens slowly, creaking ...'

'And an old man with balding white hair opens it,' said Robert. 'I can see him now. Gaunt, desiccated, yellow.'

'No. He's thin. He's about forty or fifty. He looks like a scholar who hasn't seen the daylight for too long. It's winter, of course, and he stands there in the almost darkness with a candle illuminating the side of his face.'

'Illuminating. I like that word.'

'Yes?' he asks.

'Sir, I've come about the advert. For a maid, sir.

'A maid?

'Yes, sir.

'A maid. I see. Come in.

'So she enters the house, her heart beating. She remembers all the stories she has heard, of young women being kidnapped for the Eastern slave trade. Of victims chosen for medical experiments. Dissection while alive, their body parts shared amongst students before being thrown away. She quivers as the man slowly and carefully closes and locks the door. He turns and looks at her once again, the candle in his hand. She thinks that he has intelligent eyes, but wicked eyes. They seem to be laughing at her.

'So, you wish to become our maid, do you? he asks.

'Please, sir, I need the work. I am desperate, she cries.

'Desperate, eh? Well, desperate you will need to be. Before I can hire you, you must pass a test.

'A test, sir?

'I have an elderly mother. She has many needs. She is very particular. If she says yes, then you shall be her maid. Follow me.

'So she follows this strange man upstairs. All the while, every step, her fear grows. What is wrong with this elderly mother? What sort of harridan is she?

'Or, even, is there an elderly mother? Is she being led up the stairs to a room in which she will be locked before being sold into something far worse than she could imagine?

'On each step her heart tells her – Flee! Flee! Now, while you can!

'And then the strange man opens a door and enters a bedroom. Fantine follows. Inside there is a bed, and in the bed a hideous old woman, a woman dressed in off-white bedclothes, her eyes piercing as an eagle's. A hateful, horrible old eagle.

'Maman, says the strange man, we have an applicant for the maid's position.

'About time! cries the old woman, thumping her fist on her quilt. About time, these girls expect too much. They want to live in luxury. Well, girl, you should know that we are poor. And you will have to accept it. Come in to the light, girl, I wish to see you.

'Fantine steps into the light. Because she has not been eating properly, because she has suffered from the cold, her face is blue and pinched. Because her hair has been shorn, her cap clings to her hairless head. She wears the face of ugly poverty.

'Good! cries the old woman. She is ugly. It is good that she is ugly. These sluts think they are pretty and run off to marry a man. This one will never find a man. Have you told her her wage?

'Not yet, maman. I wanted you to see her first.

'Well, stop shilly-shallying. Get her to work immediately. I wish to have my supper and retire for the night. It is too tiresome with these girls. Hurry up. Get on with it.

'Fantine and the strange man retire from the bedchamber and go downstairs. The man stops and looks at her.

'Your wage will be two sous a day, he says – I don't know the exact amount, but it was what she was earning at the factory. But, if my mother ever asks, tell her I am paying you two sous a week. There are some things she does not need to know.

'At this he giggles to himself, a strange sound, almost that of a madman.

'But she will be living in. It is a small wage, but again she can send money to the inn-keeper and his wife to support her daughter. All she prays is that the strange man who giggles will not find out, for then she will again lose her job.

'So she begins life as a maid. It is hard work, the old woman is a tough task-master even if she is bedridden, and the strange man goes out to work every day, leaving her at the whim of his mother. Not only is she a maid, but she has to become cook, washer, everything from ordering the food to making it. And the mother demands to see each receipt. Every time she buys fish the mother complains that she could have bought it more cheaply elsewhere. Each time she buys soap the mother knows that she is being cheated, soap never cost this much. Tea never cost so much! Surely this maid is cheating them!

'But Fantine learns to live with this. The strange man, Monsieur Charles he calls himself, is kind in his way. Whenever his mother rants about Fantine being a thief he agrees with her, and then winks at Fantine. Fantine learns that it is all about placating the old woman. Letting her complain. She has no other life.

'And then one day Fantine takes the old lady her morning cup of tea, only to discover that she is ...

'Dead.

'This, she realises, is the end of another story. Without the old woman she will not be required. All the money she could spare she had sent to the inn-keeper and his wife. Now she faces yet again a life of uncertainty. However, she collects herself and goes down to inform the strange man. He is sitting at the breakfast table as he always is at that time of the morning. She curtsies, apologises, and explains that she fears that his mother has passed into heaven.

'He sits there for a while, his porridge congealing. She feels sorry for him. He is a strange man, but he has been very fair to her – indeed, he has looked after her, ensuring that she eat the same as he did, and not what his mother had ordered that she be allowed. He sighed, looked at her, and sighed again.

'I will have to inform the undertakers, he says. That is a man's job, I think.

'He sat there for some minutes before moving. The whole of the next few days he seemed to be wandering in a land of his own. He hardly spoke to Fantine. He attended the funeral in complete silence. Afterward he sat down in the lounge and stared at the wall. Fantine entered to ask him if he wished to have dinner, since he had eaten hardly anything over the past few days. When she entered he gave her a small smile.

'It is over, he said. And now my life can begin.

'Fantine looked at as if he were crazy. He giggled and jumped up.

'Fantine, tomorrow we start. We will buy new curtains – bright curtains. We will clear out all the old, dark furniture. The walls must be painted. He clapped his hands. Yes! he exclaimed, tomorrow we let the sunlight in!

'For the next weeks it seemed as if there was no time to pause. The old house was redecorated from top to bottom. Everything was washed, repainted, or thrown out. Monsieur Charles even changed his entire wardrobe, throwing away his usual dark and dreary suits for something brighter. Fantine was told to buy herself new clothes. And when this was all completed, he instructed her to come to him in the library.

'Fantine, you have been a loyal and dedicated servant, he said. You have coped with my poor late mother's moods. You have always carried out my little orders faithfully. I would gladly provide you with the best of references. He paused. You realise, of course, that it is impossible for you, as a single young woman, to stay in the same house alone with me, a bachelor?

'This was the moment that Fantine had been dreading. Monsieur Charles had no longer any need of her. And what he said was true. The neighbours had already begun gossiping about the scandal of the two of them living under the same roof. Monsieur Charles would no doubt have to find some old woman as housekeeper, an old widow beyond reproof.

'Just then he giggled.

'Fantine, I am going to fire you as a maid. However I will only do that if you agree to a different position – become my wife!

'Fantine stared at him. She could not believe what he had just said. She had never considered this possibility.

'I know I am not a young man – but I am not that old yet. And though I do not have a fortune, I have inherited enough money for a comfortable life. My poor mother was always afraid of poverty, that was why she spent as little as possible, yet she never really needed to. You and I – we're alone in the world together. We get on well. We are used to each other. What better start could a marriage have? If anything, should not man and wife be best friends?

'Fantine continued to stare. What Monsieur Charles had said was perfectly true. He would never be Prince Charming, but he would make a very good real-life husband. After all her years of suffering it would be like a fairy-tale come true.

'And then she burst into tears.

'I am sorry, monsieur, but I cannot marry you, she cried.

'But why not? You are not already married, are you?

'She shook her head, tears pouring down her face, unable to speak.

'Come, Fantine, it is not because I am too old? Because I am not enough of a man for you? Why? Why can you not marry me?

'Because I have a daughter! Fantine blurted out.

'Monsieur Charles sat down. He looked at her.

'A daughter?

'Fantine nodded.

'But no husband?

'Fantine shook her head, head downcast.

'Where is this daughter?

'An inn-keeper and his wife are looking after her.

'Monsieur Charles pursed his lips.

'So, he said, this is how you repay my trust. You keep an illegitimate child from my knowledge. You are a fallen woman, yet you come into my service pretending to be an honest young girl. He leaned forward, twisting his head to look up into her face. Do you think she will make a pretty bridesmaid? he asked. And then he giggled again and jumped up, putting his hands on her shoulders. Fantine, I think I love you even more. And this old house needs the laughter of a child in it.

'But, sir, the neighbours –

'Ha! The neighbours. A fig to the neighbours. We will tell them that your husband died. We will tell them that he was a pirate whose ship was sunk by the English. We will tell them whatever we feel like telling them. Yes, a fig to the neighbours! I will plant a whole orchard of fig trees to the neighbours!

'And so, before Fantine could recover from the shock they were married and on their way to pick up Cosette. The marriage had taken place first as it was a long journey to the inn where Cosette was staying, and travel permits and other bureaucracy had delayed them.

'But there was another shock for both Fantine and Monsieur Charles. When they arrived at the inn they discovered not a happy, playful eight-year-old, but a suspicious, thin, almost starved little girl in rags, more animal than human. All the protests by the inn-keeper and his wife could not hide the fact that the girl had been cruelly treated. The only thing that prevented Monsieur Charles from physically attacking the inn-keeper was the difficulty they had in persuading Cosette to enter the carriage they had arrived in.

'After the long journey back they brought Cosette into their home. She immediately ran for the smallest, darkest space she could find, cowering there, her large, angry eyes staring out from the darkness. And so began their married life. Cosette would fight against wearing the new clothes they had bought for her, changing back into her rags as soon as they turned their backs. She refused to eat at the table, stealing food from the pantry and gulping it down in her hiding hole. Their plans for enrolling her at school were impossible. She was more a wild animal than a child. She would creep around the house, especially at night, avoiding others wherever possible.

'Fantine and Monsieur Charles were at their wits' end after six months. Doctors had been consulted, but their advice had been useless. Mostly they recommended that the girl needed a good hiding. Indeed, after her treatment at the inn, it appeared that the only thing she responded to was the threat of physical violence. It began to appear that their only choice would be to have her put into a special school which treated street children, and hope that their experience might have better effects. Yet it broke Fantine's heart just to think of such a thing.

'The choice seemed to disappear when Fantine discovered that she was pregnant. Cosette often broke things purely out of her malicious spirit. She had broken all the toys they had bought for her. She had been accused of attacking little children in the neighbourhood. She would be far too much of a danger to a new-born little baby. She would probably resent its appearance, however little love she showed for the attentions of her mother and step-father.

'Fantine's unexpected pregnancy also had an effect on Monsieur Charles. He became much more forceful and strict. He forbade Fantine any work, hiring both a cook and a maid to look after the house. He also lost patience with Cosette.

'You, young lady, are going to have to learn to behave properly! he exploded one day after she had knocked yet another vase down, breaking it. You are going to have a little baby sister or brother soon, and unless you start behaving you will be sent to a school for naughty children and never see the baby. Firstly you are going to dress properly, he said, dragging her upstairs to the bedroom which was supposed to be hers, but which she had refused to sleep in. He threw her inside. I will be back in twenty minutes. You will either have changed into decent clothes or I will change you myself! Then he slammed the door closed and stomped back downstairs.

'And a remarkable thing happened. When he returned, his anger having abated, and terrified that he might have to carry out his threat, he found Cosette sitting on her bed, eyes blazing, but dressed in new clothes. The dowdiest clothes she could find, but at least presentable.

'Now, my girl, we are going to have tea, he said, trying to retain the stern and immutable appearance of a father who would brook no opposition. And you are going to sit down like a good little lady should. Out! And no running down the stairs!

'And from that day they dated what they privately called Cosette's recovery. It was not easy, Cosette still acted like a cornered rat towards Monsieur Charles, but he learnt a skill as a rat tamer. Cosette also developed a fascination for this new brother or sister she was going to have, and she spent many hours simply staring at her mother. One day she watched her mother inspect a bowl of fruit in the dining room.

'Oh, dear, said her mother, these apples are going off. I'll take these to the kitchen.

'No! exclaimed young Cosette fiercely, the first word she had ever used in the house. Daddy says no! Mummy mustn't work!

'And to Fantine's amazement Cosette took the bowl of fruit from her and marched to the kitchen. Bad apple! she told the cook, put the bowl on the table, and ran back to her mother. Mummy mustn't work with baby, she said, scowling.

'Fantine turned her face to hide the tears which had sprung to her eyes. An idea struck her.

'Well, my darling, mummy has to do some shopping. Some cakes for tea from the bakers. And meat from the butchers.

'Cosette get cakes. And meat, said Cosette.

'Ah, my darling, but I do need the walk. And the baker and butcher wouldn't sell to you, my dear, you're too young.

'Cosette looked as if she wouldn't permit the baker and butcher to show such temerity. But she gave in.

'Cosette carry for mummy, she decided.

'Will you, darling? That would be a great help to mummy.

'Thereafter Cosette became her mother's guard. If she remotely suspected of the baker, the butcher, the maid or the cook of not treating her mother with respect she would growl at them. It took a while to train her out of this, but her glare was still sufficient to make others terrified off her. The only person she didn't try this on with was her step-father; he, she appeared to think, was an unfortunate choice of her mother's which would just have to be tolerated. And then, when Fantine went into labour, they formed an alliance as neither was permitted anywhere near the bedroom where Fantine was giving birth. Both were exiled to the library, where Monsieur Charles paced up and down, muttering and talking to Cosette about not being allowed to be master in his own house, and repeating time and again to Cosette that Fantine would be fine, giving birth was entirely natural. Cosette seemed to absorb his worries and attitude, pacing up and down behind her step-father, her hands behind her back exactly as his were, a mirror image of his worries. He tugged at his hair: she tugged at hers. He ran a finger around his collar, she ran a finger around hers.

'You must learn to say 'I', Cosette, he said. You shouldn't use your name. It's 'I love mummy', not 'Cosette loves mummy'. I'm sure your mother will be just fine. Giving birth is entirely natural. Nothing to worry about. Stop tugging your hair like that.

'You tugging yours.

'That's different.

'No, it isn't.

'Yes, it is.

'No it isn't.

'It will all be fine. Entirely natural. Nothing to worry about. Don't walk into the wall like that, Cosette, it isn't nice.

'You walked into the wall yourself.

'Did I?

'And so it went on. Until there was a sudden cry, and Monsieur Charles and Cosette looked at each other. They charged for the door and ran up the stairs. Even then they were not permitted to enter the bedroom until everything had been cleaned up. They spent another hour pacing up and down the corridor.

'And then they were allowed to see little Cosette's even littler sister.

'Cosette never looked back after that. She learnt to speak properly, having been warned that her sister would pick up her bad habits if she weren't careful. She went everywhere with her mother and sister. She no longer growled, but learnt to sing, as it was something the baby loved listening to. And in time the Charles's became a respectable, well-loved family in the neighbourhood.'

Chapter Fifty-six: It's really true

'That's it?' asked Gail.

'I think that was brilliant, sis,' said Robert. 'Excellent, in fact. You managed to combine the realism of an abused child with the happy ending.'

'I agree with Gail,' said Claire. 'I want to know more. What happened to Cosette? Did she get married and have children of her own? Or did she just look after her little sister all her life?'

'What was the baby's name?' asked Tom. Jane raised her hands.

'Whoah, whoah, I surrender. Okay, let me see. I think Monsieur Charles would have wanted the baby to be called Fantine, but I don't think Fantine would have agreed. I think in the end they would have called her Georgette, after Monsieur Charles's father.'

'Monsieur Charles's father was called George?'

'He is now.'

'And Cosette? What happened to her in the end?'

'Cosette and Georgette remained very close for their entire lives. Monsieur Charles lived to a ripe old age. He lived long enough to see both girls get married, and to see his first grandchildren. In fact he outlived Fantine. She died of pneumonia after catching a chill in her early seventies. He died a few months later, the death certificate says old age, but the truth was that he wanted to join his wife.'

'Who did Cosette marry? Some gay young blade?'

'Oh, no, she married a young lawyer, a shy young thing. She bossed him terribly, but she also loved him terribly. They had three young sons. Two of the sons died in the First World

War, but the third lived. He took over a vineyard, which his own daughter runs today, though she's getting on herself. She has a son and a daughter who do most of the work. And they have children of their own.'

'And Georgette?'

'My goodness. Georgette. Well, Georgette, after all the coddling she had as a child, both from her mother and her sister – and her father – I'm afraid she was a bit of a trial. She remained a bit of a little girl all her life. She married an older man – quite a wealthy man – he died and she then married another man, slightly younger than her first husband. All in all she had a total of six husbands and five children.'

'You're not making this up, are you, sis?' asked Robert. 'This is a real life story someone told you, isn't it?' Jane smiled.

'I stayed at the vineyard once. We were doing some work for them, advising them on their sales strategy in the U.K. Fantine's great-grandson told me the story. With names and places changed, of course. But that's enough, someone else's turn. All this talking is tiring.'

'Anyone for a top-up?' asked Gail as Jane Green yawned and lay her head on a cushion next to her daughter, holding her bandaged arm into her side.

'I'll have a small glass of wine,' Claire said. 'What about you, mum?'

There was no reply. Jane Green was already fast asleep.

'I wouldn't mind a small whiskey,' said Tom. 'Who is next in the story telling line?'

'What about you, mum?' asked Robert.

'Not tonight, my dear. I think we're all a little tired. I know I am. It's been such a pleasant day. The type of day you want to stay awake to continue, but also to drift off in sleep remembering. I think I shall just finish this sherry and be off to bed. After having woken your father, of course.'

George Browne snorted, shook his head and looked around him.

'You're right, you know, Jane. Girl needed a good clip around the ear. That's what she needed. Unfortunate, what happened, but you can't blame everything on the past, can you.' He peered at Jane. 'Gone to sleep, has she? Well, better not wake her up. Could do with a decent night's kip myself.'

Robert rubbed his chin and looked at his father.

'Dad, I remember you waking me up to send me to bed the one Christmas. I never understood that.'

'Did I? Nonsense. I'd never do that. Let sleeping children lie, that's always been my motto.' He looked at his son. 'You're off the day after tomorrow, aren't you Robert?'

'Yes, dad. Show Lucy some of London, then back to the States.'

'A pity, my boy, a pity. You know, young Lucy, I'm proud of your father. He's a professor, you know. Means a lot. Come to that I'm proud of all my children and grand-children. And great-grand-children now, of course. The times I've come to despair of them! But this Christmas just goes to show.'

'Dad?'

'Yes, Robert?'

'Lucy's fallen asleep. I think it's been a long day for her. I'd better get her to bed.'

'Of course, my boy. Reminds me of you falling asleep waiting for Christmas so that you could open your presents. Carried you to bed a number of times.'

'Happy days.'

'Happy days indeed. Well, time to turn in. I'll see you all tomorrow. Coming, Win?'

'Yes, my dear. Children, you won't forget to put the lights out and make sure that everything's locked up? And don't forget to bank down the fire.'

'Yes, gran. Sleep tight.'

'Well, I'm off too,' said Maria-Hope. She gave Tom a meaningful look as she, Peter and Rebeccah left.

'Beddy-byes for me,' yawned Valerie.

'You're off to bed?'

'I feel absolutely shattered. I could do with twelve hours of sleep.'

'I suppose I'd better wake mum,' Claire said, looking down at her mother's face. She stroked her mother's hair.

'I think that accident hit her harder than she admits,' Tom said. 'If it was just a clip on the side of the car her wrist wouldn't be so badly strained.'

'What are you trying to say, Tom? That mum is faking it?'

'What I'm saying is that, if we got a chance to look at her car, we'd probably find the driver's seat smashed in. I think she's trying to understate things. Mothers do that, you know.'

'Poor mum,' whispered Claire.

'Yes, well, let's wake her and get her upstairs,' said Gail.

Between them the two sisters woke their mother as gently as possible before each putting an arm around her and helping her upstairs. They left Tom and Patience in the lounge.

Chapter Fifty-seven: At the end of the day

'You never had the chance to carry Rebeccah out of a burning building,' said Patience. 'Any regrets?'

'She told you about that?'

'Women are terrible gossips, Tom.'

Tom looked into the fire.

'Did you know that four in the morning is the ideal time for an attack?' he asked.

'How do you mean?'

'Just that. Armies try to strike when their opponents are most vulnerable. General opinion is that four in the morning is the best time.' He rolled over and looked at her. 'It was bad enough when everybody was at daggers drawn. This sudden outbreak of peace makes me nervous.'

'It was a very nice day,' she said, standing up. 'There's a Chinese proverb about that. I can never remember what it is. There seems to be a Chinese proverb for everything. Sleep well, Tom.'

'You too. Good night.'

He lay watching the fire, until Gail dropped down next to him. He put an arm around her.

'Your mum okay?'

'Fast asleep. Claire's also fast. I'm about falling all over the place myself.'

'Better to get to bed, then.'

'Together?'

There was a silence.

'I'm afraid I'm too tired to think lustful thoughts,' Gail said.

'Me too.'

'I'll get myself to bed then.'

He stirred.

'I'd better come up with you. Otherwise I'll be found here in the morning, snoring away.'

Upstairs they kissed.

'What are we to do?' asked Tom.

Chapter Fifty-eight: Monday, Boxing Day

'Gran?' asked Claire, coming into the kitchen carrying Sarah to find her grandmother standing next to the sink. 'What are you doing up? It's not even seven o'clock yet.'

'Um?' replied her grandmother, as if returning from somewhere far away. 'Ah, Claire, let me make you some tea. I think what's in the pot is on the cold side. Did Sarah wake you up?'

'Yes,' Claire said, sitting down. 'She decided she wanted a feed. And then I thought I heard noises downstairs, so I thought I'd see who was up.'

'She's a lovely little thing, isn't she? Wakes up, has a feed and goes straight back to sleep. Such a sweet little thing.'

'Gran, are you okay? You're looking – a bit stressed.'

Her grandmother brought the teapot over to the table, sat down and poured Claire a cup. A man appeared in the kitchen doorway, carrying a heavy black bag.

'I'll be off to organise things, Mrs Browne,' he said.

'Ah, Doctor Jameson. Many thanks for all you've done. Oh, this is my grand-daughter, Claire.'

'Morning,' the man nodded to Claire.

'Morning.'

'Won't you stay for a cup of tea, doctor?'

'No, thanks, Mrs Browne, I have the various arrangements to take care of. You'll be okay? You've got company?'

'I'll be fine, doctor. The house is full of my children and grandchildren. And even little great-grandchildren. This is Sarah here, Claire's little daughter.'

'Hello, little Sarah,' the man smiled wanly at the sleeping baby. 'I'll see you later, Mrs Browne, take care of yourself.

Claire,' he nodded and left.

'What's wrong, gran? Why's a doctor here? At this time of the morning? On Boxing day?'

Her grandmother took a sip of tea and put the cup down slowly.

'Claire, I'm afraid I have some bad news for you. Your grandfather passed away during the night.'

Claire looked back at her. Her grandmother sat staring into nowhere.

'Dead?' asked Claire.

'It was a good way to go, I suppose. Painless.'

'But – but – how? He hasn't complained of feeling ill or anything. I mean, there was that business at lunch I heard about, but – He can't have –'

'It's okay, my dear. I know it must be a shock for you. It wasn't completely unexpected. He's had two heart attacks in the past two years, and a minor stroke. Doctor Jameson warned me that the next could happen at any time, and that it could well be fatal. And so it was. And so it was.'

'But – couldn't they do anything? I mean – I thought – well, heart surgery these days ...'

'You know your grandfather, my dear. The only reason he saw a doctor when he had his attacks was because he couldn't stop them taking him to the hospital in an ambulance. I got Doctor Jameson to check up on him as well as he could by pretending to come and see about my health once a month.'

'But, gran, shouldn't he have been taking tablets or something? Surely something could have been done.'

'He was taking tablets, my dear. He wasn't that silly. But he made sure they were kept in our bathroom where nobody would see them. He didn't want anyone to know that he had a weakness. That's why he kept falling asleep, because of the tablets.' She sighed. 'I don't think he took the proper dosage yesterday. He wanted everything to be – so perfect. I think he did the same the day before, that's why he had a turn. I made him take them afterwards, once we'd got him upstairs.'

Claire looked back at her grandmother, lost for words. Sarah opened her mouth and gurgled, looking up at her mother. Then she began making a noise halfway between a laugh and a cry.

'She wants her nappy changed,' Claire said, standing up. 'Oh, Sarah, you do choose your moments badly.'

'Not at all, my dear,' her grandmother said, also standing. 'Come, let's go change her nappy together. I think I'll be needing to keep myself busy today. And she's such a sweet little baby. She really makes me wish that I had more.'

It was a sober breakfast. Nobody apart from Lucy would have eaten anything had it not been for Mrs Browne encouraging them, pointing out that it was going to be a long day and they would need something in their stomachs.

Chapter Fifty-nine: Sympathy

'Grandad died last night,' Gail said.

'What?'

'I said, grandad died last night.'

Valerie looked back at her through bleary, blood-shot eyes, as if Gail was speaking a language she could not understand.

'What?' she asked again.

'For Christ's sake, Val, it's simple enough isn't it? My grandfather, remember, the one you kept flirting with, he's dead. Dead. Understand?'

Valerie stared back at her.

'Is he ...'

'Is he what?'

'Is he – still here?'

'No, Val, that's the point. He's gone to Valhalla, paradise, heaven, somewhere. He's dead.'

'I meant – is the body still here?'

'No, they took him away half an hour ago.'

'Thank God for that,' sighed Valerie, closing her eyes and lying back on the pillows. 'Being in a house with a dead body would freak me out.'

'Your sympathy is duly noted,' Gail said walking out. 'I didn't realise what a truly one hundred per cent diamond-studded fucking bitch you were until now,' she called back as she headed for the stairs.

When she walked back into the kitchen almost everyone suddenly appeared to feel the need to do something, to carry on doing something, or to start conversations about nothing in particular. Only Rob looked at her, a wry smile on his face.

'Valerie the tart say something to piss you off?' he asked.

'Bobby!' admonished his wife. 'Do you really have to use language like that?'

'It's okay, my dear,' said Mrs Browne. 'Robert has always been like that. He likes to surprise people.'

'He'll get a surprise from me if he doesn't watch it,' threatened his wife. Gail threw herself into a chair.

'She was worried about being in the same house as a dead body,' she said. 'Never mind that grandad's just died. No, first thing she thinks about is herself. Bitch.'

'Now, now, my dear,' said her grandmother. 'We all react differently at times like this. Now, there's no use moping around. I know it's been a bit of a shock for all of us, but the best thing to do is keep busy. Life goes on. Claire, you can help me prepare lunch. The rest of you find something to do, a walk would be best, you won't be able to concentrate on any games or anything.'

'I'll give you a hand, Mrs Browne,' offered Tom.

'Me too,' said most of the rest.

'No, no, don't be silly now. Gail, you can also give me a hand, the rest of you shoo, go on now. If you want to help me, do your best to carry on as normal.'

'Now,' she said once the others had left, 'I know Boxing Day is normally a day for leftovers and sandwiches, but I think today we'll have a full meal. In the dining room. Roast potatoes. Broccoli. Beans. Oh, no, perhaps not beans, can't have two greens. Or shall we?'

'I don't think anyone will have much of an appetite,' Gail said.

'I know, dear. We'll just have to do our best.'

'A few pre-lunch drinks might be in order,' Claire noted.

'Good idea, Claire.'

Chapter sixty: Boxing Day afternoon

Lunch was less sombre than breakfast. They had had time to let the news sink in. It wasn't a jovial occasion, but the pre-lunch drinks had relaxed them to the point of allowing subdued conversation. After lunch, and once the dishes and pots had been washed and stored away, they retired to the blazing fire in the lounge.

'Started snowing yet?' Peter asked, joining Robert at the window.

'It's trying to sleet. Can't see it making snow this afternoon.'

'Lousy weather.'

'We can't sit around moping here the whole afternoon,' Tom said. 'We'll end up going crazy. Anyone fancy a walk?'

'You go for a walk,' Peter said. 'We have just had a loss in the family. You probably don't share out feelings.' Tom looked at him, shook his head and walked out of the room.

'Jesus, Pete, what's wrong with you?' asked Robert softly. 'Tom's right. If we sit around saying nothing to each other all afternoon we will go crazy.'

'Yeah, maybe. I just can't stand that self-important egotist. Thinks being a journalist makes him special. He's just a jumped-up working class yob with the dirt still under his nails.' Robert looked at him.

'Nothing to do with the fact that he's Maria's boyfriend by any chance?'

Peter shrugged.

'Ex-boyfriend more like it.'

'You forgot to make a phone call on Christmas day,' Valerie said to Gail. 'Something about wishing someone a crappy histmas?'

'Oh, do shut it, Val.'

'Found somebody else to occupy your, er, mind?'

'Now what are we going to do?' asked Winifred Browne, entering the almost silent lounge. 'You can't sit around moping the whole afternoon.'

'Tom was just saying that,' Robert said. 'Why don't we have a game of Trivial Pursuit or something?'

'Where is Tom?' asked his mother.

'Gone to his room to sulk,' Maria-Hope said. 'Peter told him to get lost and he didn't like it.'

'Well, we can't have that. Ask him to come down. We'll find something to do. Maybe there's a decent film on the television.'

They looked at each other. The idea of sitting in the television room where George Browne had spent so much time sleeping did not appeal. Winifred Browne sighed.

'Well, what about carrying on with our stories?'

That suggestion was met with silence.

'I tell you what, I'll make myself a little sherry and tell a story. How's that?'

'A story, gran?'

'Yes, a story. Hope, why don't you ask Tom to come down? Let's not have any petty arguments today.'

'If he wants to sulk he can sulk, I don't care,' Maria-Hope replied.

'Oh, I'll go get him,' said Gail. 'This is just being childish.'

Upstairs she found Tom finishing his packing.

'Going?' she asked.

'Definitely. I've had enough of this madhouse. The only reason I came was because of Maria, and I can't see that relationship going much further.'

'What about our relationship?' Tom looked at her.

'You mean the quick shag we had?'

'Is that what you see it as?'

He shrugged.

'That's what you wanted, wasn't it?' he asked.

'No. I was thinking of that as a minimum. I didn't think you would split up with Hope, so I wasn't hoping for more. But if you are single again, why not?'

'You serious?'

'Yes, I am.' He looked at her again and nodded slowly.

'We can give it a try, I suppose.'

She sat down on the bed and looked up at him.

'You make it sound so romantic, Thomas.' He grinned wryly.

'Not the most romantic situation I've ever been in.'

'Oh, I don't know. Let's face it, most people get together and then meet the relations. We've done it the other way around.'

'I tell you what, I'll give you my number. You can call me when you get back from Wildfell Hall. Right now I'm heading home. A nice quiet flat in London. The neighbour plays her music too loud, her cats piss all over my garden, we no longer speak to each other, but it sounds like Arcadian bliss compared to this at the moment.'

'You can't leave now, Tom. Gran asked if you'd come down. She'd be very upset if you left.'

Tom sighed and sat down on the bed next to her. She took his hand.

'It's a toss-up, isn't it?' said Tom. 'If I go your gran would be upset, and she's had enough of that already today. If I stay Maria will have a go at me every opportunity she can find, Peter also, and I can't see that making your gran terribly happy.'

He sighed again.

'I seem to have made a real balls up of things. I'm still trying to work out where I went wrong. I thought I was in love with Maria. I thought she was in love with me. Looks like we were both wrong.'

'She is attractive, in her own way,' said Gail. She paused. 'But, Tom, honestly, she's done the same thing to every other boyfriend she's ever had. Strings them along until they're in a relationship and then just drags them behind her.'

He nodded.

'I should have known. The very first time she told me she was vegetarian. It was on our first date. I'd just ordered a steak with all the trimmings and was about to tuck in. She said to me, "You are what you eat." She gave me a smile, like she was just teasing me.'

'She's good at that look. Until you get to know her. Then you realise that it's not so much teasing as slipping the knife in.'

'The thing is – well, I looked at her plate. I thought at the time it was a bit of a warning. I was going to make a joke of it, but I thought better of it. That's when I should have known. If you're going to stifle your sense of humour for a relationship it just isn't worth it.'

'I don't understand.'

He looked up at her.

'She was eating a nut cutlet with coleslaw. She had fruit cake for dessert.'

Gail smiled. '"You are what you eat," she echoed. She patted his hand. 'Come downstairs and sit on the couch next to me. Hope and Pete will just glare at us and say nothing. Until they can get together somewhere else and talk about what a bastard you are.'

'Am I? A bastard, that is.'

'Don't be silly, Tom,' Gail said, putting her arms around him and giving him a kiss. 'Peter has never approved of any of

Hope's boyfriends. Boyfriends always had a problem when grandad was around, for all of us. But Peter was more subtle. And he was always there for Hope. To wind her up against them, that is. She'll spend a few months blaming you before finding someone else and going through the whole process again. I think she enjoys playing the martyred victim. She'll be doing it when she's ninety. Only probably more viciously. Now come on down, gran said she's going to tell a story.'

'A story?'

'Yes, a story.'

'Now this,' said Tom, 'is a story I have to hear. She's the only one who knows where all the bodies are buried.'

Chapter Sixty-one: Winifred's story

Winifred Browne sipped at her sherry, put it down next to her and folded her hands in her lap.

'I think,' she said, 'I'll begin my story some time before the war – the last World War, that is, World War Two. You see, life was totally different then. It was in the middle of the Roaring Twenties, as they call them now. Everyone remembered the Great War – apart from children, of course – it was part of their lives. Fathers, sons, brothers, uncles dead or wounded, or suffering from shell shock, something that wasn't understood at the time. Post-traumatic stress, I think they call it nowadays. Syndrome, that's it. They have to dress things up in fancy phrases these days. A bit like packaging around food. Funny, that.

'Where was I? Ah, the Roaring Twenties. You see, that's a very good phrase. It suggests people having fun. And some were. The wealthy, the connected, the aristocracy. But underneath there was great tension. There had been talk of the soldiers returning to a land fit for heroes. Well, that didn't happen. The old elite were determined that things should go back to the way they were before the start of the war, just as determined as the people they called anarchists and communists were determined that the working class should share in England's wealth.'

'Old elite, mum?' asked Jane Green. 'Anarchists, communists? I've never heard you use words like that before.'

Winifred Browne nodded.

'Yes, I'm rather sorry about that. I suppose that we were just like all parents. We wanted to shield our children from the days we had grown up in. Now I think we should have been more open. But you can't bring back the past, can you?'

She shook her head.

'Where was I?'

'The Roaring Twenties,' offered Tom. Gail squeezed his hand.

'Ah, yes, the Roaring Twenties. That's a little background. I think it helps to understand a story if you know the background. One of the things I'm always reminded of is outdoor toilets. For most people in those days, even what I suppose you would call the middle class, an outdoor toilet was – well, no-one would have found it surprising.'

She looked blankly at the carpet.

'They never showed toilets in films then, you know. Such things just weren't mentioned. Funny when that sort of thing, hygiene, sewage, or the lack of it, killed so many people. Children died through simple ignorance. Yet the effects of that sort of thing were known at the time. One just didn't speak of such things. Silly, really.

'Anyway, this story is about a family, quite a wealthy family, who had a large house in the country. It's about the family and the servants who worked for the family. They lived quiet lives. The father, Sir Edward, who was about forty-five by then, maybe fifty, had been in the war, and disliked noise. Some form of shell shock, I believe. Not as severe as those who spent so much time in the front line – I believe that he was a staff officer of some sort. But he hated noise. Loud noise.

'His sons, however, had been too young to join the war, and, I suppose, wanted something to define their own generation. They wanted parties, music, champagne.

'There was a wood nearby, and a pond in the wood, quite a large one. A stream fed it. It was a very pretty area.'

For a moment she seemed lost in reverie. The others stayed silent until she continued.

'The family. Yes. Amongst the servants was a young maid. A very pretty but naive young maid. One day she married the head gardener. It was a surprise to everybody. He was much older than her, far too old, really. They were even more surprised when she gave birth to a baby boy some seven months later. Of course there was much gossip. Working backwards the villagers noted that the young maid must have conceived around the time a wild party had been thrown at the mansion, one weekend when the parents were away. It must have been one of the sons of the mansion, many villagers said. Others disagreed – had it been one of the sons the father would have forced him to marry the girl or thrown him out of the house, for the father was a very strict, religious man. These others believed that one of the young men at the party must have seduced the girl, and the father of the mansion, not knowing which, had arranged for the maid to marry the head gardener, promising both that they would have their jobs and their little cottage in the grounds for the rest of their lives. Some said that they had been told that they wouldn't have any jobs if they failed to agree.

'I have to say that the latter was a distinct possibility. He was a man who was used to having his own way. Not an unkind man, as such, but – well, they were different days, as the saying goes.

'They say that there was never another wild weekend party in the mansion. Even when the only daughter was wed a few years later the party was quiet. She married a soldier, a lieutenant, a friend of her brothers, for they too had become soldiers. That would be about 1930. I can never remember where they soldiered, but the daughter's husband was often away and she stayed at the house with her parents. I think the era of wives accompanying their husbands to India, or wherever it was, was dying out. Or perhaps it was just senior officers who were allowed to take their wives with them.

'Anyway, she was living with her parents at the mansion when she had her first child, a little baby daughter. Now what name shall we give her? Maud, I think. It was quite a popular name at the time, I think. Oh, and the little boy's name, the servant's little boy, well, let's call him Bryan.

'Bryan was five when Maud was born. His life was not the happiest. His mother loved him but the head gardener took against him. Now the head gardener was old, but he was still strong. I know the title head gardener doesn't sound like hard work, but it was similar to having to look after a small farm. There was a large vegetable garden which had to be dug up twice a year, with a shovel, hard, manual work. There were under-gardeners who came from the local village, but everyone had to do their bit. The orchards to be pruned, fruit to be picked. Hedges trimmed with shears. There were even some pigs which had to be looked after. So the head gardener was a powerful man, and he often beat the boy, Bryan. He was the type of man who believes that boys should be beaten, and I imagine that knowing that Bryan wasn't really his son made him angry.

'I've seen that quite often in my work with the poor. I don't know whether it's what they would call genetic programming these days, but few men like their partners having had boys with someone else. But there you go.

'The boy grew up with no friends. He lived in the grounds of the manor house, so he was not seen as part of the village. Until the little girl Maud was born there were no young children in the house. When he began to go to school the other children would not associate with him. From being made to help the head gardener in the fields he was growing up to be a strong little boy, and he wasn't afraid to fight anyone, so they didn't bully him. But they all knew – from overhearing their parents' gossip – that there was something different about him. His real father was a gentleman of quality, his mother a maid, it was said. He didn't fit in. Not at home. Nor with the villagers. He was, as an old saying has it, neither fish nor fowl.

'And of course, in those days, the word bastard still meant something. They wouldn't use it to his face – not after the first time – but that was the way they all thought of him. A bastard. Illegitimate.

'As the years went by he began to take notice of little Maud. Maud's mother was a friendly woman who often sat in the gardens with her little daughter. His first sight of the gurgling little baby entranced him. Maud's mother showed him how to hold her properly. From then on he would regularly find excuses to be in the gardens when they were enjoying the sun. He was there when she took her first faltering steps. One of her first words was Biron – she was trying to say Bryan.

'And so they grew up in the Thirties. His father – the head gardener, should I say – wanted him out of school to help in the fields. As it was Bryan had to work before and after school, digging and mowing and other work as soon as the sun was up, and carrying on until it went down. No play or idleness for him.

'So he was growing up to be a powerful young man. But he also enjoyed schoolwork. The lack of friends no longer bothered him, and he knew he was good in all his subjects, better than most of the others. Normally, in those days, he would have left school when he was about fourteen, or even younger, but his teachers told his mother that Bryan was very intelligent, and should study further if she could find the money. Well, she couldn't, but the father of the mansion, old Sir Edward, heard about this and insisted that all Bryan's school fees would be paid.

'It's an old-fashioned word, responsibility, but that's how Sir Edward saw things. In a way Bryan was his responsibility, and he would do all he could to see that the boy got a chance. At the same time he would not allow anyone to speak of it. Bryan could never be a part of his world. His school fees would be paid anonymously, and Bryan himself should never know the circumstances. So he continued at school.

'That was about the time the head gardener died, of a heart attack. It's quite possible that the attack was caused by the question of Bryan's schooling, for he was determined that Bryan would give up school as soon as possible, but once Sir Edward had decided otherwise there was nothing he could do. After the head gardener died Bryan and his mother continued to live in the little cottage.

'Now, almost as soon as she could walk Maud followed Bryan around. There were no other children there, so it was quite natural that they should play together. From the first he had felt protective towards her, and as she grew up she regarded him as something of an elder brother, almost a hero. He knew all about the birds, how to fish, plants' names, even where to dig for worms. We did love worms. I don't know why. It seems so strange these days. But we did. I've always wondered whether that's what modern children lack. The chance to go out in the mud and get dirty. To hunt for worms to go fishing with. It didn't matter whether you caught anything – anything worth cooking. There was always tomorrow. Tomorrow was the day you would catch the great old pike, or trout, or whatever it was.'

She took a sip of her sherry and murmured "Tomorrow".

'Ah, yes. It seemed as if it were one long summer for both of them. But, as they say, the storm clouds were looming. He was fifteen and she ten when Hitler marched into Poland. The greatest event of their years was happening, and they did not realise it. I doubt if Hitler stood a chance in Bryan's thoughts when he considered what he could show Maude on the morrow. Certainly Hitler, for all her family discussed him, meant absolutely nothing for Maude compared with Bryan.

'At first there were few changes. Until the evacuees arrived. None were billeted on the mansion, for the army had earmarked most of that for themselves. But a large group were settled in houses in the village. The villagers didn't trust them, and they didn't trust the villagers. Each side formed gangs and fought each other. The evacuees roamed the countryside, stealing whatever they felt like, breaking whatever they found.

'It's one of those things, really. People like to pretend it never happened. But the village children all called the evacuees names like Kike and Yid. Very unpleasant words. You see they thought that everyone from the East End of London was a Jew, and to them a Jew was the worst of all creatures. I don't know if any of them were Jewish, the evacuees, that is, and even if they were it shouldn't have mattered. But things were so very much different in those days.

'So much different. Later, when the news of the extermination camps came through ...

'But one does wonder. About the whole thing. One report states this, another, later, supposedly official, states that. It makes it very difficult to work out what really happened. Rather like these days, when one day something is bad for you, and the next day it could save your life. Very strange.

'But it wasn't surprising that they went around in gangs causing damage when you think about it. The evacuees, that is. They felt unwelcome, betrayed, whatever. Torn from their parents, torn from their own little worlds. But that's the way things turned out. You can't change history. No matter how hard some people appear to try.

'A group of them were doing that – going around breaking something or other, I forget what – when they came across Maud in a pretty little white dress. She was terrified. She was alone, and they were taunting her, threatening her as children do. And up rode Bryan, not perhaps on a white steed, it was an old bicycle, but it seemed as if it should be a white steed as he set about the evacuees. As I said, he was growing into a powerful young man, and he was carrying a shovel handle at the time, and when he saw his little Maud in trouble he quite lost his temper. He was outnumbered eight to one, but the evacuees were not stupid. They took one look in his eyes and ran away. After that Bryan really was a hero to Maud.

'Sadly it left him with an intense hatred of Jews. Totally irrational, because of course the evacuees probably weren't Jews at all, but Maud meant everything in the world to him, and to see her threatened like that drove any common sense right out of his mind.

'A year or two later – probably a year and a half – Bryan received a great surprise. Well, it was a surprise to many others, but not to him. He had won a bursary to go to university to study engineering. He was extremely proud because he had worked very hard. Even then he knew what he wanted, what he hoped to achieve. And he was determined to achieve it.

'It was quite incredible. Those were the days when the idea of a head-gardener's son going to university was almost unheard of. Oh, there were a few of that class who went to Oxford, or Cambridge, but that was mainly window-dressing. And there was also the war. Very few young men in those days chose university when they knew they would be receiving call-up papers shortly. Indeed he himself was torn. He wanted to succeed. He had a driving ambition. He needed the acknowledgement to make up for his friendless youth. But, although they didn't give out white feathers to men not in uniform as they did in the Great War, there was still a great deal of pressure on all young men to sacrifice their careers for the country.

'He wanted to belong. On the other hand he had come to understand class distinctions. He knew the rumours about his real father. He knew he was regarded as a working class boy. It made him bitter. Why should he fight for a country which regarded him as a maid's bastard? But if he did not join up, would he not be forever seen as a coward, permanently different?

'He was a confused young man. I suppose we're all confused at that age. He discussed the matter with Maud. It wasn't really a discussion, since she was no more than twelve by then, but she was someone to talk with. Maud mentioned it to her mother, and her mother made a point of seeing Bryan.

'"You must go to university," she told him. "You can join up afterwards and become an officer. If you don't you'll regret it for the rest of your life."

'Bryan was still unsure. He liked Maud's mother a great deal, but he wasn't sure that a woman would understand these things. And then Sir Edward sent for him and said exactly the same thing.

'"This war will go on for many years yet," Sir Edward told

him. "Throw away your chance now and you'll never get it back. I have some contacts. I'll make sure that your service is deferred."

'That was the first time Sir Edward had ever spoken directly to the boy, now a young man.

'Bryan's mind was made up. He had a great deal of respect for Sir Edward, and he was now certain of what he should do. For a short while he was the happiest and most confident he had ever been.

'And then his call-up papers arrived.

'Sir Edward did everything he could, but it was no use. In his heart Bryan knew that if he had been the son of a lord or bishop his deferral would have come without a question. But he was just a working class boy, cannon fodder. The time came, and off he went.

'Maud was devastated. Originally she had dreamed of him in a uniform, a handsome young hero. But when he explained how important it was for him to go to university, and how afterwards he would join up and become an officer, she realised that this was his dream, and so it would be hers too. And then his dream and hers collapsed. She could feel his bitterness, his hurt.'

She took a sip of her almost empty sherry glass. Gail stood up silently, moved to the drinks cabinet, retrieved the bottle, and filled up her glass. Winifred Browne acknowledged this with a briefly upraised hand.

'Now, the last thing he did for her before he left was to comfort her over the death of her father. He was killed during the blackout in London, on his way to his club. A lorry ran over him. She desperately needed comfort, not because she had loved her father, but rather because she felt guilty about not feeling sad at her father's death. The simple truth was that he had never featured much in her life. He had always been away. Her mother did not show much remorse either. I rather believe that their marriage had ended in any real sense not very long after Maude had been born.

'Sex, of course, was rarely mentioned at all in those days. And if it was, it was by euphemism. You would think it obvious these days that when a couple stop having sexual relations it means that the relationship is in difficulty. But even now we prevaricate and search for ways of saying the un-sayable.

'I've often thought it tragic that every generation has to relearn what their parents have learnt. We protect our children from what we've been through. I don't know if that will ever change. I – well, that's the way it goes, I suppose. Maybe your generation can change that.

'Sir Edward showed little remorse at the death of this son-in-law. But I fancy that was because his sons and his son-in-law had not measured up to his standards. While alive he could always hope that they might prove themselves. Dead – well, dead, he had to face up to the fact that they had never done anything, and would never do anything. He was faced with the tragedy of a dead son-in-law who had died anonymously in the blackout, and, much worse, rumour had it that he was drunk at the time.

'One son was arrested in a brothel. I can't remember when. The other would have been cashiered for fraud, but it was in a regiment that didn't like to wash its dirty linen in public. People forget that children have ears.

'Shortly afterwards Maude was sent to boarding school. They – Bryan and Maude – wrote to each other as often as they could. She begged a photograph of him, which he sent as soon as he could. She sent one of herself. She wrote of how lonely she felt and how she looked at his photograph and cried each night. He wrote of rain, mud, marching, training with obsolete weapons. He wrote of having to live, sleep and work with people he described as "a platoon of village idiots, the only ones more stupid are the officers".

'That was before Montgomery took over, of course. After that his letters became much more positive. Much more. Apparently a number of officers were removed, much to his enjoyment. In one of his letters he wrote, "Things are beginning to move. Now we are training for the task in hand. We will be ready when the time comes."

'I reread that letter earlier today.'

She looked down at the carpet. She took a sip of sherry and looked out of the window.

'He did admire Churchill, as you will have guessed from that. He admired him inordinately. I think that, at last, he had a hero.

'And then, one day she received a letter from Bryan telling her that she wouldn't hear from him for a while. It puzzled her until news of the Normandy invasion was announced. She guessed that Bryan would be amongst the soldiers fighting on the beaches. That night she prayed extra hard, at the same time feeling extremely proud that her soldier was in the middle of the fighting. She begged God to look after him, to comfort him, until such a time that she could do the same.

'Not, of course, in the sense that the modern day world might interpret that wish. My goodness, no.

'But I do rather suspect that the modern world is pretty much the same as we were then.

'He wasn't. In the thick of the fighting, that is. A week or two later she received a letter from him. The day before the invasion one of the village idiots had accidentally shot him in his leg, and his platoon and company had left without him.

You could say that it was a blessing in disguise. Only two of his platoon ever returned.

'But at the same time it denied him of the feeling of belonging that he was still looking for. Other old soldiers might go to re-unions to discuss the times they were in battle, all he had was the clerical job he was given when he came out of hospital, once again amongst strangers.

'He was still determined to succeed. The clerical job gave him the time to return to his studies. Even before the war ended and demobilisation began he was planning on going to university. After the Labour government got into power he knew he would have his chance. And so it was he achieved that aim. In 1946 he enrolled in a university in London.

'He hadn't stopped writing to Maude, nor had she to him, though the letters were not as frequent, sometimes being months apart. In the normal course of affairs they would have eventually dried up altogether as each went their own way. But in 1947 he returned to the manor house after his mother died, for the funeral. Maude had just returned from boarding school. She was seventeen, and they hadn't seen each other for five years.

'They met in the apple orchard. It was an awkward meeting. He was now a handsome young man, and she blushed to remember all the girlish confidences she had written in her letters. He discovered that the young tomboy he remembered had turned into a not unattractive young woman.'

She smiled.

'She had developed breasts, at least.'

She shook her head.

'Each felt strange new feelings for the other, feelings which would not have been mentioned in those days.

'And, you can take it from me, they still don't. Not at that age.

More's the pity.

'She stammered out some condolences, he stammered his thanks, they each stammered something about the weather before finding some excuse to leave.

'She watched him leave. She had gone inside, and was hiding out of sight in the front parlour as he walked down the avenue – the entrance drive. There had been so much that she had wanted to tell him, but – well, we weren't called teenagers in those days, but from experience, things don't change that much, whatever the newspapers might tell you. I'm sure you've all known that terrible time.

'Three months later he received a brief letter from Maude to say that, after a sudden illness, her mother had passed away. He immediately packed a bag and set off to be in time for the funeral. He arrived the day before and, having arranged a room at the local inn, went to the mansion to pay his condolences. Maude answered the door. The time of servants was long past. After having sat uncomfortably in the lounge for half an hour he suggested they go for a walk.

'It was a cold winter's day. To make polite conversation they began a "do you remember when" conversation. It wasn't long before they were laughing over the memories of childhood, and how far away it all seemed now, with the war and a brave new peace which looked even more uncertain. After a while the talk lagged until they were silent. That was when he turned to her and said:

'Maude, I've been thinking about this since we last met. I want to marry you.

'For a moment she was stunned. Marriage was everything to young women in those days. Everything. Your whole life. And because of that she had often wondered who she would marry. She had met many young men, even many not so young men, over the past few years, but none of them had really appealed. Soldiers, officers, sailors, airmen – those brave pilots. It was only after a while that she realised that she was comparing each to her childhood hero, and all looked either foppish or shallow as a result.

'I'll understand if you say no, continued Bryan. I know I haven't got much to offer, but I'm determined to do well. It won't be easy, but there will be opportunities. I'm going to be an engineer, and there's going to be a lot of engineering work needing doing in the future. Maybe I'll be able to start my own company one day.

'He carried on like that for a while. She wasn't really listening. She knew her answer was going to be yes. She loved him beyond question. Yes, she really, really loved him. She loved him so much it gave her a physical ache.

'And so they were married. Not happily ever after, unfortunately. While Bryan finished his studies Maude stayed on in the old mansion. Their first surviving child was born less than two years after their wedding. Old Sir Edward was delighted, but Bryan noticed that Maude's remaining uncles did not even send a telegram of congratulation.

'That was very important in those days. A telegram of congratulation. It was part of the form, no matter what …

'Oh, I suppose you're wondering how Sir Edward took to the idea of his grand-daughter marrying the son of a gardener. Well, strangely enough, you could almost say he welcomed it. In hindsight it wasn't too strange, I suppose. As I said, Sir Edward had grown up believing in a world of responsibility, a world where everyone knew their place. A very paternal society. I think he was rather deluded, to be honest. People – those in power, that is – like to portray themselves in a certain way to the world, but more often than not the reality is vastly different. Bishops turn out to have had some very dubious tastes. Solid family politicians – well, look at that nice Mr John Major. He got involved with the eggs woman. And generals, well, just think of General Haig.

'But the two wars destroyed Sir Edward's ideals. I think he just managed to retain them after the Great War, but then there were the strikes during the Twenties, which showed to him that his country wasn't looking after the men who had made victory over Germany possible – the heroes. And then the Great Depression. And, of course, the Second War. Quite possibly worse than all that, his sons had been a disappointment. They hadn't had what was called a good war – a most idiotic phrase, but it was one used at the time. It wasn't that they were too old for active service. Just out of date. Sir Edward was also out of date, but, unlike his sons, he realised it. That's why he was able to accept his grand-daughter marrying Bryan. He recognised Bryan as the future, I think.

'But relations between Bryan and his wife's uncles worsened. It was about a year after the birth of their first child that Bryan, returning to the manor house for the weekend, overheard a drunken conversation between them. He had just walked in and was looking for Maude.

'"Bastard son of a maid," he had overheard. He walked into the pool room and confronted them. At first they were embarrassed, but then they laughed. That's all you are, after all. Son of a maid who was only too happy to spread her legs for any passing gent.

'He hit them. Furious, but not in a rage. He was very controlled. He always prided himself on that, control. First the one, then the other. Until both were lying on the floor, unconscious. And then he found Maude and told her to pack.

And so they left the manor house for good.

'He was now even more determined to succeed. While his wife looked after the domestic side of things he worked all the hours he could. They had few friends, but so long as they had each other and their growing family they felt that they had a fortune. He started his own engineering company, and very successful it was. Partly because of his driving ambition, but also because he had a very good idea for the right type of employee, and he rewarded hard work. He still had to struggle often against the old boy network, but the world had sufficiently changed so that people were rated against whether they could produce the goods, as the saying goes, rather than because of their name or who their father was.

'They went through some hard times, some very hard times. People look back and think it must have been very jolly, all the old photographs show people smiling. But I suppose every age is the same. It's very rare for a generation to remember only the bad parts.

'But his family remained everything to him. Possibly his worst fault was that he brought his driving ambition home. He tried not to run their lives, but he always insisted on the best schools and the best results.'

She sighed.

'And that's Bryan's story, really. The children grew up, and Maude and Bryan discovered they had become grandparents. And then the grandchildren grew up, and they felt that, with all they had been through, they had been fortunate in each other.

'And then, having worked hard all their lives they wanted a house they could spend their retirement in. One day Bryan noticed a manor house for sale. It was the very same manor house that he and Maude had left all those years before. So they made a few enquiries and bought it, and lived there happily ever after.'

There was complete silence as she finished her sherry.

'You're probably wondering why the house hadn't been bought by some major company or other. Or turned into flats. Apparently the family had lost it after the war. They managed to keep it until the mid-Fifties, but what with taxes and death duties and the general cost of living, and most of the family wealth gone, they had to sell it. It was turned into a lunatic asylum for many years. Until the late Eighties, when they appear to have closed so many asylums. They struggled for years to find a buyer. But its reputation put people off. Many people died in the house, over the years. They weren't buried here, but the locals believe the place still retains a certain, aura, shall we say.'

She put her sherry glass down.

'So who was Bryan's father, gran?' asked Claire.

'I'm afraid the only person who ever knew that for sure was his mother, my dear. Now, I think it's time for tea. After which I might have a lie down. It's been a rather difficult day.'

Chapter Sixty-two: Bad news

'I'll get it,' Gail called as the telephone rang. 'Uncle Adam!' she exclaimed after answering. 'I haven't heard from you for ages! Gran,' she called, 'it's Uncle Adam.'

'About time for the fatted calf,' muttered Jane as Mrs Browne hurried out of the kitchen.

'Fatted calf?' asked Claire.

'Sorry, darling, I'm being bitchy. The fatted calf slaughtered for the return of the favourite son. The minute your gran hears it's Adam she races out, all bright-eyed.'

'And yet he wasn't the eldest son.'

'No. No, it appears that he wasn't, after all.'

'Maybe that's why she dotes on Uncle Adam so much.' Jane sighed.

'I suppose so. But boy children were seen as far more important in those days anyway. Funnily enough, I'm glad I had only daughters. A son would just have made everything more difficult, and things were difficult as it was.'

'I think you're embarrassing Tom,' Claire said, grinning at Tom, who appeared to be fascinated by his teacup. Jane laughed.

'Oh, I think Tom will make a very good son-in-law,' she said. Tom blushed.

'I think I might take a look at that cupboard under the stairs,' he said. 'Poke a hand into the electrical wiring and see what goes fizz.'

'Tom,' Mrs Browne said, returning to the kitchen, 'Adam asked if he could have a word with you.'

'Me?' asked Tom, puzzled.

'Yes, I didn't know you knew him.'

'Only to interview, Mrs Browne. I'll see what he wants.'

'He sounded terribly down in the dumps,' Mrs Browne said, absent-mindedly running a cloth over an immaculate sink.

'I'm afraid I have some bad news,' Tom said walking back into the kitchen. 'More bad news. Mrs Browne, would you mind sitting down.'

'Oh my goodness, what is it?'

'Sit down, gran,' Claire said. 'What news, Tom?'

Tom folded his arms and looked at them grimly.

'Adam asked me to break this as gently as I could. I think he's having trouble coping with it. You see – well, it will probably be on the news this evening. He's been accused of having an affair with a sixteen-year-old girl who was on work experience at his office.'

'What?'

'You're joking!'

'It can't be true.'

'It's going to be headline news for a certain tabloid tomorrow morning. I'm afraid they're all going to be crawling over his life by the end of the day.'

'But surely it can't be true.'

'Oh my goodness,' whispered Winifred Browne. 'My poor Adam.'

'I don't know how true it is. Apparently the girl's sold her story to the tabloid in question. But I know how it works. The paper will use the words "claimed" and "alleged" a lot. Even if he manages to prove his innocence it's going to be a tough few weeks, and his career is pretty much definitely finished. He was going to come up here, but – Well, he'll have reporters on his tail, and you don't need that sort of thing at the moment. He doesn't want to bring them here. He said that he'll try to give them the slip, but it won't be easy.'

'You knew about this!' exclaimed Maria-Hope, pointing at him. 'You bloody knew all about it beforehand.'

'I'd heard the rumours, Maria. The political world is full of rumours. Who has a drinking problem, who has mistresses on the go, who's sleeping with whom. Most of the time it's difficult to tell which are true and which just gossip. Anyway, most of it is meaningless. It certainly is in my world.'

'You could have told us! Warned us!'

'About what? That there were rumours? How would that have helped anyone?'

'He did warn us,' said Gail. 'That story of yours, about the king's minister – that was about Adam, wasn't it?'

'It was loosely based on the rumour. It just sprang to mind. I thought it was a story that everyone would have forgotten the next day.'

'Christ!' exploded Maria-Hope. 'I suppose you felt so smug, sitting there watching us, knowing all the time that – well, fuck you!'

'Okay, Maria,' Tom said as calmly as he could, 'what should I have done?'

'He's got a point,' Robert said as Maria-Hope glowered at Tom. 'He could hardly say, "Hey do you know what they're saying about your Uncle Adam" now could he?'

'He could have said something,' insisted Maria-Hope.

Tom shrugged and shook his head wearily.

'I suppose you'll be writing about this in your precious little political column,' Maria-Hope accused. 'I can see the headline: from the bosom of his family. How I insinuated myself with his niece to get an exclusive look at Adam Browne's family. P.S. also almost managed to shag his niece. But did manage a fuck with a friend. Photo to follow.'

'Maria,' Tom said softly, 'I won't be writing anything about it. It's called a conflict of interest in my book. I do serious journalism, not gutter press gossip.'

'Tom?' asked Gail.

'Yes?'

'I'd like you to write about it. For our sake, the family's sake. I think you'd give an unbiased view.'

'Well I wouldn't!' shouted Maria-Hope. 'He's – he's – a total and utter shit. I know about you and Valerie, Tom. You think I wasn't suspicious when you decided to sleep on your own? Sleep? I heard you and that bitch screwing in the television room. You thought you'd get away with it because it wasn't in your bedroom, didn't you?'

'What the hell are you talking about?' demanded Tom.

'Children, children,' pleaded Mrs Browne. 'Please think of Adam. He has enough problems without coming home to all these arguments.'

'Oh, who cares?' said Valerie. 'So he found himself a nice piece of sixteen-year-old totty. Good for him, I say. You all think of him as your precious Uncle Adam, the perfect politician.'

'Valerie, shut up!' Gail shouted.

'Shut up?' She laughed. 'Shut up? I'll tell you something about "up". "Up" is the only thing the men in your family understand. Your bloody grandfather visiting you at boarding school, his eyes almost falling out at the sight of young flesh. And your Uncle Adam. Remember when we all went across to France for a week during the holidays? Who do you think crept into my bedroom in the small hours? And there's another uncle of yours quite happy to fuck me even though I'm no longer sixteen. Little hopeless Hope, It wasn't Tom you heard in the television room. He wouldn't have the balls.

It was Robert.'

She gasped as Gail slapped her.

'You bitch! Shut your mouth or I'll break your bloody neck!'

They looked at each other.

'It was Peter who went to your bed in France, and you know it,' Gail hissed. 'I wasn't that sick by that time. I saw him.'

The others were looking at Robert and Patience. Robert shrugged.

'The only time I came down was to get a drink for myself and Patience. We couldn't sleep. And I certainly didn't come down for anything else. After that drink I fell asleep like a log.'

'Well?' Claire asked an unruffled Patience.

'Bobby is quite right. He didn't wake up. He got our drinks, talked about not being able to sleep, and then promptly fell asleep. Actually I came downstairs and found Valerie asleep in front of the television. I put a blanket over her.'

'A blanket' asked Valerie.

'There was an adult movie on. That's probably what you remember. And what Maria-Hope heard.' She smiled. 'I am a Chinese wife, you see. I make sure my husband will never want.'

There was a silence as this sank in.

'My poor Adam,' sighed Mrs Browne, tears starting in her eyes.

Postscript

Three weeks later a jet plane took off from Heathrow, one of many bound for New York that day. Amongst its occupants were Robert, Patience, Lucy and little David. Robert had gained leave of absence from his university, stayed for the funeral, and for long enough to know that his mother would not be left alone. Claire had moved into the manor house permanently, and Jane had joined them. There were plans to open a tea-shop in the village. As Claire had noted wryly, 'One little baby girl, one unmarried mother, one crocked-up grandmother, and a great-grandmother, all stuck in a big house in the middle of nowhere. I think that makes us eminently qualified to take on the world.'

'You okay, honey?' asked Patience once they had reached cruising level, and Lucy had put on her earphones to dive into the entertainment available.

Robert nodded. His face was tired and worn. He had spent the previous three weeks cursing jet lag for being unable to sleep properly. Now he was struggling with the one big fear of his life. Flying.

'I bet Tom gets scared as hell flying,' he said. 'He's the kind that would. Take all sorts of risks while the bullets are flying without even thinking about it. But he'd be even more scared than I am at flying.'

Patience squeezed his hand.

'I hope it works out for him. He seems a nice kind of a boy.'

Robert seemed to think about this for a while. Patience hid a smile. She could tell what he was thinking.

'He's okay,' Robert said grudgingly. 'He's got potential.'

'I wonder if he and Hope will stay together. It seems such a waste.'

Gail had driven Valerie to the town on the day after Boxing day so that she could get a bus or train back to London. Peter and Rebeccah had also left with the children so that they could be handed over to the care of their grandparents while their parents returned for the funeral. With Valerie and Peter out of the way Maria-Hope appeared to realise that she had made a tactical mistake in estranging Tom, who had stayed on until the funeral – to "help out where he could", as he put it. He spent most of the time wondering if he had made a mistake, as he found himself the focus of attraction of both Gail and a totally changed Maria-Hope.

'He's an intelligent kid,' said Robert, closing his eyes. 'But too naive. And too soft. The sort of person who would end up with a little harridan like Hope for a wife.'

'Daddy, what's a harridan?' asked Lucy, a normal child who could both watch a movie in front of her, with headphones on, and be able to absorb any interesting titbits from her parents' discussions. There was no response. Her father was a normal father, who had chosen that moment to fall asleep.

'Mommy, what's a harridan?' she asked, turning to her mother. Patience smiled and stroked her hair.

'It's a word we use to describe a woman who is strict and severe and grumpy with her husband, darling.'

'Oh,' said Lucy, and went back to her movie.

Patience and Rebeccah exchanged many e-mails over the next few months. While they both filled most of theirs with the doings of their children, it was noticeable that Rebeccah never once mentioned Peter, although Patience always included at least a snippet on her hopes and worries about her own husband. Patience tried a few times to elicit information about Tom and Maria-Hope, but Rebeccah, possibly because Maria-Hope was Peter's sister, evaded the questions.

Winter turned to spring, without any major seasonal spasms in New York, but with continual stops and starts in England, as is normally the case. A few days of balmy weather followed by buffeting storms and howling winds from the north, more days of calm, and then a return to grey weather, windy, wet and cold. Finally winter grudgingly retreated, and the days could be counted on to be at least mild and pleasant, if not bright and summery. People began to emerge from their houses as if survivors from bomb shelters. Jane Green and Claire started work on the vegetable patch that George Browne had once spoken of. Not a twee little herb garden: the first thing Jane Green did was to hire an agricultural digger and plough up almost the entire back garden, much to Claire's amazement and delight. Somehow she had never imagined that her mother, who she remembered as perfectly coiffured and elegant, would end up in a pair of overalls, sitting on a rotavator swearing at the stones beneath her.

It was after the area had been readied and the seedlings were in, in early April that the card arrived. A similar card dropped into the post-box of an apartment in New York on the same day. Both were invitations to a wedding. At the manor house Claire came running out to her mother, waving the card. In New York Robert finished reading it before looking up at his wife who was preparing the children for a walk to the park.

'Fancy a visit to England in June?' Robert asked. 'See the place in all its summer glory.'

'Bobby, it's too early for the kids to go through another twelve hour flight both ways.'

'Lucy, show this card to your mom.' Lucy took the card, read it, exclaimed "Yes!" and handed it to her mother. Patience read it and looked at Robert.

'Well, okay,' she said, 'just this once, then.'

'Now, how,' mused Robert, 'did she manage to bag him?'

'Mum!' cried Claire rushing up to her mother. 'Guess what?'

'We've won the prize for the most irregular lines of lettuce in the world?' asked Jane Green, critically inspecting the vegetable garden. 'What possessed us to plant so much lettuce I don't know. We could have planted half as much and used the rest for rhubarb. The yuppies like their rhubarb crumble.'

'No, mum! Here, read this!'

'You read it to me, darling, my hands are too dirty.'

Claire smiled and read:

"You are cordially invited to the wedding of Tom Woods and Gail Green. It will be sometime in June. Not quite sure when, exactly, but we'll let you know.'

They looked at each other.

'I suppose it's too early to open a bottle of champagne,' Jane Green noted.

'No, but gran's just made a fresh pot of tea.'

They went back up to the kitchen, arm in arm.

'Honestly!' Jane Green said once she had scrubbed her hands and they were sitting down at the kitchen table, 'you would think that Gail had never heard of the telephone.'

'I think this is much more romantic,' Claire said, holding the card in front of her. 'We can put this on the mantelpiece and look at it every time we pass it. Telephone calls can come later.'

Indeed one did come later that day, Gail asking if she and Tom could come up for the weekend. Her grandmother told her to stop being silly, that she knew there was a room for her whenever she wanted to visit, and Tom, of course, and, oh, congratulations, and had they set a date yet?

They hadn't, it turned out, because they had wondered whether they might not be able to get married in the village church, and if there were a few spare rooms available at the manor house ...

Now Gail was really being silly! Of course there were spare rooms available. Of course they should get married in the village church. It would be wonderful. Just wonderful.

And if the vicar objected, her grandmother would threaten to tell the RSPCA about his pig.

Tom did not enjoy that weekend. He felt desperately short of male company. Or, to be more accurate, any company where the subject of discussion was other than wedding dresses, bridesmaids and real invitations. Possibly the worst moment came when Gail revealed that she would not be trying on any wedding dresses until much closer to the time, as she didn't know how large the bump would be by then.

That was met by an unusual silence, followed by an uproar of congratulations, and Tom's face going the colour of a sunburnt peach.

And so was Robert's question answered when he met the bride to be in June. The bump did indeed stand out as Gail walked up the aisle, proudly so.

'Not like in your day, gran?' suggested Claire as they sat at the main table in the reception tent afterwards. Winifred Browne smiled at the sight of Gail and Tom attempting a slow dance to open the floor.

'Well, you could say that it's a different world,' she said. 'But, to be honest, I don't think it is. I think we all grow up in different worlds. It's only when we see someone else's world that we think it different. We could just as easily have grown up in theirs. We just have to accept whatever world it is we're given.'

'To a certain extent,' said Jane Green. 'You don't have to follow someone else's script.'

Winifred Browne nodded.

'Yes, my dear, you're right. To a certain extent.'

Tom retained his job as a political journalist, despite the

cutbacks. Gail moved into the manor house with the others. Tom has bought a new car so that he can get there faster whenever he has the time. The tea-shop was opened and does roaring trade on weekends, with an occasional lost tourist during week-days.

Robert, Patience and the kids continue to live in New York, endlessly debating whether to move somewhere else for the kids' sake.

Peter and Rebeccah still live together, but no longer share a bedroom. Peter has decided to study for the priesthood. A Presbyterian priesthood.

Maria-Hope has a new boyfriend. He beats her on a regular basis. He is not a vegetarian. He also punched Peter on their first and only meeting. Her grandmother has told her to come to the manor to rest for a few weeks, but she is resolute in defending her new boyfriend. She has also refused offers from all of her family to assassinate him. Apparently she believes that her boyfriend needs her.

Mr Porker, by the way, was not destined for the dinner table. He gate-crashed the wedding, and afterwards decided that the grounds of the manor house made a better home. So they fenced off the vegetable garden, built him a sty, and found a docile mate for him. The two can often be seen wandering behind Jane, Gail and Claire when they go for an afternoon stroll. The pigs become quite belligerent when a stranger approaches little Sarah.

And, as it turned out, they regard lettuce as a special treat.

Other novels by Bill Dughaille:

The FFSG series (aka the Wellbury Chronics)

Summers

The first in the FFSG series (aka the Wellbury Chronics).

Detective Sergeant Frank Summers is a man on a mission: to keep his head down, stay out of trouble and enjoy the relaxed atmosphere of the easy-going, genteel town of Wellbury, his new posting. It's a town just made for him, where, he believes, even the criminals take bank holidays off. But, while perceptive in his professional life, he tends to miss the subtleties in his private life. In this case he fails to realise that his own tranquillity is being threatened by three women and a philanderer. The fact that the women in question are his boss, his constable and the local pathologist adds just the touch of danger to his life that he had hoped to avoid. The philanderer has been dead several decades. The women are very much alive.

The Eighty-five-percenters

The second in the FFSG series.

Detective Sergeant Frank Summers is faced with an unexpected crisis as the staid citizens of the genteel town of Wellbury rapidly descend into disorganised anarchy after a sociology professor announces on radio that eighty-five percent of the population will die in a coming cull. The prediction appears to be coming true as apparently total strangers are felled one by one according to a list of the ten-most-disliked Wellburians, from nagging neighbours to estate agents ... and the police, at a poorly performing number ten.

But Frank fails to realise that there is a graver danger closer to home. Three women have decided that he is their responsibility: his boss, his constable and the local pathologist have agreed to become best of enemies. Now they intend to re-arrange his fate the way it should be. And they aren't asking anyone's permission.

Fakes, Fraud and Deception

The third in the FFSG series.
Detective Sergeant Frank Summers is in the doghouse, despite having recently arrested an internationally sought con-artist. And since he is in the doghouse he has no intention of pointing out that there is something very strange about the attractive French police woman who has come to interview the arrested man, not to mention the two detectives claiming to be from Scotland Yard. Oh, no, he is going to stay well out of the way this time. Definitely.

Jokers

The fourth in the FFSG series.
The doctors have pronounced Detective Sergeant Frank Summers physically fit following recovery after his shooting, but his colleagues fear that his sense of humour was extracted along with the bullet. They are, as always, more than willing to interfere in his life in the pursuit of a good cause. If that wasn't enough, a bunch of criminals calling themselves the Joker Gang are laughing at him, the university students are creating mayhem during their rag week, and someone called

The Shocker is trying to kill him. The only advantage is that it take his mind off of the ultimatum the three women in his life have given him, one that he has only until the Sunday to resolve. Or leave town.

Prophecies

The fifth in the FFSG series.

Detective Sergeant Summers is under a hex, otherwise known as his colleagues. First they don't want him to get married, then it is imperative it must happen. Then they decide that a prophecy has been made which threatens the wedding. They don't believe in prophecies, but aren't sure that prophecies understand that. So they'll have to Do Something About It. And if their bumbling efforts aren't enough to ensure he never makes it to the altar, he has to cope with visiting aliens and resident ghosts. He does have tiny Squishy to protect him, but what match can even this plucky little kitten be against a prospective mother-in-law?

Loonymoon

The Inspectors Summers have tied the knot and embarked on their honeymoon in a small family-run hotel in Normandy. She has very definite ideas of what she wants out of a honeymoon: to set a seal on their love, and to form a foundation for life-long devotion. He just wants to nick a French police officer's kepi. He had a Bobby's helmet nicked from him once by a French girl while he was on crowd duty one New Year's Eve in London, and now he intends to return the favour. Neither is about to achieve their aim unless they can solve the mystery of the woman in the bath and the missing heroin. Which means pitting their minds against the French Inspectors Simenon. That's Mr and Mrs Simenon, whose marriage has gone beyond the rocks and is now beating itself to death against humdrum reality. One or either or both or neither could be the guilty crumpet. More importantly, is their marriage a portent of what could become of the Loonymooners? Ultimately the decisive question could well be: which side do the peas go?

Others:

The Window

Jim Allbright, ex-bobby and now easy-going window washer, innocently responds to an advert for window washing placed in the newspaper by the local council. The response is a torrent of paperwork, political correctness and a computer system doing exactly what it was told to do, but not quite what was intended. But if the system cannot be beaten, the interchange of letters can be used to have a little fun and get to know some of the people struggling behind it. There's Sandi, who signs herself as "(pp the Administrator)"; her four-year old little angel Helen; Graham, a shadowy computer programmer who definitely has too much time on his hands, and a slew of Project Managers and Senior Administrators eager to ensure standards are upheld no matter how many problems they create. Against a run of bad luck and circumstances Jim and Sandi aim to meet up one day, eventually. Hopefully. The window might even get washed. Maybe.

Diary of a Sane Man

In a cross between 'Last Of The Summer Wine' and 'One Flew Over The Cuckoo's Nest', set against a backdrop of the brave new world of New Labour's end of honeymoon, Fred is the Last Cynical Optimistic Realist.

Believing that he's found the perfect niche – three square meals a day plus all the newspapers he can read just for occasionally pretending to be mad – he's not going to be the one to rock the apple cart. Oh, no.
Safe from the wiles of women and the woes of the world, he's not going to rock the boat. Oh, no.
No, he's just going to sit and observe, and comment quietly on the insanity of life outside.
Well, maybe just little one tug of the loose strand of wool on life's jersey ...
Did you know they elected a monkey as mayor in Hartlepool?

The Weekend At Longwood

A whodunnit in the classic sense, set against the backdrop of World War II and the trials, tribulations and romances of nine suspects.

A group of friends get together during the last weekend of August 1939 at the rural retreat named Longwood, just a few miles from Portsmouth. They are there to celebrate the last time they will see Georgina Riley, famed American novelist and socialite, for some time, as she is scheduled to leave for her native New York in order to marry her childhood sweetheart. During the afternoon they good-humouredly assign to each other the most suitable names of the nine muses, the daughters of Zeus and Mnemosyne:

Calliope: the muse of epic poetry and rhetoric

Clio: history

Erato: love poems and mimicry

Euterpe: lyric poetry

Melpomene: tragedy

Polymnia: hymns to the gods and heroes

Terpsichore: dance

Thalia: comedy

Urania: astronomy, astrology and prophecy

The following morning Georgina is discovered in her bedroom covered in blood, her throat slit, barely alive. Her American maid is dead. A tiara Georgina had been flaunting the day before has disappeared.

Detective Inspector Rudman arrives to investigate. But with Georgina in a coma and no solid evidence there is little he can do apart from haunt their lives. With Germany's invasion of Poland a week later they disperse across the land, some to the air-force, some to the army, others to reserved civilian jobs.

But Rudman does not give up. Wherever they are he can be found. Whatever other duties he is tasked to, he will find time to keep tabs on them. Whatever the defeats and victories of the Allied cause, he has only one aim: to find the person responsible for the murder done that weekend in Longwood.

The war ends; some of the Muses have survived, some not. Some have prospered, some married, some matured, others have found despair. And then comes invitation to spend another weekend at Longwood. The message is that Rudman has found the evidence he has been looking for.

And so one of the surviving couples motor slowly down to Portsmouth, remembering the original weekend, the trials and the tribulations of the past years, and wonder: what will be revealed during the coming weekend at Longwood?

For further details on these visit:

www.dughaille.info